Praise for Suzette Hollingsworth's novels

Sherlock Holmes and the Case of the Sword Princess is a 2015 finalist Chanticleer Murder and Mayhem Awards

"Best Holmesian Book of 2015" – Amazon customer

"This is an excellent, gifted writer, with a true future ahead of her." – CHARLOTTE CARTER

"I will pimp it and be the first to buy it!" - DELILAH MARVELLE

"Sir Doyle would enjoy. It has all the classic trappings of one of his novels. From the language to the descriptions of London and its denizens, it is historical fiction at its best." – Christopher Gallagher

"A Sherlock tale with Hepburn and Tracy flair . . . It had the feel of a classic old Hollywood mismatched romantic comedy to me.... Hepburn and Tracy. It was charming and would really appeal to people who love the idea of a kind of Jane Austen meets Conan Doyle mash-up." - RaynaRed, Audible reviewer

"Cumberbatch/Sherlock meets his match!" - Jan, Audible reviewer

"Sherlock in Mr. Darcy mode . . . " - PandaRS, Audible reviewer

"Irene Adler has competition" - Mary, Audible reviewer

"This is a very fascinating novel. All the characters are very vibrant and come to life while reading them." - Coffee Time Romance & More

"Her humor is refreshing, I laughed out-loud on a few occasions, shed a few tears, and sat on the edge of my seat for most of it." -- AnaMaree Ordway, owner Wenatchee Book Co.

Also by Suzette Hollingsworth

Sherlock Holmes & The Case of the Sword Princess

published by Bookstrand
THE PARADOX: The Soldier and the Mystic
THE SERENADE: The Prince and the Siren
THE CONSPIRACY: The Cartoonist and the Contessa

To be released in 2016:
Sherlock Holmes & The Chocolate Menace

Sherlock Holmes and the Dance of the Tiger

The Great Detective In Love #2

Imprint: Mystery with romantic elements

Copyright © 2015 by Suzette Hollingsworth

ISBN: 978-0-9909952-8-9

First Printing: November 2015
Cover Design by Fiona Jayde Media
Inside artwork by Clint Hollingsworth

PUBLISHER'S NOTE:
This is a work of historical fiction. As such, there are historical figures who actually lived contained within the pages of the book; the author has attempted to represent them honestly, but some leeway must be given as she has never met them in person. There are also fictional characters within the book which seem more real than historical figures, namely those created by Arthur Conan Doyle. For all the remaining characters, names, places, and incidents either are the product of the author's imagination or are used fictitiously, and any resemblance to actual persons, living or dead, business establishments, events, or locales is entirely coincidental. So what is real and what is not? We no longer know. That's grand then, Ted.

Printed in U.S.A.

PUBLISHER:
Icicle Ridge Graphics

Sherlock Holmes
and the Dance of the Tiger
by Suzette Hollingsworth

The Great Detective In Love #2

**Sherlock Holmes solves the most perplexing mystery of his life—
unlocking the human heart.**

Dedication

The subtext of this book and the original title was
Sherlock Holmes and the Spy Who Danced on Horses
Hence, the dedication.

To Donna Weiss
the dearest and truest of friends
who is not a spy (to my knowledge),
but who certainly dances on horses

To Bill Green
who is a spy—and probably a mad scientist as well
Watch out Moriarty!

and to my wonderful, delightful grandmother
Omah Lock Hewitt
a tiger and a fire-eater who loved me into existence

Chapter One
St. Petersburg, Russian Empire
13 March 1881

"I signed it this morning," stated Alexander II, Czar of Russia.

"You signed what, Father?" Alexander III, Czarevich and next in line for the throne, asked with trepidation. He sat across from the Czar and beside his twelve-year-old son and the Czar's grandson, Nicholas II.

Was the document in question an alliance with Germany? Or perhaps with France? Something told the Czarevich it was nothing so deducible.

It was Sunday and the three royals were seated in a closed bullet-proof carriage, a gift from Napoleon III of France. They were travelling to the Mikhailovsky Manège, the riding academy, as they did every Sunday for the military roll call. The carriage was accompanied by six Cossacks sworn to protect the Czar, first in the processional, followed by two sleighs. Among the open sleighs' inhabitants were the chief of police and the chief of the emperor's guards. The route, as always, was via the Catherine Canal and crossing the Pevchesky Bridge. The people of St. Petersburg lined the sidewalk for miles along the narrow passage.

"I signed a draft decree to establish a democratically elected parliament," the Czar stated nonchalantly, as if he had just announced the name of his new tailor rather than the drastic alteration of a government which had been in place for centuries—since 1547 under Ivan IV. Adding a democratic branch to a heretofore totalitarian government.

Is the Czar mad? Many an aristocrat thought so, and his son and heir apparent was not far behind. Alexander II had initiated even more reforms than Peter the Great.

But this went far beyond reform. Alexander II had freed twenty-three million serfs, little better than feudal slaves, from their bondage to the landowners. And he had wrested eight-five percent of Russia's land from private landowners. In the Czar's mind that land belonged to all the Russian people, not only to the select few.

Alexander III almost choked. "You signed a duma?" he asked, disbelieving. "The first step towards a constitutional monarchy?"

"I did," the Czar stated without apology. "Who else will help the Russian people? This is what we were born to do."

No, Father. We were born to rule.

"The people they are very poor," the Czar continued. "It is better to abolish serfdom from above than to wait for the time when it will begin to abolish itself from below."

"What do you mean 'from below'?" Alexander III asked.

"An uprising. An insurrection," Czar Alexander II replied. "*And it will happen, son*, if changes are not instigated. Attempting to control will never work; you must give the people their freedom, and they will choose to follow if you are a just and good ruler."

"And is that how it has worked, father?" Alexander III asked, attempting to keep the bitterness out of his voice. He would never consider being anything but respectful to his father.

"Regrettably, no," Czar Alexander II shook his head.

"And how have the people repaid the Czar for his unfathomable kindness which has earned him the hatred of the aristocracy?" Alexander III asked in his quietest voice because he was never to question the Czar. But he could hold his tongue no longer, a duma was madness. "And the earlier reforms, father? What have they achieved? The peasants are angrier than ever. There have been five attacks on the Czar's life in the twenty years since the Emancipation of the Serfs was signed the first of March, eighteen hundred and sixty one."

"But I will correct the mistakes I have made. Hence, the duma."

"*Your* mistakes?" Alexander III sighed. "Why do you help the people when they hate you? I know that you mean well, father. But the peasants don't appreciate anything you have done for them, as always happens when people do not earn their own reward."

The Czar's expression remained resolute. "Freeing the serfs backfired. The landowners held onto the best land, while the serfs had to buy back their land from the nobles at an inflated price. The majority were unable to afford the cost. The peasant, freed from serfdom, was no better off than he was before. I see this now. And I waited much too long to correct it—twenty years. Everything can generally be reduced to the basic principles of economics: the serfs are no better off, so they think the emancipation was all a trick and that I am not to be trusted."

"I agree with you that they do not know the heart of the Czar," the Czarevich muttered.

"It is the day of my enlightenment, so to speak, and everything will be different henceforth. You will see, son."

What next? A *democracy*? In spite of his shock, Alexander III saw one benefit to a democracy: no elected official could have given away the land of the wealthy—he would have been tarred and feathered and run out of town. Only a monarch could get away with such a thing. A monarch could be true to his own principles. An elected official must answer to the powers that be.

"What is that?" Nicholas II asked. Alexander III looked out the window in the direction of the boy's eyes to see a man carrying a small white package wrapped in a handkerchief. In an instant the man threw the package under the horses' hooves.

BOOM! There was an explosion so great that it knocked the thrower of the package into the fence.

"AEEEE!" People were screaming and running—those that were not left on the ground in pools of their own blood.

"No! Nicholas, do not look!" Alexander III commanded, taking his son under his arm as he shielded him with his own body. While keeping his head back, the Czarevich could see through the window that there were bodies strewn everywhere. The three of them were unharmed due to having been in the bulletproof carriage.

Police Chief Dvorzhitsky stepped over the bodies to arrive at the carriage, opening the door slightly at the Czar's nod to report. "One of the Cossacks has been killed. Let us leave the area at once, your highness."

"No," the Czar replied, proceeding to get out of the carriage.

Alexander III bit his lip. One was never to argue with the Czar's authority, but inside he was screaming. Alexander III touched the Czar's arm, imploring his father with his eyes to stay in the carriage. He had no doubt that his meaning was understood. But the sovereign turned away, proceeding to get out of the carriage.

"Dlya matushki-Rossii!" *For the Mother Russia!* There was a scream. And then Alexander III saw it. A man standing by the canal fence raising both his arms. In an instant there was something at the emperor's feet.

KBOOM! A second explosion.

"Help!" The Czar was half-lying, half sitting on his right arm. Both of his legs were shattered, and blood poured out from what was left of his limbs. Twenty or more people lay scattered about on the sidewalk and the street, some crawling, some attempting to free themselves from bodies which had landed atop them. Debris and body parts were everywhere, the red blood vivid against the white snow.

Police Chief Dvorzhitsky, also wounded, in a matter of minutes managed to orchestrate applying tourniquets to the Czar's body in an attempt to stop the bleeding, followed by moving Alexander II to one of the open sleighs, as it wasn't possible to navigate placing the wounded man in the more confined carriage.

Alexander III looked to his son Nicholas, tears streaming down the child's face as both watched the patriarch of their family, his legs torn away, his stomach ripped open, and his face mutilated.

Czar Alexander II was returned to his study where, almost twenty years earlier to the day, he had signed the Emancipation Edict freeing the serfs. Alexander the Liberator was given Communion and Last Rites while his family, the Romanovs, looked on.

"I will never forget," Alexander III murmured as he held his father's bloody hand, looking into a face he did not recognize except for the eyes. Grief filled his being for the father he loved while hatred filled his heart for the men responsible.

"Proklyat'ye!" He cursed the man who had murdered his father in his mind. *You have just killed the only person in the world who was on your side! These vermin do not understand your liberal principles, Father. They were not educated by a pacifist romantic poet as you were. Clearly the idiocy of that education must now be clear to you as you lie dying, your life's blood draining from your body.*

Czar Alexander II squeezed his son's hand, a smile of pride revealed somehow through his mutilated features.

And then Alexander II, King of Poland, Grand Prince of Finland, and Czar of Russia died.

Things will be very different now. In his moment of grief, Alexander III, the new Czar of Russia, the largest country in the world covering more than one-eighth of the Earth's inhabited land area, knew precisely what he would do.

I am now one of the most powerful sovereigns in the world. He was the ruler of over one hundred million people and the leader of both the Imperial Royal Army and a brutal police force. Alexander III had never known a people to hate their own ruler more than the Russian people. They did not deserve his father. He might not agree with his father's politics—or his personal morals—but no one could have worked harder. Alexander II had instigated elected judges in the judicial system, abolished capital punishment, promoted local self-government, ended some of the privileges of the nobility, and promoted universities.

And the very people Alexander the Liberator had done this for had killed him.

All of which I will now reverse, the new Czar promised himself.

Perhaps it is the greatest irony in the history of the world that the terrorist who threw the bomb wanted freedom for his people. Energized with a savage anger, he felt the bomb gave him power. And it did. The future of Russia and her ninety-seven million inhabitants was determined in that moment when this violent act destroyed any hope of democracy for his people, sentencing tens of *millions* to death in the century to come.

In the process of eliminating any democratic structure, there was no system in place to fight tyranny when it arrived.

This member of the revolutionary "People's Will" thought he was killing his enemy, but, instead, he opened the door for the enemy to enter.

Czar Alexander III was a man of principles. He counted himself a sensible man: he knew what he was dealing with. He had been taught his views by the blood of his father and those determined to bite the hand which fed them.

The new emperor of Russia now knew what his people needed: a supreme ruler. The only hope was no deviation: one language, one ruler, one religion. And anyone who deviated would be dealt with in the harshest manner—before they could plot and plan and hurt someone else.

Czar Alexander III vowed then to destroy the democratic systems.

Constitutional monarchy? Alexander III felt a tear roll down his cheek as he released his father's now cold hand.

I will rule with an iron hand. *I will cancel the policy my father signed only this morning.*

Autocracy will be unlimited.

Chapter Two
Scotland Yard
March 1882

Crack!

"Aim with your thumb, girl," Sherlock Holmes admonished.

Snap! She popped the whip. The jar shattered where it sat on the post behind Scotland Yard. Mirabella Hudson, niece to the Great Detective's landlady and chief bottle washer of his laboratory, glanced to the water's edge to see a police rowboat in the distance patrolling the Thames.

The odor of hops and malt from the Lion Brewery filled her nostrils, still strange to her after a country upbringing in Dumfries in southern Scotland in the county of Dumfriesshire, the sounds and smells of her family farm unimaginably different from London life.

"I abhor repeating myself to the inattentive." Sherlock Holmes tapped his finger on his chin in obvious perplexity while studying her stance. "I know there was nothing lacking in my precise and expert explanation so I must ask myself why you fail to perform, Miss Hudson."

Mirabella breathed deeply: even the scent of the coal and the Thames—an odor which could charitably be described as "muddy" on its best day—excited her.

Everything about this city of over four million people of every nationality thrilled her. This city of universities, government, sinister underground crime, newspapers, silk-weaving, fashion (in equal parts elegant and disturbing), tanning, exotic foods, and manufacturing.

And what was manufactured that was not manufactured in London? Soap, bricks, precision instruments, furniture and clothing, and even ships and railroads! In seeing London she had been allowed to see the world.

I thank my lucky stars. Even on this cold day in early spring—or late winter, some might say, depending on one's optimism.

"Miss Hudson!" Sherlock commanded. "I am speaking to you!"

I could hardly call that volume speaking. But I am not one to split hairs. "Yes, Mr. Holmes?" she murmured.

"I said why do you fail to perform?"

"I am trying, Mr. Holmes. This is only my third practice with the whip. Please do allow me time to master the skill."

"There is no time, Miss Hudson! While you daydream and spin about in your game of play, criminals prey on the innocent. For every moment you are idle, someone is being hurt. Do not fail me, girl," he admonished. Her tormentor standing before her had the physique of a middle-weight boxer and was in the prime of his life, both physically and mentally. He commanded, "Again!"

"Yes, sir." *Whirrr!* Mirabella snapped the whip and missed the jar altogether, the sound of the popper slicing through the air, rising above the tugboat horns and the children shouting as they played ball. The crisp air, longing for spring, made every sound and smell more vivid in her mind.

Mirabella knew that she was fortunate by anyone's estimation. Due to her independent streak and her difficulty in keeping her opinion to herself, she was wholly unsuited to domestic work and had been dismissed from her first London position. She had been unemployed and unemployable when her Aunt Martha, with whom she lived, found her a position with one of her tenants: Sherlock Holmes. Mr. Holmes was a young detective, not even thirty years of age, but fast gaining a name for himself.

Thankfully no one wished to work for Mr. Sherlock Holmes or her present position might not have been available. Sherlock had, one might say, difficulty in social situations.

"I directed you to wrap the popper around the jar, not to wave at it. Are you deaf, girl?"

"I am not," she murmured, her eyes now fixated on her target. *But there is every likelihood I will be soon.*

"In that case, if you could be so good as to strike the target," he commanded.

Her arm was already sore as she lifted the bullwhip over her head, almost five pounds in weight! Sherlock had insisted that, though the heavier bullwhips did not lend themselves to fast movement, they were more accurate.

And then the humor of her situation struck her involuntarily. *How have I arrived at this strange and unforeseeable place so quickly?* She smiled to herself as she estimated the speed of wind blowing eastward by the breeze hitting her cheek.

Initially, she had simply kept the laboratory clean and documented fingerprints—if anything involving Sherlock Holmes could be termed simple. Then Sherlock had needed a female operative. Mirabella quickly learned that the Great Detective had more in store for her than washing jars and labeling specimens: pistol shooting, fencing, boxing, and *Jiu-Jitsu.* And as if that weren't enough, finally, the ultimate persecution: *Miss de Beauvais Finishing School for Distinguished Young Ladies.*

"Miss Hudson! If you could strike in this century, I would be much gratified!"

Her concentration broken, her arm fell, four meters of cord landing on her feet.

She stared at the formidable man before her, so devoid of the social niceties, which annoyed her all the more because she knew very well that he knew how to behave—he simply chose not to do so in her presence. Though the Great Detective did not favor the company of women, he was generally able to wrap them around his little finger. He was almost genteel in the company of noblewomen and "proper" ladies—a class within which he clearly did not place his oppressed assistant.

"Do you not hear me or are you merely inept, Miss Hudson?"

"How could I not hear you, Mr. Holmes?" reiterated Mirabella with a curtsey, turning towards him. She whispered under her breath, "You never stop talking."

"Ah, the mystery is solved: I must conclude from your reply that you are listening; it is your ability which is wanting. And, my dear girl," he added, brushing his dark, wavy hair out of his eyes, "when you do it correctly I will cease speaking. Silence is therefore unlikely.'"

She glared at him.

"Do you wish to say something, Miss Hudson?"

"Certainly not. I wish to perform as I am directed." *Simply because you are ill-mannered does not mean I should wish to be so as well!*

"An excellent decision, Miss Hudson."

Ever since the Christmas Ball at *Miss De Beauvais Finishing School for Distinguished Young Ladies*, Sherlock had been . . . well . . . *mean.* Cantankerous, easily annoyed, overly critical, unfair—and just plain grumpy! Well, that was Sherlock Holmes, everyone knew that.

But he had been so nice to her at the ball . . . It had seemed almost *romantic.* If anyone could use such a term in connection with Sherlock Holmes, which, of course, one could not.

"Well?" he demanded. "Why do you not proceed?"

She sighed heavily, turning to face him. "Might you consider, Mr. Holmes, that perhaps you are breaking my concentration?"

"It is ludicrous to suggest that I have any part in your ineptitude, Miss Hudson." Sherlock paused, rubbing his unshaven chin.

"And why do you ignore your behavior while exaggerating mine, may I ask, Mr. Holmes?" In spite of her best efforts, her anger was mounting. She threw herself into every manner of hardship at Sherlock's request, had learned everything put before her, and had even assisted in solving one of his cases! Granted because he could find no other female stupid enough to accept the role and to subject herself to his tyranny, but the fact remained that she had played a necessary part.

"The reason for your difficulty in performing the tasks put before you, my dear girl, as you well know, is that you are *not concentrating*."

"But can you eliminate your part in my difficulties from the realm of possibility, sir?"

"There is no need to. I have already resolved the question. As to your concentration, I cannot break that which does not exist. Nor would I attempt it." He placed his hand on his waist, his blousy white cotton shirt open at the chest, revealing his sculpted muscles. His pants were dark and form-fitting.

Mirabella felt her cheeks turning pink and she had no idea why. She didn't feel angry—*precisely*.

Well, she did feel angry. Very angry. But she felt something else too, she knew not what.

She averted her gaze, fingering the whip as she contemplated the next jar on the post. "You complain often enough that the sound of my voice is interfering with the workings of *your* great mind. Could not the reverse be true?"

An uncommon sound met her ears. The sound of Sherlock Holmes laughing.

"Do you presume to compare our respective intellects, Miss Hudson?" She made the mistake of turning to look at him again. His stormy grey eyes, his most terrifying characteristic, were intent upon her. "Amusing."

But he did not look amused. His gaze was like that of a madman's; when he looked at her like that she knew beyond a doubt that there was a thin line between genius and insanity. And that Sherlock Holmes walked that line.

"We are both of the human race, after all," she replied. *Except for you.* "And anyway, our comparative intellects are irrelevant to my point." Though she had to admit that, despite his youth, Sherlock was fast gaining a name for himself as a private detective. Certainly Scotland Yard knew of him. In her opinion, it would not be long before they relied on him.

"And your point is, Miss Hudson?" he demanded.

SNAP. She missed the jar altogether.

"I only repeat that which you have oft said to me, Mr. Holmes, that incessant chattering distracts one."

"How could it be otherwise? But do you imply with your misdirected intellect that Sherlock Holmes *chatters*?" He indulged in a sudden fit of laughter as he threw his head back, his dark curls flying every which way. "A preposterous notion, indeed, no doubt brought on by your overly emotional state, a characteristic of the female sex I have observed."

Pop! The end of the whip grabbed the jar, flinging it to the ground where it shattered. She seethed, "And if you have observed it, sir, it must be so."

"I cannot ignore the facts: I am rarely incorrect. It would be strange indeed to pretend otherwise."

"Please do forgive me for pointing out the obvious, Mr. Holmes, but I do not think that you are best qualified to make the current analysis," Mirabella offered. "Some might claim that the observation and assessment of one's own mind incorporates an inherent bias."

She glanced at him sideways and was rewarded to see the Great Detective raising his eyebrows at her.

"And . . ." she added, smiling, ". . . is *unscientific.*"

She was pleased to note his silence for a long moment as he gaped at her before reclaiming his jaw.

"Sherlock Holmes not qualified for analysis? Sherlock Holmes *unscientific?* My dear girl, I have introduced forensic science, and, in fact, the scientific method to Scotland Yard. Tsk! Tsk! I never imagined you to be stupid nor insane, Miss Hudson, only inexperienced and incompetent. It is my great hope that competence will come with experience; I pray that I do not delude myself. *But look*! I told you not to break the jar! Why do you not do as I tell you, girl?"

"I did, Mr. Holmes. My aim was accurate. The whip touched the jar and knocked it over . . ."

"The popper will follow your thumb when the arm is extended. Granted, it takes a bit of extra skill to wrap the leather around the jar—and I have not seen much evidence of skill in your execution—but no doubt you would improve if you would only focus rather than stringing incoherent attempts at language together."

Why do I stay and tolerate this treatment?

Studying the genius before her, so gifted and yet so oblivious to elementary manners and human kindness, she sighed heavily.

I stay because I have never felt so alive in my life. For a girl to be able to learn more than needlework, music, and water color—well, it was positively thrilling.

In the short time this farm girl had been working for the Great Detective keeping his home and his laboratory in good order—Sherlock Holmes was perfectly slovenly as his mind could not attend to the mundane—she had learned more than in the previous eighteen years. It was the most challenging—and the most exhilarating—time of her life.

She had learned science, forensics, dissection, finger-printing, cataloguing, and autopsy. She could analyze blood stains and identify vegetable toxins. She had learned disguises and accents. The most difficult to achieve of all the things she had learned: to pass herself off as either a lady or as a scullery maid.

Mirabella sighed. The scullery maid had been notably easier, what did that say about her?

She had learned the fighting arts. And now how to use a whip. And yet . . . Sherlock Holmes had taught her that she knew practically nothing. *That is still his favorite lesson to impart.*

She had learned to bear the lack of warmth, kindness, and appreciation. And she had learned to put up with his moods, his drive, and his critical and mechanical approach to her.

"You might wish to consider, Mr. Holmes—" she sighed heavily, "—that a teacher who incites his student with unrelenting insult and torment may block the pupil's access to knowledge."

"No doubt, but I don't see how that applies, Miss Hudson. You are blessed to be in the service of the greatest mind of the century. I have shared with you much of what I learned when I was in contact with the Chinese Embassy, knowledge which is unavailable to most Westerners. My knowledge I generously bestow upon you—while paying you no less!" He chuckled. "If one in your situation is agitated, that is a lamentable failing in your character which must be addressed."

"And you shall no doubt address it," she seethed.

"Very likely I shall. But not now. Return your too easily diverted attentions to the matter at hand and illustrate that you can wrap the cord around the object without breaking it. You have wasted enough of my time this morning. However amusing you may be, Miss Belle, I am not here to be amused. Which is all for the best, as you have not accomplished that either. *Please, dear girl, succeed at something today.*"

She turned to face him, livid, even as she stepped back several steps. She knew her great fortune, but that did not make her cross any easier to bear. And being that her greatest flaw was her temper, as her mother was wont to tell her, there were times when she lost the battle with herself.

There was no one who could lead her to battle more quickly than Sherlock Holmes.

A woman is always to be refined, docile, and agreeable. She heard her mother's voice pleading with her in her head, even as her hand firmly clasped the handle of the bullwhip and lifted it over her head, the five pounds of weight suddenly as light as a feather.

But their situations were different, now weren't they? Her mother had married a country curate and was surrounded by the godly and the pure each and every day. Mirabella glanced at Sherlock. She, on the other hand, was cavorting with the underbelly of London.

Mirabella snapped the popper and quickly wrapped it around the greatest detective the world has ever known and spun him several times before dropping her newest weapon.

"How was that, Mr. Holmes?" she asked demurely.

He glared at her forcefully as he disengaged himself from the whip, but she recognized the appreciative gleam in his eyes, though she had rarely seen it directed at her. She knew she should feel guilty, but that sentiment was strangely absent.

A long silence ensued, and she wondered if she had imagined his reaction.

"That is grounds for dismissal, Miss Hudson."

"But I meant to grab your hat, Mr. Holmes! You know what an incompetent I am—you said as much yourself!"

Sherlock Holmes was completely silent. *Nothing could be worse.*

Her heart fell in her chest, but she could not let it go. "Don't you see, Mr. Holmes? I had to take extreme measures to prove myself capable because you refuse to entertain such a notion. And in proving the great Sherlock Holmes to have made a mistake, I also showed him to be deliberately cruel and unmannerly in his insistence on my inadequacies. What other explanation can there be?"

He stared at her for a long moment, the crease in his brow revealing his twenty-eight years. His slim, muscular structure stood completely erect, appearing even more solidly formidable than usual. "You are, as I recall, still in my employ, Miss Hudson, or at least you were a few seconds ago; you had best remind yourself of that fact. I have my limits—and you are fast imposing upon them, my girl."

"Yes, sir." *As always, I never know when to stop.* She felt her lip shaking now, for the gleam in his eye was gone. She had stepped over the line, she had amused him, but of course she had to take it one step further and turn amusement to anger.

And now dismissal from the most wonderful situation any girl had ever been blessed to have.

Certainly you may always be yourself, but don't expect other people to wish to have you about when you are doing so. She heard her mother's admonitions clearly, dismayed that her headstrong daughter had more in common with her boys than her girls.

"I am sorry, Mr. Holmes." She felt a rumble of anxiety in her chest, always a sign of foreboding for her. "It's just that I try so diligently to do as you ask—more than anyone else would do—and I do very well, and yet it is never good enough."

Staring at her accuser, all hope vanished. She knew that when Sherlock Holmes made up his mind there was no turning back.

"If it is *not* good enough, do you wish me to pretend that it is, Miss Hudson?" His voice was darkly quiet. "I do not pretend and I do not engage in falsehoods. Truth is my quest and my life's purpose."

"No, of course not." *And let's be honest, Mr. Sherlock Holmes: the game is your life's quest.* "I mean, yes, I—"

"And when a real circumstance arises in which your life or the life of another is at stake and you are ill-prepared, will I have paid you a service to have cosseted your fragile, feminine ego?"

"No." *If, indeed, I had such an ego.*

"Excuse me?" demanded Sherlock.

"I didn't say anything."

"Yes, you did. Your expression told me everything."

I cannot be blamed for having a face. God gave it to me, and He no doubt had a purpose in doing so.

"You are not invincible, Miss Belle," he murmured. "This attitude of yours is precisely what concerns me. You must always be on the alert—and you rarely are!"

I know what that expression means. He means to dismiss me. Terror gripped her as she read the meaning in his dark countenance.

If I lose this position, I will be cleaning the privy—if anyone will have me. I won't make enough to live on and I'll never go to university.

How could I have made this mistake again? No one wanted a vocal, intelligent girl with ideas—no matter how good those ideas were, as her last position proved.

Well, technically the reason she had been dismissed was that she had started a fire in her former employer's laboratory—but she had had an idea to help solve his formula, which had merely backfired. Literally. Honestly, could she be blamed for that?

"Pick up the whip, Miss Hudson." Sherlock's silver grey eyes appeared almost slate today, considering her as he frowned. "Describe it to me. Once you truly understand the weapon, perhaps you shall be able to wield it."

She sniffed, not making eye contact with him, containing her tears with great effort. "Y-you see these four leather strands come together to form the ball."

"And the end of the whip?"

"T-the end of the whip is the popper," she whispered.

"Hence its sound. And what causes the sound?"

"The popper travels at some seven hundred miles per hour—surpassing the speed of sound."

"Correct. Speak up when you address me, Miss Hudson. Now let us try again."

She stepped forward on the opposite foot, her eyes glued to the post ahead.

Crash! She successfully wrapped the whip around the jar, but it once again plunged to the ground and shattered.

It was the Great Detective's turn to sigh heavily.

"When we return to Baker Street you are to pack your bags, Miss Hudson." Sherlock turned on his heel and began to depart the courtyard.

"Pack my bags?" She dropped the whip where she stood and stared at his back, the reality far worse than her worst fears. As much as she wished to run and never return, she knew that her heart would break were she to do so. "But why? I said I was sorry, Mr. Holmes . . ."

"As am I." He turned his head only slightly, his body still intent upon departure.

"Then why . . . why must I pack my bags?" she asked in a whisper, barely managing to add, "Where am I going?"

"The more appropriate question is 'where are *we* going?'"

"Very well," she gulped. "Where are *we* going?" In her anguish, her mind began playing terrible tricks on her. She pictured herself being escorted to Millbank Prison where Sherlock would promptly leave once she was behind bars.

"Paris." He raised his left eyebrow at her, his dark hair curling around his strong features. "I am taking you to Paris, Miss Belle."

"*What*?!? Do you mean . . . I am not . . . do I still have a position?" she asked, looking up at him through wet lashes.

"That is yet to be determined. In the meantime, there must nonetheless be consequences for bad—no, *inexcusable*—behavior. There will be punishment for your insubordination."

Paris. Sherlock might have many faults—and he did—but he never lied to her. He meant precisely what he said. *She was going to Paris.*

"You certainly know how to punish a girl, Mr. Holmes!" she managed to exclaim, astonished, clutching her hands to her chest.

"You don't know the half of it, my dear," he smiled, his raven hair waving around his face as he returned to her side and picked up the fallen whip. Throwing the bullwhip forward, he perfectly wrapped it around the last remaining jar, pulling the glass jar towards him entirely intact.

Chapter Three
A Wish Come True

"It appears you have a visitor, nyet?" The beautiful woman scantily clad in scarlet chiffon harem pants, her face covered with a veil, opened the door to the tiger's cage. In this outfit she both blended in with the other circus performers—and was unidentifiable.

"Are you insane? What are you doing?" Beckham exclaimed in horror.

"Getting rid of evidence, naturally." With the door placed between herself and the tiger, she effectively gave Beckham nowhere to escape, the tiger now in between him and the gate she held onto. In point of fact, the predator was fixated on the trapped man, with little to no interest in the gate or the woman behind it. The scent she had rubbed on Beckham's clothing was proving to be effective.

"M-me? I don't know anything!"

"Soon you will not." She smiled. "*Shishka!*" she murmured as the tiger inched towards him.

He reached in his jacket for his gun, only to find that it was now gone. "Where is my pistol? . . . how did. . .?" His speech was erratic as the terror of his situation struck him.

"You really should check for gun when you put your clothes back on, da?" She advised.

"You'll never be able to cover your tracks, Mademoiselle!" he exclaimed, frantically looking about him for some form of weapon, the only thing available being a long wooden pole leaning against the wall, which he snatched up.

"Oh, I think I will, dahling," she purred. "I already have, in fact."

"The British government will find you—and you'll hang! But it's not too late. Throw me my gun."

The woman laughed a taunting laugh even as the tiger advanced upon him, the animal's curiosity now intense.

Beckham kept his eyes glued on the striped carnivore, even though the circus beauty was his only hope at this point. The pole was a temporary barrier at best. "Help me! I promise I won't say a word!"

There. That was better. She resented his lack of attention on her. This was the part of the game she like the best, when her victim understood her power.

"*Nyet*, Mr. Beckham, you should not have spied on me. How you think you can outsmart me?" she asked, almost singing the words.

"This is inhuman! I implore you, don't do this! Shoot me if you must, but this is too cruel by far!"

"Death is occupational hazard in our business, but how wonderful when can be dealt in such creative way, da?"

"How can you? You're not a woman, you're a monster!" he exclaimed, covering his body with the pole as he jutted it into the jaws of the tiger. He was doing fairly well at keeping the tiger at bay—for the time being.

But if the tiger decided to win, win he would.

"Sheltered life you have led," she replied tersely. "In Russia, no shortage of cruelty. Czar provides example daily." Her own beloved father had killed himself after he lost his land under the Emancipation of the Serfs, his family starving—and her mother too weak to do anything about it.

She, on the other hand, had the power to control life.

Every life. Man, woman or beast, it didn't matter. She always initiated the first—and last—strike.

The tiger was positively mesmerized by the scent she had placed on Beckham's clothing. She made a mental note to experiment further with the method. And yet, it was not enough: circus animals were uncertain, having learned to obey man. Some of the wildness had been trained out of them.

This is boring. The tiger was not ready to attack. But she had anticipated this, as she always thought of everything, she congratulated herself. She was so much smarter than everyone gave her credit for—so much smarter than the men she flattered. She shrugged. *So much smarter than everyone, in fact.* Everyone thought she was nothing more than a beautiful performer.

But Beckham had figured it out. Anger rose up in her for his audacity to think he could trap her.

The same anger she had felt when she had found her father dead.

A small bucket sat in a corner, the contents of which she had obtained from a local butcher. Beckham's back was now to her as he had inched closer to the cage door while keeping the tigers at bay. Apparently he expected to find a way to overpower her. *Foolish, foolish man.* As they all were.

Lining up carefully through the bars, she splashed the entire contents of the bucket over him.

"What is this?" he cried out, "My God! *Blood*!"

"Do svidanija, Mr. Beckham. *Good-bye*."

It annoyed her that a drop of blood had splattered on her outfit. Now she would have to change. *How inconvenient.* As she left the caged area with the now empty bucket to be cleaned out, she locked the outside door, dropping the key into her cleavage.

"AEEEEE!" She heard the screams of the man as the tiger attacked him, the scent of the blood irresistible. The tigers were kept hungry to improve their performance. A man would have no chance against a determined tiger, particularly with no weapon. Funny how the sound was barely noticeable amidst the noise of the circus all about them.

As she had known it would be.

It was disappointing that it would be over in seconds; tigers were efficient killers, in most instances severing the victim's spinal cord. She consoled herself with the knowledge that a murder committed quickly was always to one's advantage, making it much more difficult to place anyone at the scene. Amateurs had no place in the tiger cage and it would be assumed the British gentleman had made a foolish mistake.

Which he had. He had underestimated her.

She had wished Beckham would suffer more—she wanted him to know who was responsible for his death and why—but sometimes it just wasn't possible to enact her revenge as she would like to.

On the positive side, by the time the lock to the door was opened no one would be able to tell that the extra blood was not Beckham's. He would be in no position to contradict that notion, being quite dead.

His secrets would die with him.

She had made certain that Stanislav, the tiger trainer, would be far away from the scene of the murder—waiting for her at a proposed liaison, which would likewise provide her with an alibi. The only other person who might have been present, Stanislav's assistant, was even now completely encased in bandages in the hospital.

Quiet ensued inside the tigers' cage except for a few low growls.

My revenge is complete.

Feeling a strange satisfaction, she knew that she had the power and was the victor. She was always the victor.

It is as if I cannot lose. She smiled. Just once she would like to come up against someone who posed a challenge for her.

A flash of lightening crossed the sky—as if she might get her wish.

She nodded to the heavens. *Even control the future do I.*

Chapter Four
London from a Hansom Cab

"You won't be sorry, Mr. Holmes, I will double my efforts," Mirabella promised as she attempted to remove the mud from her boots before stepping up into the Hansom cab.

"221 Baker Street," Sherlock commanded before seating himself beside her in the cab. He brushed his coal black curls now wet with perspiration away from his face. "I already am sorry. But it can't be helped."

She sighed. *Proof that her lovely memory of dancing with Sherlock was nothing but strange imaginings.*

"This is important, Miss Hudson. Please pay attention. *It could mean life or death for you.*" Sherlock turned towards her, his expression pained. "In addition to your purported abilities in science, I admit that you do keep my laboratory well enough. Your jar washing skills are excellent." He paused momentarily before a frown washed over his face, as if something were weighing heavily on him. He muttered under his breath, "I wish we had left it at that. Far less treacherous."

"Left it at *what*, Mr. Holmes?"

"Much to my astonishment, your family wishes for you to continue under my tutelage despite the inherent dangers."

"What does my family have to say to it, Mr. Holmes? I am earning my own income. And if I am to be risking my life, the question should be put to me, not to them, don't you think?"

"Ah, yes, well in the absence of a husband to ask . . . "

Ask the husband? Of all the infuriating . . . ! She bit her lip, coming dangerously close to making it bleed before realization struck.

This was not the Sherlock Holmes she knew. Was he attempting to dissuade her from going to Paris by using the tactic of enraging her? She fingered her whip.

Well, it wouldn't work!

At least not twice. Not on this girl.

His expression was pained as he added softly, "Mrs. Hudson informs your family that she has never seen you happier."

"She is generally seeing me when I am not with you, Mr. Holmes," she murmured under her breath, as they turned onto Northumberland Street, near Charing Cross Station. In her vision was the Northumberland Arms, a public house and restaurant. She knew from Sherlock and John Watson's conversation that it was always crowded and the ales were good. Naturally she must rely on their assessment as such an establishment would not be appropriate for a respectable girl.

"True, it is difficult to always be in the company of one's superiors. Even so, it is terrifying to consider the state of your being if that which I see before me constitutes happiness for you."

I am deliriously happy. She fingered the whip beside her. *I have a weapon and you are unarmed, Mr. Holmes.*

They approached another pub: the Museum Tavern. She knew that Sherlock had lived around the corner when he first arrived in London. *And yet Montague Street is still standing.*

"You're still angry about the whip, aren't you, Mr. Holmes?"

"Yes I am, Miss Hudson," he replied without the slightest pause. "And yet, the incident provided me with some relief. It illustrates that you are in possession of the anger, initiative, and reaction time which you will need to survive in my employ."

"Oh." Her mouth snapped shut. That was not what she had expected to hear. She was, for once, speechless.

Almost. "Did you . . . Mr. Holmes . . . did you incite me to anger . . . on purpose?"

"My dear girl, when will you ever learn? *Nothing* is an accident where I am concerned."

Ask the husband? She repeated the words in her mind. She knew very well that Sherlock Holmes was forward thinking in such matters and believed that women should learn to both think for themselves and to protect themselves. He might come to the aid of helpless women on a daily basis, but he respected those few who displayed independence. Heavens, he kept a picture of Irene Adler in a prominent location and looked at it daily! Mirabella had never met the female deity who held a unique and exclusive place in Sherlock's esteem—a place Mirabella would have thought impossible to attain—but from all accounts Miss Adler was a woman who most certainly had determined her own destiny.

And Sherlock had said more than once that he had a high regard for her father, Henry Hudson, a curate and a man of God, who had even educated his girls at home and taught his children that the husband is to love and cherish his wife, not to possess her—unlike the dictates of many behind the pulpit.

The Great Detective turned abruptly towards her, his grey eyes suddenly smoky, as if he were pleading with her. "Miss Belle, this is important! This is not a game. You must tell me, do you wish to continue working on my cases? Or do you wish to remain our cook and housekeeper?"

"Of course I wish to work on the cases! How can you not know that, Mr. Holmes?" She laughed. "For such a brilliant man, sometimes you say the most ludicrous things! I am an open book. If there is anything you wish to know you have only to ask."

"There are things which are better left unsaid, Miss Belle." He looked away.

That would be a first for Sherlock Holmes!

"I must be assured that you understand the type of work we do. And the inherent dangers," he stated, adding softly, "And that you enter into them willingly."

"I do." Mirabella received the very clear impression that her proximity was uncomfortable for Sherlock. She who revered him so much and who was never so alive or inspired as when she was in his company. "Do give me some credit, Mr. Holmes. I did help to solve the case of the Sword Princess, after all."

She determined not to let Sherlock pull her in with these moments of emotion—unfathomable and unreadable but emotion nonetheless—which tugged at her heartstrings. She knew very well that she was like a fly to be lured in—and then to be swatted when it got too close to his lifeblood. His cases. *His work.*

They passed the Diogenes Club, Sherlock's brother Mycroft's club. They were approaching Piccadilly Circus when she saw the Eros statue followed by the Criterion Bar, where Dr. John Watson had first learned of an eccentric scientist needing a roommate.

"For the time being you still have a position, Miss Hudson, but you must promise to take my instruction more seriously. Why should I waste my genius and my valuable time on a thankless girl which might otherwise be spent undermining crime and saving lives?"

"Oh, I am grateful, Mr. Holmes, believe me." *Especially when you are asleep.*

"As you should be. But I assure you that you will be punished for your insubordination. And your tendency to lie, which I abhor above all things."

"Lie?" she replied indignantly, turning to stare at him. "I do not even know how to lie."

"You just did." He consulted his pocket watch. "Not two minutes and fifty-seven seconds ago."

"Whatever do you mean, Mr. Holmes?" she asked, genuinely dismayed.

The carriage turned onto Paddington Street where she saw James Taylor & Co., shoemaker to Sherlock Holmes. As if to commemorate the occasion, he tapped his foot in annoyance. "I refer to the Case of the Sword Princess, which you claim to have solved."

"I did not say that I solved the case, I merely said that I *helped* to solve the case," she replied.

"It is nonetheless an incorrect statement."

"Of course," she murmured, understanding dawning. "You were not the star of that discourse, therefore it must be untrue."

"You are becoming more like Lestrade every day, Miss Belle." He stifled a laugh, an expression of uncharacteristic amusement crossing his features. "Being abducted by the villains does not constitute solving the case."

"I managed to save myself and four little girls!" she replied indignantly, crossing her arms in front of her waist.

"And would you still be alive today if Watson were not such a crack shot?"

"Probably not."

"And would Watson have been there to fire the shot if I had not deduced where you were and led him to the location?"

"No."

"So who solved the case?"

"You did, Mr. Sherlock Holmes, and I am a wretched, evil girl." She added in a whisper, "And I owe you my life."

"Think nothing of it, Miss Belle. Many people do."

She sighed heavily. "You seem to forget, Mr. Holmes, that I saved Princess Elena from a terrible fate."

"*I forget nothing about you, Miss Belle.*" He stared intently at her before looking away. "Most notably, I recollect that you allowed your revolver to be separated from you, unlike the princess of Montenegro who had the forethought to have hers within her grasp."

Will we ever put that behind us? If Jesus forgave my sin, I should think that would be good enough for Sherlock Holmes. She added in her own defense, "We did work together."

"Miss Hudson," he turned to face her, his expression severe. "I will admit that you have had every success on your side thus far—despite your inattention, incompetence, and carelessness."

"You are too kind, Mr. Holmes," she demurred.

"I am, Miss Hudson. You have been astonishingly lucky." She saw his hand clenching his ivory cane and feared it might split in two.

Chapter Five
221 Baker Street, London

"Mr. Holmes, please do tell Dr. Watson." Mirabella gulped, offering the doctor his after dinner sherry in the comfort of 221 Baker Street. She didn't believe it herself and wanted to hear the news from Sherlock's lips again—in the company of a witness. "I am going to Paris . . . *aren't I?*"

"Yes. With Watson and myself," Sherlock stated, taking a sip of sherry.

"Going to Paris, are we?" asked Watson with the raise of an eyebrow, a slight smile forming on his lips. The good doctor was dressed immaculately, complimenting a physique created by competitive rowing, a sport he had taken up since his injury at the Battle of Maiwand. Rowing only required upper body strength, not the use of his wounded leg. Although Sherlock kept Watson running about London, if the truth be known.

John Watson is going with us! Mirabella felt her heart jump in her chest even as she made a concerted effort for her expression to remain unchanged. Something exciting had now turned into something *wonderful*.

If it weren't for Dr. John Watson who was always kind, always willing to offer encouragement, to laugh and to see the humor in it all—well she didn't think she could have borne it. Just as no one could be more infuriating than Sherlock Holmes, no one could be dearer or more charming than John Watson.

John Watson had his own demons as a result of his time spent as a military doctor in Afghanistan. Was that why he took so many risks with Sherlock? Throwing himself into Sherlock's cases seemed to keep John's memories at bay—until the night came. Mirabella knew from Sherlock that John often paced the floors at night, the young doctor's bedroom being on the third floor above Sherlock's room.

Mirabella glanced at Sherlock. Everyone was tortured in some way. It seemed to be the human condition.

Sherlock leaned back in his wing-backed chair beside the beginning flames of a fire, his open shirt casting his physique in a favorable light. His curls were still damp from a combination of initial perspiration and a light drizzle they had encountered. "I must warn you, Watson, there is a certain danger."

"Naturally. I wouldn't have it any other way."

"Grrrrr! ZZZ-Zzzz-ZZzzz SNORT!" Sherlock's outstretched legs rested on Dr. Watson's bulldog who vacillated between snoring and growling. Prinnie was a formidable and fearsome hedonist, much like his namesake.

"But why are we going to Paris?" she asked, picking up the duster and applying it to the marble fireplace.

"Beyond a doubt I would tell you if you needed to know, Miss Belle. This is a matter of utmost secrecy involving the highest levels of government."

Please, please, dear God, don't let it be another finishing school. What a horrific experience that was, attempting to sit, sew, smile, converse politely, paint, play the pianoforte and be on display in corseted splendor all day. She shivered at the thought.

And then she remembered being shot at and attacked by men with knives, which was almost as bad as the finishing school.

"I must protest, Mr. Holmes." She turned around from the fireplace. His belligerent mood was beginning to wear thin. She said quietly, "I may be your student, and I may be a domestic, but I deserve to know where you are taking me—and, in particular, how much danger I will be in."

The good doctor looked up at her from his chair opposite Sherlock's, surprised, which immediately made her feel ashamed of her protests—although John Watson should be the last person to trust Sherlock without question. She bit her lip and moved to stoke the fire in the black marble fireplace surrounded by dark walnut wood.

"Why?" repeated Sherlock. "When you need to know why I shall tell you, Miss Hudson. Is that clear? This is a highly confidential matter. As to the danger, I thought we had already resolved the matter in the carriage. I have great concerns about your safety which is distracting me from my work—and that *I cannot tolerate* above all else."

He was truly angry now. This was not Sherlock's usual verbal sparring and his unemotional assessment. It was as if something suppressed had finally burst forth. "You are here to assist with my work and not to distract me from it! You must choose once and for all, Miss Hudson!"

"Really, Holmes, I don't think—" John protested.

Oh, no! I've gone too far! As I always do. *Please, please let me go to Paris.*

"Mr. Holmes is quite right, Dr. Watson. I am sorry," Mirabella stated softly. "It isn't that I don't wish to go, I merely wish to be informed."

Sherlock threw the paper down on the stand next to his chair. She didn't think she had ever seen him so impassioned.

Where was the man who had held her in his arms at Miss de Beauvais' Christmas Ball, smiling down at her, congratulating her? Treating her as an associate.

Almost treating her as an equal, if that could be imagined. Sherlock Holmes didn't treat *anyone* as an equal! He had even called her the *world's first lady detective*! High, high praise coming from one so intelligent—and one who considered himself so far above others.

She would never forget the look of admiration in his eyes. Almost *gentle*, if Sherlock Holmes could ever be called that.

It had been a moment of heaven. She stole a glance at the harsh profile of the man sitting beside her.

That moment was gone.

"You told me, Miss Hudson, that you wished to make the decisions about your future as opposed to having your family or myself make those decisions," he continued. "So be it. If you consider yourself to be grown, then act it. I assure you, Miss Hudson, that I cannot re-visit this subject every hour on the hour. I must have the entirety of my energy focused on my work. Do you or do you not wish to work for me, Miss Hudson? If the answer is yes, then we shall not discuss this again and you shall be going to Paris, is that quite clear?"

"Well, of c-c-course! It just seems *unusual* that you should be taking me to Paris. Two men and a woman that is." She searched for anything to say, glancing at Dr. John Watson, whose usual laughter and cordiality had been replaced by surprise.

"Two men and their assistant, you mean," Sherlock corrected, who seemed to be regaining his composure and returning to his usual mechanical state.

"She's quite right. We cannot, Holmes," Watson interjected. "It would destroy Miss Mirabella's reputation."

"I do not care a feather for such things," stated Mirabella, raising her chin. "I do not plan to ever marry. I will be a scientist." She was indeed saving to attend the University of London. For the first time in England, almost two years ago in eighteen hundred and eighty, four women were awarded Bachelor of Arts degrees. And only last year two more women were given Bachelor of Science degrees from the University of London, precisely the degree she wished for.

"There you have it, Watson. Scientists are not in need of a

reputation." Sherlock picked up *The Globe* as if the matter were now finalized. "And I might add that all of Miss Belle's activities will be in the context of detective work. Surely there can be no objection to that, the highest of callings."

"Do not risk Miss Mirabella's future, Holmes," Watson commanded. "She is young and may not yet have settled on what she wants."

Oh, I know what I want. Mirabella's eyes rested on Dr. Watson's blonde-streaked hair, perfectly cut, falling into his concerned eyes in a most stylish manner.

"Miss Belle is a person of decided opinions. I have every confidence that she knows precisely what she wants," Sherlock murmured as if reading her mind, his eyes not moving from the paper, adding under his breath, "and will stop at nothing to get it."

"I will not bend on protecting Miss Mirabella," John Watson insisted.

"Very well then, we shall take Miss Hudson's aunt as a chaperone." Sherlock glanced up from the paper, his manner now calm but resolved. "Mrs. Hudson will go as far as Paris and from there will return home, as other arrangements have been made for a companion of sorts upon our arrival."

"What do you mean *of sorts*, Holmes?" pressed Watson. "Miss Mirabella will either have a companion or she won't."

"Miss Belle will have numerous companions, Watson, I guarantee it," Sherlock replied. "Even so, given the nature of our business in Paris, I must disclose that it would appear quite odd for her to have a lady's maid or attendant."

"As long as Miss Mirabella is not alone in our company and there are other females present, I believe it will be deemed acceptable," concluded Dr. Watson.

"I must advise you, Watson, that if Miss Hudson continues in our service—and that is a very big 'if'—" he glared at her as if issuing a warning, "it can only be a matter of time before she is found to be a person in our employ. Servants are generally not afforded the same requirements as a lady of quality without occupation. Miss Hudson will have to be the final judge if the risks to her matrimonial future are worth the benefits of an apprenticeship. It would be very unlikely that she should marry outside her class anyway. Maids marry footmen, and so on, and they adhere to a different set of rules regarding chaperonage than the upper class."

"To the contrary, Holmes, maids and other women in service are held to much stricter rules of conduct than upper class ladies," remarked Watson. "Female servants might be allowed one dance per year only to mix with eligible young men—outside of conniving to meet the butcher's son at the servants' door in the back of the house. That or a chance conversation with the footman might be a maid's only stolen moments."

"I bow to your superior and no-doubt first-hand knowledge on the different ways which female domestics might contrive to engage in liaisons, Watson," remarked Holmes, setting down the *Globe* and picking up his pipe from the marble end-table beside his chair.

"I have no objection to occupation," interjected Mirabella, finding some difficulty being included in the conversation purportedly about her as she continued to dust. "I wish to be included on the cases. I didn't mean . . . I merely asked . . ."

"Why are you always asking questions, filling the air with pointless sounds and otherwise obstructing the functioning of my mind?" Sherlock sighed heavily, pressing the tobacco into his pipe.

"When are we leaving?" asked Mirabella, suddenly turning from the fireplace. "Or is that too much of a drain of your superior resources to bestow that information upon the lowly and undeserving likes of myself?"

"Beyond a doubt it is." The beginnings of a smile fought to be formed on the Great Detective's lips, causing his mouth to twitch as if he were determined not to be amused.

Sherlock motioned to her to light the candles on the mantelpiece as the last light was now coming through the open window. Between the hand-held gas lamp, the various kerosene lamps in the apartment, the candlelight and the wallpaper of questionable taste in rose and dark brown with hints of purple in the triangular design, the study had a warm glow in the evening. Mrs. Hudson had refused to install gas lighting saying that Mr. Sherlock bloody 'Olmes didn't need any help blowing up the building.

Mirabella herself often sat in front of the fire with Sherlock and Dr. Watson after their dinner—she was a decent cook though one would never know it by Sherlock's matter-of-fact response to all meals, they were mere fuel to him—before retiring to her Aunt's quarters on the first floor.

"Do you have a headache this evening, Miss Belle?" Sherlock directed his attention towards her again.

"Yes . . ." she replied slowly. "How did you know, Mr. Holmes?"

"Your coloring is not at its usual glow. And you are not wearing your glasses and yet are engaged in close-up work. Generally you forfeit your glasses when you have the headache." He pulled a jar out of his pocket. "Here, take one of these. It will help your headache. And it will help you sleep."

She took the jar, reading its contents aloud. "Barbituric acid." She glanced at Dr. Watson, who shook his head. "No thank you. I'll manage."

As she returned the jar to Sherlock, a ringlet of her hair fell forward.

"I see you've tried a new shampoo, Miss Belle."

"W-w-why, yes."

"From your expression, it is not clear to you how I know."

During this interchange, Dr. Watson handed her a bottle of aspirin, from which she took a tablet.

"Thank you, Mr. Holmes, but you needn't trouble yourself." She felt a grave apprehension rising.

"It's no trouble at all, Miss, Belle, I assure you. For one thing, your hair is curlier, as if it is less encumbered," Holmes continued, undeterred. "You now have curled wisps about your face. I certainly hope none of that hair finds its way into my specimens."

"I am ever watchful, Mr. Holmes. And now, if you have no further need of me—" All of her instincts told her it was time to retire for the evening.

"And for another," he continued, "I am accustomed to the smell of tar about you, which I presume would not be your perfume. And I am acquainted with the smell of your laundry soap as it is my own."

"Tar?" she repeated indignantly. "Well, I never! I'll have you know that I finish every rinse with rose water. Of all the rude remarks you have made to me, Mr. Holmes, which are innumerable—"

"Yes, the rose was the overall scent, no doubt contrived to hide the smell of the tar. You went to great pains, and most would never have noted it."

"I never detected it," remarked John.

"It was very faint," agreed Sherlock. "Therefore, I must conclude it is your prior hair shampoo for the purpose of controlling the flaking of the scalp, which I can assure you is a problem you do not have. Probably a long standing habit from childhood initiated by your well-meaning country mother."

"My mother is a very intelligent woman with a wide range of helpful remedies." Mirabella raised her chin. "Why, everyone in the Dumfries parish went to her when they were sick—"

"She also has outmoded ideas of feminine behavior, surprising since your curate father is obviously very forward-thinking in educating his girls. I must say, I put your being spoiled and brash at his door. But that is a different topic to be sure."

Thank the heavens for small miracles.

To her dismay, Sherlock continued. "The lavender shampoo you are now utilizing is a decided improvement over the tar shampoo, Miss Hudson. Which I presume was also chosen to help you sleep. If you would but take the Barbituric acid . . ."

"I can't sleep because you're playing the violin at 3:00 a.m., Mr. Sherlock Holmes!" exclaimed Mirabella, wincing as she managed to swallow the aspirin with her hot tea, the bitter taste dissolving in her mouth.

"Playing helps me sleep," remarked Sherlock in surprise, looking up from placing the tobacco in his pipe.

"And wakes everyone else up!" chimed in Watson.

"Do accept my apologies, Watson. I didn't realize."

"How can someone be so observant and yet so oblivious?" asked Mirabella.

"An interesting question," considered Sherlock, taking a puff on his pipe. "And one which deserves reflection. But first, there is another matter which concerns me." His eyes rested on Mirabella.

Heaven help me. She had completed the lighting and moved to stand beside the door. What was keeping her from running for her life? A full day in Sherlock's company had long since grated on her nerves. She asked reluctantly, "Yes?"

"It appears that you have taken up drink, Miss Belle."

Dr. Watson stared at her in alarm.

"I certainly have not!"

"There is a certain melancholy to your personality of late and a tendency towards being annoyed."

"I assure you I had no such tendency before meeting you, Mr. Holmes."

"To drink or to annoyance?" he asked innocently.

"I do not drink spirits!" she exclaimed. *To excess anyway. An occasional sherry with my Aunt Martha. In fact, I will very likely have one tonight.*

"Yes, clearly there has been a change in your chemistry in the last six months." He continued, ignoring her as if she hadn't spoken as he was wont to do. "Naturally we can rule out the change of life for a young girl or an older woman as you are neither. Next to consider would be a change in sleep patterns or a lack of proper nutrition. We can all be assured it is not the lack of good food, you have the appetite of a horse. You have only just informed me that your problems with sleep are musically rather than chemically related. Therefore, there can be only one other explanation for a person of your gender and age if you have not dipped into drug use."

"While we're on that topic, let us discuss your drug use, Mr. Holmes," she seethed, raising her eyebrows at him even as she placed her hands on her waist. "There we actually have some facts to support the theory."

"And what *is* the explanation for Miss Mirabella's purported mood changes, Holmes?" asked Dr. Watson, bending forward in his mahogany wing-backed chair of rose satin, a smile on his lips. It appeared both men were completely ignoring her this evening.

How charming.

"Please don't answer, I beg you," pleaded Mirabella, placing her hand on her head. "I don't wish my headache to grow."

"Elementary, my dear Watson. Miss Belle's is the behavior of a young woman in love."

Oh, my aching head! She bit her lip and closed her eyes, quickly discovering that his stating the truth was far worse than his hurling unfounded and false insults at her.

The truth. This was the reason people hated Sherlock Holmes. It was all becoming vividly clear to her now. He always spoke the truth.

"But Miss Belle is not generally in the company of any male persons except for me and you, my esteemed companion," Sherlock continued his musing, as if he had not inflicted enough damage for a lifetime in the past few moments. ". . . both wholly ineligible due to the nature of our relationship and our respective ages. I must confess that even I am somewhat baffled, a state to which I am most unaccustomed."

Even through her squinted eyes she could see that John glanced at her, both interest and skepticism written across his expression.

Does he guess? She couldn't help feeling some relief that the idea did not appear to repulse him.

"I have to disagree with you there, Holmes."

I was wrong, the idea does repulse him. She bit her lip. *I should have known. Dr. John Watson is handsome and dashing, always flirting with the ladies, and I am a plain girl with brown hair and brown eyes—and definitely without a twenty-inch waist.*

"On what point, doctor?" Sherlock raised his eyebrows at his friend.

"I do not hold either of us to be too old for Miss Hudson. I am nine and twenty and you are not far behind me. We are young men only just established in our careers—or beginning to be so—Miss Mirabella is a young woman not much more than a girl, granted, but she *is* out of the schoolroom. The Queen herself took the throne at Miss Hudson's age. I am certain some of Miss Hudson's contemporaries are now married, and very likely to men of approximately ten years their senior."

Does he mean—could he mean—the idea of being with me is not unappealing to him? Or is John only humoring Sherlock? Observing his smile and his eyes alighted upon her, Mirabella could feel herself coloring even as her head swam. She reached for the doorknob, strangely unable to place her hand on the protruding metal handle in the dismay of the moment.

Hers was a strange mix of elation and fear: it filled her heart with terror that Dr. John Watson might guess the truth. She would rather jump off the London bridge than he should discover her feelings.

"Y-y-you forget, Mr. Holmes, that I v-volunteer at *Lady Graham's Orphan Asylum for the Female Children of Deceased Officers of the Police*," she managed to utter, stumbling across the words as she spoke. She swallowed hard, determined to sound nonchalant. "I encounter many young men in my comings and goings, so I don't know why you should think it would be Dr. Watson or yourself—if there were any truth in your supposition, which there is *not*."

"I am well aware of every move you make, Miss Belle," Sherlock stated quietly. Upon reflection, he added, "And are there a great deal of young men in that establishment? I would be most surprised to learn it."

"Y-y-yes, of course. There is a young solicitor who is at *Lady Graham's* at times, there is a gardener about the grounds, and a bookkeeper in the office."

"The young solicitor you refer to," considered Sherlock. "Would that be the same solicitor who is engaged to a Miss Bethany Allen?"

"Well, y-y-yes, I believe so."

"I sincerely hope your affections are not engaged there, Miss Belle, because that shall lead to nothing but heartache. And Miss Bethany is your *friend*."

"Well, of course, I didn't mean, I only meant that I do encounter other young men—"

"Ah. And tell me about them." Sherlock leaned forward in his chair.

Yes, I will do that. Right after I am crowned the Queen of England and just before the second coming.

Dr. Watson watched attentively, strangely silent. She could usually count on the good doctor to come to her defense when Sherlock was drilling her, but she was noticeably alone. What could it mean? No doubt he had considered the idea of being her beau—and withdrawn in horror.

Praise God, I found the doorknob. Now if I am able to turn it with all the sweat on my hands, it will be a miracle. "You know, I think it is time for me to retire to my rooms. I should not have trespassed on your time this long. You have been fed, you have your evening tea and brandy, and your papers and your laboratory are in order."

"Not at all," remarked Dr. Watson. "Do tell us about your young man."

Praise the heavens! He hadn't guessed. She bit her lip in relief.

"There is no young man, I assure you, Dr. Watson." She smiled shakily at John. Though she would happily barbecue Sherlock Holmes and throw him to the wolves at this moment she had no wish to be rude to dear John Watson. "And I would much prefer to hear about our assignment in Paris. You know I must pack my bags and prepare for the journey."

"I shall tell you in the interest of peace," agreed Sherlock, watching her. "You will have a task in Paris. And when it is time for you to know the specifics of your engagement, I will tell you. My brother Mycroft in the Foreign Office believes it has implications at the highest levels of government."

"Mycroft?" demanded Dr. Watson. "Must be important."

"I see," murmured Mirabella, comprehending positively nothing at this moment in time.

"Good. So let us return to the former topic which I had not quite concluded," Sherlock mused.

"I have concluded it," she replied through gritted teeth.

"Ah, yes," nodded Holmes in obvious dismissal of her wishes. His expression bore that intensity of curiosity which she had come to fear. "But I must be apprised of the emotional state of those in my employ. Utilizing my powers of both observation and deduction, I do see, Miss Belle, that you are not so very much in love. I will admit that I am relieved to know it."

"Why do you say so, Holmes?" asked Watson, his curiosity now piqued as well.

"It is very unkind of you to discuss my feelings right in front of me as if your opinion were fact," protested Mirabella. "I can be the only actual judge of *my* feelings."

"Having observed your skills of deduction first hand, Miss Belle, I beg to differ," replied Sherlock appearing to consider her words with interest.

"Of all the arrogant, rude—"

"Arrogant and rude? Perhaps. But wrong? No."

"Sherlock Holmes!" she huffed indignantly, grabbing the doorknob tighter and managing to crack the door open, her back to him now.

"Oh, have I upset you, Miss Belle?" He asked innocently, his voice wafting through the room like the spread of the Black Plague. "Well then, let's say 'Good night'. Watson and I will simply discuss the matter in your absence if that is what you prefer."

She slammed the door shut and turned to face him. "I would prefer that you minded your own business, Mr. Sherlock Holmes!"

"I will tell you how I know, my dear Watson, that the charming Miss Hudson is not so very much in love," murmured Sherlock, leaning towards his friend as if to whisper. "She is wearing the perfume, *Jacinthe Blanche*. I went down to Harrods' perfume counter, which has an extensive collection, to verify the scent. Most revealing."

Both Watson and Mirabella stared at him in an obvious state of disturbance.

"And?" ventured Watson after some moments, his expression one of some concern. "Is *Jacinthe Blanche* a perfume which is only worn by girls who are not so very much in love?"

"Don't be ridiculous, Watson!" Sherlock lit his pipe.

"I would certainly wish not to be. I was only repeating your words, Holmes."

"Tell me this, Miss Belle. Are you, in fact, wearing *Jacinthe Blanche*?"

"I am," she glared at him. *And you should be wearing a straight jacket.* She knew full well there was positively nothing Sherlock could deduce from the perfume she was wearing, however arrogant he might be.

"But don't you see, Watson?" pressed Sherlock, turning to his friend.

"I do not," sighed Watson, tapping his finger on the stand beside him.

"An expensive perfume purchased by a girl who won't part with her funds for anything: everything must go to her savings for her college education. Quite illuminating."

"Then why do you say she is not in love?" asked Watson.

"I did not say that she is not in love." Strangely, his pronouncement gave her some comfort. "I said that she is not so very much in love. One must be accurate in one's speech as well as in one's observations."

"Dr. Watson! How revolting that you encourage him!" Mirabella balanced herself against the door, somehow managing not to fall, though she could not quite will herself through it. Not until she had heard the entirety of her employer's insanity.

"There is no complexity to the scent," stated Sherlock, snapping his fingers in the air as if revealing one of the mysteries of the universe. "It smells of violets with no undertones. Miss Belle is a multifaceted young woman deserving of a complex fragrance—a mosaic, if you will. And she must surely be attracted to such a one. She has changed her shampoo and her perfume, that is all. The fact that she has selected a simple scent tells me that she is unsure of her course and is second guessing herself. My conclusion: her heart is not fully engaged."

"There is a certain logic to that," Dr. Watson agreed.

"Even madmen consider themselves to be brilliant," she muttered under her breath.

"Hmmm," Sherlock nodded, his eyes alighting on her. For the first time in their acquaintance, she perceived a strange longing in those dark, intense eyes which pierced everything they alighted on. With a sudden uncharacteristic sensuality, he added, "Miss Belle is a girl who would leave no stone unturned were she decided."

She looked away, wanting so badly to be angry that Sherlock sometimes understood her better than she understood herself—wishing that she might turn that stone over and throw it at his head—and instead she felt . . . she felt . . . she didn't know what she felt. *Intimate and violated at the same time.*

So she did what she always did when she felt uncomfortable and confused: she talked. "If I might interrupt your tirade, Mr. Holmes, only that I might pack the appropriate things so as to better serve you—what clothing will I need for Paris?"

"Very little," replied Sherlock, closing his eyes as he relaxed further into his chair. "And what you will need would fit in a purse."

She opened her mouth in shock, but in a mere instant in time the Great Detective had tuned her out completely, as was his inclination. His eyes were now fixated on the last embers of the fire, as if he were no longer aware that she was in the room.

Mirabella found that she wished Sherlock's fiercely impassioned gaze was still absorbed with her.

She passed through the door, possibly closing it a bit more loudly than was entirely necessary.

Chapter Six
Palace of Westminster

"It's much more complicated than that, isn't it?" asked Mycroft Holmes, mid-level official in the Foreign Office, who was repeatedly asked to assume a higher level position—and who repeatedly refused. Some said Mr. Mycroft Holmes, though only thirty-five years old, might have been the most rapidly promoted man in the history of the British government if he had not been so utterly disinterested in personal advancement.

"More complicated than a ring of spies in Paris determined to kill the Czar?" asked Spencer Cavendish. The War Secretary, the 8th Duke of Devonshire and the Marquis of Hartington laughed, but he was clearly not amused.

"My little department has long known that the anti-Czarist movement is strong in Paris," considered Mycroft, who momentarily wondered that Cavendish was having this conversation with him rather than with the Foreign Secretary. "Stronger even than in Russia."

"Naturally. No one dares breath a word against the Czar in Russia." Cavendish frowned. "That would mean sudden death."

"Not sudden," Mycroft corrected the War Secretary without hesitation. "Death would come after torture."

"At any rate," Cavendish leaned back in his chair. "You did an excellent job, Holmes, of pin-pointing the Cirque d'Hiver as the location of a known nest of spies."

"Indeed. The *Winter Circus*, situated in Paris." Mycroft nodded distractedly. "We were getting very close to identifying the ring of spies when one of our most valuable operatives, Beckham, was found mauled to death by a tiger."

"You don't think it was an accident?"

"No." Mycroft shook his head. "Proof that we were getting close, I should say."

"The Queen is as mad as hornets over the dead agent, I can tell you," Cavendish said.

"I don't believe Beckham was too thrilled with the outcome either," Mycroft added, untroubled at the news of the Queen of England being in a tether over the functioning of his department. He was considerably more distressed at the loss of a man. Her royal highness had been upset before, and would likely be again.

"And now, with everything in utter chaos, Prince George wanders into the web of spies, cavorting with a circus bare-backed rider," Cavendish exclaimed, shutting his eyes momentarily.

"The Commander-in-Chief of the British Army," Mycroft repeated, whistling under his breath. "In the middle of a spy ring."

"Prince George is a good soldier—but a bit of a muffin where women are concerned."

"As many have been before him." Mycroft shrugged, himself indifferent to females outside of the amusement they offered, but aware of the weaknesses of his gender. "I should think the Queen could dissuade him from this course."

"She is his cousin, Holmes, and reluctant to do so. I fear she has left the resolution to us." Cavendish shook his head. "I'd say we have an emergency on our hands, Mr. Holmes."

"I'd say we do, Cavendish. I don't think it can be overstated: if we're not careful, we could have another dead Czar on our hands—and an international altercation." Mycroft frowned. "And though we might be friends with the Czar's government in theory, I can't think we'd want the Russians knowing British military secrets. If this bare-backed rider is a spy for the Russian Czar and Prince George is loose-lipped in a moment of weakness—"

"*Damnation*! Let's hand over our secrets to a country with thirty million soldiers, shall we?" Cavendish swallowed hard. "I know you hate to leave the office, Holmes, but I fear you're going to have to travel to Paris. There's no one else we can trust to see that the thing is handled. Very delicate situation."

"I fear it as well." Mycroft sighed heavily. "But shouldn't the job fall to the Foreign Secretary? I don't wish to step on anyone's toes. It is very disruptive to one's digestion, you know."

"I shall handle the Foreign Secretary," Cavendish replied sternly. "There is too much at stake to let politics get in the way. The peace of the world is at stake!"

"If you insist," Mycroft agreed reluctantly, sighing heavily. "But I won't be going alone. Naturally I won't be involved in any undercover work. Doesn't suit me in the least. There is a little boutique hotel I like in Paris—the Hotel Pont Royal—excellent food. I'll reside there while my operatives attend to the matter of the espionage—under my supervision, of course."

Cavendish raised his eyebrows, well aware of the expense of such a fine establishment, but he offered no objection. "Certainly you must be comfortable, Holmes."

"I wouldn't think of being anything else."

Cavendish cleared his throat. "Who are you going to take with you, Holmes, to unravel this mess, identify the spies and the persons responsible, and to disengage the Chief?"

"*The best*, Cavendish. Nothing less than the best."

Chapter Seven
The Winter Circus
Paris, France

"By Jove! We're at the circus!" Dr. John Watson whistled as he stood outside the *Cirque d'Hiver* at the juncture of rue Amelot and rue des Filles Calvaires.

"So, we're at the crossroad between Amelot street and . . . the street of Calvary Girls?" Staring at the street signs, Mirabella attempted to make the translation in her mind, 'rue' being the French word for 'street', she knew.

"Although the translation is technically accurate, the inference is significantly misleading," Sherlock said. "I believe the reference is to the Congregation of Our Lady of Calvary."

"Calvary being Golgotha, where Jesus was crucified," Dr. Watson stated.

"That doesn't bode well," Sherlock muttered.

"The crucifixion was not gloomy or foreboding at all. It was an act of intense love," Mirabella murmured.

Sherlock was never superstitious, or religious for that matter, but he was consistently serious and usually somber. His expression turned even darker than usual. "I do not see much evidence of love in this world. Only darkness and destruction."

"And the fun begins," Dr. Watson muttered.

From where Mirabella stood, she could see numerous horse drawn carriages, a stylish lady of quality walking her poodle alongside her lady's maid, a milliner's shop displaying every manner of color and feather in elaborately fashionable hats, French soldiers walking together, a horse-drawn subway bus with customers swaying back and forth atop the bus, and a man pulling a cart of vegetables while watching a young lady dressed in black mourning attire.

"Sherlock Holmes, I dare you to feel something," Mirabella stated under her breath. "How can you not? Isn't it sweet to see that older gentleman feeding the pigeons? Or the girl selling flowers? Each of them has a life, with people they love and care for. Every person is a magnificent universe unto himself. Look at that beautiful young woman in mourning, such a becoming sheer black veil she is wearing, doesn't it touch your heart to see her longing for her love, Mr. Holmes?"

"She is a lady of the night selling her wares," Sherlock stated. "It is a disguise."

Mirabella gasped, placing her hand on her mouth. "You don't mean it, Mr. Holmes!"

"I wish that I did not," Sherlock replied. "Most morbid. But the costume is apparently stimulating to some men—clearly it is to the fellow pulling the vegetables. As for the older gentleman feeding the pigeons, he is homeless and has very little to eat, and yet he spends what little he has to feed his only friends."

Mirabella bit her lip, making a mental note to buy a loaf of bread and a slice of cheese for the gentleman seated on the bench. The birds would have no use for the cheese, so at least the old man might eat that.

"See here, Holmes!" Dr. Watson interjected, apparently attempting to divert his friend even as he forcibly turned Mirabella to face the building. He was never one to approve of ungentlemanly conversation in her presence. "Consider the Cirque d'Hiver, if you will. What you see here is a twenty-sided masterpiece of architecture, a Corinthian column at each of the twenty sides so as not to obstruct the views of the central circle. And it holds *four thousand people*! I know architecture to be an interest of yours, Holmes."

Sherlock bestowed an expression of disdain upon the structure before them. "The Cathedral of Notre Dame is a masterpiece. This building before us, however, is the effort of one who did not know when to stop. Simply because one exerts effort does not mean that the effort is useful or worthwhile. Take Scotland Yard, for example."

Giggle. Mirabella was finding Sherlock's sarcasm surprisingly amusing today. But then, anyone could please her today!

I'm in Paris! Mirabella had thought she could not be more impressed when she first saw London, but she had never seen such a beautiful city in her life or with more fashionable people than Paris.

She smoothed her beautiful peach silk crepe de chine gown, feeling very attractive, a most unusual feeling for her to have. She was, after all, too shapely for the fashion of the day, added to the fact that she had plain brown hair and plain brown eyes—and was too tall.

But if one were lucky enough to be here, how could one not be gay in *Gay Paree*?

And what a thrilling trip it had been! The three of them along with her Aunt Martha had taken a train from London Charing Cross to the Dover Priory station. The train had boarded a ferry at Dover—it was astonishing! They never even left the train!—then the ferry took the train to Calais where she entered France for the first time in her life. From there the train brought them to Paris. Once they had landed here at the *Cirque d'Hiver*, Aunt Martha had left to visit a friend before her return trip to London. Although Mirabella didn't expect to have a ladies maid at her Paris lodgings, presumably she would have a companion. Being a domestic in a gentleman's home was one thing, but travelling with two gentleman unchaperoned was another.

"I never saw so many columns," Mirabella exclaimed, returning her eyes to the home of the Parisian circus. "And look at the statues of the Roman soldiers!" The soldiers stood on podiums guarding the entrance, a green marble sign above the massive doorway embellished with gold. A wrought iron fence surrounded the astonishing structure.

"When in Rome, do as the Romans do," Dr. Watson stated, taking Mirabella's arm and leading her towards the entrance.

Giggle. "We're not in Rome, silly! We're in *Paris*!" Mirabella wanted to pinch herself.

"What are the paintings all around the circumference of the building?" Mirabella asked, glancing up some twenty feet. "Horses?"

"It must be obvious that it is the history of horsemanship depicted in pictorial form," Sherlock replied. "As if it needed to be done. Artists appear to have a great deal of time on their hands."

"Have a care, Holmes! We're at the circus! Fun, excitement, entertainment!" exclaimed John Watson, echoing her thoughts, the grin returning to his face. "Can't we enjoy ourselves for a day?"

Sigh. She returned her gaze to Dr. Watson, who looked to be closer to twenty-five than thirty. His boyish looks had never shown to better advantage, Mirabella thought as she smiled up at him, studying his blonde-streaked brown hair which was always neatly and stylishly cut. Unlike Sherlock Holmes, who ordinarily never got a haircut until it interfered with his work—and sometimes not then if he was too absorbed. There was nothing in Sherlock's mind except his work: everything he did was to that purpose alone.

"Why are you gasping for breath, Miss Belle?" demanded Sherlock, observing her.

"I'm just so very happy, Mr. Holmes. How could I not be?"

"Now see here, Holmes," Watson continued, "Do lighten up. There is every manner of entertainment before us!"

"It is quite astonishing!" Mirabella agreed, taking in all the posters even as she took Watson's arm. "Jugglers, clowns, elephants, tigers—even tight-rope walkers! There are midgets, giants—and mermaids! They even shoot a lady out of a cannon!"

"Yes, it certainly speaks to the sad condition of the human race that in these times the circus vies for popularity with the music-hall and the cabaret as the most popular entertainment of the day," Sherlock commented.

"I wouldn't for the life of me approach life with the cold analysis you apply to everything, Holmes," mused Watson. "Where is your emotion, old chap?"

"Literature, opera, and theatre impart every manner of emotion," countered Sherlock. "We have the immortal Shakespeare—and you imagine that I am in need of the bearded lady?"

"You are not without your vices in the popular realm, Holmes," Watson suggested, smoothing his tweed jacket.

"I do like a good boxing match—but it is critical to the conditioning of the body—and mind," Sherlock replied, pushing his long, dark curls out of his eyes. Sherlock had attended to his toilette for the purposes of the mysterious assignment, and was looking rather dapper himself in an embossed blue velvet vest, silk ascot tie in navy blue, and white cotton shirt.

No doubt someone at the hotel had ironed his pants for him. Mirabella wondered why she had not been shown to her lodgings yet. Her things had been put somewhere, that was a fact in evidence since they were missing. She was not particular, she did not need a fancy hotel: a ladies' boarding house with a private room would suit her fine.

"Must every form of entertainment be a venue to self-improvement, Mr. Holmes?" asked Mirabella. "Can you never experience the magic of the moment?"

"I assure you, Miss Belle, that I am neither entertained nor improved by this moment."

Mirabella giggled in spite of herself. Sherlock Holmes might be the world's most trying man, but his brain never stopped, and though he might find most experiences dull—there was never a dull moment with *him*.

The only thing wanting was some sense of being in a relationship *with* him rather than being an outsider watching a spectacle: some sense of being connected to him. She saw that connection between Sherlock and John Watson, but she herself was like a wheel on a bicycle, to be replaced when its usefulness had expired. It was clear that her admiration for and enjoyment of the Great Detective was one-sided, and it did reduce her pleasure in her situation somewhat.

She pursed her lips, determined to savor and appreciate her special situation for however long it might last—all the sights she never expected to see, the people she never expected to know, and the things she never expected to learn.

"You mustn't take Holmes too seriously, Miss Mirabella," pleaded Watson, taking her hand. "I can't believe we are arguing about the circus! In *Paris*! Let us be gay and forget the old duffer!"

She stared hard at Sherlock. "When do we attend the circus, Sherlock?"

"We shall attend at eight o'clock this evening. And by *we*, I mean Watson and I," stated Sherlock, straightening his silk ascot. "You, my dear girl, will be performing."

Chapter Eight
rue des Filles Calvaires, Paris

"Perform in the circus? Are you quite mad, Mr. Holmes?" Mirabella exclaimed, dropping John's hand, feeling that she might hyperventilate on the spot. Fortunately the good doctor took her by the elbow and steadied her.

Wait, I know the answer, you are!

"I am not a circus performer!"

"Did you think I brought you here for pleasure, Miss Belle?" asked Sherlock, glancing at her disinterestedly. "I told you very clearly that this is a working excursion."

"But if you had told me you expected me to perform in the circus, I never would have come!"

"That is precisely why I didn't tell you." Sherlock twirled his ebony cane. "I hope that you are not allergic to animals or that would make you entirely un-useful to me, Miss Hudson."

"How horridly selfish of me if my inability to breathe should inconvenience you, Mr. Holmes!"

"Indeed it would," he replied upon reflection.

"Oh, you . . . *you* . . . I could . . . !"

"Ha! ha! ha!" John Watson began laughing with his characteristic delight and optimistic outlook.

Sherlock turned and raised an eyebrow. "You, too, have an important undertaking to perform, my dear Watson."

John Watson stopped laughing abruptly. "But I thought you said we would be attending, my dear fellow . . ."

"And so we will. But you have perhaps the most important part to play of this entire charade, old chap." Sherlock tapped his cane on the ground, adding emphasis.

"To suppose that the success of the mission rests on my shoulders fills me with a deep foreboding." Watson took out his handkerchief and wiped his forehead.

"Never fear, Watson, it is a role imminently suited to your talents and abilities."

"And when did you plan to tell us this, Holmes?" John demanded, suddenly joining the ranks of the offended, his handkerchief held in mid-air.

"Let's see, it is now two o'clock. Miss Hudson will be performing at eight o'clock. Is that sufficient notice?"

"You are far too accommodating, Mr. Holmes," Mirabella uttered through barred teeth.

"Even I am entitled to a shortcoming, Miss Hudson. I realize it boggles the mind." He sighed with regret. "And I fear that a tendency towards duty and service is mine."

"Either that or the constant need for excitement and stimulation," muttered Watson.

"Realized through the persecution and torment of anyone who is foolish enough to associate with you," added Mirabella.

Chapter Nine
The Girl who Danced on Horses

The white plumed horses moved at a slow gallop in the circular ring below them, all strung together.

"I say, Holmes, look at that girl!" exclaimed Watson, as they sat in their box seat watching the bare-backed rider jump from horse to horse for the evening performance of *Cirque d'Hiver*.

"Am I to understand that you approve of the young lady, Watson?"

"You would understand correctly, Holmes," John Watson stated in between the applause of the crowds.

"Curious. You haven't even met the girl. How can you bestow your good opinion so freely, my dear Watson?"

Sherlock knew that Miss Belle would be performing in the next few acts and was watching the sidelines for her. Only a hand was visible, clutching the red velvet curtain in such a manner that caused one to imagine the domed ceiling collapsing upon the central ring. *That would be Miss Belle.*

"Not freely given at all," Watson argued. "The gold spangles on her pink tights are quite exquisite."

"Most unnecessary. I do not perceive their function."

"They draw attention to her assets," Watson muttered, his eyes not moving from the performer.

"I only just forwarded that you can have no opinion of her assets as yet, my good man." Holmes lifted his eyebrows at his friend.

"I have a reasonably good notion where they lie," Watson murmured.

"As you have informed me. Gold spangles on pink tights." Sherlock tapped his finger on the metal bleachers. "Most ornamental."

"That's not the term I would use, Holmes." Watson sighed with obvious impatience.

The rider had initially worn a beige-colored leotard which made her appear naked. To those, such as Watson, who wished to envision such a thing. Sherlock did not. Quite a cheap—and uninteresting—trick, in his opinion.

The lady had then been strapped to a so-called wild horse which had reared and galloped about the stage to the apparent delight of all

but himself. When the audience had endured that performance to its
predictable conclusion, she had quickly changed into a pink leotard with the
aforementioned gold spangles and was even now hopping about on moving
horses.

"What a beauty! So lithe! She looks to be dancing in the air."

"Technically she is jumping, Watson, not dancing."

"Look at her now! She's riding on two horses at once, one leg on
each horse!"

"That's what she does. Did it need to be done? And what purpose
does it serve?" Sherlock yawned, looking away momentarily to study the
crowd, which proved equally uninteresting. He and Watson were seated in
the reserved box seats allowing them some privacy and the best views.

Astonishing that I can be bored in this cornucopia of stimulation.
Was there any locale which bombarded the nose more between the smells
of the animals, the people, and the assault of salty and sugary foods? Not
to mention fatty meats and spicy condiments. Perhaps a street fair in India
could offer as much, but Sherlock didn't think so. Warm caramel, popcorn,
apples, peanuts, lemonade, lager, hot dogs, cotton candy, assorted frying
meat which one wished never to have identified, perfume, sweat, flowers, all
mixed with the smell of dirt, hay, and animals.

"I do not understand how you can see this beautiful girl moving
her body with such artistry and athleticism and not be . . . *inspired* . . . by it,
Holmes."

"And I do not see why you would care to waste your time watching
it." *And the lights.* There were lights everywhere, not to mention every
color visible on the clothing of both the performers and the spectators, the
brighter the better. As if the smells and sights weren't staggering enough,
the sounds were deafening between the squealing children, the braying
and roaring animals, the applause and shouts of the crowds. For Sherlock
Holmes, who felt stimulated in the most mundane of circumstances and who
noticed things others did not, it was less than pleasurable.

And yet, he who both thirsted for stimulation and was repelled
by it found the Circus underwhelming in its bombardment of the senses.
It was not the type of stimulation which provided any information or
required anything of his intellect; it was mindless and purposeless. It was
meant to provide pleasure, but he could not find the amusement in it—he
who desired, longed, *craved* the mindless thrill. Even the drug promised
enlightenment: the circus only reinforced his low opinion of the human race
which he willingly and devotedly served.

The deafening shouts of the prize fights could not compare in volume, boxing matches which Sherlock entered, not for the money, but because the endangerment of his life erased his boredom. Boxing was very different from this because, in a fight, along with the stimulation came the physical release. Boxing was an exercise for both the mind and the body.

"That's because you're not normal, Holmes. You're a machine and not a man. How can any man watch this exquisite creature and not be besotted?"

"Not normal?" Holmes reflected. "If your behavior is normal, Watson, I count myself fortunate to be otherwise."

Fortunate to be who he was—the Great Detective. Destined to live his true vocation, which was the air he breathed.

Sherlock's profession was the expression of that intelligence which was the drive behind all his actions, his reason for being, the source of his elation—and the venue for his daily torture.

John Watson chuckled. "I know you take great pride in not being like the rest of us, Holmes."

"You have lived with me for almost a year at Baker Street, Watson. I am comforted to learn that you have deduced something in that time." Sherlock cleared his throat, the discomfort of being imprecise manifesting itself in a physical form. "Eleven months, fifteen days, sixteen hours, and seven minutes, to be exact."

"It is a wonder I am still alive and un-incarcerated," Watson murmured before becoming suddenly animated. "Look at that, Holmes! She's doing the splits across both horses! What agility!"

"Astonishing."

Damnation! Sherlock searched his pockets for his pipe. He had somehow left it in his other jacket. He had grown distracted of late.

"*Zounds!* Holmes! You didn't even blink an eye when Madame Zazel was fired above the audience from a cannon!"

"Ah, the stuffing of a woman in a spring-loaded catapult and the lighting of same. Who would have thought it had the power to excite?"

"Haven't you been entertained by any part of this spectacular show, Holmes?" Watson managed to tear his eyes from the stage and narrow them at Sherlock.

"The clown who taught Tom to sing to the accompaniment of bagpipes, a trombone, and a violin was amusing, I must admit."

"The singing donkey? That was the only part of the circus you enjoyed?" Watson repeated, dazed.

"*Enjoyed* is a bit of a stretch, Watson. Except when Tom refused to sing, that was pure bliss, to be sure."

Watson stared at him in disgust or disbelief, it was difficult to tell which, and perfectly immaterial as far as Sherlock was concerned.

"To be quite honest, my dear fellow," Sherlock added, "I believe Tom was bored with the entire proceeding. That tells you something, don't you think, when you find pleasure in something which bores an ass?"

"Look at the girl!" Watson stood up and pointed to the bare-backed rider. "Now she's on her head showing off those gorgeous legs!"

"I wouldn't expect her to do anything else."

Sherlock motioned to one of the attendants, who handed them each a beer.

"Ha! Ha! I just had a thought, Holmes," Watson said when the attendant had withdrawn.

"That is a welcome and unexpected development."

"You said that I have a role to perform here." Dr. Watson chuckled. "Would that my task were to court that young lady."

Sherlock turned abruptly to study his friend. The Great Detective was not one to be surprised.

"Why do you stare at me, Holmes?"

"That's precisely what your job is, my good man."

Watson kept his eyes glued to the lovely spectacle, muttering under his breath, "Don't toy with me, Holmes."

"I wouldn't dream of it. Her name is Miss Joëlle Janvier—though naturally that is not her real name—and your assignment here is to wine and dine that young lady."

Watson turned abruptly to stare at him. "You can't be serious, Holmes."

"Have you ever known me to be anything else?" Sherlock scrutinized his companion, feeling like a teacher witnessing his pupil's first success. "And how did you deduce your primary role in this case, Watson?"

"Deduce?" Watson chuckled. "It was wishful thinking only. And still I don't believe you for a moment."

"Believe me, it is true." Sherlock felt a grave disappointment in the knowledge that Watson's astuteness was attributable to a longing born of infatuation rather than a deduction derived from reason. "It is essential to the case that you should be at your most amorous with Miss Janvier and convince her of your unrivaled love and devotion."

"You astonish me, Holmes."

"Do I? Beyond a doubt I astonish most of the people most of the time, so I suppose that is not surprising. Although I might have thought you would be accustomed to it by now, my dear fellow."

Watson returned his eyes to the beauty and let out a low whistle.

"Steady, boy. I told you it was an occupation perfectly suited to your abilities," Sherlock said.

"But not my pocketbook. The girl must have dozens of suitors—no doubt with pockets to let. Of what possible interest could she have in a poor doctor?"

"You wouldn't be poor if you wouldn't fritter away your money, my good man. At any rate, the money is the least of your worries, Watson."

"Money is always my greatest worry," Watson muttered.

"You shall have a carte blanche, my dear fellow. In fact, the more you spend the better."

The young doctor had the look of child who had just opened the toy of his heart's desire. "You want me to romance a beautiful girl with a pocket full of blunt?"

"Didn't I just say so?" Sherlock looked at Watson in some dismay. His generally capable companion was remarkably slow-witted this evening. "Really, Watson, don't force me to say everything twice. Do let us move on."

"As much as I love the idea—and it is a *definite* step up from our last undertaking traversing the London sewers—of what possible benefit would my romancing a circus beauty be?"

The audience burst into clapping.

"Just play your part, Watson, as painful as it is for you. It shall all become clear shortly."

"If it's all above board, why don't you romance her yourself, Holmes? It's your case."

Holmes raised his right eyebrow at his companion. Watson was uncommonly dull-witted this evening. Proof that a strong interest in women diminished a man's intellectual powers.

In an instant Sherlock Holmes felt something he never expected to feel: a slight longing to take pleasure in all this nonsense. Of late he had wondered what it would be like to experience the joy he saw in Miss Belle's expression, her joy of both discovery and of every day, simple life.

Sherlock frowned. *I must have work.* Ever since *Miss de Beauvais'* Christmas Ball he had been agitated and angry. *Nothing will interfere with my work. I must pursue my life's ambition.*

"Right," Watson murmured. "I only thought because you're a genius and all, that if you applied yourself to the task at hand, surely—"

"I would have no idea how to romance a woman. And particularly a . . . a . . . circus performer," Sherlock interjected. "What would I discuss with her? Faraday's research on refrigeration? No, Watson, that is entirely out of my skill set and completely within yours."

"It isn't that difficult, Holmes. Instead of being underhanded, devious, unkind, and cryptic, flatter the girl. *Be nice.*"

Holmes began to grow concerned. "Do you have a fever, Watson?"

"Right," Watson murmured. "Foolish of me, old chap. You have the right of it, it could never work."

"Just so."

Perhaps having vacuous sisters and growing up with a much older brother who was the pride of the family and who had dressed him in girls' clothing had formed Sherlock into the person he was, having a distaste for the feminine. For that, he was not sorry. He was a man who revered logic and method above all else and who had no time for the mundane, dramatic, and ridiculous. From his observation, women were inclined to make the smallest, most insignificant incidents into the greatest importance (such as the selection of chinaware and lace) and to overlook those things of true importance (such as the twenty-seven brands of tobacco sold in London, the time it took a body to decay, and the solving of crime). Certainly Sherlock felt warmth and respect for his own mother, but it was a fact that he was a man's man while his brother Mycroft was the apple of his mother's eye. In truth, outside of Mycroft, who in his eccentricity was not a kindred spirit in every way, Sherlock had no true friends.

Until Dr. John Watson that is.

Sherlock found that he liked having a friend.

"But what purpose could my romancing that gorgeous girl have?" Watson demanded. "As much as I love the idea, I refuse to do it unless you tell me what this is about, Holmes. Why are we here?"

"We are here, my good fellow, to determine if that lovely lady is a danger to our beloved England."

"Of what possible harm could a little gal jumping from horse to horse in pink sequined tights be?"

"Cavorting with the Commander-in-Chief of the British Army?" It was Sherlock's turn to laugh heartily. "All the harm in the world, I should say! It doesn't take an espionage genius to tell us that."

Watson almost choked on his beer, lunging forward. "That girl is seeing Prince George, the Duke of Cambridge?"

"Indeed. I just said so didn't I?"

"And you want me to go after Prince George's girl?"

"Why do you keep making me repeat myself, Watson? Most

tedious."

"Now I know you're crazy, Holmes."

"But don't you see, Watson? You're destined to court the stunning bare-backed rider. No one better."

Even from their private box overlooking the ring, the noise was deafening each time the crowd clapped and roared, but the box did allow for some privacy.

At this moment the tightrope act was in progress so the crowd was subdued except for the occasional cough or sigh.

"Of course I see, damn it!" retorted Watson under his breath, running his hand through his hair. "I see that Prince George is courting Miss Janvier and I don't have a bat's chance in hell with her—and that it might be dangerous for me if I did!"

"Come, come, Watson, Prince George is indeed Commander-in-Chief of the British Army, with obvious ties to the Foreign Office, but I doubt very much that he'll call you out."

Drum roll! Rat-a-tat-tat! Rat-a-tat-tat! The tightrope walker had reached the center of the tightrope some hundred feet in the air.

"I am most comforted," Watson muttered.

"Prince George *is* married after all—on paper anyway. Scandal, don't you know." Holmes took a sip of his beer.

"Everyone knows the Duke of Cambridge has a preference for the ladies. Doesn't strike me as the type who is afraid of scandal—may derive a great deal of pleasure from it, in fact."

"No doubt he does."

The next act was now underway, none other than the high wire acrobatic act. The female acrobat in a shiny sparkling orange outfit did a triple somersault in the air before her partner in cobalt blue tights caught her from another swing. Next they swung precariously back and forth.

Sherlock hoped that the fact that the female tightrope walker was having an affair with the clown in the wings watching her did not make her partner less inclined to catch her.

Possibly I am jumping to conclusions. The performer dressed as a clown could be a brother rather than a lover, but the man definitely had an attachment to the lady tightrope walker. He seemed at great pains to avoid others observing his interest, so it seemed more likely he was a lover.

"Ha! Ha!" laughed Watson abruptly, throwing back his head. "I don't know why I'm so worried about a duel."

"Neither do I," agreed Holmes before reflecting for a moment.

"Damnation! If my life is of so little interest to you, I assure you it is of some interest to me!"

"See here, Watson, I am painfully aware that you have a demented love of humor—and I might add that it is not your strong suit—but this is no time for jokes."

"Jokes?" Watson demanded. "Do you believe me to be jesting, Holmes, when I say that I fear for my life if I pursue this girl?"

"Mycroft believes this mission to have implications of the utmost importance," Sherlock stated. "*World-wide* implications."

"Your brother?"

"Mycroft is behind all this, didn't you guess? Even you might have been able to guess it if not deduce it."

"You said earlier that your brother was involved with the case. But what the deuce does Mycroft have to say to a beautiful girl in sequined tights?" repeated Watson, but his tone was somewhat calmer. "Hmmm . . . he works for the British government, doesn't he? In the Foreign Office?"

"*Works* for the British government? Mycroft *is* the British government. To say that they work for him would be more to the point."

"Ha! Ha!" Watson smiled but his expression was disbelieving. "If Mycroft ran the government, more people would hear of him."

"My dear brother doesn't care about power and yet he wields it with a word or a nod."

Watson stared at Sherlock, stunned. "I thought Mycroft was merely a mid-level official."

"Very true. With no ambition whatsoever. He's far too lazy."

"What the devil are you talking about Holmes? Make sense, man!"

"*Quiet*, Watson! Keep your voice down."

"I would be positively shocked if anyone could hear us over the din," Watson muttered, glaring at him. "Besides, my days are numbered, why should I care? Prince George's girl, indeed!"

"Let us return to the subject at hand, Watson." Sherlock could see that there was going to be no peace until he explained the whole. "If I am conveying the truth to you, and I could do nothing else, then it must be your pursuit to make sense of it. Only consider: everyone at the highest levels of government consults with Mycroft—even the Prime Minister and the Queen." Sherlock chuckled to himself. "He hates to be bothered. And yet—if there is a secret in the government—Mycroft knows about it."

"How does Mycroft come into such knowledge?" demanded Watson, apprehensive.

"Mycroft is quite unable to avoid taking in everything around him." *Quite exhausting, really. At times one would wish to think of nothing.* "He has a mind which observes and analyzes, remembers it all, catalogues and re-arranges it, and makes conclusions—which turn out to be accurate."

"No doubt he sees things which other people miss," shrugged Watson. "But how did that propel him to the limelight in the world's most powerful government—"

"He solved a few puzzles, came to some correct conclusions, identified problem areas and questionable people—not least of which was a spy in the government—and voila, word gets around. And then because of this, of course, people confide in him." Sherlock shrugged, setting down his beer. His eyes scanned the floor for Miss Hudson. Ah, there she was, on the sideline, some twenty feet from the clown. He smiled. "Taking into account that Mycroft is in the unusual position amongst government officials of knowing right from wrong, has no ambition, and would therefore never utilize the information for personal gain, he becomes everyone's confidante."

"And Mycroft is interested in a bare-back rider in pink sequined tights?" asked Watson.

"On a personal level, no." Sherlock stared at him, abashed, unable to hide his amusement.

"Blasted, Holmes! Of course not on a personal level." Watson pulled on the vest of his three-piece suit, immaculate as usual. That the retired army doctor found the funds to always be dressed to the nines led Sherlock to conclude that his friend must be hocked to the hilt. It was time to invest some of Watson's funds for the doctor's own good—in order to maintain his lifestyle, if nothing else.

Sherlock drew near to his associate. "Possibly the lady is a spy attempting to find the troops' movements, weapons, headquarters. Everything that an enemy of the crown wishes to know, Prince George *does* know."

Gasp! The crowd all seemed to sway to the side, even as the male tight-rope walker almost missed catching his partner for the second jump. She gave him a look of complete anger, which seemed to please him.

Yes, they have been involved as well.

"Ah, but surely Miss Joëlle Janvier has been thoroughly investigated. What is known about her?" Watson asked with a sudden show of interest.

Now we're making progress. Why did it take so long for others to get to the work? *The case.* That was the place of true bliss.

"Hmm . . . Quite a lot is known about her and almost nothing."

"Whatever do you mean, Holmes?" Watson asked, but his interest was only partially engaged as yet, of that Sherlock was certain.

"She is of Russian descent. Countless duels have been fought over her. A young Italian opera singer with a promising future at *La Scala* committed suicide when she refused to see him again; apparently his wages were not commensurate with his talent. A high-ranking employee of the Bank of England became obsessed with the idea that if he were to fulfill our lovely horse rider's unorthodox desires that she might fulfill his. But life doesn't always go as planned: now our former bank employee is enjoying all the sensual delights a prison cell has to offer."

"And the stolen funds?" asked Watson, unable to conceal the interest in his expression. *Excellent.*

"None of the money has been recovered. What might you conclude from this Watson?"

"That the young lady has a power over men, that she is fond of money, and that her moral compass does not point north."

"That is putting it very politely, Watson. Most gentlemanly of you."

"Of course," Watson smiled, nodding to his friend. "How would you describe her then, Holmes?"

"I would call her an enchantress, a seducer, an adulteress and a very dangerous woman." Sherlock tapped his fingers on his knee. "And I can't help but wonder if she had anything to do with Beckham's death. She had an iron-clad alibi, however, she was with a man, naturally—"

"An adulteress?" Watson inquired, his interest apparent. Clearly the idea that she might be a murderess as well was of relative unimportance. "And you don't fear for my safety, Holmes? Under the influence of this Jezebel?"

"Not in the least," Sherlock murmured with a smile. "I do not, my good man. She may yet meet her match."

"What's this? You think me to be immune to the charms of women?"

"Quite the opposite," replied Sherlock without hesitation. "But as I love the game, so do you. You would not forego the pleasure of the game for any woman."

"Holmes! Really!" Watson protested. "Most unfair of you."

"Perhaps."

"I take it that you wish me to determine the barebacked beauty's motives."

"Precisely. Is she simply after a rich benefactor, is it all a game of power for her—or does she have another goal in mind?"

"And how do you propose that I come by this information?" Watson asked pointedly. "Aside from the fact that I am a cold, heartless charlatan immune to the pain a female can so expertly inflict upon the honorable."

"Elementary, my dear Watson. If a young, handsome man with more wealth comes along and is able to sway her attentions from Prince George, the Duke of Cambridge, then clearly she's a mere fortune hunter. If, on the other hand, a man of your extraordinary charm and good looks is unable to sway Miss Janvier's attention from an elderly duke with grandchildren, the young lady is a possible threat who requires further investigation." Sherlock moved forward, emphasizing under his breath, "So give it your best effort, Watson."

A slow smile illuminated Watson's face as he watched the shapely beauty gracefully glide from horse to horse as both the acrobats and the horse riders converged upon the ring.

Now I've got him! Sherlock nodded his approval. *Let the games begin!*

Watson sighed. "I would love to apply myself to the task at hand . . . but she can't possibly prefer me to a prince."

Sherlock took out a wad of bills and placed it in the good doctor's hand. "You've developed a great deal of appeal all in the span of a few minutes, Watson."

"I suppose I should buy myself some ravishing accoutrement and give myself a title," considered Watson, thumbing through the wad of bills appreciatively before putting them in his pocket.

"Your attire is second to none," Holmes shrugged. "And the title of *Doctor* suits you fine and is actually more to our purpose. We wish to know which is the greater draw for her: riches or power."

"And Prince George? How will he be removed long enough for me to make my bid for the fair maiden's favor?"

"Ah," chuckled Holmes. "Mycroft has that well in hand this evening. Is it necessary to remind you, my good man, that Mycroft works in the foreign office? The way has been paved for you to meet the young lady in her dressing room after the show."

Watson glanced to see the ravishing Miss Joëlle Janvier bowing and posing for the crowd.

A wicked smile crossed the good doctor's expression as he glanced towards the dressing rooms, raising his glass in a toast. *"To God and Country."*

Chapter Ten
Out of the Schoolroom and Into the Ring

"Oh, and bye the bye, Watson, in your spare time, when you are not romancing Miss Janvier, I would like you to look in on Miss Veronika Vishnevsky, one of the Baghdad Dancing Girls and a young lady who was being investigated by Beckham as well. Miss Vishnevsky is also Russian and a member of the anti-Czarist movement."

"And why is Miss Janvier of more interest than Miss Veronika, then?" John asked.

"Because Miss Vishnevsky has not shown any interest in Prince George." Sherlock raised his eyebrows. "Or vice-versa."

"But are Beckham's murder and the concern over Prince George's alliances necessarily related?" Watson asked.

"Most certainly."

Watson pointed to the ring. "Look, Holmes, there's Miss Mirabella! She's on now. Oh, if the girl isn't positively beautiful herself! Who would have thought she had such long legs under those dowdy skirts." Watson whistled under his breath. *"And a very shapely girl she is . . ."*

"It doesn't take a genius to have deduced that." Sherlock felt himself to be strangely silent on the matter as he watched Miss Belle in a red sparkling outfit move about the stage, the tassels striking her shapely hips as she walked in silk hosiery and red high-heeled shoes. He cleared his throat in discomfort.

"Quite true," Watson murmured, his eyes fixated on Mirabella.

"Just because she wears serviceable clothes . . . Keep your mind on your duty, Watson. Remember, Miss Hudson is a mere girl. She's not a woman of the world like your bare-backed rider. And she is our ward— well, an employee to be sure, but under our protection and care, depending on us for guidance and instruction. It is completely inappropriate that we—I mean, *you*—should entertain such thoughts."

"Holmes, I never meant . . ."

"Indeed you did, Watson. I am no simpleton." Sherlock drained the remainder of his beer before allowing his eyes to rest on her for a long moment. "Besides," he muttered, "Miss Belle is more like a man than a woman."

Watson turned his head suddenly to stare at his companion. "That's the most senseless thing you've said all evening, Holmes, and that's saying something." He raised his eyebrows. "Whatever does Miss Mirabella have in common with a man?"

"Fearless. Logical. In the pursuit of knowledge. Hungry for the game. Without the need for constant adoration."

"Miss Hudson likes to be flattered as much as any woman."

"Woman?" Holmes laughed. "She is still a child."

Mirabella moved to open the cage, taking long strides with her lovely, long legs, her thick chestnut brown hair swinging as she walked. Sherlock had correctly surmised that her hair was long and lustrous despite generally only seeing it pinned atop her head, but somehow seeing her tresses long and loose gave him an unexpected feeling.

Ridiculous! She held the whip over her head and pushed her chest out; no doubt she had been taught to parade about in that contorted fashion.

Watson suddenly grew pensive. "Holmes, are you sure it is perfectly safe for Miss Mirabella to be on stage with those tigers?"

"Perfectly."

"How can you be certain? Those are wild beasts. In the end no one can control them one hundred percent of the time. And she a novice."

"She is merely the presenter. She is not the trainer."

"The Bengal tiger with his eye on her seems unconcerned with her precise title."

"Don't be absurd, Watson! The tiger contemplating her title indeed!" Sherlock turned to stare at his friend. "Surely you can see that Miss Hudson is simply opening and closing the cage door while the Russian trainer does everything else with the tigers. Mycroft made it clear that Miss Hudson is not qualified to be in contact with the tigers, only to clean out the cages, feed the tigers, and open the cage door, fully protected by the iron door in between herself and the beasts. She is only to stand about and look pretty." He paused. "Which she does very well. Even in that limited capacity, she may be able to learn something while she is in close contact with Mr. Afanasy. Her youth and her gender are her protection against suspicion. Someone to be overlooked, as it were. Much to our advantage."

"Ah, I see. The circus is comprised largely of Russians, hence the breeding ground for the anti-Czarist movement—and the fact that it is in Paris, out from under the eye of the Czar. And do you think there is a connection with Beckham's death, Holmes?"

"Most assuredly."

"And how is it that there was an opening for Miss Mirabella to assist Mr. Afanasy?"

"There was *an accident* with the former assistant . . . and the tigers. That is why Mycroft was so clear about Miss Belle's limited role."

There was a long silence for a time before Watson recommenced the conversation. "Miss Mirabella certainly is looking all of her eighteen years."

"Seventeen," muttered Sherlock.

"You know very well that she had a birthday some months ago, Holmes. You were at her party." Watson muttered under his breath, "You gave her a completely ridiculous gift, as well you know."

"Ah, yes. The party." Sherlock moved in his seat uncomfortably while Mirabella turned her back to the audience, her well-formed derriere in full view. He coughed, looking about for an attendant and seeing none. "I believe I shall go in search of a beverage. My throat is dry."

"Is it?" asked Watson, his gaze not wavering from the stage.

"Decidedly. And I'll have you know, my good man, that a mouth-blown German Geisler tube is an excellent gift. When hooked to voltage coils, the fine instrument reveals how different gasses fluoresce."

"Indeed. Miss Hudson was almost beside herself in girlish delight, I recall now."

"She is a very sensible girl."

Dr. Watson glanced up at him. "I haven't seen you like this since we encountered a Miss Irene Adler, Holmes."

"Like what?" Sherlock knitted his brows in reflection as he took the handkerchief out of his pocket and wiped his forehead with it.

"Never mind."

"Now that you mention it, Irene Adler does share some common characteristics with Miss Hudson."

Watson began chuckling uncontrollably.

"What amuses you, Watson?" Sherlock raised his eyebrows.

"Sweet, lovely, faithful, loyal, Miss Hudson has something in common with the devious Irene Adler?"

"Beyond a doubt."

"Holmes, despite the reminder you continually provide, you still astonish me with your lack of understanding." Watson moved in the rickety box seat, repositioning the red cushion beneath him. "Miss Hudson is the type of woman one would eventually wish to settle down with. Irene Adler is the type of woman one would expect to poison one's dinner."

"Odd that you should suggest it, Watson, I believe Miss Adler did just that on one occasion."

"Not odd at all. Irene Adler is deceitful and manipulative to the extreme," Watson continued. "She never stops plotting. Miss Adler doesn't know the meaning of love. She would stab her own mother in the back if there were a tuppence in it for her."

"If you put it that way . . ." Sherlock shrugged.

"What other way is there to put it?"

"Like Miss Belle, Irene Adler is fearless, clever, driven, and unstoppable."

"As is a venomous snake. You only admire Irene Adler because she was clever enough to deceive you. Which is no reason to admire her at all."

"I should say that being able to out-think one of my superior intelligence is every reason to admire her."

"Your narcissism may yet kill you, Holmes," muttered Watson under his breath.

"Self-adulation is only narcissism if it isn't *true*," Sherlock replied with disinterest.

Watson appeared to be choking to death before he added, "At any rate, Miss Adler was only successful because she used her feminine wiles."

"Oh, no," protested Sherlock, shaking his head. "That wasn't until after she deceived me. I can honestly say that Miss Adler outwitted me with her intelligence—it had nothing to do with this biological indulgence you are constantly responding to but which has little to say to me."

Mirabella bowed to the audience on her high-heeled red shoes, her not insubstantial cleavage showing to advantage.

"What was I doing? Ah, yes, I was going in search of a beverage."

"For your dry throat." Watson studied his friend, his eyebrows raised. "Holmes, you know very well that, ever since the conclusion of our first case with Miss Mirabella, you have been acting strangely towards her. You watch her more, you are quicker to anger, you take more reckless chances—throwing yourself in that infernal boxing ring with men twice your size—and even your drug use has increased. Just when your reputation is starting to be established, when you have solved two international cases, *Scandal in Bohemia* and *The Sword Princess*, when you should be the happiest you've ever been, you're discontented. What is bothering you, Holmes?"

"Watson, you're delirious. Honestly, I have no idea what you're rambling on about." Sherlock ran his hand through his hair, his eyes still watching Miss Belle.

"Holmes, we're not just two boarders who share a flat. We've risked our lives for each other. We're *friends*." He pulled on his leather suspenders. "I wouldn't say this if it didn't concern me as a friend—and as your doctor. What is going on between you and Miss Hudson?"

"*Bloody hell*, Watson!" Sherlock felt a burst of anger overwhelm him when he had heretofore been absorbed in Miss Belle's performance. He loosened his neck cloth as he turned towards Watson, his anger no longer containable.

Sherlock was mindful of the fact that Watson was his best friend—his only friend—and he did not wish to repulse the good doctor as he had the others. But he was never one to lie, no matter the cost. "That is the question I should be asking you, Watson! You who are always looking at that trusting, innocent girl like a lecherous old man. You who will never take her seriously and who has no serious intentions. To you, Mirabella Hudson is just a game. But to Miss Belle, it all means something." *It is you whom Miss Belle is interested in, Watson. She has no eyes for anyone else. And look how you fling that precious treasure about just as you disregard flippantly everything of value.*

Watson looked at him aghast. "Of course it does. And it is you—not I—who is too hard on Miss Mirabella."

"Not a bit of it. She loves every moment of it." Sherlock allowed his eyes to rest on Miss Belle as he regained his composure.

"She doesn't love being in the skimpy outfit facing the tigers," Watson said.

Ah, but we do.

Sherlock rose, determined to go in search of drink. "We must assure no harm comes to her. Keep your eye on Miss Belle."

"Gladly."

Chapter Eleven
All for Show

Roar! The Siberian Tiger, orange and white with black markings, opened his mouth to reveal sharp teeth each four inches in length. Mirabella didn't know if she was shaking from the anxiety of being in the ring with a man-eating predator—or because her outfit wouldn't keep a polar bear warm on the equator.

Please, please, dear God, let me go back to the finishing school. I promise to never complain again and to be thankful for each and every lace doily. How I long for those insipid remarks and dreamy watercolor paintings.

Granted, she had a metal cage door between herself and the tigers. Her only job was to open the cage door and to look pretty. From there, the tigers leapt forward towards Mr. Stanislav Afanasy, the trainer, who popped his whip, did summersaults, and directed the tigers as they rode on horses and even jumped through hoops.

She was merely to pose and smile to the crowd—and to walk to the cage to both open the door and close the door once Mr. Afanasy had the tigers back in the enclosure. If one could call it walking; it was more like a continual state of vibration while inching forward or backward as the case may be. Then she put the lock on the cage door, her hands trembling. She carried a whip to make it look as if she was doing something, but it was only for the show.

Quite Simple. Straightforward. Uncomplicated. She felt a great deal more frightened than was warranted. She was perfectly safe. It must be the proximity of the tigers which gave her the illusion of being unsafe, even though she was fully protected on the other side of the open cage door.

But something about this show was disturbing. Let's see: the entire premise was to take a situation where man was prey and the animal was predator and to puff up one's chest and show off that one had reversed the relationship.

In other words, the philosophy was to break the animal's spirit. She hoped the poor creature didn't become so angry that it decided to fight back and retrain its "trainer." The trainer became the trainee, so to speak.

Not only that, but Mr. Afanasy kept the tigers hungry so they would perform in anticipation of the meat after the show. Facing a hungry tiger just did not seem like a good idea to her. Maybe she was only a country girl from Scotland, but it certainly hadn't worked out so well for Mr. Beckham, that was a fact in evidence.

Thank goodness she had nothing to do with any of this and was merely the door opener!

Something is very wrong. What is going on?

Grrrr! The Siberian roared. He was acting strange. He wasn't following any of the orders. He seemed . . . quite . . . *angry.* All of the other five tigers started acting in an agitated fashion, as if they were following the Siberian's lead.

A prison break-out.

SsssssSNAP! Stanislav snapped his whip, ordering the Siberian to go through the fire ring. *Honestly, I would have let it go this one time.* Anyone could see that something was not right.

GASP! The crowd all inhaled as the male Siberian, instead of jumping towards the fire ring, jumped towards Stanislav.

"Zatk'nis!" Stanislav snapped his whip, causing a slight retreat, but all the other tigers began to circle the large, muscular Russian. Mirabella could see in Stanislav's expression, not fear, but the belief that he was doomed. And he was accepting it like a man.

She looked around. No one was coming on the stage to assist.

What am I thinking? She remembered now: she had been told that no one worked with the tigers except Stanislav and his assistant. Frantically she looked towards the stage curtain. And where was his assistant?

Oh, that must be me.

She clenched the bullwhip in her hand—which she wasn't supposed to need!—and moved from around the metal door, her teeth already chattering.

I am the only one. I have to assist. I can't stand here and watch a man be mauled by five tigers! And, after that, maybe the tigers would go into the audience—where there were *children*!

Perhaps between herself and Stanislav, they could get the tigers back in the cage. *Perhaps not.*

Heaven help me, I do not wish to be savaged by tigers! The only hope she had was to persuade the tigers that she, too, was in charge. Or at least give them pause to wonder.

I pray to God I can convince the tigers better than I can myself. Mirabella mustered all the courage she had, walking about the stage and snapping her whip as if she were the one to be feared.

She distracted the Siberian, who moved away from Stanislav.

ROAR! The beautiful white Bengal tiger weighing three quarters of a ton and with the strength of fifteen men moved his attention from Stanislav to her.

This is a terrible idea! And the Bengal looked hungry. She knew that the tiger hunted mostly at night, killing his prey by severing the spinal cord—or by inflicting a suffocation bite.

She continued snapping her whip, shouting to increase her courage, as did Stanislav, whose confidence had clearly increased with her presence.

Heaven help me! The Bengal was charging her! Her grip tightened on the whip as her mind raced. *What do I do? I'll be dead within seconds if I don't do something.*

Mirabella tried to move her legs and could not, frozen in fear. But she could still feel her fingers. She struck the whip. Somehow, miraculously, she struck the Bengal on the nose with the popper.

Oh, my goodness! I didn't mean to do that. But it was quite the move that saved her. The huge cat looked stunned for a moment, a bleeding welt starting to appear on his snout. The other tigers who had been moving towards her stopped in their tracks.

Stanislav popped his own whip an inch from the Siberian's nose and the tiger finally began to get the message, backing up.

I saved myself from a tiger! How can this be? Mirabella was more astonished than she had ever been in her life. This success increased her courage—as well as her determination to live. She had certainly given Stanislav new hope, she could see that in his now robust movements.

Snapping the whips and yelling, the two managed to herd all five of the tigers back into the cage. Her fingers shaking, Mirabella put the lock back on the cage, slamming the shackle home.

And then at the moment of her success, her legs began shaking uncontrollably. She tripped on her high-heeled shoes, falling to the ground. Stanislav helped her up, holding her firmly by the waist. Her entire body shaking now, tears streaming down her cheeks, Stanislav forcibly turned her to the audience and executed a bow for both of them.

There was a roar of applause, all four thousand people rising. The act had not gone off as planned, but everyone in the audience knew that this had been a close call.

Mirabella wondered herself if the Siberian had been drugged. He was still in a rage in the cage. Something had gone very wrong.

How had I let myself be talked into this?

I am here against all reason because it is my duty. Sherlock had explained the situation, that she was to be in the inside, to watch, listen, and learn anything she could. She was not one to shirk her duty.

Perhaps it was time to re-think that dangerous sort of idealism.

Chapter Twelve
Tiger Girl

"You were goot zis evening. You saved life," said the large, muscular animal trainer, a softness in his eyes which seemed out of place. "Want train you to be Tiger Girl."

He began moving the tigers one by one into their night cages with his large whip while Mirabella watched from the greatest distance possible.

"Tiger Girl?"

"Da. You be on stage with me. Performing. Girl before is . . . um . . . *sick*."

"Oh, no, no. Mr. Afanasy. I wouldn't be good at that at all." *I would rather die. Oh, wait. That's precisely what would happen.*

"You not want job, girly?" He looked at her suspiciously. "Why you here if you not want work in circus?"

Oh, no. He is testing me. Any real circus performer would jump at the opportunity to be trained by the head tiger trainer.

She glanced at her lovely red heeled shoes, covered in dirt, which would have to be washed, as did her red satin outfit—what there was of it—now drenched in the perspiration of her fear.

"Of course I want the job! I simply don't wish to ruin your show. I thought I would have more time to learn. I haven't had any training at all. I actually know very little about tigers." *I am rambling. Terror does that to me.*

"I teach you." He motioned to the bullwhip. "You know whip. You look pretty in red. You brave. That all I need."

"GRRRRROWL!!!!" the Bengal who had circled her earlier replied.

What was that part about being brave? In that you are utterly mistaken!

"You crack whip around tiger. Don't have to hit animal, but must crack whip." He illustrated his point.

Mirabella cursed the day Sherlock had taught her to use the whip.

"Luck was with us this evening, Mr. Afanasy! What if the whip makes the very large man-eater with the long, sharp fangs angry?" Mirabella pleaded, wrapping her arms around her waist as she attempted to back up. The smell of the raw meat, the animals, and the dirt made her slightly queasy, though she was not ordinarily one to have a weak stomach. "I truly, *truly* don't wish to make him angry!"

"You had bad night, but will feel better in morning. Cannot be afraid! Tigers know you afraid." Mr. Afanasy twirled his long, black moustache with one hand while he easily maneuvered the tigers with the whip in the other.

"Why should I be afraid of an animal with fifteen times my strength who could kill me in playfulness if it *loved* me but which, instead, gives every indication of loathing me?" She glanced at the cage.

"What you saying, girly?" he narrowed his eyes at her. He was tall, dark—and ominous. His defined muscles were easily revealed by a skin-tight black sequined suit, a match to his long black hair falling loosely to his shoulders. The hair closest to his face was pulled back and braided. He was actually quite a handsome man. Large. Very large. "My English not so goot."

"*I am saying* what a wonderful opportunity." She swallowed hard. She had no intention of complying with Mr. Afanasy's wishes, but she had to maintain her cover until she had time to think. She couldn't jeopardize the mission and risk the lives of others—of entire countries, to hear Sherlock speak of it.

"The big cats they must know who is master." He closed the lock on the last cage.

Between me and the tigers, I think we all know who is the master.

"Mr. Afanasy, doesn't it seem odd that the Siberian was so agitated tonight—and still is? Do you think . . . maybe . . . he was drugged?"

Stanislav shrugged. "Tigers they not like light and noise—not predict—sometimes too much for them."

"But, shouldn't we try to find out why—"

"Girl must *work*. This much better than Russia. Easy. Time to feed tigers. No more talk. I show you."

Suddenly his attention turned elsewhere as the most beautiful woman Mirabella had ever beheld entered the tented area for the animal cages, just outside the main multi-sided marble structure. The visitor walked on the ground as if she were gliding, and as if dirt would never dare touch her slippers as they had coated Mirabella's.

Her long, lustrous black hair fell past her shoulders. Their glamorous guest with violet-blue eyes had a figure that could make a man melt. And which did, from the look of things.

She was petite, as was the style, Mirabella reflected with envy. Naturally the visitor was not as tall as Mirabella—and yet was every bit the athlete. She had a tiny waist and was cushioned in all the right places. Her outfit was beige so as to make her appear almost nude, with sequins, and she wore a sheer lilac jacket which added to her allure. She walked with the confidence of one who knew her power over men.

She would have to be an idiot not to know that. And if there had been any doubt the raven-haired beauty would have known it by the fact that the dark, muscled man, threatening only a moment ago, was now a puddle on the floor.

"Joëlle," he bowed, his wide grin somehow strange on so masculine a face. "Beautiful performance."

"Stanislav," she nodded, but there was condescension in her smile, as if she thought him much beneath her.

"Are you . . . what do you do in the circus, Miss?" Mirabella asked of the beauty, attempting to be polite.

"What I should do?" The beauty turned momentarily to stare haughtily at her. "I *am* ze circus. "

"Joëlle is bare-backed rider," Stanislav explained.

"Circus is nothink without me." She lowered her eyelids. "You may call me *Mademoiselle Janvier.*"

"And are you a trapeze artist too, Mademoiselle Janvier?" Mirabella swallowed hard. "You must have very good balance to ride the horses."

"Who is zis?"

"Her name is—"

"Does not matter. What she doing here?" Joëlle demanded.

"New Tiger Girl. New assistant until Ashanti get well from tiger attack . . ."

"T-t-tiger attack?" Mirabella stuttered, feeling the room spin around her as she backed into the tent, the canvas rough on her skin. Mirabella's eyes opened wide, but she could not find words.

"We have supper together, Joëlle?" Stanislav asked hopefully, his attention focused on the violet-eyed beauty as Mirabella did her best not to swallow her tongue. She reached for a pole or a chair but instead found the side of the canvas tent. No doubt it was an act of Providence that the tent was stabilized to the degree that she was unable to knock it down upon them all.

"*Nyet.*" Joëlle laughed as if the idea was absurd. "There is fine Englishman who wishes to meet the beautiful Zsh-oëlle."

"Who he is?" demanded Stanislav.

Joëlle shrugged. "Young and handsome doctor, only arrived from London. I go dressing room and await him."

Oh, no! Could it be . . . *Dr. Watson? Please, heavenly Father, tell me this ravishing beauty is not the reason we are here.* Mirabella was able to inch herself to the ground and sit in the dirt, her head spinning. Tiger Attack. *I do not stand a chance.* John Watson and this femme fatale! *He does not stand a chance.*

Mirabella touched her hand to her cheek even as she watched the two of them verbally sparring, feeling the dirt smear her skin. *This is nothing like the Parisian holiday I had envisioned.*

This case was so much worse than anything she could have imagined. Only eight hours ago she was in ecstasy, now she felt that fear might make her explode.

"An Englishman! What is it with English, Joëlle?" He spit on the ground before a wicked smile crossed his lips. "Look what happened last Englishman. Tigers got him."

Oh, no! Could Stanislav have killed Beckham out of *jealousy*?

Mirabella watched Joëlle intently, but the bare-backed rider gave no sign either of concern or remorse.

"Sometimes wonder if you are traitor to Mother Russia, Joëlle." His eyes narrowed at her.

"Like you, Stanislav?" she asked seductively, both appearing to forget Mirabella's presence.

Understandable. Who could notice her in the presence of the beautiful Joëlle?

"I not traitor!" he exclaimed indignantly. "I for Russia, not for Czar and pile of riches built on people's labor."

"Not say where others can hear, Stanislav! If you could speak decent Russian, we would not need speak in English. But you are peasant Ukrainian. Naturally Joëlle does not speak Ukrainian." She spit on the ground. "And as for English, at least they have money. Not just animal trainer!"

"I worked all life, no time for school. What wrong working for day's wages? You always say you for worker, Joëlle, in meeting, but actions they are different."

She shrugged, turning away from him. "*Nyet*, a girl she has to eat."

"And anyway . . ." he took her by the arms, spinning her around and holding her very close in a familiar manner, "I am more than animal trainer. You know this."

"Humph!" she laughed. "You might hold a position in . . ." She glanced at Mirabella before returning her eyes to Stanislav.

Miss Janvier had not forgotten Mirabella was there after all.

But the two bantering back and forth had already told her a great deal. Clearly they assumed the inept tiger presenter to be a foolish, harmless girl. Her attempts to knock down the tent were probably doing nothing to dispel that notion.

Perhaps my fumbling has worked to my advantage. Mirabella felt a moment of enlightenment, realizing that she had something to contribute to Sherlock's case. She had learned a valuable tool in acquiring information: being too stupid to worry about.

Perhaps being a complete incompetent is the role I can play best.

Her interest in the case momentarily surpassed her overwhelming desire to enact bodily harm on Sherlock Holmes. She couldn't help but deduce that Stanislav clearly had another role in an organization outside the circus, however little Joëlle thought of his importance—if indeed her disdain was not an act to further manipulate him. And Stanislav and Miss Janvier were in the same organization.

What was the organization? Stanislav had mentioned the bourgeoisie in derogatory terms and Mother Russia with a glow in his expression.

The organization in question must be an anti-Czarist group. Stanislav had a position in the group, and he clearly expected Miss Janvier to be impressed with his position.

Maybe Stanislav had more power than Joëlle would lead one to believe.

And maybe he had killed Beckham.

She swallowed hard. That would mean she was in close contact both with tigers and a murderer. *Lovely.*

"*We will succeed, Da,*" Stanislav insisted. "And what do you see in lazy bourgeoisies? None of them they work! Live off labor of others, all soft and flabby! One hanging about you now could be grandfather!" He smiled broadly as if surely she would see his point.

Mirabella was desperate to ask a question which might reveal more about Beckham's killer, but she thought she'd better not press her luck at this time. Her life was hanging by a threat as it was, and she had used up all the luck of a lifetime in this one evening.

"Georgie?" she laughed. "He is *prince.* And what you, Stanislav? Circus *clown.*"

Prince George!?! This woman was seeing Prince George?

"He is English clown. Do you believe will *marry* you, Joëlle?" Stanislav sniffed loudly. "The English, they know what you are."

She lowered her eyelids, as if very proud of what she was. As if to say, 'and yet you all want me.'

He shook his head at her but there was longing in his eyes. "And English prince is married."

She shrugged. "Would not be first time married man choose me over wife." She turned to look back at him over her elevated hip. "Maybe I get lucky one of these days. In meantime I dine on caviar and champagne instead of horsemeat and cheap wine."

Chapter Thirteen
The Bend in the Road

"I'm not going back in there!" Mirabella exclaimed despite her earlier promise to Stanislav. That was before she learned about the 'accident' with the prior 'Tiger Girl'. Her hands were shaking, along with her knees and even her teeth. She couldn't stop shivering. She wrapped the red satin robe more tightly around her body, which was a wasted action as the thin, shiny fabric provided absolutely no warmth. Involuntarily she looked up, catching a glance at the stars overhead. It was a clear, moonlit night, and the sky was filled with stars.

"Not going in *where*, Miss Hudson?" Sherlock asked.

Mirabella was standing behind the elephants' cages, a predetermined meeting place. It was dark and noisy, and most would not care for the smells or the ground cover. She and Sherlock were guaranteed some privacy to discuss the case.

"In the ring with the tigers, of course!" she sighed heavily, surprised at his denseness which could only be deliberate in the case of Sherlock Holmes. "Mr. Afanasy wants me to come out from behind the cage door and be the presenter—replacing the hospitalized 'Tiger Girl'—while he is the tiger trainer."

"Excellent!"

"*Excellent?* What is 'excellent' about my impending massacre?"

"This is working out much better than I could have anticipated." His manner was one of uncharacteristic excitement. "You'll have much more time with Afanasy. No doubt you can incite him to talk when you are on friendlier terms."

Horror struck her as she studied Sherlock's face: even in the dark she recognized immediately the dawning of an idea in his eyes.

Sherlock Holmes with an idea is the last thing I want. In her mind's eye she envisioned Sherlock assigning her to the elephant ring in addition to the tiger ring. This terrifying idea was followed by a mental picture of petite Kemberly, whom she had only just seen laying on the floor of the circus ring while Purdy Girl the elephant raised her huge hoof just above Kemberly's perfect face.

Right after Purdy Girl had swung Kemberly about in her trunk a bit.

Naturally the gigantic animal would not do so well if Mirabella Hudson were the girl in the trunk, she reflected, picturing herself dropped by

Purdy Girl from the strain.

Staring with apprehension at Sherlock's determined expression, Mirabella's mind wouldn't slow down. She then had a vision flashing before her eyes of beautiful Rochelle suspended over the pool of black alligators. Only it was her own face in Rochelle's body.

Imagining one's death isn't helping! Which of these options was worse? Alligators, elephants, or tigers?

They would all be effective in putting an immediate period to her existence, so it was difficult to pick one.

How did my life come to this? In the terror of the moment, Mirabella couldn't remember how her life had become intertwined with Sherlock Holmes—or why.

"EWAAAAAAAAAA!" The occasional bellowing roars interrupted their conversation.

"Mr. Holmes, don't you understand?" she exclaimed. "I might have been killed in the circus ring tonight! If it doesn't seem real to you, it certainly does to me!"

"Miss Hudson, this evening four thousand people—myself among them—watched you save yourself and a seasoned animal trainer. I'm as astonished as anyone, I assure you." There was a slight smile forming on his lips. "And I'm not accustomed to being astonished."

"I might have saved Stanislav, but I certainly didn't save myself! I've no doubt signed my own death warrant!"

"Mr. Afanasy certainly thinks you are capable of handling the tigers. He is in a position to know."

"What Mr. Afanasy thinks is that *he is safer* with me in the ring—having had his last assistant mauled by tigers—and that, if something happens to me, someone else will readily fill my place. It's no loss to him either way!"

"What do you want, Miss Hudson, more pay?" Sherlock Holmes demanded, turning on his heel in one swift movement, so close now that she could feel his breath on her cheek.

He looked particularly demented and fearsome, she could see that even in the dark. Darkness and Sherlock Holmes went together, and that was never more evident than now as he glared at her through the faint moonlight, his face unshaven and his frown naturally sinister. And his clothing added to the effect: he wore a knee-length black frock coat and a blue and gold striped satin neck cloth, along with a black top hat better suited to the opera than behind an elephant cage. His coal black curls peaked out from under the top hat lodged atop his head.

"I believe I have stated my position clearly," she murmured, somewhat uncomfortable that their breaths were intertwined in the moonlight. She whispered, "I am not going back."

"I know I can always buy you with money, Miss Hudson," he added. "Despite the fact that you appear to have no interest in baubles or clothes. Saving to attend your illustrious university."

"And what good will money be if I am not *alive* to go to university? I need a body in order to attend!" His proximity making her uncomfortable, she backed up, carefully watching where she placed her foot in the beautiful red satin shoe.

She might hate this place, but her beautiful outfit—as skimpy as it was—was nonetheless expertly made. It had to be, or the material would no doubt be torn off her body with the extreme movement required. She felt an obligation to take care of it.

"Don't be ridiculous." He shook his head. "You are surrounded by professionals, Miss Hudson."

"Then *you* go in the cage and face the tigers if it is so easy, Mr. Holmes!"

"Screech! Owwww!" Mirabella could hear the laughter and chattering of the monkeys nearby.

She peered around the corner of the cage to see a juggler practicing with his five or six wooden miniature clubs in every color of the rainbow in the gas lamplight.

"To be sure, it would not be a pretty picture," Sherlock murmured, twirling his hand and motioning to her outfit as he spoke, as if he were searching for words. Even in the dim light, she could see that Sherlock looked away in embarrassment.

Impossible. Sherlock Holmes was never embarrassed.

His voice grew suddenly rough. "It looks decidedly fine . . . You are quite *convincing* in it . . . I mean to say . . . it becomes you very well, Miss Belle." He took out his handkerchief and began patting his face although there was a chill in the air. "At any rate, I have been a female on numerous occasions, but I am neither attractive nor convincing in tights."

"I was meaning to speak with you about that, Mr. Holmes! How could you, in all good conscience—oh, wait! You have none!—expect me to appear half-naked before thousands of people without discussing it with me first!"

He tapped his cane on the ground. "Miss Hudson! I'll thank you to take a more appropriate tone with me."

"And I'll thank you not to throw me in the ring with man-eating predators, Mr. Holmes!" she replied in the least appropriate tone she should manage. She was generally at great pains to bite her tongue, but something about fighting for her life against deadly carnivores had loosened her reserve.

It's deuced annoying how I am forever needing a female operative. I cannot play every role," the Great Detective concluded. "It can't be helped."

"Yes, if there were no females in the world, it would be a much better place."

Sherlock appeared pensive as he tapped his ebony cane on the ground, as if considering the merit of her words. He was silent, which she found even more annoying than his long tirades.

But his eyes were never still. She might wear a robe, but it adhered to her form, and she noticed that his eyes continually returned to assess her.

Perplexing. He was obviously thinking about how well suited she was for some devious plan, she knew not what.

"Miss Belle, the thing that gives me hope is that you are generally able to behave like a man and look like a female."

Even his compliments sound like insults. "Whatever do you mean, Mr. Holmes?"

He looked away momentarily. This was the most peculiar conversation: Sherlock Holmes was never hesitant, he was only straight forward. "Feminine and soft when it's called for, powerful and confident when needed."

She placed her hands on her hips. "I am no different from other women."

"I beg to differ, Miss Belle," he murmured without hesitation. "I am accustomed to women who are helpless, vulnerable, and unable to think for themselves, and, though I am pledged to help them in their very real dilemmas, I would not wish to be long in their company."

"I was not born yesterday, Mr. Holmes! There are many capable women. My Aunt Martha for one. And I will never believe that the mother of Sherlock Holmes is unable to think for herself. As I know mine is not."

"True," he agreed reluctantly. "But my mother is not in need of my assistance. Moreover, she can be . . . demanding, histrionic, and ridiculous in her turn."

Sounds like someone I know.

"Do try to be sensible, Miss Belle," Sherlock continued with raised eyebrows. "And return to the subject at hand. You have only been in the ring once; as with anything it will become easier with practice."

"Well, this female is not going back in the tiger ring!" she retorted. "It can be no less than an act of God that I am still be alive. I will not tempt fate, whatever nonsense you may choose to spout, Mr. Sherlock Holmes."

He stepped back, staring at her in surprise, as if he were astonished that she did not care to be someone else's dinner.

"Very well. If that is your final decision, Miss Hudson." He twirled his ebony cane. She knew the cane contained a sword and it wouldn't have surprised her if he had pulled the sword out and demanded that she throw herself into the tiger cage.

Instead, he seemed resigned to her decision.

"You . . .you are agreeing with me, Mr. Holmes?"

"What else can I do? I cannot force you to do that which you refuse to do, Miss Hudson." He removed his top hat, rubbing his hand through his hair and turning away from her altogether.

"Quite right," she agreed shakily.

"I shall look for a new assistant." Returning to meet her eyes, he smiled perfunctorily at her and bowed, to be interpreted as either a gesture of departure or a supposed attempt at politeness.

It had to be the former.

She stepped forward in an attempt to gain his attention and stop him from leaving. "Are you saying, Mr. Holmes, that I cannot keep my position washing bottles, documenting specimens, and dissecting bodies at the morgue, if I don't face tigers?"

"It will be difficult to find another situation so effortless and yet with so many glamorous elements in such illustrious company, I grant you that, Miss Hudson." He shrugged, smoothing the lapels of his frock coat. "But I have never understood where your priorities lie, my girl. Perhaps it is for the best."

"You cannot be serious."

"I am always serious."

And she knew Sherlock Holmes always spoke the truth.

This was no exception. She could feel it in his very manner, as if he were relieved at the idea that she would no longer be in his life—as if she created some difficulty for him.

"But . . . why?"

"Why do I always have to point out that which should be apparent by this time, Miss Belle?" He sighed heavily, looking away again. He was suddenly stiff and removed from her, as if they were strangers to each other. Sherlock Holmes was, once again, a machine. "I need a female assistant who is willing to go undercover on my cases when I need it. One who doesn't ask questions and who does as I ask. I cannot perform every role—and I cannot hire two assistants."

"Not for what you pay me."

"EWAAAAAAAAAA!" Teensy accentuated.

"Precisely. And my career is far from established. True, I have had a few successes, but the public is very fickle. All it would take is one high-profile case unsolved, and my life's work is over." He turned towards her and placed his hands on her arms, his voice almost a whisper but somehow louder than she had ever heard it. "*My life over*. Why is it so difficult for you to understand that you were hired to perform a function, Miss Belle? And that you, like myself, must be extraordinary in everything you do? My future, and our future together, depends upon it."

Our future together. What a strange sound that had.

"Tell me, this, Sherlock." He released her and she and brushed the hair out of her face. "What if I were to be attacked by the tiger, and supposing I lived, I were to have a large scar across my face?"

"What if? What do you mean by that, Miss Hudson?"

"Would you still keep me in your employ, Mr. Holmes?" She braced herself for the answer.

"Hmmm. You would not be as useful to me, as you are no doubt aware, Miss Belle."

"Enlighten me, Mr. Holmes."

"If you are not able to reason that out, we have been remiss in your education, Miss Hudson. There are some roles which call for a pretty female. A scar we can add, but it would be much more difficult to remove one. And . . . " he considered. "It would make you identifiable."

She felt her jaw clenching. "And, what if, instead, I were to die after a tiger attack?" Inadvertently she reached down to rub her leg from a strained muscle.

"I can't see that I would then have to choose whether or not to retain you. The choice would be made for me. Surely you must see that, Miss Hudson."

"Would you not feel some sadness—or regret, Mr. Holmes?" she blurted out without meaning to.

As soon as Mirabella asked the question, she wondered why she had asked it. She had accepted the position, she knew the risks. She couldn't have her feelings hurt anymore than an enlisted man should have his feelings hurt when his commander sent him in to battle.

But Sherlock's lack of attachment to her was both disturbing and painful. She was so devoted, so loyal to him—it took man-eating tigers to scare her away! She couldn't bear to be off the case—she began to wonder if she couldn't bear to be deprived of Sherlock's company—while he could dispose of her like yesterday's newspaper.

Her eyes met his, where she searched for the answer, and saw nothing, which hurt her far more than she expected. She dare not ask for his feelings, for she knew he had none.

"Well? Would you feel anything if I were to die, Mr. Holmes?"

"Obviously I would not wish to see you dead, Miss Belle, or to learn that evil had prevailed. The idea has concerned and disturbed me for some weeks now." He shuddered, adding in a whisper, "I never thought to feel such things—or wished to."

"To feel what?" she asked.

He looked away and his tone was once again emotionless. "Though I must say it is my devotion to the execution of justice which propels me and not any personal feeling."

"It is touching indeed that the thought of my death is so debilitating to you, Mr. Holmes."

"What do you suppose I hired you for, Miss Hudson? Companionship?" He laughed. "I am not an old woman or a doddering fool requiring an attendant."

You're not an old woman at least. "I beg your pardon, Mr. Holmes, but you do require an attendant."

"The fact remains that I am a world-class detective without time to spare, time which you are wasting at the present moment. Something which appears to have become a habit with you, Miss Belle."

"Forgive me for taking up moments of your precious time which could very well determine whether I shall live or die."

He tapped his cane on the ground, creating the sound of rock hitting wood. "I won't say I'm not fond of you, Miss Belle. I approve of your drive and persistence. But unless you are able to not only try but succeed, you are of no use to me."

"How kind."

"I am not attempting to be kind."

"I am relieved to know it, and it diminishes the sting."

"Do you wish something more from me other than that of being your employer?" His voice became suddenly and uncharacteristically thin, and it seemed to her, almost anxious.

"Of course not!" she exclaimed, his words setting her ajar. *What a ridiculous thought!* She didn't know why she was asking these questions herself.

And she didn't know what she wanted him to feel. Nothing like the devotion she felt towards him obviously, but perhaps warmth, loyalty, friendship. At the beginning, she had disliked Sherlock while perceiving that he was somehow necessary to her future. And now to her very being, to all that she wanted to be.

Someone so utterly and thoroughly distanced from her.

And yet I have my answer. I am nothing more than a tool. A tool to be used and discarded. She stiffened.

"I understand now, Mr. Holmes," she stated softly.

"You see, Miss Hudson, you are becoming illuminated as well. Ours is a professional relationship. And while we're on the subject, allow me to dissuade you from setting your cap after Watson. There's not a better chap among men—but I wouldn't advise a woman to get within two continents of him. Particularly a lady of your inexperienced years."

"Oh? Why, may I ask?" she murmured distractedly.

"Watson is . . . well, he's knows his way about . . . that is to say, he's a ladies' man."

"He likes women, certainly." *Unlike some unnatural men.*

"It will take an eyelash fluttering, adoring, feminine flower of quiet demeanor to hold Dr. John H. Watson's attention. Someone who is willing to manage him. I don't see you in that role, Miss Belle."

"And how do you see me, Mr. Holmes?"

"I do not necessarily see you married," he added gravely, as if it were the worst of situations. "But if you choose that life, I advise you to find someone willing to run the race with you, Miss Belle." He paused. "Someone who prefers a strong-willed, incorrigible, troublesome, pigheaded, unmanageable, opinionated woman of education."

"Since you mention it, Mr. Holmes, as it so happens, I am far too busy pursuing my studies and saving my money for university to pursue Dr. John Watson." *And if you believe that, you're not the detective I thought you were.*

"Good. It appears our business is concluded." His sigh was palpable. He bowed again, tipping his hat to her. "I wish you the best of luck, Miss Hudson, in your future endeavors."

"So this is 'good-bye'?"

"I may be able to keep you on in a small, domestic capacity unless my new assistant is able to meet all of my requirements, as you are not." He moved to depart.

She bit her lip, terrified at the idea of Sherlock's final departure, trying to think of anything to stall for time. "I do have some news.

Stanislav is Ukrainian apparently."

Sherlock turned his head to view her, even as his back was now to her. "Interesting."

"I wondered why he and Miss Janvier spoke in English around me. Either she will not lower herself to speak Ukrainian, or she doesn't know it. Clearly Stanislav cannot speak high Russian."

He moved to face her again. "Unless Miss Janvier desires that you should hear what she is saying . . . "

"But why? It was clear that they both belong to a political organization—and my guess is that it's an anti-Czarist group."

"Why do you say so, Miss Belle?" He moved closer, clearly interested.

"Because everything Stanislav says is derogatory about the Russian upper classes—and, I would presume by association, the Russian government. Not so with Miss Janvier. She apparently goes to the meeting and is accepted, but it is evident that she aligns herself with money. She loves everything to do with established wealth, she made that quite obvious."

"Excellent work, Miss Belle!" Sherlock pointed his cane in the air. "It doesn't quite fit, though: the Ukraine is largely rural, but there is a growing nationalist movement among Ukrainians aligning themselves with the Russian empire. I would have expected Stanislav to support the Czar."

"I'm quite sure he doesn't. Miss Janvier, on the other hand . . . she's much more difficult to read." Mirabella shrugged. "Now may I cease going in the tiger ring—and keep my position?"

"Absolutely not! You are ideally placed to gather information, particularly since they clearly do not consider you to be a threat."

"Perhaps my being in a continual state of terror causes them to think of me as powerless and unimportant," she suggested.

"Perhaps," he considered, leaning on his cane, now frowning. "And what is your decision, Miss Hudson? Are you staying on the case or returning to London in search of a new profession?"

She felt a sadness well up in her chest, having the strange feeling that their association was at an end. "Are you truly prepared to replace me if I do not risk my life and get into the cage with the tigers, Mr. Holmes?"

"That is the need I have today," he nodded, lighting his pipe "If you do not do it, I will find someone who will."

"Forgive me, Mr. Holmes, but does it not seem a bit *cold*?"

"It?"

"*You*, I mean."

"Logic is without emotion. It simply is. At any rate, it is of no interest to me what it seems, only what it is. Am I to tell you that you can sit on pink cushions and eat chocolates while I pay you, Miss Belle? There are criminals out there ready to slit someone's throat, entire countries on the brink of collapsing, and dictators ready to subjugate a population while you ask me to cosset and admire you. Who will die while I am flattering you and satisfying your every feminine whim?"

"I do not wish to be cosseted and admired!" she sputtered, furious. "I merely wish to *be alive* to see tomorrow!"

"Then live," he remarked politely, raising an eyebrow at her. "But while you are living, do you wish to be in the employ of Sherlock Holmes or not?"

She turned to leave, distressed, disillusioned, and heartbroken. She took a step towards her tent, glancing at the ground just in time to avoid the voluminous and slimy deposit from an elephant. In the process, she lost her balance, landing in a puddle of water.

At least the ground was soft and her tailbone was still intact.

If not her pride.

Chapter Fourteen
Key to the Case

Mirabella returned to the ladies' tent to wash and change her clothing. Every tent dweller had a small sleeping area—not partitioned—a blanket, and a trunk for her clothing, which most ladies balanced on its end to allow for the hanging of clothes. In addition, Mirabella had a kerosene lamp which Sherlock had provided for her. She had claimed a space on the edge of the tent so that she might watch outside through the slit in the canvas. Sleeping was definitely a luxury on this case.

En route to the shared wash basin, Mirabella saw something which caught her eye: Veronika's scarlet chiffon outfit had been thrown atop her bedding rather than hung or folded.

Mirabella looked about her, grateful that no one was watching her despite the openness of the area. She gasped as she saw that there was a red stain on the gold trim of the bodice, almost hidden by the scarlet chiffon. Could it be blood? The garment had been washed several times, but the stain was still evident.

She looked around again, insuring that no one was watching her. The sheer volume of activity in a circus environment was ever her friend. She hoped it might remain so.

Mirabella then placed her hand under the folded clothing in the trunk, the neatness in contrast to the garment thrown on the bedding, and found—a key! Mirabella pocketed the key and scurried to her own bed comprised of multiple blankets, turning her back to everyone as she compared Veronika's key to her own key.

It is identical! This is a key to the tigers' cages. Mirabella felt her breathing increase as the implications hit her.

Veronika has a key to the tigers' cage.

This was shocking. Veronika was such a shy, quiet girl—so sweet. Mirabella liked her and would never have thought her capable of murder. Veronika had her wounds—her father had died at the Czar's hands, she had said—but everyone had an inner wound of some type or another, Mirabella was learning.

Veronika might be involved in the anti-czarist movement—but many Russians were. It was not surprising that the orphaned girl should be opposed to tyranny.

Mirabella re-traced her steps to return the key and had only just slipped the key under the clothing when Veronika appeared from around the vertical trunk, her expression one of betrayal. "What are you doing, Mirabella?"

"I saw the key protruding out from your clothing," Mirabella lied, much to her chagrin. "And I picked it up." Mirabella cursed herself for being caught—what if she was face-to-face with Beckham's murderer?—but her only course now was to obtain Veronika's reaction.

Since Mirabella was in this unenviable position, she must make the best of it. "It is a key to the tiger cage. Why do you have it, Veronika? Stanislav said there are only two such keys: I have one and he has one, and it is forbidden to make a copy."

Veronika stepped back, but there was anger written across her expression. "I have never seen the key before. I don't know how it got there. And anyway, you should not have gone through my things. I thought you were my friend."

"And what about your outfit, Veronika?" Mirabella pressed. "It looks like there was blood on it."

"Why are you asking me these questions, Mirabella? It can be none of your business."

"It is my business! There was a man murdered in the tiger cages!" Mirabella replied with an indignation she certainly felt. "I have the right to insure the same doesn't happen to me!"

Veronika hung her head a bit, obviously distressed. Was it the distress of guilt? "Someone took my costume and returned it with blood on it. I do not know how the blood got there. It is as if they are trying to make me guilty. Like Russia. They did the same thing to my father. They broke his spirit." A tear dropped down her cheek.

"Did the red stain appear on your outfit the same day as Beckham's murder?" Mirabella asked.

Veronika nodded.

Is she telling the truth? Mirabella hoped so, because, if Veronika was lying, she might be extremely dangerous. It wouldn't be the first time a shy, wounded person was deadly.

And if Veronika was telling the truth, someone was attempting to diffuse attention away from herself and onto Veronika—either because Veronika was convenient, or because the true murderer disliked Veronika.

Or both.

Chapter Fifteen
Napoleon and Josephine: Le Grand Véfour

"You must have very successful hospital, Doctor Watson," Joëlle Janvier smiled giddily even as she ran her hand seductively along the distinctive red sash of the French Legion of Honor draped across the bottle of *Cordon Rouge* champagne. She was dressed in a strikingly low-cut black silk gown which was an unmistakable copy of Madame X's daring evening gown, the mere portrait of which had caused a recent scandal when displayed in the Paris Salon.

The Russian beauty leaned towards him, her plunging neckline vividly more scandalous than the painting she brought to mind.

A mind that momentarily went blank.

"Hospital?" John laughed forcibly. He removed his white gloves but left his black top hat on his head. He might be in Paris, but he was still British and still civilized. One did not remove one's hat in public venues. "No. I'm strictly private practice. And you, Miss Janvier, may call me 'John'."

"And what do you *practice*, Zsh-ohn?" she murmured, her lavender eyes bright with promise, even more stunning against her raven hair, as she took another bite of caviar. Like Madame X, Joëlle apparently used henna to cast purple hues into her shining black locks, but unlike Madame X, Joëlle had the lavender eyes to match.

"I practice . . . whatever is asked of me." He added in a seductive murmur, "I seem to be able to anticipate my patients' needs."

John was enjoying himself and the sensual awareness this woman evoked immensely. He even relished the continual glances their way, he in his black suit with tails, white vest and white bow tie, and she in her black evening gown with the revealing neckline. His heightened awareness increased his enjoyment of every detail.

The glances of admiration were a welcome balm to the war wounds still visible to the public. And even those which were not. Of all the things John hated, the stares and sympathy his limp evoked was the most aggravating to him.

As if his wounds were an open book for strangers.

"Mademoiselle Joëlle." Apparently everyone had a certain familiarity with Miss Janvier. "And *monsieur*." The waiter appeared, bowing before them. His tuxedo was so fine and so expertly fitted that

John, who always took pains with his own appearance, could not help but feel admiration in the presence of an obvious man of fashion. "Have you decided monsieur?"

"Ah, yes," murmured John, scanning the menu a final time. He took a moment to relish the knowledge that he could order anything he wished. Being a person whose pockets were always to let, he was utterly delighted by this *carte blanche*.

John smiled at the beautiful Joëlle. *Along with the other benefits.*

"We shall begin with a shredded crab and radish salad, my good man. And, of course, more caviar and champagne. Then a tomato bisque. For the main course, let's see . . ." He considered several items on the menu. ". . . perhaps a monkfish on mango with coriander mousse. Or would you prefer the lobster, Miss Janvier?"

"Which more expensive?" asked Joëlle without hesitation.

Le Grand Véfour's waiter raised his eyebrows, making no effort to conceal his disapproval despite the obvious advantages to his gratuity of the more expensive dish.

"The lobster, Mademoiselle," he murmured with condescension. "But let me assure you that all of the dishes at *Le Grand Véfour* are —"

"We take lobster," she pronounced. She glanced at her date, who smiled, nodding his approval at whatever she might choose. She positively glowed, and it pleased John more than he could almost endure. His senses told him that this was a dangerous woman, but that did not preclude him from enjoying himself.

Perhaps the knowledge increased his enjoyment, in fact.

The garcon bowed slightly, the tails of his tuxedo miraculously unperturbed in spite of his movement.

"For dessert, we try cherries flambé, *Zsh-ohn*? I have sweet tooth. And--"

"And?" John asked, wondering with interest where this was going.

"Everyone turn to look." she smiled charmingly. Even in her constant need for admiration, she was delightful.

John felt himself blush with a slight embarrassment, realizing that he shared a sentiment with this vixen: he did not mind the stares, not at all. The diva was beautiful. But more than that, he had never before met a woman who was more flirtatious—and more bold.

And glad I am of it! She was the only woman of his acquaintance so without morals that he need not feel guilt for an indulgence—*any* indulgence. The two of them might have a good time—and each was getting far better than they deserved in the bargain.

She could enjoy his company under the pretense that he was the real thing, and he could enjoy her attentions knowing full well that there was nothing real about her.

"Of course, Miss Janvier, the cherries flambé." Her appetite, combined as it was with a figure a man might only see in his imagination, revealed her to be an athlete. He hoped his imagination did not disappoint in other respects. "Whatever you wish."

"*Bon.*" The waiter bowed, the slightest frown on his lips, having much the expression of a royal who was obliged to endure the peasantry. With his every exchange, his air of superiority left no doubt that he was a waiter of sophistication.

"Miss Janvier . . ."

"My name Zsh-oëlle," she pronounced with a sly smile, leaning forward and displaying her cleavage to advantage. It was odd that she had chosen names which began with "J", which was not a sound in the Russian alphabet. Her pronunciation made the letter sound as if she were breathless, "Zsh-oëlle Zsh-anvier".

Perhaps not so odd.

It was about time that they exchanged names since the first course was en route—the shredded crab and radish salad—along with the second bottle of champagne. Although generally a gentleman did not call a lady by her first name unless she were family or they were engaged.

"Miss *Janvier?*" He considered. "It doesn't sound Russian somehow."

"Is stage name. Last name Bezborodov."

"Ah, I see why you chose a different name."

"Ze English, they like ze French. Russians, not so much."

"Oh, I wouldn't say that. Some English love the Russians," he leaned towards her, kissing her fingertips, something he would have never been able to do with a respectable girl. Which made it all the more enjoyable.

She did not withdraw.

The tomato bisque arrived, which they began to eat. *Delicious*! He couldn't remember when he had had a more enjoyable dining experience.

"It is easy to see why Napoleon and Josephine's love affair blossomed here," John murmured, tearing his eyes from her and glancing about the restaurant so as not to appear too interested. He gathered that besotted men were putty in her hands.

He wished it to be the other way around.

Gaslight from the street lamps poured through the windows,

further brightening the gold walls and ceilings, as did the numerous candle chandeliers. Mirrors were everywhere. The furniture was almost black, being a dark walnut, while the cushions were red; the carpet was black and gold.

Le Grand Véfour was somehow opulent and quaint at the same time. Small tables with white tablecloths were scattered throughout.

"Is that what you wish might happen?" she asked with a coy smile. "Love affair?"

"I am most interested in romance." John reflected that he might be enjoying himself a touch too much.

He reminded himself that he was not here for an *affaire de coeur* but to discover information. If he ascertained what he needed to know before the relationship heated up, all the better.

If he didn't, well that was much to be regretted. One did what one must.

John Watson smiled appreciatively at the sight of the beauty before him. He was with the exquisite Joëlle Janvier, but he did not require exceptional beauty.

Though he certainly had no objection to it. John Watson liked women, selfish or foolish he didn't mind: they were simply delightful.

Unlike his illustrious flat-mate, John's one requirement in a female companion was that she not attempt to poison, injure, or kill him—qualities which appeared to pique the interest of his mystifyingly brilliant companion—though Miss Janvier might prove to be the exception to John's heretofore unwavering rule.

As a point of fact, Holmes had warned him to be on guard at all times with Miss Janvier. Holmes would know—he recognized danger in a woman immediately.

Holmes. John owed Holmes most of his aggravation. And everything good in his life.

Sherlock Holmes had brought John Watson back to life and given him a reason to live. Holmes had taught him—by example, no less—that one might be unhinged and a bloody disaster. But was that any reason not to enjoy oneself?

Holmes had illustrated the co-existence of bliss and despair, efficiency and destructiveness, genius and insanity all too well. Certainly, their weaknesses lay in entirely different areas. Holmes cared little for dalliance or for money, despite always seeming to have plenty of blunt.

As for himself, John knew that he had always been attractive to women, but he had taken it to the next level since the war—he had become a bloody rake.

He wasn't proud of it, but he was now damaged goods—and he wasn't just talking about the leg. When the nightmares came, sometimes he feared he had lost his mind. So why not have a bit of fun since he could hardly saddle a respectable woman with the unworthy ravages of the war?

"It is the strongest wish of my heart that we should be on more familiar terms, Miss Janvier. Why don't you start with telling me more about your background? I want to know everything about you."

"First you tell me."

"Not much to tell," John replied with a shrug. "I am a military doctor, I was in the war in Afghanistan not so long ago, now I am here with a beautiful woman."

"And your friend? Who is he?"

"My *friend*?" He feigned confusion. "I have many friends wherever I go."

"The man with unwelcome stare who appears to have fight with bear." Her expression was perplexed. "Has wild look about him."

"Ah. Yes, I know who you mean. The gentleman, he is a business associate. We have been involved in a profitable business venture as a result of my contacts in the military. *Very* profitable."

She smiled, her eyes suddenly shining. The word 'profitable' seemed to be the word which was the key to all things Joëlle Janvier. "You should buy him comb, then."

"Yes, a trip to the barbershop is in order." John paused. "Although he shows longer hair to advantage, in my opinion."

She turned her body towards him, although there was really no need. It would have been difficult to reveal more than was already revealed without undressing. "I raised in Moscow, is there I started in circus, you know."

"So you came to Paris with the circus, Miss Janvier?"

"*Nyet*, I to prominent doctor was married, moved to St. Petersburg." She nodded proudly. "He saw Joëlle perform and no other could he have despite protests of his family."

"I am gratified to learn that you have a preference for doctors, Miss Janvier," John remarked with laughter.

"*Nyet*. Not to do with that. He was very *rich* doctor. From old family."

"And you were happy with this doctor?" John asked.

"I to death was bored!" A lilting laughter escaped from her lovely lips. "Like bird in cage I was."

A beautiful bird in a cage. Ah, there was something Miss Janvier cared even more for than money. What was it? Danger? Adventure? Adoration?

Being hidden away in a rich man's home, no doubt she disliked being unable to observe the effect she had on men. Joëlle Janvier was a ravishing creature—and he had yet to discover that the awareness of anything else was in her consciousness.

Of course, Miss Janvier was not without talent. It took much practice and skill to perfect her show and he wondered how much of that competitive nature permeated her other endeavors.

"I will make it my business not to bore you, Miss Janvier," he murmured.

"Greater adventure and *danger* I need," she pouted, the look in her eyes shooting a current through his body, even as she began to answer his questions.

"What type of danger?" he asked with some degree of aloofness, a manner she was clearly not accustomed to, and which seemed to make her more determined to win his interest.

It was a calculated risk, but it paid off.

"All type, *Zsh-ohn*," she smiled, her lavender eyes twinkling.

"And your husband? Is he deceased?" John asked.

"Nyet."

"I did not know it was possible to obtain a divorce in Russia . . ."

"Did I say I divorced?" she shrugged, taking a sip of champagne.

"You are still married to this doctor?" John sat straight up in his chair, affecting a look of stern indignation. Exhibiting a moral indignation made his interest appear personal and less like that of a spy's interest, increasing his safety level all around.

"What difference it makes?" she demanded.

"None whatsoever, it appears." John raised his eyebrows. "But marriage is a sacred vow. Forgive me if I do not take such a thing lightly."

Involuntarily, it occurred to him that Miss Mirabella had everything this Russian starlet had to offer: beauty, excitement, a taste for adventure. Along with faithfulness and purity of heart.

John brushed those thoughts away. In the first place, he did not deserve Miss Mirabella Hudson. All that aside, her intelligence was a bit intimidating.

There was a girl with ambition. He wanted a girl who could put him first—or, at the very least, put their life together first. The man who married Miss Hudson—if she ever found the time—would always be competing with her goals and her drive.

John chuckled to himself. And of late she was forever commenting on a complex scientific principle completely out of context to the social conversation. Her mind never stopped—much like Sherlock's.

He envisioned those long, shapely legs in the red satin outfit in the tiger's cage. *But, damn, she was a beautiful girl.* He smiled to himself. *Playing second fiddle to Miss Mirabella's ambition might be worth it.*

"Let me understand your position, Miss Janvier." He fixed his gaze on Miss Janvier, keeping his manner aloof. "You do not consider marriage to be a sacred vow?"

She shrugged with indifference. "In fact, I make not one but three vows at that time." Joëlle replied without apology, taking another sip of champagne. "Only one I keep."

She is bragging about being above any sort of moral code. John felt his heart beating more quickly, knowing that this was the information he had been waiting for. The effects of the champagne were telling him what he wished to know.

And clearly Miss Janvier did not consider him to be a threat. This was generally the response people had to him, he wasn't sure why. His non-threatening manner was serving him well in his newly found career of espionage. But neither did she give any indication of revealing her three vows to him. Her only intent was to entice, not to impart information.

He might yet outmaneuver her.

John saw the waiter approaching and shook his head, indicating that under no circumstances was the Frenchman to approach the table.

"And I am to be impressed that you kept one of your three vows?" he laughed with unbridled amusement, hoping to goad her further. He wondered whether she kept that one remaining vow out of honor, deliberation, or mere happenchance, the answer to which might cast a poor light on an already miserable record. He murmured, "I already know you did not keep the marriage vow by your own admission."

"*Da.* Did not take marriage vow so seriously." Her eyes were ripe with illicit promise. "But one of three vows I kept. So you will know I am not *all bad.*"

"Oh, I sincerely hope that you are, Miss Janvier."

He felt himself shiver; he was not accustomed to this type of conversation from a woman and it was inviting at the same time he was appalled. "But, just as a matter of interest, what were the other two vows?"

"You must guess that too, *Zsh-ohn.*" She ran her fingers along the yellow and red orchid placed in a silver vase between them. She clearly didn't think he stood a chance of deducing the answer, but she had nonetheless given him permission to discuss the vows. That was something.

John took a bite of caviar, appearing bored as he glanced about the room in an effort to increase her desire for his attention. "Give me a hint."

"I went to university in St. Petersburg."

"Oh, let's see. You're Russian. You were a student in St. Petersburg." He smiled playfully. "You took an oath to kill the Czar."

Shock crossed her expression, followed by a frown. "Why you say this? This is not funny to Russian." She feigned indignation, but he didn't think it was because he had insulted her—but because he had hit the mark.

"Are you quite serious, Miss Janvier?" He stared at her aghast, which appeared to please her, before he burst into laugher. "I was only making a joke. University students. St. Petersburg. I didn't suppose you would be part of a knitting group with your oath to make a blanket before the winter set in."

John leaned back in his chair, laughing to ease the tension while his mind raced. So, perhaps she belonged to a revolutionary group which plotted to kill the Czar—and which succeeded. If this was the vow she kept, then the second vow she hadn't kept—along with her marriage vow—was that of *protecting* the Czar. A truly successful agent would have pretended to work both sides in order to obtain information.

"I told you not funny! That was Ignacy Hryniewiecki. The first bomb which failed was Nikolai Rysakov. They have both been executed." He thought he saw a smug smile cross her expression. "All Russian know this."

"Of course." He shrugged, feigning indifference as he motioned to the waiter. "Dull dinner conversation at any rate."

A blush crossed her expression, an experience he was certain was quite uncommon to her, followed by intense anger. Inadvertently he placed his free hand on the pistol inside his jacket.

She looked as if she were through speaking—and through with dinner. She withdrew her hand in a pronounced fashion, starting to rise from her chair, and it was obvious that she was furious. If she was indeed a spy, having her cover blown was extremely dangerous for her—and for him.

Life or death, he didn't care, but he did want to succeed at this and to protect his country. He decided to try a different tactic, attempting to prove to her that he was harmless.

"There, there, my dear," John murmured. "I would not offend the magnificent Miss Janvier for the world. And remember, it was your game, not mine. I assure you that I have little interest in your empty oaths to political groups." He hoped she believed him. Taking a box from the inside of his coat, he handed it to her, afraid that if he didn't, she might leave. "Please take this as an apology and a token of my admiration."

She opened the box to behold a double strand of perfect pearls, her eyes suddenly growing wide with appreciation.

"Am I forgiven?" he asked, helping to put the pearls on, which looked magnificent against her bare skin, framed as they were in black silk.

She fingered the beautiful pearls, looking at him as if to decide if he was just a foolish, wealthy man or an actual threat. Her eyes narrowed.

"No more talk of such things," she said.

"Certainly not. I abhor politics. Frightfully dull."

The lobster arrived, and he was glad she had ordered it, succulent and delicious as it was.

John didn't know if it was the champagne or her idea of manipulation, but she seemed to suddenly think it better to make light of the entire situation. "Is true, I heard of the revolutionary groups, I went to a few meetings, but I had no interest."

"Why did you go then?" To withdraw at this point would make her more suspicious.

"Is many handsome young men in revolutionary groups. Also, it annoyed husband."

"Ha! Ha!" He gave the reaction he thought she would like but studied her eyes, taking her hand in a patronizing manner. "But you could be hung for such an offense, Miss Janvier. Belonging to such a group was extremely reckless of you."

"Is true I reckless." Her seductive smile accentuated her words. "But if caught, would simply say I was spying on revolutionaries."

Not unless she had an official position with the Russian Imperial Police to protect the Czar. She wouldn't be believed otherwise—and would hang.

He effected a sudden frown, hoping to display his displeasure. Perhaps playing the jealous besotted fool would be more to the diva's liking.

"Revolutionary groups is where I met Stanislav," she said, in an obvious attempt to make him jealous.

John frowned, attempting to give her the reaction she wanted. "He seems a bitter young man, always complaining about the bourgeoisie and the injustice of things. He seems to greatly resent anyone with money."

"Stanislav is fool. Why not just take money?" she laughed. "He not know when to keep mouth shut. Or how to get what he want ..."

"And you do, Miss Janvier?"

She nodded, taking another sip of champagne, a sensual light in her eyes. He had to admit that he was drawn in.

"It stands to reason. And yet—what would be your reason for associating with him, my divine Miss Janvier? He is poor, and you seem, forgive me, rather fond of, let us say, *affluence*."

"Why not? What poverty can offer?" She took a bite of the succulent lobster, staring at him sideways in a manner which sizzled.

"Ah, but do you love wealth more than danger and adventure, Joëlle?" he laughed, easily goading her on.

She shrugged, but there was amusement in her expression.

Most of all, he wondered, *Are you still planning to kill the Czar?* An action which could entirely destabilize Russia. If the rebel forces succeeded in taking over the government of the world's largest country, who knew what else it might lead to on an international plane?

John wondered. *Am I as clever as I think myself to be?* Was this all bedroom games? Or simply that she thought him to be harmless? Or was her improved disposition an act? He sensed danger in proceeding, but he had to attempt to find out if she would tell him more. Now for the information he had been directed to procure.

The timing felt right; he prayed that he did not delude himself. He leaned back in his chair, studying her. "Prince George—I saw you speaking to him. Is he one of your beau, Miss Janvier?"

"Georgie?" she giggled. "Not be silly, Zsh-ohn. He is old man." She shrugged, but it was obvious she liked the turn of the conversation.

"That is not what I asked. Are you keeping his company?" He raised his glass to her, but kept his expression severe.

There was fire in her eyes, but she was amused. This was a game she liked. "You telling Joëlle who she may see and who may not see?"

He raised his eyebrows in disapproval, patting his lips with his napkin as if he were ignoring a spoiled child having a tantrum.

But he knew very well that threats would not hold her. She was for sale to the highest bidder and the only way to keep her was to offer more than anyone else. Since his discretionary income was now the equal of Prince George's thanks to Mycroft and the British government, he did have an advantage. He was young and fully functional, not an old man, all other things being equal.

"Do not pout, love," he murmured, lightly touching the pearl strand around her neck. "I am willing to lavish every manner of gift on you."

"I like every manner," she murmured.

"But I am devoted to only one woman at a time, so naturally I do not wish to share."

"Humph! I saw you talking to Veronika." Slowly she lowered herself back into her red velvet seat. It appeared that jealousy was a useful tool. She did not care to be second to any woman.

"She is a beautiful girl, certainly. You see, I like the Russian girls."

"Stanislav like Veronika too. How dare you tell Joëlle not to see other men when you look at other women!" she retorted venomously.

"A mere child!" He laughed, taking her hand and kissing it, bestowing his most devastating smile upon her. "You, my dear, are a . . . *woman.*"

Her lips began to form a smile before she caught herself.

"And I am a man who does not share. Those pearls, for example." He ran his free hand along her pearls, in the process touching the skin along her neck, even as he watched her shiver. "The luminescent quality of a genuine strand of pearls becomes your translucent complexion so well, don't you think, Mademoiselle Joëlle? And would you not like the earrings to match the necklace?"

"*Da.*" She blushed before the fire returned to her eyes. "Is it gift or bribe?"

"Spend time with whomever you like, Miss Janvier. Keep the pearls. If you prefer the company of an old man, I shall look elsewhere. There are many ladies who like jewelry and fine dining. I prefer you—so beautiful, so *experienced*—but I shall not be alone long. "Do I . . ." he ran his hand along her cheek, "*please* you?"

"*Da,* Doctor Zsh-ohn," she replied, breathless.

"But you must have more than one man, is that it?"

John could see the reluctance in her eyes, but it wasn't because there was something he could not provide. Whether it was for the game—or the political benefit, he did not know.

He knew that at some point he had to force the issue, even if it made her bolt. *Especially* if it made her bolt: that would tell those in the service of the Queen all they needed to know.

John looked at the ravishing beauty before him. On second thought, it was too early to press the point and demand a choice. It was necessary to romance her a bit more.

"Are you ready for dessert?" he asked seductively, leaving some question about the dessert that he had planned.

She nodded, a slight smile forming on her lips.

I know my duty. It was a tiresome, thankless task, but he had made a promise to his government.

John snapped his fingers to the waiter, motioning for the cherries flambé.

"It is in your hands then, Joëlle. I shall let you decide. But once you have made your decision, I shall not be revisiting it."

He was bluffing. *Did she suspect?*

Chapter Sixteen
The Walking Dead

"HRRRRRR!" As the wild animal ripped into the flesh, Mirabella could not help but imagine it as her own.

Of all her numerous revolting tasks, feeding the tigers was the one she hated the most. Right after being in the cage with the tigers. Even cleaning the tiger cages was better than the feedings—and the resulting carnage.

"There, there, Pasha, I p-promised you a t-treat!" *And I never break my promises to anyone with fangs capable of eating me for dinner.* Mirabella spoke as soothingly as she could manage to the four-hundred pound Bengal as she cautiously placed the raw meat on a stick through the bars of his cage, her heart still pounding. It was a wonder her heart hadn't pounded out of her chest during the last twenty-four hours.

Mirabella told herself that she might never go back into the ring, that was yet to be decided, but in the meantime she had responsibilities to fulfill. However much she might wish to ignore them. And now, of course, she had to tell Sherlock about Veronika and the missing key.

She hoped she might do so before she was eliminated—by man or beast, neither would surprise her. But there was no way to get word to Sherlock. She didn't know where he was staying. And John Watson was dining with Miss Janvier.

"Such a magnificent animal in such a small space," she murmured with a sigh, admiring Major's orange fur from a distance after pushing the meat into his cage.

"You deserve so much better," she added in a whisper. Despite her fears, she felt sorry for the animal and felt the cat's anger to be legitimate.

"ROAR!"

Still, she did not wish to be shredded with that same anger. As much as she hated the idea of leaving Sherlock Holmes' employ—at the moment she loved the job and hated the man—she was not willing to sacrifice her life for the honor.

Or was it loved the man and hated the job? She didn't know anymore. But she was certain she hated something.

After leaving her delightful meetings with each Sherlock and Veronika, Mirabella had first washed herself followed by washing her satin high heels and her outfit (it was, as yet, unknown if they were ruined). She had then done what she should have done to begin with: put on some serviceable shoes and warmer clothes. Sherlock had been in such a dreadful hurry to speak with her that she had not changed before following his summons.

Mirabella pursed her lips as she thought of Sherlock. She had never met a person with less patience for anything outside of his own agenda.

"Yes, yes, I am so sorry to keep you waiting!" she apologized to all the tigers. "I know that you expect to be fed immediately after the performance, but I was with someone with an even louder roar than you!"

RRROOOWAH!!!!

Strange that Sherlock Holmes could have the patience of a saint for a task which might drive anyone else to jump off the London Tower and yet be feverishly intolerant towards anyone who did not share his perceptions and was not on his time schedule.

Mirabella felt a twang of guilt for her own part in Sherlock's annoyance. If the truth be told, she was not doing that which she was hired to do. As yet, he wasn't aware that she had learned anything of significance.

Just as Dr. Watson had been instructed to pay close attention to Joëlle Janvier. It was clear that Dr. John Watson had that covered in spades.

Evangeline roared, impatient for her dinner.

"Believe me, I feel the same way," she murmured to the rarest of all the tigers, the beautiful golden, feeling a sudden kinship.

Mirabella felt her stomach growling with hunger, hoping to someday purchase something greasy, salty, and fatty from the food stand in the park set up for the circus employees. She placed the meat in Evangeline's cage on a stick.

It was the height of torture to know that the ever-so handsome and debonair Dr. John Watson was gallivanting about with a woman-of-the-world: a beautiful and *experienced* woman whom she could never hope to compete with.

Did she wish to be like Joëlle Janvier? Ravishing and bewitching, desired by men?

Of course I do! Well, not all men. Just one in particular.

She sighed. John Watson. So nice. So uncomplicated. So *handsome*.

Mirabella sighed. The mysteries of attraction went far beyond appearance. Except where Dr. John Watson was concerned—who was far and away the most beautiful man she had ever beheld.

"Evangeline! You were resplendent tonight in the ring!" Mirabella returned to admire the gorgeous golden.

"Rajah, you were the best of all the tigers tonight, you will receive an extra treat. You are a perfect gentleman." She sighed, a picture of the handsome John Watson flashing before her eyes, wining and dining the beautiful Miss Janvier. "Unlike most men!"

As she contemplated the lovely time everyone else in her entourage was having, the difference in their circumstances was glaring. No doubt Sherlock was staying in a local hotel with a *private* toilet and *hot* running water while she slept in a tent with the female circus crew and used a public wash basin filled with cold water to hand bathe herself behind a makeshift curtain, as did all the other ladies, the water so cold that the soap never properly dissolved.

And that is the best part of my day.

Grateful she was to have the soap, even a shared bar. It was a fact that Londoners and Parisians were competitive with their scent. And it was no wonder: the smell of soap or the lack therein was a strong indicator of one's station in life. A bar of ordinary soap was roughly the cost of a good piece of beef, and a lady's scented bar of soap well beyond that. To obtain water required effort after a long day of labor; how well she knew since she had had to carry a new bucket to the basin after washing her clothes.

Mirabella glanced at the small cage of the magnificent cat torn from her jungle home. Perhaps one wasn't so afflicted after all.

"We all have our role to play, don't we?" she asked Pasha, who, with his big golden eyes, almost tempted one to place one's hand in the cage, so sympathetic was his expression. She murmured to the tiger, "At least I chose my vocation voluntarily."

It was true. She had wanted to do detective work, which was not an occupation that came with luxurious surroundings. One was to observe for long hours in probable discomfort; that was her job, and the purpose was not to provide her with entertainment—or luxury.

Mirabella was well aware of these facts. But Sherlock bloody Holmes should at least feel something if she were to die! Was that asking too much? Particularly when she was willing to sacrifice everything to perform well *for him.*

"Good Zamba!" She placed the meat in the cage with a stick and then backed up, even though she was a decent two feet away and there were bars between them.

And why? Why am I willing to do so much for Sherlock?

"Don't eat so fast, Prince! You'll give yourself indigestion." His golden fur glistened in the light.

The tiger ripped and shredded his meal. Well, that was time well spent, teaching dining etiquette to a hungry tiger.

"He is magnificent animal, nicht?" she heard a voice behind her ask. "You see Evangeline, in small house. She is of large size for female."

Mirabella turned suddenly to see a girl covered almost entirely in bandages with crutches under her arms.

Angels above! Mirabella stared at her visitor stupefied, unable to reply.

"I saw you in show today—you looked frightened," the mummy girl continued in a shy voice. "You must come to love them."

"How were you injured?" asked Mirabella abruptly, finding her voice somehow. It sounded so rude, but the words seemed to erupt from her mouth.

"It was mine fault. I was with tigers when—"

"Heaven save us all!" Mirabella reached out to brace herself, the sight of the bandages and crutches dissolving what little remaining courage she possessed. "The tigers did that to you?"

"It was my fault. I lost my footing in a muddy arena, and it startled tigers when I fell."

"H-h-how is that *your* fault?" Mirabella asked, remembering how recently she herself had had such a fall.

"It is their instinct to attack when you run or become like prey. There can be no sudden movements, you see."

Gasp! "They attacked because you fell?" Mirabella repeated, wrapping her arms around her waist, thinking of the high-heeled shoes she was required to wear which were so difficult to walk in.

"Ja. They go in for kill when they see one who is weak. It is instinct." Mummy Girl nodded her head. "So don't trip and you will be fine."

Mirabella felt her head spinning. "Even as the presenter, I thought I was merely supposed to stand about and look pretty, maybe crack the whip about. I thought Mr. Afanasy took care of the tigers."

"That is true. All you must do is not fall." The girl moved forward, waving her right crutch in a circle, adding, "And do not look like prey."

Mirabella felt herself hyperventilating as she clutched her throat with her hands.

"Do not worry. You have only to be presenter. I want to be trainer."

"Whyever would you wish to do that, Miss?" Mirabella exclaimed, her terror momentarily displaced by shock. *Have you lost your mind as well as your body?* Mirabella thought the wise course would be to run from the circus and to take the first boat for London.

"Ich liebe sie," the girl replied tenderly. *I love them.*

"After they did . . . this . . . to you?" Mirabella motioned to the girl's body, entirely covered in bandages.

"Of course. They do what they are made to do." Mirabella thought of the singularly disturbing Sherlock Holmes, doing precisely what he was made to do—solving crime. The world's first consulting detective. If Sherlock were any less annoying that he was, he would not be *the best*. The mummy girl added, "And usually—they do whatever I ask them to do— even though they don't wish it. The tigers they are my friends."

"Who are you?" Mirabella asked abruptly. She did not wish to be impolite, but she had never before talked to a girl covered in bandages bearing tidings of her imminent death.

"Ashanti Van Horn." Somehow the mummy girl's strange accent was comforting in that it was distracting Mirabella from the fatal prophecy. The girl spoke English but as if her native language were something close to German.

"And what is your name?" Ashanti asked.

"Mirabella." *But you can call me 'Dead Girl'.*

"Is your accent . . . German?" Mirabella asked.

"Dutch," she replied. "But I know a little German."

"And you work in the circus?" Studying the poor girl, even through the bandages Mirabella could tell that her guest was tall and muscular, with an athletic build. Her bone structure was slim but shapely and her legs were unusually long like her own. Standing out in an appearance which was surprising in every way was her visitor's puffy lips. Possibly the girl's mouth was accentuated because the mummy girl was covered in bandages and it was one of the few parts of her body visible. Or possibly she was swollen from head to toe and her lips were no exception.

"I will never leave circus," the girl murmured, moving towards Pasha's cage.

Oh, you may leave quite suddenly, Mirabella reflected. *But not in the way you imagine.*

Pasha began pawing at the cage. Ashanti put her face very close to the cage and the tiger licked her bandaged cheek.

"Stand back!" Mirabella commanded in a whisper through gritted teeth. "You shouldn't get that close!" Clearly the girl had no concept of danger, had lost her mind, and was, in all likelihood, insane.

The mummy girl put her hand next to the cage—which one was never to do!—and Pasha licked her hand.

"You must nicht be afraid. Your fear they can see."

"The blind in Siberia can see my fear," Mirabella murmured.

"They're so big." The mummy girl said, stating the obvious. "Even when they love you and play with you, can hurt you without meaning to. You know damage a ten-pound housecat can do. Pasha, he is Bengal tiger and weighs four hundred pounds."

"That makes me feel a great deal better." Mirabella swallowed.

"They're *tigers*," Ashanti giggled, which was a strange sound emanating from a mummy just risen from the dead. "Look at tiny cage. In wild tigers are most territorial and roam the large spaces. A cage would make any creature miserable, but it inflicts particular suffering on tiger."

Mirabella looked at Pasha's huge head, gazing lovingly at Ashanti.

She was coo-ing at a wild beast. Such a bizarre sight. Particularly since one moment ago the girl had been shy and cautious in front of a harmless female laboratory assistant. How odd that the girl should feel more comfortable with the ferocious beast who had attacked her than with a human being.

Mirabella somehow managed not to make a sound although her strongest instinct was to run from the circus screaming. She didn't want to startle the tiger while Ashanti's hand was near the cage.

"What do you think is biggest cat?" Ashanti asked, withdrawing her hand.

"The Lion, of course. King of the Jungle," Mirabella answered mechanically.

"No," Ashanti shook her head. "Lions seem larger because of their mane, but the tiger, she is bigger. Male lions, they weigh 320 – 500 pounds, but the male tiger he weighs 500-700 pounds. Shikar, the Siberian, weighs six hundred, but the Siberians, they can weigh up to seven hundred pounds."

Mirabella swallowed hard, whispering, "Twice as big as the Bengal."

"Look at how they are treated. And yet he licks my face and my hand. How can you not love him?"

"I suppose he can't help being a ferocious killer," Mirabella said.

"Ja," Ashanti nodded. "That is how the gods they made him. I tell you secret."

"Yes?"

"I never use whip myself. I carry it because I am required to, but I use it not."

"How do you get the wild beast to do what you wish?"

"I *talk* to him. He knows what I say, and he choose to do it. I find what each of them they like to do. Some they like to roll over, and Evangeline she will go through a ring of fire. Unusual for a cat. They fear the fire."

"Is this the animal that . . . did Pasha do this to you?"

She nodded. "He is sorry for what he did. Stanislav, he teaches them with fear. But because Pasha loves me, he did not kill me. If he had feared me, in the moment that the fear it was overcome, he would have killed me. You hear of many injuries, but very few killings. Believe me, if the tiger he wants to kill you, it will be over in a second. It was a *warning*."

"My heart begs to heed the warning." She swallowed hard. "Do you know why the tiger attacked the English gentleman?"

"How you know about that?"

"It was in all the papers. Are these tigers particularly ferocious?"

Fury crossed Ashanti's face. "Goro was killed after that. Not right. Goro was sweet tiger."

"*Sweet?*"

"Something was done to make Goro mean." There was pure vengeance in Ashanti's eyes. "If I find out who did it, *I will kill him*."

"Are you . . . will you get better, Miss Van Horn?"

"I'll perform again. The wound almost severed my leg, I had face lacerations and a hole in my shoulder."

"*Why do you stay?*" gasped Mirabella.

"*I love them.*" Ashanti answered simply. "And I had very bad life before this."

"Worse than . . . *this?*"

"Much worse," she murmured. "And when the bright lights they come on, the chute door it opens, and the tigers they leap into the air roaring, there can be nicht to match the joy I feel in my heart in that instant."

"I am quite happy without joy," murmured Mirabella. "Ecstatic, in fact."

"That I have seen. I have watched you. I had to make sure you deserve my tigers."

"What do you mean?"

"You are not animal trainer. You are not circus performer. Why are you here, Miss?"

Mirabella looked deep into Ashanti's dark eyes, still black and bruised, knowing that she would never be able to fool her. "I can't tell you, Miss Van Horn, but I assure you that I mean no harm to the tigers."

"*Why are you here?*" Ashanti repeated, unmoved.

"I must work if I am to eat," Mirabella replied. This was entirely the truth.

"But you have not worked with animals, Miss Mirabella. That is not your occupation."

"Everyone must have a first day sometime." Mirabella felt discouraged and embarrassed; she was clearly incapable at pretending to be anyone other than herself despite having the master of disguise as her teacher. Every time she had gone undercover she had been most unconvincing: first as a debutante, now as a circus presenter.

Ashanti tapped her gloved finger to her bandaged face. "Is something you want to find out. Is why you are here."

"Something I want to find out?" Mirabella repeated suspiciously.

"Ja." Ashanti nodded. "Like spy."

"You think I am a spy?" giggled Mirabella, acting amused though feeling alarmed. *Oh, Goodness! If this young girl can see right through me, can someone else?*

"It is nicht so easy to fool me," admonished Ashanti, as if continuing to read her mind. "Mine auntie she has taught me the old ways. And . . . there are others."

"Other spies?" Mirabella giggled, attempting to appear as silly and foolish as possible.

Ashanti pursed her lips, saying nothing.

"I am sure I would be no better at spying than I am with the tigers!" exclaimed Mirabella, attempting to lighten the mood.

"Probably you are right about that," agreed Ashanti, nodding. "You do not know how to lie."

I'll have to work on that.

Mirabella motioned to the tigers. "Do the tigers like to do the show?"

Ashanti laughed at her foolishness, which seemed to be a general source of amusement in every court. "They are solitary. They require much less light to see than humans. And their hearing it is best sense—even better than sight. The high pitches and loud noises on tigers is very hard."

"It is all some have ever known, I suppose. And perhaps they live longer than in the wild," considered Mirabella.

"Do you know, I adopted a sickly tiger cub, Rajah, and he lives with me—when I am well. We are working on a show."

"You live with a tiger? How ridiculously dangerous!" Mirabella glanced at Rajah in his cage, aghast at the idea.

I live with a tiger as well, Mirabella reflected upon further consideration. One learns to adjust.

"Not dangerous with Rajah," Ashanti smiled, watching the direction of Mirabella's eyes. "When I can care for him he will come back to live

with me. Stanislav thinks I am verrückt-crazy-but every now and again
there is special one, Ja? *You can just tell.*"

Yes, you can. And you should run for the hills.

Ashanti sighed, her eyes caressing Rajah. "I cannot bear to see
him in this little cage. And he loves the bath. Most people don't know that
tigers they love the water."

And meat. They love the flesh.

Ashanti turned to stare at Mirabella with disapproval.

"What is it? Is something wrong?" Mirabella asked.

"I saw you let Shikar get broom handle in show tonight."

"Of course I did! Shikar weighs six hundred pounds; if he wants
the broom, he can have the broom!" she swallowed hard, remembering
the tug-of-war with the tiger. "Honestly, I didn't like the broom that much,
anyway."

"You can't let the tigers get away with anything. Even small things,
Especially small things. It is little actions teach them you are in charge."

"Oh, have you been misinformed, Miss Ashanti? Why can you
not see what is to obvious to me and everyone else? It is the *tiger* who is
in charge! All the tiger has to do is grab you, shake you a few times, and
you're dead."

"You must call them by name," admonished Ashanti, ignoring
her outburst. "They know when you have not taken trouble to learn their
names."

"Of course! I don't want to make the nice kitty mad! Let us
practice their names." As a matter of fact, Mirabella knew all the tigers'
names, but she wished for a disruption in the mummy girl's stare, which was
torturous in that it was almost as penetrating as Sherlock Holmes' piercing
gaze.

"Siberian Tiger—largest tiger—that is Shikar," Ashanti began,
reviewing their names. "The white tiger, and sweetest and most beautiful—
that is Rajah. Golden, the rarest of all the tigers, is Evangeline. Bengal—
male is only around four hundred pounds—that is Pasha, Andrei, Major,
Prince, Cleo, and Zamba."

"Can you teach me how to manage the cats, Ashanti?" Mirabella
gulped. "I so wish to live."

Ashanti laughed as she waved her crutch in the air, her smile the
only thing visible beneath her bandages. "I'll teach you everything I know,
Miss. I don't know why you're here, but for some strange reason, I trust
you. I don't trust anyone. But whyever you are here, I would hate to see
you die."

"I would truly hate that too," Mirabella murmured. She swallowed hard.

Run! A voice inside her head was screaming to her. *Leave the circus!*

But instead, like an idiot I will ignore the voice of reason and do as the great Sherlock Holmes commands. Staring at the crazy girl covered in bandages, when she should have been the most afraid, somehow Mirabella knew in her heart in that moment that she would go forward. That she would complete this assignment—even if it meant she had to go back in the tigers' ring.

I must be insane too.

Do I do this for Sherlock? Or is it an insatiable desire to solve the case?

At that moment Mirabella made a commitment to herself to act in spite of her fright—it was an impossibility that she should overcome her fear of a very real danger, but act in spite of it she could. And she made another commitment: she would never again wear the red high-heeled shoes. Only the slippers. She would have every possible advantage on her side.

She frowned. The cut of her costume was surely low enough to take attention away from her feet. As a matter of fact, her usual undergarments revealed less than her performing outfit! Her chemise, drawers, and corset alone covered more than the red satin circus costume!

Mirabella didn't know which was more terrifying—the tigers or the humiliation of parading herself about like a loose woman. She was a decent, God-fearing girl, but no one would believe it who saw her in that ensemble. It was the height of embarrassment. If she weren't so frozen in fright from the tigers, she wouldn't be able to present herself half-naked before all those people.

And yet, reflecting on her humiliation over her costume, the other ladies she knew in the circus were just working girls like herself trying to feed and house themselves while attempting to live long enough to have a life.

Mirabella sighed. Somehow she knew that, if she survived, she would never be afraid of anything else again.

That was a big 'if'.

Staring at this girl who looked like a walking mummy, Mirabella's peculiar companion seemed the most unlikely teacher in the world.

And very likely this mummy girl was her angel.

Chapter Seventeen
Aladdin's Lamp

"Tell me, my dear Watson," Sherlock asked, "are you enjoying yourself?"

"Absolutely not," murmured Watson. "Dreadful piece of business."

"Hallo, Doctor John!" waved one of the four dancing girls of Baghdad, all dressed in sheer outfits and looking as if they had only just emerged from Aladdin's lamp.

"Hello, Chloe´," Watson smiled, nodding. "Elise. Francine. Veronika." A blur of giggling gold, chartreuse, indigo, and scarlet chiffon floated by.

"And what progress are you making, Dr. Watson?" asked Mycroft, motioning to his minions to place a small table with refreshments next to their seats just off the stage in the Cirque d'Hiver.

"I should think Watson's progress is fairly obvious," murmured Sherlock, his eyes trailing after the dancing girls.

"I understand that Miss Vishnevsky—the dancing girl in scarlet—was a particular favorite of Beckham's," Mycroft murmured, studying the trail of color.

"Beckham, like Watson, was pleased to spend time with the ladies," Sherlock said, turning a critical eye to Watson. "Beckham's interest wasn't necessarily part of his investigation."

"And did you travel all the way from London merely to see us, Mycroft?" Watson asked cordially, taking a seat.

Sherlock muttered under his breath. "The death of a British agent and the head of the British army walking into a Russian spy ring would warrant a slight effort, even on Mycroft's part."

"It isn't far, just across the channel," Mycroft drawled lazily, sitting down. Even before his black tails touched the chair, his attendants were obviously in the process of procuring refreshments for the small party of three. The elder Holmes brother was impeccably dressed in the highest style, as if he were going to a fancy dinner party—which he no doubt was after their meeting on the circus grounds. "I come to Paris often. All the fashionable people are here."

"Except when you're in London, old boy," interjected Sherlock.

"Very true," agreed Mycroft. His slight paunch as caused by his lack of physical activity and hedonistic lifestyle was easily hidden as well by his height and superb tailoring, which did not deter in the least from his dashing good looks. Only in a boxing match would the differences in the brothers' comparative physiques become apparent, Sherlock reflected, being in the habit of analyzing appearances for the purpose of disguise.

Whizzzzz! The Whirling Dervishes of Constantinople somersaulted by. This was followed by a duel by the sword fighters, shouted on by the knife throwers, which gave every appearance of being a fight to the death.

Mycroft turned to the doctor. "And have you learned anything about Miss Janvier, Watson?"

"She is reluctant to give up her relationship with Prince George," replied Watson, his expression contemplative. "Whether or not it is the game she enjoys or there is a political reason for her interest in Prince George I have not yet determined."

"You don't seem in a great hurry to conclude the case, Watson," murmured Sherlock under his breath. He could not help but feel some relief that Watson's attention was diverted from Miss Belle by Joëlle Janvier and Miss Veronika. But Sherlock knew his duty to his friend. "I assure you that Miss Janvier is not one to play with. You might find that you are the mouse and she the cat, Watson."

"TO THE DEATH! KILL THE BLAGGARD!" The knife throwers shouted the sword fighters on.

Mycroft took a sip of the lemonade just provided. He turned to his aide who was standing beside him. "Do see if you can procure some of that pink spun candy, my good man. It looks quite appealing."

The attendant nodded and vanished.

Mycroft pulled an ornate oriental fan from his pocket and began fanning himself with it, but his gaze remained fixed on Watson. One of Mycroft's aides moved forward in an obvious attempt to take over the fan duties, but Mycroft motioned the attendant to keep his distance.

Excellent decision. Sherlock nodded in approval. In addition to the security concerns, waving the thin fan about might be all the exercise Mycroft had that day.

"Rowwwwwwaaaaaa!!" an elephant roared on the stage below them as its trainer urged the animal up on two legs, a sort of domino game with ten thousand pound animals being played, four on each side of center. A midget standing on his head moved in and out of the elephants.

Mycroft glanced about him. "It is rather like the Roman army collided into a rainbow, is it not? Gad, the resplendent cerulean blue and pulsating pink is atrocious! The blinding lights and screaming color positively give one a headache!"

"To hell with your headache, Mycroft!" retorted Sherlock through a clenched jaw, lowering his voice with effort. "Why the devil did you call this meeting here in this public place?"

Mycroft sighed heavily. "Miss Janvier already knows you and Watson to have a business arrangement of sorts, our meeting only confirms it if word were to get back to her." Mycroft knew very well that he stood out wherever he went—an effect he worked ardently to promote. "And who am I? A mere mid-level government official. No one has the slightest idea who I am—or cares."

"Stated in your characteristically modest fashion," Sherlock murmured.

"Humility is apparently a family characteristic," muttered Watson.

"As far as anyone knows I am your brother come to visit Paris. To attempt secrecy is the worst thing we could do, making it appear that we have something to hide. Someone would see us beyond a doubt." Mycroft tapped his manicured finger on the small table, lowering his voice to a whisper. "Moreover, if Miss Janvier does get nervous, that tells us a great deal. A mere circus girl would have no way of finding out who we are—and would not care."

"It must be delightful to always be so confident in the thoughts and behavior of everyone around you, in the laws of nature, and even in the weather," Sherlock muttered. "And in the meantime, if Watson is murdered, we shall write it up to a miscalculation."

"The weather? Not at all!" Mycroft pointed to his umbrella leaning against the wall. "And I must say, Shirley, you are a bit of a curmudgeon today—even for yourself."

I had thought it myself. Usually I am in a state of ecstasy when working on a case. . It seems I have not been able to do anything but worry about Miss Belle's safety for the last month—and now Watson . . . I who hire children to work for me—the Baker Street Irregulars—whom I worry less about than these two adults. "Curmudgeon? Nothing of the sort. I am a pragmatist and a teller of truth, neither of which suits you, Mycroft."

"To be sure," Mycroft replied smugly.

"The relevant point is that I can understand being confident in oneself, but do not be overconfident about the forces of evil around us—or in the predictability of behaviors," Sherlock mused.

"Strange coming from you, Holmes," Watson said.

Mycroft languidly took a sip of lemonade. "And Dr. Watson has successfully become one of the divine Miss Janvier's suitors, not so easily accomplished for the average *bon homme*."

"It is my patriotic duty," murmured Watson, a wicked smile forming on his lips. He was handsomely dressed in a dark jacket and vest teamed with beige trousers, his face shaven and his sideburns and hair stylishly cut. The man was a veritable advertisement for male grooming.

"I don't believe you are fully aware of the sacrifices which this dear fellow has made, Mycroft," stated Sherlock solemnly, his glass still untouched.

"Reasonably aware. I have seen the bill," said Mycroft, patting his forehead with his handkerchief. "At least the lady is much less in Prince George's company since the good doctor came upon the scene. To be quite honest, I am simply mortified the old duke will say something he shouldn't to our beautiful sequined rider."

"I fear Watson will over-exert himself," Sherlock said. "He has been romancing both Miss Janvier and Miss Vishnevsky, with attentions to the latter in a purported attempt to determine her likelihood as a suspect in Beckham's murder."

"Indeed. It is too much for one man," Mycroft said, now holding the candy cone in his hand, meticulously pinching off small bites so as to preserve his immaculate dress while clearly enjoying the spun sugar. "Exhausting."

"I am managing. It is better I should do the job than you should hire two men," Watson said.

"True. It simplifies things," Mycroft agreed.

"And at the close of our case we shall have only one more dead agent instead of two," muttered Sherlock.

"I have confirmed that Miss Vishnevsky is both Russian and in the anti-Czarist movement," Watson added.

"Definitely a suspect," Sherlock said.

"Yes," Mycroft agreed. "Miss Vishnevsky would certainly not wish to be exposed to the Czar's government."

"But does Miss Vishnevsky have the temperament and the intelligence to enact such a cold-blooded murder?" Watson considered.

"Miss Vishnevsky's family history is not good. She puts her father's death at the Czar's door," Mycroft added.

"As does Miss Janvier," Sherlock added.

"Miss Janvier did say something interesting," considered John Watson, shaking his head at the pink fluff offered to him.

"Ah. And what is that, Watson?" asked Sherlock.

"Joëlle said that, about the time of her marriage, she made two additional vows for a total of three vows—and that only one of the vows did she take seriously." He cleared his throat. "I can guarantee you that it isn't her marriage vow."

"An extremely revealing comment," considered Sherlock.

"Hmmmph," suggested Mycroft, his mouth full with candy.

"The three vows were—" Watson began.

"—Hello!" Sherlock sat up suddenly, speaking over Watson in the excitement of his sudden realization. Finally they were making progress! "I have no doubt one of the vows would include revolutionary activity."

"Yes, and, the other—" continued Watson patiently.

"—but we now know that Miss Janvier is on the Okhrana's payroll," interjected Mycroft, his eyes meeting Sherlock's in the excitement of discovery.

"The Okhrana? The Russian Imperialist Police and protector of the Czar?" exclaimed Dr. Watson. "That might have been very helpful information to convey. When did you intend to inform your operatives of this fact?"

"Oh, didn't I tell you?" Mycroft asked politely.

"It is for the best that Mycroft didn't tell you, Watson," Sherlock said.

"Better not to lay the facts before me?" demanded Dr. Watson.

"Beyond a doubt. It could only lead to mental laziness," Sherlock replied matter-of-factly.

"Holmes, I should land you a facer!" Watson muttered, a flash of anger in his eyes.

"Giving you too much information would only skew your observations and interject your conclusions with a bias," said Sherlock. "And I suppose it is all irrelevant. Simply because she is being *paid* by the Okhrana, doesn't mean that's where her allegiance lies. She could be a double agent."

"QUIET!" ordered Watson. "I'm trying to tell you what I have learned, if you could only but stop speculating theoretically for an instant!"

"Really, my man, we're all ears," murmured Mycroft, his eyes running over Dr. Watson with disapproval. Mycroft shrugged, holding out the empty cone of his cotton candy while one of his attendants rushed forward to take it from him. In general the entourage stood just far enough away so as to be out of hearing range but to be immediately available should Mycroft need his lips patted with a handkerchief or his shoes tied.

"Why don't you tell us, Watson, rather than keeping us waiting? We've a case to solve," Sherlock said. "Clearly the vows were to her husband in marriage, to the revolutionaries, and to the Czar, the latter two being on opposite sides."

Watson sighed heavily. "Yes. Precisely my conclusion. Joëlle let it slip that she once made a vow to kill the Czar—that vow was unquestionably made to the revolutionaries."

"Is this the vow she kept?" Mycroft posed. "And, if so, did she assist with the murder of Alexander II? And is she still plotting to kill Alexander III?"

"She claims that she had nothing to do with the assassination," Watson said. "But she became noticeably angry, as if I had come close to the mark."

"I wonder," Sherlock murmured. "If Miss Janvier was on the Czar's side, she was sadly ineffective in protecting him from the assassination."

"Ah, with friends like that, who needs enemies?" Mycroft agreed.

"Why wasn't the Czar told not to go out in the carriage that day? If Miss Janvier knew of the attack . . ." Sherlock grew pensive.

"Maybe he was," Mycroft added. "If Alexander II had not left the bullet-proof carriage either, he would not have been killed. It was insanity to do so given the circumstances. He didn't show the best of judgment. Perhaps he believed himself to be invincible."

"Whether or not she is still part of the revolutionary movement, Miss Janvier indicated that she was never loyal to it," Watson added.

"If she was telling the truth, that only leaves the Okhrana as the one vow she kept," Sherlock said. "A fairly big 'if'."

Watson paused, as if running her words through his mind. "Yes, she was strangely emotionless in revealing her true allegiance."

"Capital work, Watson!" Mycroft exclaimed, staring at Sherlock's friend in surprise. "You shall make a detective of him yet, Shirley."

"I must admit that I was initially perplexed," stated Watson, leaning back in his chair. "The Okhrana is the opposing force to the revolutionaries. It didn't precisely make sense to me that one of her vows would then be to the revolutionaries."

"Ah, but it does," said Sherlock. "If she were, in fact, working for the Czar, it would be quite natural that she should be spying on revolutionary groups pretending to be one of them. I would expect her to do nothing else."

"Yes, Miss Janvier would naturally have to take a vow of allegiance to the revolutionary cause while infiltrating the group," agreed Mycroft.

"But the question remains," posed Sherlock, leaning back in his chair and looking quite content, "where does her true allegiance lie—with the revolutionaries or the *Okhrana*?"

"Clearly she has no difficulty in lying," Watson said.

"And, in fact, may take some pride in it," Mycroft agreed.

"I think there is a way to resolve the question of where her allegiance lies," stated Watson. "Even though Miss Janvier has made excellent work of confusing the issue, for my part I would expect her loyalty to be wherever the most money lay."

"Assuming she has any loyalties, Watson," murmured Sherlock. "In my mind Miss Janvier is a wild card."

"True. To be quite honest I would be very surprised if the elusive Miss Janvier held to any ideals at all," chuckled Watson.

"What do you think motivates the beautiful Miss Janvier then, Dr. Watson?" asked Mycroft pointedly.

"Her own pleasure," Watson replied off-handedly. "And nothing more or less."

"The Czar can offer far more money than the revolutionary groups, which are no doubt unpaid, being formed on high ideals. A shortage of money is the primary reason the revolutionary groups exist to begin with. And yet," mused Sherlock. "It all begs the question."

"Who killed Beckham?" asked Mycroft. "And why?"

"And to which cause would we wish any of British military secrets leaked?" Sherlock posed. "The Russian Czar or the Russian revolutionaries?"

"Neither," stated Mycroft.

Sherlock turned to Watson. *"So have a care."*

Mycroft added, "We know that anti-Czarist activity is widespread here at the Circus. But was Beckham killed because he had the names of all those involved—or because he had learned something about the murderer personally?"

"Indeed." Sherlock nodded. "Beyond a doubt there are dark days ahead."

Chapter Eighteen
The Seeds of Revolution

As Sherlock's mood was darkening, a slight young man of medium height approached. Looking nervously about himself, he wore a loose smock, a wide-brimmed straw hat as might be seen worn by a laborer in the fields, and a moustache which appeared too thick for his young age. One of Mycroft's guards stepped in between the party and the young man with a decidedly threatening stance.

Sherlock cocked an eyebrow at the intruder, a slight smile on his lips, adding in quiet undertones, "Here comes our other operative."

Mycroft motioned to his guard to allow the visitor in overalls to join them, all seated in the shadows behind the Cirque d'Hiver stage, inasmuch as anything in the Cirque d'Hiver was in shadow.

"Ah, Miss Hudson," Sherlock murmured in a low tone as she sat down.

"And how did you know it was me, Mr. Holmes? I thought my disguise was reasonably good."

"You cannot simply put on different clothes and add a moustache, Miss Hudson. You must also speak the part—and move as your subject would move," Sherlock admonished, shaking his head.

Sherlock was certainly one to criticize one's presentation! He looked half-mad, his eyes jutting everywhere. His hair was tousled, and he was unshaven. And yet, somehow he managed to look . . .well . . . *masculine* instead of disheveled. His dark, navy pants were neatly pressed at least. No doubt the hotel where he was staying took care of that.

The hotel with hot water.

And a private room in which to bathe. How she missed her room, her wash basin, and her bar of Pears' soap at Baker Street!

She closed her eyes momentarily. Who would have thought one might have such sweet dreams about a bar of soap?

"And how should I have moved?" she asked as complacently as she could muster, biting her lip.

"Most certainly not with that sway of the hips which you employ."

Moving her eyes to the other two men in the party, now visible even in the shadows and through the blind of a straw hat, her jaw dropped.

Sherlock's older brother is positively exquisite.

"My brother, Mycroft," Sherlock muttered, as if knowing where her eyes alighted.

"There is no need to tell me that," she murmured, quickly tipping her hat up that she might get a better view.

"They are very much alike, are they not?" John Watson asked.

She nodded, experiencing a rare moment when she was unable to find words. After a long pause she whispered, "And yet, so different."

The resemblance was uncanny, Sherlock and Mycroft were clearly related, but where the Great Detective was inattentive to his appearance and managed to blend in when he wished to, this striking brother of his was of a larger build and taller. Mycroft Holmes could not blend in if it were the greatest desire of his heart.

The elder brother was impeccably dressed in a modish style with a crisp white shirt, a silk grey paisley vest the color of his steel-grey eyes, black top hat, and black tails, as if he were going to a society dress party rather than the circus! The tips of his shirt collar were very high and starched and he wore a fancy bowtie in a grey satin, further accentuating his melancholy—but dreamy!—grey eyes. She wasn't man crazy, truly she wasn't, Mirabella assured herself, but neither was she blind.

Her eyes moving to Sherlock, Mirabella reflected that Mycroft was at least three inches taller than his younger brother. Sherlock was only somewhat taller than average height, allowing the Great Detective to successfully utilize his various disguises, at times requiring a slight bending of his torso. An overly tall man would be too easily identifiable, as well as one in possession of any remarkably distinctive features. In point of fact, Sherlock had chiseled, aristocratic features. It was a credit to his abilities in disguise that had learned how to make himself less identifiable.

"An honor to be sure, Monsieur Hudson." Mycroft bowed his head momentarily, a teasing smile on his lips, as if conveying a compliment to her costume.

Trill! While she sat down at their secluded table, she could hear the flute-like sound of a snake charmer luring the cobra out of its basket-home. She loved Bahadur, the white-bearded yogi, from the moment of meeting him. She could just catch a glimpse of his orange turban, yellow cotton tunic, and brown beige linen pants from behind the stage curtain.

"A lemonade for our guest." Mycroft motioned to an attendant standing some distance from them, obviously thinking of her comfort.

She inhaled deeply, feeling as if she might swoon from the kindness. In an instant, she imagined that she saw a glow of light, not unlike a halo, around Mycroft Holmes' head.

"And what have you learned in the *Cirque d'Hiver*, Hudson?" Mycroft asked.

Even in Mycroft's addressing her as if she were a boy, the elder

Holmes was definitely more playful than his brother. Sherlock was not without wit, but he used it to sting more often than not. And with those few words it was apparent that Mycroft Holmes was treating her with respect.

"I found a key to the tigers' cages among Veronika's things," she said without further ado. "And there was a red stain on her scarlet outfit—pale but there nonetheless."

"It certainly makes Miss Veronika appear to be our murderer, doesn't it?" asked Mycroft. "She is a member of the anti-czarist group, we know: she had motive, means, and opportunity."

"Unless the real murderer was attempting to frame her," Sherlock considered. "The murderer would have destroyed the outfit, leading me to think that the key was planted."

"Veronika said as much," Mirabella replied.

Sherlock raised his eyebrows in disapproval. "Miss Vishnevsky knows that you know about the key? That was exceedingly careless of you, Miss Belle, and could put you in grave danger."

"I know. But I can't help but feel that Veronika is not the murderer. She's too sweet. Unlike Miss Janvier."

"Ah, but sometimes the cruel ones work harder to appear sweet," Mycroft said. "Those who are themselves sometimes have less to hide."

Mirabella recounted the scene and her conversation with Veronika, to which Sherlock said, "Interesting." He was often a man of few words while he was deep in thought, which was fine with her. He added, his mood now darkened, "And have you learned anything else, Miss Belle?"

"In truth, I am too busy trying to stay alive to learn much!" She hated to waste everyone's time with a plea for her continued existence, but if it was not an important topic to them, it certainly was to her.

"Stanislav does seem to disappear at regular intervals. Always on Sunday night," she added. "Or so Ricardo—he cleans the animals stalls—informed me."

"A regular outing," Mycroft murmured. "Does Stanislav come back rowdy and smelling of drink?"

"Stanislav sleeps in the men's tent, of course, and I in the women's, but I do keep an eye out through the slit in the tent." *Someone has to do the detective work here, and clearly no one else intends to.* "He's not stumbling or anything when he comes back. I have asked Ricardo and he says Stanislav has been drinking but not to excess. Ricardo says that Stanislav always comes back disturbed—and quiet."

"I hope that you were discreet in your questions, Miss Belle," Sherlock interjected.

"Naturally," she replied. "Ricardo likes nothing more than to share his observations. I barely have to say a word."

"Not believable," Sherlock considered.

"I don't doubt it," murmured Dr. Watson. "All it takes is a pretty girl in the young man's vicinity and he starts talking."

"What pretty girl?" Mirabella asked before understanding dawned, shaking her head in surprise. "*Oh, no!* He's simply being friendly. Nothing of the sort."

"It was the part about Miss Belle not saying a word which I don't find believable," Sherlock stated, his expression reflective. He added languidly, "I do not dispute her beauty."

Compliments from Mr. Sherlock Holmes. The moon must be full.

"When does Mr. Afanasy leave?" Mycroft interjected.

"About six o'clock on Sunday nights," recollected Mirabella.

"We'll have him trailed," Mycroft remarked definitively, tapping his finger on the table.

"Joëlle was not available on Sunday night," considered Dr. Watson, rubbing his chin. "I assumed it was Prince George, but now I wonder . . ."

"Don't you have anyone trailing Miss Janvier, Mycroft?" Sherlock asked.

"Of course. Dr. Watson," Mycroft replied, waving his hand which revealed his diamond and gold cufflinks.

"And you, Miss Belle, did you observe Prince George with Miss Janvier on Sunday night?" Sherlock asked.

"No I didn't," Mirabella considered. "But she has a private room, she doesn't sleep in the tent with the rest of the ladies. It is possible she has escaped my notice. Now, if you were to obtain a private room for me . . ."

Mycroft pulled his watch out and glanced at it. He motioned to one of his staff who appeared to be his number one man, the same man who had attempted to stop her from joining the party. He was a large man and she was relieved she hadn't had to engage in fisticuffs with him.

"What time is my dinner engagement?"

"Seven thirty, sir."

"Very good." Mycroft nodded. "Do see if you can round up some fruit and cheese, my good man. Something light, I don't wish to spoil my appetite."

"An impossibility, to be sure," Sherlock murmured.

"And some tea, please," Mycroft added.

"Certainly sir."

"We'd best add someone else on Sunday nights," suggested

Sherlock, once the attendant had withdrawn.

"To trail each Miss Janvier and Stanislav? Definitely," agreed Mycroft, who had apparently already mentally filed away the agenda despite appearing distracted.

"We also must consider the animal trainer's assistant as a murder suspect," considered Sherlock, rubbing his unshaven chin with his hand.

"I don't think Ashanti thinks about anything except the tigers." Mirabella shook her head. "Honestly. Ashanti is a lovely girl: quiet and shy. And she has taught me a great deal about the tigers—probably saved my life." *Thankfully someone cares about my life.*

"If Miss Van Horn can manage the tigers, she may be Beckham's murderer," Mycroft suggested.

"Oh, no! I can't believe Ashanti would do such a thing!" Mirabella exclaimed.

Sherlock raised his eyebrows at her. "And why is that, Miss Hudson?"

"Because Ashanti knows right from wrong," Mirabella stated definitively.

"Ah. So Miss Vishnevsky isn't the murderer because she is sweet. And Ashanti didn't do it because she is righteous," Sherlock stated.

"And Miss Janvier: what dealings have you had with her, Miss Hudson?" asked Mycroft.

"Oh, Joëlle taunts everyone: Stanislav is obviously in love with her—and she is so cruel to him, telling him how he is worthless. Why doesn't Joëlle just leave him alone if she doesn't like him? She is even mean to Ashanti! I have seen Joëlle whispering to the poor girl, and Ashanti running off crying. Ashanti wouldn't tell me what it was about."

"Miss Janvier unkind?" Watson raised his eyebrows at this, as if surprised by the revelation. Dr. John Watson was a good man and a loyal friend, but sometimes he struck Mirabella as naïve. Particularly where women were concerned. "It's difficult to believe someone so warm-blooded could be so cold-blooded," John murmured.

"Tsk! Tsk! Watson, I beg you to have a care." Sherlock turned to Mirabella. "Try to find out what Miss Janvier is taunting your friend with, Miss Hudson."

Why not? I'm doing everything else. In between the tiger attacks I shall do so.

"Yes, sir." Mirabella sighed, inwardly agreeing that there must be a great significance to Ashanti crying. Whether or not it was relevant to their case, Mirabella didn't know, but if it was relevant to her friend, it mattered to her.

"Obviously the bare-backed rider has something she could hurt Ashanti with," Sherlock mused.

"If Joëlle hasn't already done so."

"Excellent work, Miss Hudson." Mycroft looked up to bestow his dazzling smile upon her.

Mirabella shrugged. She couldn't see that she had accomplished anything—though no one could say she wasn't giving one thousand percent.

"The existence of the red-stained outfit has enormous implications," Sherlock said, appearing to be deep in thought.

"Do you think so, Holmes?" Watson asked.

"Veronika Vishnevsky has no reason at all to encounter blood as she is removed from the animals, her act being one of dance. Neither is she prone to accidents in her act. If the harem outfit is, in fact, the garment worn by Beckham's murderer, further promoted by the existence of the key, we now know that the murderer was a woman." He tapped his finger on the table. "Which I suspected by the fact that Beckham was separated from his gun. More easily accomplished by a love interest."

"To our knowledge, only Miss Vishnevsky fall in that category," Mycroft said.

"Ah, but the murderer would have taken pains to be discreet."

"Discreet? Miss Janvier?" Watson laughed.

"This is considerable progress," Mycroft agreed. "Oh good, the refreshment is here. I am positively wilting." Mycroft placed a grape in his mouth as he motioned for the tea to be poured.

"Miss Hudson." Sherlock turned to her once the servants had retired. "Do you still have the gun I gave you?"

She nodded.

"And do you keep it with you at all times?"

"Where would I keep a gun in my costume, Mr. Holmes?" She knew it was not appropriate for women to discuss such things, but it was a particular sore point with her among many. "There is not enough material in my costume to cover my body! My aunt would be quite scandalized to see it!"

"There is a pocket in the cape, is there not?" asked Sherlock.

"I recall a lovely pink velvet cape," remarked Watson.

"Pink velvet is a complement to your chestnut brown hair, Miss Hudson," Mycroft remarked, enjoying a strawberry. "Very advisable."

Watson turned to stare at the government official.

"Have I offended you, my good Dr. Watson? I am not color blind."

"To be sure," nodded Watson, his expression stiff.

"Miss Hudson?" demanded Sherlock, his usual gruffness returning too quickly for her pleasure. "I asked you a question."

"Well, yes, but . . ." She was somewhat perplexed by all that had passed, not being accustomed to so much attention from men. But rather than all this male attention—the main purpose of which was to assign her more duties—if one or the other might simply arrange for a hot bath and a hot meal, that would warm her heart far more than compliments she could not take to the bank. Or to the wash basin as the case may be.

"I desire you to have a weapon with you at all times, Miss Hudson," Sherlock ordered sternly.

"And do you think it is safe that I should be seen speaking to you?" Mirabella asked. "You have already said that my disguise is not convincing."

"She has a point, Holmes," considered Watson. "Though in that disguise I would never have known her . . ."

"We will resolve upon a better place to meet," Sherlock nodded.

"And where are you staying, Mr. Holmes?" Mirabella sighed heavily, turning to Sherlock.

"At Le Grand Hôtel de la Paix," answered Dr. Watson, nodding appreciatively. "Sometimes referred to as the *Paris Le Grand*."

"It is quite nice?" she asked breathlessly, staring into turquoise eyes.

"Nice? I suppose so," shrugged Sherlock. "I chose the hotel because it is only steps from the metro station."

"And close to the *Opéra Garnier*, the *Louvre*, *Place Vendôme*—and with a view of the Eiffel Tower," interjected Mycroft as if he were being forced to undergo a great trial but was enduring it due to his devotion to discipline. "An acceptable location."

One thing Mirabella had observed in her short acquaintance with the Great Detective's brother was that, in contrast to Sherlock's almost compulsive discipline, his brother was devoted to enjoying himself. Most certainly Mycroft performed well in his trade, but it appeared to be rather an aside for him whereas Sherlock slept, ate, and breathed his profession.

"Though I personally prefer the *Hotel Pont Royal* on the Left Bank," murmured Mycroft.

"On Saint-Germain des Prés?" asked Sherlock. "And why is that, brother dear? It is much smaller is it not?"

"Precisely the point, Shirley," agreed Mycroft," and thus the *Pont Royal* is able to provide exceptional service. I, of course, do not require much, but it is desirable that my associates should have all they wish."

"The food is very good at the *Pont Royal*, I understand," Watson said with a knowing glance.

"Yes. Again, my needs are simple, but the food is good," agreed Mycroft, taking a sip of tea. "Predominantly I like the *Pont Royal* because it is so fashionable. I adore style—and it is a marvelous place to host a party. Beautiful décor, always fresh flowers. Everyone of importance has been there."

"And at the *Pont Royal*—do they have baths—with *hot* water?" she sighed longingly.

Sherlock replied mundanely, "Now, my talkative agent, if we are quite finished discussing meaningless and pointless topics—and I assure you we are—let us return to the matter at hand."

"I expect that food and hot water are of little importance to you because you have them," said Mirabella.

"To each according to his abilities," replied Mycroft without the slightest hesitation, accenting his words with a winning smile at precisely the right moment. "The most difficult pursuits must necessarily go to the most capable."

Goodness sakes, the elder brother was in possession of a charm so great he could make one believe that it was a great honor to be shot by the firing squad. She began to doubt that he and Sherlock came from the same womb.

What struck her immediately was that Mycroft Holmes was in possession of an unmatched charisma. Whereas the electrical field about Sherlock propelled him on in jagged bursts of flame, reminiscent of insects hovering about one in the most annoying fashion—or of lightning bolts frying one's intestines—Mycroft obviously harnessed the field as a warm glow emanating from him.

"*Tsk. Tsk.* I can assure you, my dear Mycroft, that were we to outfit Miss Hudson in the Queen's Palace she would complain about the accommodations."

"I rarely complain." She glanced at Sherlock who was smiling sardonically as if it were all a joke.

"You never heard anyone protest so much as when we enrolled her in *Miss de Beauvais Finishing School for Distinguished Young Ladies*," Sherlock continued, unabated, pulling on his brocade vest in a decided but genteel manner. "We outfitted her in jewelry and gorgeous gowns. All she had to do was sit about and drink tea, embroider and chat all day and you would have thought we had placed her in a medieval torture chamber."

"All I had to do?" she objected indignantly. "I was also required to learn fencing, *Jiu-Jitsu*, and boxing in addition to hand-to-hand combat. To which I never objected."

"Never objected? You, Miss Belle?" Sherlock laughed heartily, a sight which seemed to both surprise and amuse Mycroft exceedingly.

"Miss Hudson," interjected Mycroft. "You work for my brother. I should think the tiger's den is not that great of a change for you."

Mirabella saw that her cause was lost. She studied Mycroft. "If I may ask, that you are so apparently social, while your brother—"

"—Could give a rat's ass?" finished Watson, laughing.

"We are much more alike than you might think," remarked Sherlock. "Rest assured that Mycroft, like myself, could care less what anyone thinks of him. However, unlike me, he enjoys people immensely. But we don't have time to go into that here."

"Very true," agreed Mycroft. "I only have two hours to dress for dinner."

Mirabella stared at the elder Holmes brother in disbelief. What more did the citadel of fashion need to do?

Dr. Watson tipped his hat to the debonair gentleman seated beside him. "Now the truth comes out, Mycroft. The fact is that you like to socialize as much as the Lutheran Ladies' Knitting Club of Paddington Place likes to gossip."

"Socializing and gossip are synonymous." Mycroft demurred. "And, if I were not a gossip, I should not have made a name for myself in government. Gossip is the essence of politics."

"What do you mean?" Mirabella asked, perplexed. "You have a respected position in government, Mr. Holmes!"

Sherlock patted his lips with his handkerchief, smiling smugly. "The very nature of Mycroft's work is that the information of every government department descends upon him wherewith he assimilates, discards the useless, reorganizes the relevant, and spits out the conclusions which were invisible to everyone else."

"So *information* is Mycroft's trade?" asked Watson, his lips curving in amusement.

"Precisely," nodded Sherlock, taking his pipe out of his pocket. "*Gossip*."

"I had understood that serving the people is the essence of politics," suggested Watson.

"Ha! ha! ha!" laughed Sherlock with unusual merriment.

"Oh! Ho! ho!" joined in Mycroft, lightly punching his brother in the arm in an uncharacteristic moment of camaraderie. "Where did you find him, Shirley?"

"Most amusing," added Sherlock, taking out his handkerchief and wiping his face. The Great Detective was in a rare state of joviality. "Though I shan't say that Mycroft has a servant's heart, he does know right from wrong, unlike many of his contemporaries, and he cannot be swayed from his principles. He could care less, frankly, about the opinions of others."

"Like some others I know," Watson murmured.

"So now that we have established Mycroft's purpose, let us turn to Miss Hudson," Sherlock said. "Your job is to attempt to find out what Miss Janvier is holding over Miss Van Horn. Also, probe Miss Van Horn—and Stanislav—about Beckham: try to discern how the tiger could have killed him."

"Ashanti said there must have been interference," Mirabella offered.

"Yes, that we already know. But were the cages locked? How did the tiger get out? Why did the tiger attack? Discern if they were genuinely surprised by the attack: this is the important thing. We can piece together what happened, but I want to know their reactions, which will confirm or refute my conclusions. Ask Stanislav if there could possibly be a third key to the tiger cages in existence. We, of course, know there is, but find out if Stanislav believes there to be another key. I want to know if he was involved in the murder."

"Yes, sir," Mirabella replied.

"And I wish to search Miss Janvier's room. With your assistance of course, Miss Belle."

Her heart fell in her chest. Her last search had not gone that well.

"As for you, Watson," Sherlock continued, "Press Miss Janvier to cease seeing Prince George. While you're exhibiting your jealous rage, perhaps approach the topic of her relationship to Beckham: try to find out the extent. But be careful. She is dangerous. Many of her former lovers have died or been incarcerated."

"I'm always careful, Holmes," Watson replied.

"Perhaps," Sherlock said unconvincingly. He studied his friend before him. "But you may underestimate your foe, Watson. "

"And what will you be doing, Holmes?" Watson asked.

"I'll be undercover at the Sunday night meetings—disguised of course—to learn what I can about Miss Janvier, Stanislav, Veronika, and the plans of the group." Sherlock tapped his finger on the table. "And you, Mycroft?"

"I'll be paying a visit to the local key makers to attempt to determine who commissioned the additional key. We must turn mere speculation into fact," Mycroft said.

Chapter Nineteen
Animal Attraction

Mirabella was possessed by a strange curiosity; respectable ladies didn't wear make-up.

Joëlle Janvier was not a respectable girl. Still, Mirabella's instincts told her that this warranted further investigation. Mirabella removed the lid of the rouge pot on Joëlle's dresser, smelling the contents.

"It doesn't smell right, Mr. Holmes. It has a decided . . . *animal smell* . . . for want of a better word."

Sherlock looked up from his search, moving swiftly to her side to smell the rouge pot. Sherlock and Mycroft had brought her along to search Miss Janvier's room while John Watson took the circus performer to yet another elaborate dinner after the evening's performance.

"Fascinating. I believe 'animal smell' is precisely the right word, Miss Belle. An alarm substance as described by Jean-Henri Fabre."

"I recall that paper," Mirabella said, searching her memory for the various scientific papers of Sherlock's that she was in charge of filing. Technically she wasn't supposed to stop working to read them, but she had learned to scan the introductory and closing paragraphs for the summary. "What is the term for the substance?"

"Chemical messenger," Sherlock replied. "The scent has meaning only to the animal of a particular species. It could communicate danger, the desire to mate, or other survival needs."

"It affects the neurocircuits," Mycroft added, seated in the lime-green winged back couch and fanning himself profusely. "Something which might incite a beast but leave a human unaffected."

"I wouldn't think such a substance would be needed," Mirabella said. "The tigers are kept hungry. They don't need much incentive to attack."

"Added incentive. Perhaps the straw that broke the tiger's back . . ." Sherlock considered. "Take a small sample and put it in the bag, Miss Hudson."

"What if Miss Janvier notices?" Mirabella asked.

"It is important that she doesn't. We don't wish her to alter her behavior." He emphasized, "Or to put Watson in danger, who doesn't appear to be proceeding with care."

"And yet, Miss Hudson has a point," Mycroft said. "We may be able to prove that Miss Janvier attempted to use chemical messengers to provoke a tiger attack—but it doesn't necessarily mean that she succeeded or is the killer. She had an alibi, in fact."

"It is difficult to establish the exact time of the murder," Sherlock said distractedly, continuing his search.

He went through her clothing, pulling out a heavy beige overcoat. "What would a woman who delights in showing off her figure want with a large, loose garment such as this?"

"To disguise herself?" Mirabella asked.

"And these boots," he continued. "Much too serviceable."

"Precisely. And there are an inordinate amount of books in this room." Sherlock began opening Miss Janvier's books, apparently in search of missives which might have been placed inside the books. "I don't expect Miss Janvier is an extensive reader."

It was shocking to be in the same room with so much brain power, Mirabella reflected. "Mr. Stanislav brought up the tiger attack, and he seemed quite smug about it," Mirabella said.

"Oh?" Mycroft asked, interested.

"He is very jealous of Miss Janvier, and it could be a motive," she said. "What if Beckham's murder has nothing to do with the spy ring and it was simply a jealous boyfriend?"

"If we can match the scent from the rouge pot to Beckham, indications are that Miss Janvier was the murderer," Sherlock said. "It is fairly clear that the idea was in her head. Animal hormones are not the type of things one generally finds in ladies' toiletries."

"But what about the duplicate key in Veronika's things?" asked Mirabella.

"The key would be a simple item to plant on someone else," Sherlock said. "Not so the chemical messenger. Only the murderer would have such a thing. And why would anyone plant it here? It is very unlikely to have ever been found—or understood."

"Quite so. If not for Miss Belle's instincts, we never would have found it," agreed Mycroft.

"And the blood-stained clothing which was not burned is further support of the idea that someone is attempting to frame Miss Vishnevsky. Who better than the actual murderer?" Sherlock said.

"If Miss Janvier is the murderer," Mirabella considered. "That would mean that John . . . *Dr. Watson* . . . is in danger."

"Indeed." Sherlock didn't look up from the book. "But he has his revolver."

"I'm sure Beckham did too," Mirabella replied flatly. "How could a trained spy be separated from his weapon?"

Sherlock looked up. "I asked myself that same question when you were in the parlor purportedly protecting the princess of Montenegro on your first case and became separated from your pistol."

"I take your point, Mr. Holmes," she murmured. "That was probably the only five minutes of the day when my gun was not with me."

"Hmmm. Pistol in the parlor purportedly protecting the princess. Most poetic, Shirley."

Sherlock frowned. "Personal safety is not a laughing matter, Mycroft."

"Certainly not, Shirley. Nothing is." Mycroft suddenly appeared deep in thought. "I can think of another way Beckham may have been separated from his weapon."

"Seduction," Sherlock stated simply, returning his eyes to his search. "I believe that Miss Janvier is more dangerous than one might suppose."

"She wasn't seducing him in the tiger cages, I can assure you," Mirabella said. "Not romantic *at all*."

Sherlock smiled to himself. "I shall remember that, Miss Belle."

"So now we have the means," Mycroft stated. "Beckham was killed by a tiger, which could have been accomplished with the alarm substance and a key to the cages. Assuming Miss Janvier could have wrested Beckham's gun from him."

"But why?" asked Mirabella.

"Most likely Beckham knew too much," Mycroft considered. "Perhaps the names of all the spies in the ring—or perhaps even their plans. The murderer got to him before he had time to convey the message via telegram. Communication is rarely instant in this business."

After a moment's reflection Mirabella added, "Stanislav had a key too. Just because Miss Janvier has a key doesn't mean she is the one who used it."

"Aha! I've found something!" Sherlock exclaimed, flapping a piece of paper about.

"I wonder what it says," Mycroft considered, fanning himself.

Sherlock handed the paper to his elder brother. "I believe you know Russian, Mycroft."

"Certainly. One must do something in the evenings when one is not dining with friends. And it is a language indispensable to the British government."

Mirabella made a concerted effort not to drop her jaw.

"It is a personal letter to Miss Janvier," Mycroft replied, his voice somber. "From the Czar. Inviting her to the palace in appreciation for her services."

"Proof that she is on the side of the Czar," stated Mirabella, feeling her disappointment. She added in a whisper, "It has to be Stanislav, Ashanti, or Veronika who murdered Beckham—they are the only ones who had access to the tiger cages."

"To the contrary," muttered Sherlock, shaking his head. "I'd say this letter is proof positive that Miss Janvier plans to murder the Czar herself."

Chapter Twenty
Le Grand Hôtel de la Paix, Paris

"To be honest, I am most impressed with her," John Watson murmured, staring into the fire of the suite he shared with Holmes at Le Grand Hôtel de la Paix. It was early Spring and the evenings were still a touch on the cool side.

"She is a very good bare-backed rider," agreed Holmes, taking a puff on his pipe.

"Oh, no, I'm not speaking of Miss Janvier." Watson chuckled, taking a sip of his brandy.

I miss the familiar comfort of the Baker Street flat, Watson reflected. Despite the opulent surroundings and every convenience—even oil lamps and a private bath!—he was surprised to realize that he missed home.

And he was surprised to learn that the flat in Baker street had become home. After a harrowing tour in Afghanistan where he almost lost his life in the Battle of Maiwand. And he would have died had it not been for his orderly Murray who had thrown his commanding officer on a pack horse and led him through enemy lines.

Not surprisingly, John Watson had lost his fear of death. And yet, he had begun to fear living. Sherlock Holmes had given the army doctor not only a second chance at life—but this unlikely friend had given John Watson a new life. John soon came to relish this life of adventure which helped him forget all he had seen in the war.

And here he was pining away for an outdated, foul-smelling flat in London! In eleven months of living with Holmes he had become a sentimental old fool.

Damnation! He was having the time of his life in circumstances he never would have thought possible. Not that long ago he was recovering in an army hospital—merely lucky to be alive he was!

"You're not impressed with Miss Janvier then?" Holmes asked, eyeing him with a scrutiny Watson had come to dread.

"Hmmm? Miss Janvier is beautiful, certainly. Devious, crafty, and intelligent. But, no, I was speaking of Miss Mirabella."

"Miss Belle? Hmmm." Sherlock closed his book, appearing completely at home in his maroon satin robe as he took a puff on his pipe.

"Miss Mirabella has been the real star of this show—as she is of every endeavor she undertakes." John Watson looked intently at his friend.

"As well you know, Holmes."

"Do I?"

John looked about him as he set his pipe on the Louis IV stand. The hotel rooms were elegant and subdued in taupe and mahogany with cream-colored carpets. The wallpaper was an ornate white and taupe curli-cue pattern reminiscent of Versailles and the kings of France. His room, just off this suite, contained a 4-poster bed, comfortable when he slept in it.

He could not help but chuckle as he thought of the not-so subdued décor of 221B Baker street: the purple-maroon wallpaper, the bear skin hearth rug, the stacks of papers, the experiments in progress, and the deadly chemicals. A smile came to his lips as he recalled the gramophone, the pictures of criminals on the walls, even the dreaded violin in the corner.

"And why is it you are impressed with Miss Belle?" Holmes' voice was strangely suspicious.

"She got in a ring with tigers. Not a handful of women would do that."

Holmes shrugged, taking a puff on his pipe. "It is her job."

"I believe that the tiger aggression during Miss Mirabella's first performance unnerved her and she is not yet recovered." John added under his breath, "Much like a war trauma." He slouched in his elegant satin winged back chair, not nearly as comfortable as the chairs in their London flat, and opened his newspaper. "And that's not the point. Miss Mirabella had the nerve to go back on the stage despite her understandable terror. And why did she do it? Because you, Holmes, asked her to. You might at least acknowledge that."

"Miss Belle cares very little for my wishes, I assure you Watson. It all has to do with her savings, her entrance into university, and her continued employment." Holmes frowned. "But true . . . she does surprise one at times."

"Oh? The great and all-knowing Sherlock Holmes surprised? In what way?"

"She is generally willing to step up to the plate," Sherlock conceded. "Striving, learning and always willing to stretch herself, as it were."

"She's made of strong stuff," Watson agreed, scanning *The Times*.

"Or she can't bear to leave the puzzle unsolved." Holmes shrugged. "Risking all to solve the case. Much like a compulsion and not necessarily to be admired."

"Ah. Like gambling, drinking or the illicit use of drugs, Holmes?" John looked up from his paper.

"Yes, something like that, Watson." Sherlock continued after a long pause. "Miss Belle has an incredible intellectual curiosity. Very driven. More like a man than a woman."

"I don't believe curiosity is the exclusive domain of men, Holmes." John shook his head in disagreement, his eyes returning to scan the news. "And for a man Miss Mirabella has decidedly feminine curves."

"I bow to your knowledge of the fair sex, Watson. But I do not think you will find Miss Belle an easy one to decipher." He added in a low tone which sounded strangely threatening. "And I do not recommend that you attempt it."

"Perhaps I have no need to *decipher* her as you put it."

"Are you saying your intentions are honorable Watson?" Sherlock laughed robustly. "And you cavorting with a circus bareback rider and presumed spy. Let us not forget the Dancing Girls of Baghdad."

"Let us not," John mused, a smile forming on his lips. "That would be a shame."

"Clearly you haven't, Watson." Sherlock set his pipe on the stand beside him, the amusement fading from his eyes. "Do be reasonable. You are not a man who can find satisfaction in one woman. Consequently, respectable girls are not in your line. And Miss Belle is, above all else, a respectable girl."

"Precisely. I had always assumed I would be married by now. I wish to marry someday, and a finer girl than Miss Mirabella Hudson I will never find." And it did seem, if he was not mistaken—and he rarely was where the fair sex was involved—that she was interested.

"I have no doubt of that, Watson. I am not arguing if she is worthy of you, but I am questioning if you are worthy of her." Sherlock leaned forward in his chair, his expression ominous. "And advising you to leave her be."

"To answer your question, Sherlock, where Miss Mirabella is concerned, yes, my intentions are honorable." Watson snapped his newspaper. "Do you know what I think, Holmes?"

"No, and it holds no interest whatsoever for me, Watson. We are here to perform a function. A very important engagement of international significance."

"I think that you have feelings for Miss Mirabella, and in your determination to deny them, you are ignoring her, ignoring her safety, and throwing her in harm's way. As if to ignore her will resolve your feelings. *It will not.*" He muttered under his breath, "Believe me on this."

"Ridiculous, Watson! I am merely concerned about Miss Belle—

because she is my employee. I have no feelings for her whatsoever! I have no desire to have a woman in my life—now or ever. And I've told you, it is perfectly safe. She is merely on the stage for show—"

"Holmes, sometimes your brilliant mind is your worst enemy. It allows you to build walls and to convince yourself of anything you wish to believe."

"Outrageous!" Holmes appeared truly aggravated now, displaying a rare show of emotion. "The scientific method is my god!"

"Sherlock Holmes is your god! I will never forgive you if you allow something to happen to Miss Mirabella." Watson's voice was rising now to match his friend's. "You have the right to be reckless with your own life—or with mine, of course—but Miss Mirabella is special."

"Of course she is special. Beautiful and intelligent." Holmes turned to study his friend. "But then, so is Miss Janvier. Or do you forget the woman you are currently embroiled with? It is, frankly, impressive that Miss Janvier can maintain her balance and does not fall to her doom hopping about as she does on the horses," Holmes continued convivially, impervious to Watson's cues. "I am still attempting to determine why none of the fillies ever startle."

"I'd be more concerned about the stallions than the fillies."

"Believe me, I am, Watson," Holmes said, his piercing gaze intent upon his companion.

Chapter Twenty-one
The Ring of Fire

"What in the world…" Mirabella turned abruptly, hearing a noisy metallic click behind her. She spun, seeing that the door to the cage had been shut. Mirabella sprang towards the door in an instant. Locked.

Frantically she patted her training suit for the key.

Heavens! She had left the key, as well as her pistol, in the pocket of her cape, which she had taken off outside the cage.

And then she saw what filled her heart with terror: blood splattered on the floor.

Her hands began shaking uncontrollably. *No! No!* She wrung her hands, glancing in the direction of the tigers, who were now aware that she was frightened.

They feed on fear.

Who locked the door? Looking frantically about her, Mirabella saw a figure standing in the gloom of the tent. She could make out few details, as her captor obviously intended. Dressed in a long baggy coat and wearing a wide-brimmed slouch hat, the fiend had made sure that identification would be extremely difficult if not impossible. A woman or a small man, not very tall. The figure, deep in shadow, watched her for a moment.

"Release me!" Mirabella cried. "What is the meaning of this?"

The culprit turned and walked towards the lever between the two tiger cages. Mirabella felt her heart suddenly beating like a stallion at full gallop. She had been lured into a trap—enhanced with blood—in which she would have to face aggravated predators. *Just like Beckham.*

Except there were three tigers, not one.

"Stop!" she yelled. "This is inhuman!" She knew her plea would most likely fall on deaf ears. "I don't have a pistol, I don't have anything . . ."

"Ha! ha!" her captor laughed, and she heard that it was a woman's voice. It was strange that the attacker let this be revealed, as if she were certain of success.

Mirabella refused to accept defeat until it was the only outcome. Sherlock Holmes had taught her that.

Think. Think. Mirabella admonished herself. *Do not put your hope in this viper. Put it in yourself.*

In spite of Mirabella's pleas, the mysterious woman walked through the door, closing it behind her, but as she left Mirabella saw something strange trailing behind the bulky overcoat: a wisp of scarlet chiffon.

Scarlet. Fire. Inadvertently the murderer had given Mirabella an idea. *The ring of fire.*

I will use the tigers' training to my advantage. Mirabella hurried to the props, finding the whip. The tigers feared the whip, with its small end-tassel moving faster than the speed of sound.

But the ring might also prove to be an asset. This the tigers associated with a specific movement—the act—and with a reward. In the act, she was not prey. The act put her in the role of both alpha animal and of the provider of the reward.

Beckham might have faced one tiger and she three, but neither had Beckham ever been in the role as alpha. She had that advantage.

Mirabella heard the grinding of gears, seeing what she had feared. The door between the two tiger enclosures was opening, and the big cats were immediately taking an interest in the blood—and in her.

She took care not to move too quickly and to remain facing the tigers. Continuing to search the props she found a bowling pin which the cats batted about. She also found the ever present steel ring, with its groove for holding flammable liquid for the Ring of Fire act.

Shikar, the largest of all the big cats at six hundred pounds, stepped through the entrance and began to walk towards her. He began pacing only a few feet from her. *Not a good sign.*

Mirabella waved the hoop at him. If she could make Shikar believe it was time to practice, he might not be so inclined to attack. And if she could command Shikar and entice him to return to his enclosure before the other two came through, Mirabella thought she could reach the door lever between the cages.

It was a slim chance, but any chance at all was better than waiting for a horrible death . . .

"Pereyti!" She called out and held up the hoop. To her amazement, Shikar complied and performed his trick, moving to his place in the imaginary row. Mirabella glanced at the other two tigers and was dismayed to see Evangeline, the beautiful, rare Golden Tiger, approaching the gateway.

Oh this is very bad. Evangeline's mate had tasted human flesh. Mr. Beckham's flesh. The tiger who had killed Beckham, Goro, had been destroyed, but Evangeline was Goro's mate, and Evangeline had never been the same since losing Goro. It was as if Evangeline knew. She was angry.

An angry tiger was simply not good.

"Come! Shikar!" She tried to coax the first tiger back to the gate, but he had scented the blood on the floor, which left him in a great state of confusion. Shikar began a combination of purring and growling. Shikar remained in his place, but the noises he was making prompted Evangeline to enter the ring, as well as convincing the ordinarily more peaceful Rajah that there might be something of interest where Evangeline was going.

Control your fear, Mirabella. Panic will not aid you in any way here. Do not act like prey.

Mirabella slowly backed towards the edge of the cage while Evangeline sniffed and licked the blood. Mirabella grew horrified when the female tiger looked up at her, eyes calculating.

Tigers in the wild only occasionally went man-eater, avoiding their two legged cousins in general. But Evangeline had lost her fear of lone humans.

To Mirabella's horror, the huge tigress began to stalk her. Evangeline crouched down, tale whipping, preparing to pounce.

Use the ring of fire! Use the show! Mirabella admonished herself.

At just the right instant, Mirabella managed to jump to the side, placing the ring perfectly so that Evangeline had to jump through it, reinforcing the idea that this was a show, not a kill.

Crack! Mirabella cracked her whip as she might during the show. "Good Girl, Good Evangeline!" she managed to say.

Evangeline whirled around, a look of confusion crossing her expression even as the tigress took her place in the row.

"Excellent!"

Mirabella held the ring out for Rajah to take his turn. "Jump, Rajah!" she commanded, snapping the whip.

Rajah did as he was told, jumping through the hoop and moving to stand beside Evangeline.

I love Rajah. God bless Rajah. And God bless Ashanti, who had trained him.

All the tigers now lined up, she commanded them to roll over, which they did.

I am in command again.

As could happen at any time with wild animals, in an instant she lost everything she had gained. Mirabella took another step back and tripped over the bowling pin, falling with her back against the bars. This was all the invitation that Evangeline needed. The huge beast roared a terrifying blast of sound and sprang forward, fangs exposed and claws extended. Mirabella could see or hear nothing but the charging death.

Evangeline's charge was ended prematurely by a *snap*, loud as a gunshot, and the tiger halted in mid-lunge, confused. Mirabella looked towards the door and to her astonishment saw Sherlock pulling back his arm for another strike with Stanislav's bullwhip. In her moment of terror, she had not seen Sherlock enter the cage.

The tigress growled at the detective, her blazing yellow eyes burning into the human, but Sherlock's sea gray eyes blazed back with a like fury. They locked stares for a moment, both apex predators, before Sherlock cracked the whip once again, this time an inch from Evangeline's nose. The report was like a gunshot.

"Back you devils! Back, damn you!" he roared in a voice that would have done a lion proud. He snapped the whip at Shikar, who had little stomach for this sort of interaction. The young tiger joined Rajah who had already returned to the other enclosure.

Evangeline, however, was made of sterner stuff. She charged Sherlock. As she got close, Mirabella made full contact with the whip, resulting in a splash of blood on the tiger's head. Evangeline yowled.

"We tried to warn you, Tigress," Sherlock said.

The pain of the bullwhip is considerable whether one is man or beast, and Evangeline, for all her fury, quickly decided that the benefits did not outweigh the cost. She returned to her two comrades in the other cell and Mirabella leapt to the lever, closing the second gate.

"Miss Belle! Are you all right?" Sherlock's face, normally a dry mask of logic, was contorted in a sudden terror.

She ran to him and threw her arms around the Great Detective, something she had never done before, tears streaming down her face.

"Praise the heavens you came when you did, Sherlock!"

"There, there, Miss Belle." Sherlock said, his own composure returned while he tapped her back mechanically. "You were performing admirably without me, I assure you. I expect you would have saved yourself in all eventuality."

"No, I would have died!" she sobbed, holding onto his lapel.

"As would I," he said softly. "You saved me as well."

She felt his body stiffen, as if he were completely uncomfortable. Facing man eaters was nothing to Sherlock Holmes, but holding a woman in his arms made him uneasy. "That was a bit of an adventure, wasn't it? It's all right now, brave girl."

"S-someone set a trap for me! They locked the cage…" She looked up at him. "How did you have a key?"

"Naturally I had a duplicate made from yours."

"But I swore I wouldn't let anyone copy it!"

"That is precisely why I did it without your knowing."

She wailed, "Oh, what if you hadn't had a key, Mr. Holmes?"

"Calm down, Miss Belle!" Sherlock commanded, and she felt her hysteria abating with the strength of his command. He grabbed her by the arms and looked down into her eyes. "Did you see who did this, Miss Belle?"

"No," Mirabella shook her head. "It was a woman from the sound of the laugh. . . And there was something else. I saw a wisp of scarlet chiffon."

"Like Veronika's outfit," Sherlock considered. "Could your attacker have been Miss Vishnevsky? What was her height?"

"I'd say . . . about Ashanti's height," she sobbed. "Veronika is closer to Joëlle's height."

"Which might make for an excellent disguise—if one were attempting to implicate someone else," Sherlock considered, his steel-grey eyes full of fury. "The two women are remarkably similar in appearance. And could the attacker have been either Miss Janvier or Miss Vishnevsky?"

"The woman was taller."

"Perhaps heels or elevated shoes were worn?"

"I couldn't say. My attentions were elsewhere as I was fighting for my life."

"Do you think it could have been Ashanti?" Sherlock asked.

"No," Mirabella shook her head, still crying.

"Because she is your friend?" he asked softly.

"No, because she is the tigers' friend. She would never do anything that might result in the death of one of her tigers. She never forgave Beckham's murderer—not for killing Beckham, but for killing Goro."

"Ah, excellent reasoning, Miss Belle. Even so, I always confirm my suspicions and intend to search three ladies' wardrobes within the hour."

She nodded, biting her lip.

To her surprise, Sherlock leaned towards her, his breath on her neck, and she felt a strange sensation.

"The scent is on your training suit," he pronounced, frowning. "And once again you don't have a pistol."

"I didn't imagine . . . I was only practicing and the tigers' cages were closed . . ."

But his anger did not seem to be directed at her, but elsewhere. "I believe I know who made the attempt, Miss Belle, and I guarantee that I will hunt her down and kill her myself, as need be. Her reign is, as of this moment, *officially over.*"

Chapter Twenty-two
First Kiss

"I saw you in the show today, Miss Mirabella. You were marvelous."

"Was I?" Mirabella cracked her whip in the center of the arena without turning towards John Watson. She had changed into the form fitting white training suit which she wore while fencing and practicing jiu-jitsu.

"And I saw you as well leaving Miss Janvier's room quite late, Dr. Watson." She had not recounted her attempted murder to Dr. Watson, as she and Sherlock had agreed it was best that John not treat Miss Janvier any differently. Sherlock was closed-lipped about the entire episode and adamantly opposed to discussing it further. She had never seen him in such a dark mood.

"It is my job," John shrugged. She caught a glimpse of him out of the corner of her eye, displaying his usual happy-go-lucky attitude. His long sideburns were pronounced underneath his brown top hat and his expression had an easy-going frivolity about it.

Which utterly annoyed her. Ordinarily she would find that countenance most attractive, but she had seen a new side to John Watson which made her question the direction of her regard. It seemed to her that John Watson was a bit too enamored of feminine attention—and a bit too free and easy with his affections.

She smiled to herself. Funny that Sherlock Holmes had no desire whatsoever for such attentions, and John Watson could not have enough.

Mirabella glanced in the direction of the tiger cages. It seemed that she was destined to be surrounded by extremes.

As for the tigers, her charges were all sleeping. It was becoming easier to manage them. Insofar as anyone managed a tiger. Her near death experience had actually increased her courage aground the tigers, a surprising outcome.

Ashanti had taught her a great deal about loving the tigers—while reminding her that one must be on her guard at all times. Mirabella had most certainly not lost her fear, but that was the sign of a good trainer, Ashanti had said.

She turned momentarily to face the indecorous doctor and he tipped his hat to her, smiling. She sighed. Almost instantly, he was able to work his magic. But at least now, she knew what was happening: *it was all a lovely game.* Which would be fine were she the only other player.

Smiling at her, John Watson looked ever-so-dashing instead of guilty (as he should have!) in his white pin-striped shirt with pearl cuff-links, brown leather suspenders, and grey wool slacks. In fact, far from looking remorseful, he appeared to be having a most delightful time of it.

"What? Are you angry because I've been spending time with Miss Janvier?" John moved closer to her and she felt a pleasant awareness of his proximity. "I didn't know you cared, Miss Mirabella."

"It's none of my affair, I am sure." She stepped away, returning to her whip. She executed an overhead crack, circling her own head. "And I'll thank you to return to your *affairs* so that I might attend to mine, Dr. Watson."

He took her gently by the wrist, willing her to look at him, his entire manner elegantly seductive. "There's nothing to it, Miss Mirabella."

"Nothing to *what*, Dr. Watson?" She let out an exasperated sigh, letting her hand fall and turning to him.

"To the whole thing with Miss Janvier," he replied breezily. "Just following orders."

"So," she murmured. "Are you telling me that you're not enjoying yourself?"

"Did I say such a thing?" he smiled boyishly, looking alarmingly charming.

"Or that you haven't . . . that you didn't . . . that you aren't . . . doing more than the role requires?"

"Miss Hudson!" He winked at her. "A gentleman would never speak of such things—and, for a woman to do so is considered quite forward!"

"What an odd turn of events that a forward woman should repulse you, Dr. Watson." She yanked her arm from him and snapped her whip in a figure eight beside her, just missing him.

"I'm not repulsed at all," he remarked, moving closer to her in the moment her whip dropped. He took her chin in his hand, and she felt her heartbeat increase. "I am, Miss Mirabella, excessively flattered."

"And why should you be flattered, Dr. Watson?" she demanded breathlessly, backing up, even as she felt flushed. He took her into his strong arms, looking down at her, and she held onto the whip with some difficulty.

"Because you, Miss Mirabella, are *jealous*."

"J-j-jealous?" she gasped, but she did not attempt to move away from him. Instead the whip fell out of her now limp hands as she gazed into eyes the color of the sea, utterly focused on her. "You can't be serious!"

He moved forward to kiss her.

She thought about pulling away from him. Truly she did. But he was so focused on her. John Watson was a wonderful man and an incomparable friend. *And so handsome.*

"Miss Mirabella," he continued. "Would you like me to kiss you?"

"Why?" she demanded coolly, but her heartbeat was rapidly increasing. "Are you not being kissed enough, John?"

"I won't lie to you, Miss Mirabella. I am being kissed. But I venture to state the warmth of those kisses are based on the state of my pocketbook. Were that to go empty . . . Well, enough said on that. I would prefer to kiss someone I . . . have some feelings for."

"And what feelings might those be?" she asked lightly.

"Admiration. Affection. *Fascination.*" He took off his top hat and held it in his left hand. With her chin in his right hand, slowly he bent towards her lips even as she felt her chest rise and fall in anticipation.

Stop! She knew she should stop him since she wasn't seriously considering a relationship with the good doctor any longer. Only a strumpet would encourage a man in such a way!

And yet—he was so dreamy!—what was the harm? She had wondered for so long what it would be like to kiss John. Would he think her a loose woman? Clearly that was precisely the type of woman he liked!

Her lips were shaking she knew. But she shut her eyes and allowed herself to enjoy the kiss—perhaps the only real kiss she would ever have.

Which was quite wonderful to be sure. A magical foray into the unknown. She felt that she might melt as the softness of his lips touched hers.

His kiss was teasing, enticing, *exciting*.

But it felt more like playing around than love—or even desire.

Chapter Twenty-three
Jump Ship

"John," she pulled away. "This wasn't a good idea."

"It's the best idea I've had all day," he murmured. Boldly, he moved his arms around her waist. She was a beautiful woman, and her performances in every manner of shimmering and revealing costume had made him inescapably aware of that fact.

And what a form! The girl was slim, but muscular, amply endowed, and with gorgeous long legs. Her chestnut brown hair sat atop her head, and her large, warm brown eyes were mesmerizing.

How could I have not seen it before?

Mirabella Hudson was also everything a man could want in a woman: pure, loyal, engaging—all this, and without airs. There was nothing manipulative about her.

She wouldn't know how.

The fire in her eyes thrilled him. She was alive with a passion not yet expressed.

A *real* passion. Not a contrived passion which Miss Janvier utilized to manipulate men. He sometimes wondered if the Russian femme fatale felt anything at all.

He leaned down to kiss her again.

"Watson!" commanded Holmes, entering the arena. "What are you about?"

Holmes' eyes moved from one to the other. Anger flushed his face, but he regained his composure almost instantly, one of his remarkable gifts.

And yet, Holmes' manner was even more brusque than usual as he moved towards them. "Miss Janvier is calling for you. Make haste, Watson."

As John reluctantly headed for the tent entrance, their paths crossed, both of them some twenty feet from Miss Hudson but within hearing range of each other.

"Miss Belle is not for you, Watson," Holmes muttered under his breath.

"How do you know, Holmes? I never met a finer girl," John replied. *And so inexperienced.* He would love to teach her the art of love. He had always planned to settle down at some point; he was not strange like Holmes. He wished for love and family.

But the war had happened, then he had almost died, then Holmes had saved him. In the meantime, women found him appealing and he was not one to disavow them of the notion.

The truth be told, he wasn't ready to settle down yet, but when he was . . .

Sherlock's expression grew somber. "Do catch a clue, my good fellow."

"It appears I am without one," John replied, ducking out of the tent.

*****

Ah, well, then let me provide you with a clue, my friend—but I warn you, I shall not repeat it, so you had best take note of it. Sherlock turned to move towards Miss Belle, furious. He knew she was not truly to blame with such an experienced ladies' man as Watson, and yet Sherlock felt an intense anger which required a release.

"What are you about Miss Hudson? Do you find it utterly impossible to behave in a professional manner?"

Why am I so angry? If she wishes to throw herself at libertines, who am I to stop her? She shall learn soon enough.

"Why? Because I like John Watson?"

"Because we three have a professional relationship and you are to treat both Watson and myself as such. Do you have no sense of propriety, Miss Hudson? Do you wish to compromise every mission with your childish pranks and girlish whims?"

Man, get a hold of yourself! You won't be pursuing Miss Belle—that you have already decided—so it is nothing to say to you.

"Oh, for heavens' sake, Sherlock, it was only a kiss." Disappointment crossed her face, which was even worse.

"Only a kiss. *Only a kiss*? And what next? Is that how you regard being in a man's arms? As a playful interlude?"

"I suppose so," she retorted. "Yes, it was rather like that."

"Miss Hudson!" he exclaimed. "I am sorely ashamed!"

"No doubt you are, Mr. Holmes." She raised her eyebrow at him. "But I don't see how it is any of your affair."

Sherlock stared at her, aghast. The beautiful woman before him, no longer a girl. He recalled when he had held her in his arms at Miss de Beauvais' Christmas ball, what an enchanted evening that had been.

That was a lie—as all emotion was.

Emotion and women were not to be trusted. *Get a hold of yourself, man! You are eight and twenty years! These are the rules you have lived by all your life—with great success!*

This is no time to jump ship.

Chapter Twenty-four
On the Clock

"Actually it wasn't even a kiss." Sherlock didn't need to know that there had been a kiss before the second one which he had—thankfully—broken up. She had wanted to know what it would be like to kiss a handsome, wonderful, grown man—outside of a peck or two at home with a country boy when she was young, it was her first real kiss—and she didn't regret it, marvelous as it was.

She was unaccustomed to the attentions of men—much less worldly, debonair, *handsome* men—was it any wonder she had fallen for John Watson?

Not this girl. Not any more.

She was older and wiser now, and that was a thing of the past. She had no use for a man who was only playing the field. She would prefer to be alone than to pine over that type! Besides, she and John Watson would remain friends and colleagues, she had no doubt.

Which was where she should have left it to begin with. She loved John as a friend, but she could not envision a more serious commitment—on either side.

She could thank Joëlle Janvier for that lesson and for opening her eyes. Wasn't it the oddest thing how so often a person one wholly disliked brought important lessons into one's life?

"Thank the heavens I was there to put a stop to this nonsense!" Sherlock pulled at his blue satin vest.

Yes, thank the heavens Sherlock hadn't seen the kiss. He was so often a mind-reader, she began to wonder if not actually seeing the act made the slightest difference in the world.

"I had thought Watson was the one to watch, but perhaps it is you, Miss Belle!"

"Sherlock Holmes!" Her mouth flew open in shock, her face now flushed. "How dare you!"

"How dare I *what*?"

"Oh, that is outside of enough!" She was furious. "I have the right to determine for myself whom I wish to kiss, and you, Mr. Sherlock Holmes, have nothing to say to it!" He almost made her want to pursue John Watson again.

Almost.

"Miss Hudson, there is no employer in the world who would not dismiss you for kissing a man while on his clock, and well you know it."

"I am always on your clock, Mr. Holmes," she fumed.

"Good. I am glad that we finally come to an understanding."

"But John . . . Dr. Watson . . . he is kissing Miss Janvier—at your request, no less!" She felt a fury to match the look in his eyes. "Forgive me, Mr. Holmes, but how can you be such a hypocrite?"

"Romancing Miss Janvier is Watson's assigned task—which, I might add, he has performed with admirable eagerness. Perhaps you should remind yourself of that before allowing Watson to take liberties with you, Miss Belle," he retorted, his voice cracking as he spoke the words.

"Remind myself of what?" she demanded.

"That his services are for sale."

"Mr. Sherlock Holmes, I greatly resent your taking that tone with me—not to mention talking that way about your friend!"

"John Watson is the best of friends—perhaps my only friend. And you, my dear, are my only employee. Remember that. Your affections you may give freely to whosoever you so wish, but do not jeopardize my work. *That I can never forgive.*"

"So you have said. I am well aware that nothing else matters to you but your work, Mr. Holmes." She pursed her lips. "You are the most unfeeling man on the planet—almost a machine. And yet, I have the strange sense that you would not wish me to like any man." He moved closer to her and she felt her skin tingle as she felt his breath on her neck.

He loosened his necktie. "Naturally, it would interfere with my work. And, again, there is not an employer in the world who feels differently. Girls who become *involved*, shall we say, are dismissed. There are no married maids, only the upper servants would be allowed to marry."

"In the first place, I am not a maid, by your own admission," she retorted. *He had called her the world's first lady detective!* "And second, I don't think that it is quite fair to expect me to have no warmth or feeling for anyone—as you do not."

"Would that it were so."

"You don't wish to have any feelings, Mr. Holmes?" She studied him.

"I do not." He tipped his hat to her. "And nor should you. Good day, Miss Hudson."

She placed her hands on her hips. "Good day, *Mr. Holmes.*"

Chapter Twenty-five
One's Patriotic Duty

"There is no need to proceed to Miss Janvier's dressing room, Watson," Sherlock intervened, taking his friend's arm, which required no small amount of force given Watson's forward movement. "The case is solved."

Dr. John Watson's broad smile diminished instantly at the news of their success. He carried a bottle of champagne and a large bouquet of red roses, a complimentary contrast to his olive green tweed three-piece suit. A brown top-hat and pearl cuff-links completed the doctor's ensemble, giving him the appearance of one who was both eager and dapper.

"Your services are no longer required, Watson," Sherlock repeated.

"What? Excuse me?" The good doctor's fallen countenance was pronounced.

"You have fulfilled your duty."

"Do you have all the answers you seek?" Watson asked, brushing blonde hair out of his eyes with his free hand. "Surely there is something else I can discover?"

"No doubt, but it would be of no interest to national security." Sherlock stared at his friend pointedly. "We have concluded that Miss Janvier murdered Beckham—the results from the lab conclude the match between Miss Janvier's red rouge and a scent on Beckham's body. The fact that the scent was in her room rules out Stanislav Afanasy and condemns her."

As well as the attack on Miss Belle by a person too slight to be Stanislav and the scent on Miss Belle's cape. Sherlock had thought it better to keep the attack from Watson as any alteration in the good doctor's behavior towards the femme fatale could have put Watson in imminent danger. Sherlock still held to this opinion until the resourceful Russian spy was behind bars. John Watson was loyal above all things, and he would be furious were he to be apprised of Miss Belle's endangerment.

Sherlock smiled to himself. As was he. But he intended to enact his revenge with a cooler head.

"It's difficult to believe Miss Janvier murdered Beckham," Watson considered.

"There are indications that she has designs on the Czar even though she is officially working for Okhrana," Sherlock said. "We're going to take her in for questioning. The British government wants her for Beckham.

The Czar's government is interested in her as a possible double agent. We believe she attempted to get information from Prince George to pass onto the Czar in order to gain favor and access. But none of this can be made known to Miss Janvier—yet."

"So I can still be of use, Holmes?" asked Watson hopefully.

"No. You're lucky to be alive, Watson. I want to pull you out while you still are." Sherlock tapped his can on the ground. "At my insistence, Prince George has been advised in the strongest terms to sever the relationship."

"He must be quite disappointed," sighed Watson.

"He is bearing up as best he can," replied Sherlock.

Watson sighed. "Are you certain there is nothing more I can do? If there are unanswered questions, I'm sure I can oblige . . ."

"We all appreciate the great sacrifice which you have made, old chap." Sherlock bowed his head with reverence.

"It was a regrettable piece of business."

"Indeed. Your feelings on the matter were obvious to even the dullest of observers, Watson."

Suddenly Watson's countenance rose. "At least I should tell Miss Janvier I won't be able to meet her this evening. We had a dinner planned. It's the gentlemanly thing to do."

"Decidedly." Sherlock sighed heavily, taking a step back. He removed himself from the pathway, doubting that he would be able to physically retain Watson without knocking him out. Thankfully Mycroft had placed a French policeman outside Miss Janvier's door—for her safety or for the safety of her suitors was a question debatable.

Sherlock considered forcibly detaining his friend, but the good doctor was already half-way down the hall, clearly determined to pay his regards.

"Prince George has already headed in the same direction to say his farewells. I don't advise you to meet him, old chap," Sherlock called out, certain to reach Watson's ears. Receiving no reply, Sherlock wondered that the army man who walked with a limp was already out of earshot.

Some minutes later Watson returned looking downcast.

"How did she take the news?" Sherlock asked, now seated and enjoying his pipe as he watched the knife throwers, always ready to learn a new technique.

"Rather well, I should say. If I didn't know better, I would say Miss Janvier has a new love interest."

"And why shouldn't she?" Sherlock laughed, turning towards his friend as he took a puff on his pipe. "Surely you didn't expect to be the last of her lovers, Watson?"

"Why no, it's just that Prince George had only just left and she seemed rather happier to see him."

"She's dead! She's dead!" Miss Janvier's maid came running into the main coliseum.

"Who is dead?" demanded Watson, spinning around.

"Joëlle!" the maid replied, tears running down her cheeks.

The French policeman in charge of watching Miss Janvier's room arrived on the maid's footsteps, turning toward Dr. Watson. "*Arrêtez s'il vous plaît*! That makes you the murderer! There were only two people to enter that room since I last saw Mademoiselle Janvier alive: you and Prince George. Prince George swears the mademoiselle she was alive when he left."

"She was fully alive when I left as well, Lieutenant," Watson replied indignantly. "But before I would let the British Commander-in-Chief hang for the offense, I would hang myself."

"*Bon.* I don't believe that will be a problem, Monsieur le Doctor."

***

"*Entendre! écouter!* Either it was Dr. John Watson or it was the English Prince," Lieutenant Dubuque argued. "No one else went in or left. I stood by the door the entire time."

"I saw Mr. Afanasy heading that direction as well," Sherlock stated.

"Mr. Afanasy he came wanting the entrance, which was *denied* by moi!" Dubuque pulled at his jacket. "Then maid ran out screaming girl was dead."

"I beg your pardon, my dear lieutenant," Sherlock said, "but the maid had to have gone in after Dr. Watson, or who found the body?"

"The maid she was in ze room not ten seconds before she began screaming!" Lieutenant Dubuque retorted. "*C'est impossible* to have killed someone in that time."

"Absolutely untrue," Sherlock murmured. "I wish to speak to the maid."

"Let me remind you, Monsieur, that this is not your case. This is *mon.*"

"Also not true." Mycroft suddenly appeared, entering the room, "you are both on the case. I have it on a high authority."

"And who says zis?" Dubuque sputtered.

"A Monsieur Alphonse Bertillon," Mycroft replied without ceremony.

"*Sacre Bleu!*" Dubuque dropped his jaw. "L'Inspecteur of le Forensic Identification Département Français?"

"The very same. Inspector Bertillon holds my brother in some regard for a paper he wrote on the use of fingerprinting as a method of identifying criminals," murmured Mycroft, waving a telegram about. "And if that is not sufficient for you, Lieutenant, there is the Queen of my beloved homeland who sends her regards."

Chapter Twenty-six
Ebony Butterfly

"Ouch!"

"Careful, don't flinch!" Mirabella pulled hard.

"Oooooh!" Ashanti bellowed.

"Be still! It's almost done." Mirabella took her hand, attempting to console her.

The bandages came off. And there before Mirabella was one of the most beautiful women she had ever beheld.

And her skin was as black as ebony.

Another startling revelation was that, now that the bandages were removed, one could not miss that there were extremely fine diamonds in Ashanti's ear lobes. Large, beautiful diamonds. So dazzling were the jewels that, despite the young woman's beauty, it was difficult to tear one's eyes from them.

They must be worth a fortune. Anyone who had diamonds like that did not have to work, much less work in a circus facing life-threatening predators. In fact, it was likely more dangerous to be out in public with the human predators with something that valuable visible.

Mirabella felt her mouth open wide, even as she attempted speech.

"Why do you look at me so? At what are you staring?" Ashanti demanded.

"I thought you s-s-said you were *Dutch* . . ." Mirabella swallowed hard.

"Do you mean hair blonde, eyes blue, Dutch?"

Mirabella nodded involuntarily.

"You could see my eyes were not the blue."

"No, but I never dreamed, I never imagined . . ."

"You never imagined that I was not *like you*?" Ashanti raised her chin.

"Y-y-yes. I mean, no!"

"I am still girl like you. I am same as ever I was. What is it you do not like? My color?"

"There is nothing I do not like about you, Ashanti!" Mirabella pleaded with her. "You're quite beautiful. Just not what I expected with the name of Ashanti Van Horn."

"Ashanti is Afrikanische name. Van Horn is the name of Boer

family I served after was captured. It was easiest." Ashanti looked down at the ground momentarily.

"*Captured?* Whatever do you mean?" Mirabella demanded, somehow finding the presence of mind to place the robe lightly around her friend, motioning her to sit on the bed that she might sponge her clean and apply the lotion.

"I am daughter of Cetshwayo." Ashanti raised her chin as she sat down.

"The Zulu king Cetshwayo?" Mirabella managed to stutter.

"The last king of an independent Zulu nation." Ashanti rolled her eyes at her, as if to say, '*Who else?*'.

"*You are a Zulu Princess?*" Mirabella put her hand on her mouth.

"As I said." Ashanti put her hands on her hips, clearly exasperated, but did so too forcefully. "Ouch!"

"Then why . . . why are you *here*? In the *circus*?" Mirabella attempted to regain her composure, the sponge in her hand.

"When the English they killed my father, I was to be given to John Dunn as one of forty-eight Zulu wives."

"How perfectly horrid!" Mirabella exclaimed, placing the sponge in the basin full of warm soapy water which had been set by the bed. She began gingerly sponging the royal princess of the Zulu nation.

"As thought I. For all I know, Dunn he has never noticed that he only has forty-seven wives."

Mirabella giggled before she grew somber. "But *why*?" asked Mirabella, looking up momentarily. "Why were the Zulu attacked? The slave trade was abolished in Britain since 1807, and slavery has been abolished since 1833."

"I don't know your English laws and dates. I know that I was taken captive. Why? It is for glistening rocks . . . the *diamonds* . . . " She touched her earlobes. "Europeans they value them over all—above life even."

"People killed over *diamonds*?" Mirabella exclaimed, pausing to close her eyes momentarily, the sponge in her hand in mid-air.

"They said the war was over the many wives," Ashanti shrugged. "But it was really for the diamonds."

"Do you mean . . . polygamy?" Mirabella asked. "I doubt if you are a great supporter of polygamy yourself, Ashanti."

She shook her head. "No. But even less do I support those who kill my family. All I know is, except for missionaries, the white man he was not in Africa before the diamonds. Polygamy, it was there always. Polygamy bother the white man all the sudden when the diamonds discovered." Ashanti added, "And I know also that most of my family—the royal family—is now dead and our nation destroyed. Because we are the *black savage.*"

"Oh, Ashanti, I am so sorry." Here before Mirabella was a beautiful, talented and gifted woman. A princess. *Royalty.*

Tears welled up in her eyes. Prior to the Zulu wars, Mirabella had read in the British newspapers that Shaka Zulu, Cetshwayo's uncle and a former king of the Zulu, was as psychotic and vicious a murderer as any man who had ever lived, even killing his own mother. Also in the papers were the stories of polygamy.

Because of these newspaper articles, Mirabella herself had thought the black Afrikaners to be devils. So must have the British troops. Mirabella's curate father, a good and righteous man, so progressive he had educated his own daughters along with his sons, had been appalled by the reports.

The British citizen had been given a picture of the Zulu, an image to be despised and loathed. The white soldier had stood before the black warrior, repulsed, thinking him a demon, and wishing to eradicate him from the face of the earth.

Mirabella felt her heart breaking at the destroyed life before her. It was not the Zulu who had done this to her friend, but her own people.

"Was Shaka Zulu as bad as they say?" Mirabella asked.

"He was very bad man." Ashanti began to choke on her own words, fighting the tears. "But not my father, Cetshwayo. He was man of honor."

And who has the diamonds? Someone had spun a story—with some basis in truth—so that the British solder and the Zulu warrior would die on the fighting field—while someone else absconded with the diamonds.

Under the tutelage of Sherlock Holmes, Mirabella reflected that she was beginning to question her well-meaning upbringing and everything she had been taught.

Who benefits? She began to ask herself, when someone spins a tale of hate to the masses?

Mirabella swallowed hard, somehow finding her voice. "You must come and live with me, Ashanti. We can share my room. I am sure my Aunt Martha –"

"I belong here. With the tigers. They are only family I have now."

"Ashanti, the tigers cannot be your family." Mirabella put her arm gently around her friend who flinched. Mirabella removed her hand and forced herself to begin applying the lotion that they might finish.

Ashanti must be very cold, though one would never know it from her stoic composure. "They are not safe. They would as soon kill you as not."

"The man—he is same as the tiger—a cold-blooded killer. But he pretends to be something else. The tiger, he never pretends. He would never lie to me."

"And your people?" Mirabella asked warily. "Do the Zulu pretend?"

"No." Ashanti shook her head. "We speak the truth. We are *like the tiger*."

"Ashanti, I must ask you, why do you wear such valuable jewels in your ears where everyone can see them?"

"They are for tigers. I want to build bigger cages for them."

"Why not put the jewels somewhere safe?"

Ashanti laughed. "I have not anywhere I can put them. This is safest place. To get them, someone will have to kill me."

They may do just that. "Why not sell the diamonds and put the proceeds in a bank?"

"In the bank of the white man?" Ashanti laughed again, but there was no amusement in her eyes. "White man would take my money and say I have not give to him."

"Oh, no, they couldn't—" but Mirabella saw in Ashanti's eyes that she would never be able to explain the rules of her people. It was acceptable to kill the Zulu and to steal their diamonds, provided that they were of a different religion, but there were laws and a code of honor within the white man's institutions.

From a distance Mirabella heard the tiger's scream. Mirabella glanced at the bandages lying all about them on the floor, the remnants of an accident that had almost cost Ashanti her life.

And Ashanti trusted the slayer who had almost killed her more than she trusted man.

Chapter Twenty-seven
Voodoo Murder

Once in Miss Janvier's room, Sherlock studied the body without any regard for the police, much to the Lieutenant Dubuque's annoyance. "What is your diagnosis, Watson?"

Dr. Watson raised her eyelids after examining the body for some minutes. "Ruptured capillaries," he murmured before pronouncing, "Indicative of asphyxiation."

"It would be difficult to strangle such an accomplished athlete with one's bare hands," Sherlock stated, glancing about the small but opulent surroundings. "And no rope visible in the room . . ."

Dubuque's eyes rested on Watson, his expression one of suspicion. "The killer he took the rope with him."

"Ah, yes." Sherlock raised his eyebrows. "When the killer left the room without going through the door. May I remind you, Lieutenant, that you searched Dr. Watson yourself and found no weapon?"

"*Attention!*" The lieutenant commanded. "The doctor he disposed of the rope between the time he left the room and before he reached you, Monsieur Holmes."

"I presume your men have searched that small area which comprises the hallway traversed and found nothing?" Sherlock asked.

"Not as yet, Monsieur!"

"Precisely," Sherlock muttered as he continued to study the body.

"What do you see, Holmes?" asked Watson anxiously.

"Nothing. That is what is so interesting." Sherlock examined the neck more closely.

"Nothing? What do you mean by that?" demanded Lieutenant Dubuque.

"There are only the slightest marks on her neck," considered Sherlock. "She died by asphyxiation. But the marks are almost invisible."

Watson glanced at the body with an expression of perplexity. He murmured, "I noticed."

"A rope or a chord would have left clear marks," Sherlock stated. "The murder weapon was not a rope."

"The doctor, he did it with his bare hands, then," Lieutenant Dubuque stated, pursing his lips.

"Not likely." Watson shook his head. "It would have still left marks—and not the strange marks we are seeing here. The marks would be deeper than those here—which don't look at all like the imprints made by human hands."

"Why do you say this?" Dubuque asked moving closer.

"Take a look yourself," Sherlock murmured. "Look at these strange, round marks on the neck, all the same size—very faint, but there nonetheless."

"Could they be self-inflicted?" Watson asked.

Sherlock chuckled sardonically. "You knew Miss Janvier. She was having far too good a time to do such a thing."

"But she was about to be investigated."

"Miss Janvier thought herself to be invincible," Sherlock stated. "She was a true narcissist."

"Someone might have entered through the window," Watson suggested, glancing at the closed window.

Lieutenant Dubuque moved to examine the window. "*Alors!* The window it is locked from the inside."

"Correct. If someone were to enter and leave through the window, he could not have locked it," concluded Sherlock, placing his hands in his pockets while his eyebrows knitted together as he looked out the window. "And there is no ledge on this third story and no stepladder in sight."

Sherlock studied the area around the window, even as he donned white gloves and began dusting for fingerprints and collecting hairs from the area.

"What do you do, Monsieur Holmes?" Another Frenchman entered the room and approached Sherlock.

"I'm dusting for fingerprints as I am sure you are well aware," Sherlock replied with a raise of the eyebrow. "L'Inspecteur Bertillon, I presume."

"How did you know this?" the gentleman asked.

"You have an air of confidence, which infers that you are in charge," Sherlock replied. "I know from Mycroft that Bertillon has an interest in the case. And the deference which was shown to you by Dubuque when you walked in the door."

"You are correct, Monsieur Holmes." The newcomer clicked his heels together and bowed.

"Naturally." Sherlock bowed his head slightly, which was far more respect than he was generally inclined to show anyone. "I have read your paper which established a method of identifying criminals based on the assigning of numbers for each characteristic, resulting in a single summed figure. Most systematic."

Bertillon beamed. "And I have read your paper on fingerprinting, Monsieur Holmes—most intriguing. But I am not convinced that it will yield much result."

"I certainly admire your orderly approach, Mr. Bertillon, and the humility which inspired you to name your method 'bertillonage'. In all truth, it is a vast improvement over anthropometry."

Bertillon stroked his perfectly trimmed goatee beard. "And yet, you are dusting the room for fingerprints, Monsieur Holmes?"

"The system of bertillonage will be replaced by fingerprinting, I assure you Inspector, which is more conclusive, far less complicated, and therefore less prone to errors."

Bertillon frowned.

Sherlock was never inclined to conceal the truth in order to placate others. Why should he stroke egos, particularly those egos with a strong personal interest in incorrect conclusions? Every fiber of his being revolted against it. "In addition, bertillonage is limited to characterizing known criminals and comparing the results to the reports of eye witnesses. We do not have the criminal here to take his measurements. Nor have we identified any eye witnesses. If we already knew who the criminal was—necessary to utilizing bertillonage—the case would be solved." It was astonishing that bertillonage was considered the highest form of criminal identification. These were the times they lived in. Criminology was still a field dwelling in darkness.

"But we do know who the criminal is!" Dubuque insisted. "It is your friend the doctor! He strangled Mademoiselle Janvier with his bare hands."

"Impossible," Sherlock murmured. "The marks on her neck are not commensurate with that theory. And there was no weapon on the doctor, you said so yourself."

Sherlock observed a box of chocolates by the bed. He hadn't seen Watson carrying any chocolates, only the roses and champagne. "These aren't from you, are they Watson?"

"No."

"Did you see Prince George holding any chocolates, Lieutenant?"

Dubuque raised his eyebrows at Sherlock. "Non."

"Do you know who they are from?" Sherlock insisted.

"Non," Lieutenant Dubuque replied.

"Have them analyzed for poison," Sherlock commanded.

Lieutenant Dubuque frowned. "But we already know Miss Janvier was strangled—according to your doctor!"

"I did not say she was strangled. I said she died of asphyxiation," Watson considered. "The point Holmes is making is perhaps Miss Janvier was given something to reduce her resistance."

"Exactly. On the other hand, Miss Janvier had many enemies. Perhaps there was a separate, completely unrelated attempt on her life." Sherlock turned his full attention to Watson. "Did she appear at all subdued, Watson?"

"Indeed she did. She was not at all interested to see me."

"Ah, but being uninterested in a suitor is not the same thing as being under the influence of a drug."

Sherlock returned his eyes to the body laying lifeless on the pink carpet, without blood or injury, as if she were sleeping—except for the look of horror crossing her expression. The Great Detective pronounced, "On the surface it would appear inexplicable . . . unless . . ."

Sherlock moved to study the artifacts on the white marble nightstand beside Miss Janvier's bed.

"La magic noire!" exclaimed Lieutenant Dubuque, moving to stand beside her bed decorated in a silk floral pattern. *Black magic.* "Très mal."

"What is it, Holmes?" Watson asked, moving towards them.

"Roots, herbs, bark, snake skins, and dried animal parts," replied Sherlock, adding in a murmur. "Voodoo. *Black Magic.*"

"Disgusting!" moaned Mycroft, entering the room while fanning himself. "Put it in the report, but I don't wish to see it."

"Ha! ha!" chuckled Sherlock. "Yes, Mycroft, you will reflect upon it in your easy chair in front of a fire while drinking a brandy."

"Certainly, and I could solve the case were all the facts to be laid before me," murmured Mycroft indignantly. "But I need your fine eye for detail to do the leg work for me, Shirley."

"And here is something interesting," Sherlock considered, picking up white and yellow blossoms amidst the roots and herbs. He added in a low tone, "From the borrachero tree."

Mycroft turned towards him abruptly, expressing an increased interest. "To induce a sudden stopping of the heart."

"But why, then, the strangling if a drug to stop the heart was administered?" considered Sherlock.

"It does seem a bit of over diligence to my mind," Mycroft said.

"Every action is a bit of over diligence where you are concerned, brother dear."

"Miss Janvier does not appear to be the victim of a heart

malfunction," Watson said.

"And yet, I predict we will find a poison in her system derived from the petals of the borrachero tree."

Sherlock spotted a gold coin on the floor near the animal remnants, as if it had been knocked off, which he picked up and examined. It was a Chinese coin. He murmured, "Most interesting."

"What avez-vous?" Dubuque asked. Sherlock showed the lieutenant the coin.

"I do not see what it is so important?"

"There is a hole drilled into the gold coin," Sherlock explained. "Interesting."

Dubuque shrugged.

"May I take the coin and examine it for fingerprints?" Sherlock asked, though he had every intention of doing so regardless of the answer. When there was a nod from Bertillon, Sherlock placed the gold coin in a handkerchief, pocketing it.

"Do you think Miss Janvier was poisoned, Dr. Watson?" Mycroft asked.

Dr. Watson shook his head. "I don't seen any indicators, but it is difficult to be certain before the autopsy."

Sherlock moved to Miss Janvier's wardrobe and fingered an outfit in . . . *scarlet chiffon*. Hung next to a man's overcoat. He returned his eyes to the remnants of voodoo so out of place in a room rampant with lavender and pink, chiffon and silk, and huge gilded mirrors squeezed into every spare inch of space. He noted that the room was surprisingly devoid of personal pictures outside of photographs and paintings of Miss Janvier.

"But would everything be left out here in the open?" asked Mycroft.

Sherlock tapped his chin with his forefinger. "True, it seems to be more a part of a ritual than a poisoning, which the murderer would have gone to some lengths to conceal."

"For my own part, I suspect that these remnants of voodoo were purposely left here to make it appear that the death was a case of magic—further adding to the mystery—given that there is no evidence of another presence in the room," Watson said.

Sherlock turned to the lieutenant. "You will have to examine the body for poison. I would prefer to see Watson do it, but it's an impossibility since he is a suspect."

Dubuque nodded.

"On the surface, logic tells us that the killer must be the maid," Sherlock continued. "And yet, if that were the case, she would have to be very strong unless poison were involved—which perhaps it was."

Mycroft stooped to pick up a lace handkerchief. "Ah-ha!"

"Nothing unusual in a lace handkerchief in a lady's boudoir," Watson remarked.

Mycroft turned the handkerchief over, a wry smile forming on his lips as he handed the fine silk cloth to the lieutenant. "What would a handkerchief with the initials 'SF' be doing in Miss Janvier's room?"

"Très intéressant!" Dubuque held up the handkerchief smiling. "You would expect the initials to be 'JJ', would you not?"

"Unless the 'SF' stands for the Russian lady's real name," Bertillon considered. "The stage actresses, they always have the false names."

"No," Watson refuted. "Her last name was Bezborodov. I don't know her first name."

"Natasha," Mycroft murmured as if in a trance, his face suddenly ashen white. "And the Duke of Cambridge's wife is Sarah Fairbrother."

A silence fell over the room until the maid was brought in, whimpering and crying. She was indeed a frail looking thing. But Sherlock had seen many a dainty murderer before.

"What is your name, Mademoiselle?" Bertillon asked.

"Francine." She dabbed her eyes with her handkerchief.

"And what did you see when you entered the room?" Sherlock asked.

"I saw Miss Janvier lying on the floor, Bien sûr!" She sniffed.

"Did you touch anything, Mademoiselle Francine?" Sherlock asked politely, attempting to put the woman at ease.

"Non," the maid shook her head vehemently.

"Were you and the mistress close?" Bertillon asked.

For a moment an expression of amusement graced her face. "Non. She was close to no one. And I was the maid."

"Did you see or hear anything odd, Mademoiselle?" Sherlock asked.

"I thought I heard a sound beneath the window," she replied.

"Did you investigate?" Bertillon asked.

"Non." She shook her head. "I was too afraid." And indeed she was shaking, either from fear or guilt.

"Had you seen the voodoo items before, Mademoiselle Francine?" Sherlock pointed to the items on the desk.

"Oui," she nodded. "Miss Van Horn brought them."

"You are dismissed," Sherlock pronounced. This appeared to annoy Bertillon, and certainly Dubuque, but Sherlock did not have time to waste with the niceties.

Sherlock moved again to the window. "I will need to examine the courtyard and speak to everyone who might have seen anything through the window." He pointed to the floor, where something was just under the bed. "Look, there's a piece of paper lying on the floor here."

"Indeed," Mycroft said, fanning himself.

Picking up the paper, Sherlock handed it to his elder brother. "It is in Russian."

"What does it say?" demanded Bertillon.

"It is a personal letter to Miss Janvier," Mycroft replied, his voice somber. "From her husband. Offering her a large sum of money for a divorce."

"We will never know if she intended to accept or not," murmured Bertillon.

"To the contrary," muttered Sherlock, shaking his head. "It gives us a strong motive for murder either way."

"Precisely," agreed Mycroft.

Sherlock tapped his forefinger on his cheek. "And yet, it is not only the nature of the missive which is revealing—which only confirms that which I already suspected—but the *location* of the paper," said Sherlock, turning to glance at the window.

"What are you getting at, Holmes?" Watson asked, perplexed.

"I would have thought it more likely for Miss Janvier's reading material to have been on this table," Holmes suggested. "There is no breeze, the window is shut, how did it fall to the ground?"

"Not important! *Mon Dieu!*" Dubuque exclaimed. "Paper on the ground or the desk is no matter. It is the content which is of import, *naturellement*."

"We are here as requested." Mirabella curtseyed in the doorway, joined by Ashanti.

"What are they doing here?" demanded Dubuque.

"Lieutenant!" Bertillon commanded, causing Dubuque to bow his head.

"I sent for them," replied Mycroft. "And the tiger trainer." Both Mycroft and Sherlock stared at Ashanti for an uncharacteristically long moment.

"And how long have you been out of your bandages, Miss Van Horn?" Mycroft asked.

"Two hours," Ashanti replied.

"And were you with her the entire time, Miss Hudson?" Sherlock asked.

"Not the last hour," Mirabella replied. "Ashanti said she had something to do."

An alarmed expression on her face, Ashanti looked at Mirabella who gasped as their eyes met, only that moment seeing the body on the floor. The surprise exhibited by each of them was not lost on Sherlock.

Watson took Mirabella's hand in a too familiar gesture and she looked up at him in a trusting fashion, which infuriated Sherlock.

One body was not yet cold and Watson was in search of another. *I warned Watson to leave her be. I will not have Miss Belle preyed upon by an experienced libertine.* Sherlock felt a resolve which was now irreversible.

The lieutenant, who had been going through the drawers, now let out a long whistle.

"What did you find, Lieutenant?" Mycroft asked.

Opening a velvet pouch, a breathtaking display of diamonds was revealed.

"Magnificent!" murmured Watson. "And worth a fortune."

Sherlock glanced at Ashanti and observed her looking away with a pained expression as she bit her lip.

Definitely more to the lady than meets the eye.

"Miss Janvier was not murdered for theft. The jewels were precisely where a thief would look," surmised Mycroft, glancing at Watson. He added in a low voice, "Without a doubt this was a crime of passion."

Chapter Twenty-eight
A Crime of Passion

"Quite so." Sherlock returned to the body on the floor. "It cannot have escaped your notice, Bertillon, that there would very likely be wounds on Miss Janvier's attacker. Miss Janvier was an accomplished athlete. She would not have gone into the next world easily: she would have used her nails, her teeth, and anything else available to her. Even if she was drugged, there would be marks. I suggest that you thoroughly examine any of your suspects for signs of a struggle: Prince George, Francine, Watson. If you don't find any wounds on your suspect, it is very unlikely that he or she is the assailant."

"Of course!" L'Inspecteur Bertillon agreed.

Watson's face turned suddenly ashen, turning to stare at his flatmate.

Sherlock raised his eyebrows, stating under his breath, "Please tell me, old chap, that you have no marks on you from . . . from . . . ?"

Inspector Bertillon asked the ladies to leave the room, Mirabella bordering on hysterical, and ordered Watson to remove his shirt.

There were, in fact incriminating marks, appearing as if they were made by fingernails and teeth.

"Tsk! Tsk!" Sherlock muttered, shaking his head.

"But it's not what you think!" John Watson exclaimed.

The Lieutenant eyed Dr. Watson suspiciously, approaching him with handcuffs. "Every man he has his breaking point . . ."

"My good man, you are being hasty." Sherlock raised his eyebrows. "Dr. Watson is needed for the case. You have not, as yet, found the weapon. You don't even know what the weapon was."

"But Monsieur Holmes," L'Inspecteur Bertillon argued, "You are the one who told us to check for the marks."

"Indeed you are, Holmes," Watson growled, glaring at Sherlock and looking very much like a murderer indeed.

"You were their prime suspect, my friend, it was only a matter of time before they took you. I merely wished to make a point." Sherlock stared at him pointedly. "At any rate, it doesn't prove anything. I said that the killer would likely have marks on him. I did not say that all men with marks must be the killer. It was a test for innocence not for guilt."

"Then Dr. Watson, he is not innocent!" Lieutenant Dubuque stood to attention, blustering.

There is some truth to that.

"I am telling you, only two men they entered the room," Dubuque continued, as if a fire had been lit underneath him. "First, the English Prince George, and second, Dr. Watson. No one entered after the doctor left except the maid. I was on duty myself. I know that the doctor, he is the killer. This just proves it."

"*Bon*," Bertillon muttered, shaking his head. "And he has the marks indicative of a struggle."

"She was alive when I departed!" Watson repeated, blushing profusely, which seemed to further seal his guilt.

"Hmmm," considered Bertillon. "Prince George arrived first and had already left when Watson entered. Essentially the doctor is the Duke of Cambridge's alibi."

"Precisely," pronounced Watson. "And I have none."

"But do you protect Prince George?" Mycroft demanded of Dr. Watson.

"I would," admitted Watson. "But I am telling the truth!"

"Never fear, Dr. Watson. I spoke to Prince George and I don't believe he did it, there is no need for you to rush to his defense," remarked Mycroft.

"Prince George is not the one in need of a defense," murmured Sherlock, taking his black top-hat in his hand and rolling his fingers along the rim.

Chapter Twenty-nine
Time for Reflection

"But we have to save Dr. Watson!" exclaimed Mirabella as they placed the handcuffs on John Watson. "He is so kind. He would never hurt anyone, even someone as horrible as Joëlle Janvier!" She glanced about the room, the wallpaper a lavender floral, the carpet pink with blue hues like a sunset, and huge gilded mirrors placed at every angle reflecting pink roses, a favorite of the theatrical Russian spy. It was difficult to believe that the life which had inhabited this ornately feminine space was gone. And that the siren could potentially take another life with her.

A life so dear to her!

"Damn it, man!" snapped Watson as the cuffs clicked.

"He didn't do it!" Mirabella turned to John Watson, wrapping her arms around her waist. "You didn't do it, did you, John?"

Watson raised his eyebrows at her. "Your confidence is underwhelming, Miss Mirabella. And why should the French police believe me if you don't?"

"I do! It is so very wrong of them not to believe you! I never suspected you for a moment," she emphasized, closing her eyes momentarily. "It's just that she was so evil, she might turn anyone to the devil. And where were you at the time of the murder, Dr. Watson?"

"I was with Holmes!" John Watson exclaimed as he was being dragged to the door against his will.

"Watson was in Miss Janvier's room to hear the police tell it," considered Sherlock, staring reflectively out the window while a pink chiffon curtain caressed his face as the French police pulled his struggling friend to the door. "Prince George came out, Miss Janvier was alive. Watson went in. Not five minutes later the lady's maid comes running towards us yelling that Miss Janvier is dead, followed by the good lieutenant stating that no one has entered the room since Watson left except the maid."

"Yes, yes, thank you for that recounting of events, Holmes," exclaimed Watson, bracing his body in the door, his top-hat having fallen to rest on the pink carpet.

Sherlock took his pipe out of his pocket and began filling it with tobacco, exhibiting far more energy and interest towards that endeavor than the rescue of his friend, which appeared to be a matter of some indifference to the Great Detective. He glanced over his shoulder at his friend momentarily. "It's not looking good, old chap!"

"Oh, why did you kill her?" moaned Mirabella, genuine concern overtaking her as she dropped into the lime wing-backed couch beside Mycroft who was strangely quiet and reflective. "We all wanted to, I'm sure, but . . ."

"I *didn't* kill her," John Watson exclaimed.

"Rest assured, Miss Belle," Sherlock glanced towards her. "Watson here did not hold Miss Janvier in the same abhorrence which the rest of the world felt for her. He was quite *delighted* with her, shall we say?"

Sherlock's eyes motioned to the canopy bed adorned with wispy chiffon sheets in pink and lavender. Mirabella turned to stare at John Watson, aghast at the idea. She felt more disgust, in fact, than she had with the possibility that he had murdered the she-devil. That would have been understandable, after all.

"I was not precisely delighted with her as you say, Holmes!" shouted Watson from the other end of the room. "I merely did not find her so offensive as others did."

"Indeed," smiled Holmes, lighting his pipe. "Not so offensive, you say? Yes, that would seem to be a true statement."

"Monsieur le Doctor, you'll need to come with us, *s'il vous plait.*" Dubuque latched onto John Watson's arm at L'Inspecteur Bertillon's nod. The French lieutenant's aggressiveness was out of character with his adorable uniform: a little blue box hat, white slacks, a black belt with silver buckles, and a long blue over jacket adorned with over a dozen silver buttons decorating the lapel. Between the ensuing struggle, it looked as if the officer and his prisoner might do a tap dance together.

Much to Mirabella's surprise, Sherlock made no effort to interfere with the policeman's advance, seeming to put more energy into enjoying a few puffs on his pipe.

John Watson's body turned stiff, as did his expression, but he held his ground to glare at Sherlock. "I did my duty, that is all." Through barred teeth he added, "At your insistence, Holmes!"

Very true, Mirabella reflected. It was, after all, an affair John Watson had been forced to undertake out of duty. As she had faced the tigers, so had John Watson.

"Indeed it was, but I never imagined the enthusiasm you would bring to it, Watson," stated Holmes, winking to Mirabella. "All those days and nights making passionate love meant nothing to him."

Mirabella turned to stare at John Watson, watching for a response. Sherlock had a point however reluctant she was to admit it.

"I did it for Queen and country! I assure you, Miss Mirabella," muttered Watson through gritted teeth, "I had very little feeling for the woman."

"You see, Miss Belle, only a few days ago the good doctor was embroiled in an amorous love affair—and note how revived his mood is now. As if her loss had no effect on him at all. To be sure, Watson did not kill her. He has not sufficient feeling for that. You may rest easy on the matter."

"Where are you taking me?" yelled John Watson in a heightened voice, now being shoved again through the doorway.

"Never fear, Watson, the incidences of brutality and murder in La Santé Prison have declined and may someday approach an acceptable number. La Santé is one of the most famous prisons in France with a most respectable wing for the wealthy and well-connected," Sherlock yelled after the captive who had been pushed into the hall. He added under his breath. "Of course you won't be in that wing; you'll be in the high security wing, old chap."

"Holmes, you son of a b----" Watson yelled as he was drug down the hall. Mirabella burst into tears, resting her head on Sherlock's shoulder.

"There, there Miss Belle, all will be well." Sherlock patted her shoulder.

"He didn't do it, Mr. Holmes! I know it!" She looked up at him, knowing he would never lie to her.

Sherlock shook his head in the negative. "Of course he didn't." Sherlock glanced at Bertillon who was still in the room and who attended the conversation with interest.

"And the marks on his body? I overheard . . ."

"Beyond a doubt, the murderer has not a single mark on him inflicted by Miss Janvier," Sherlock stated, looking out the window.

"But the struggle . . . " She studied Sherlock, utterly perplexed. "Then why did you let them take Dr. Watson?"

"Two reasons, Miss Belle. First, it will be easiest to prove the good doctor's innocence if he is locked safely away. If other criminal acts are committed, to be jailed will exonerate him of all charges."

"Someone else . . . *murdered*?" she managed to whisper. "Do you really think?"

"It is a possibility. There are already two murders, are there not? Let us then solve the case with haste, shall we?"

"And what is the other reason, Sherlock?"

He took a puff on his pipe and she thought she saw a sparkle of amusement in his eyes. "Let's just say that Watson needs time to reflect upon the sincerity of his affections."

Chapter Thirty
Blackmail

Some moments later Sherlock was in the courtyard framed by three red brick walls. "Yes, the grass has been flattened. Someone was recently standing here." He bent to examine the grass.

"Of course someone was standing here!" Lieutenant Dubuque laughed. "This is a circus with every manner of person providing the entertainment most populaire à Paris!"

Ashanti was brought to the French police officers wearing loose clothing but still walking with some stiffness Sherlock observed. "Did you see anything . . . Miss Van Horn?" he asked. "You were here, there is a piece of white bandage."

"I was here. But was at least thirty minute before the murder."

"And where you were between the time you left and the time you entré the chamber of Mademoiselle Janvier with Mademoiselle Mirabella?" Lieutenant Dubuque demanded.

"I went to the tiger's cages."

"Was anyone with you, Miss Van Horn?" Sherlock asked.

"No."

"Did anyone see you?"

"Not until Miss Mirabella came running to find me after the murder, to go to her room. We did not know was murder at time."

"Why were you standing outside Miss Janvier's window?" Sherlock asked in his most consoling tone.

"Practicing. The wall is good for the practice."

"Practicing what?" Dubuque pressed.

"Striking my whip."

"You are well enough to utilize the whip, Miss Van Horn?" asked Sherlock, his eyes scanning her patches of swollen skin and awkward stance. "I would not have supposed it. You have only just had your bandages removed."

"I am tired—and stiff," Ashanti agreed. "But doctors they say I have healed good and will perform again."

"*Bon.* And did you Mademoiselle Janvier observe when you were in the courtyard practicing, Miss Van Horn?" asked L'Inspecteur Bertillon politely.

"How could one not observe her? Joëlle, she made certain all see her," replied Ashanti. "She opened window and told me to go away."

"*Alors!* Mademoiselle Janvier, did she give a reason for this *request*?" Bertillon asked.

"She said the noise it bothered her." Ashanti smiled. "And it was not *request*."

"Assist me if you please! And Mademoiselle Janvier, did she generally have the window closed or open?" asked Inspector Dubuque, making notes in his notepad.

"Open. She liked the air fresh."

"Ah, but not the noise," Sherlock considered. "And you, Mademoiselle Van Horn, were you practicing outside her window simply to annoy her? You weren't truly exerting yourself very much, were you?"

Ashanti shrugged noncommittally.

"*Comment?* Mademoiselle Janvier, you did not like her?" Bertillon persisted.

Ashanti shook her head.

"Pourquoi?" *Why?*

"She was not kind, that one."

"In what way?" L'Inspecteur Bertillon asked while Dubuque wrote furiously.

"How many ways are there not to be kind?" Ashanti stared at the inspector. "Joëlle, she was all of them."

"The People they have seen Mademoiselle Janvier speaking with you on beaucoup occasions," Dubuque pressed. "What was she saying to you?" It was clear that Dubuque was accustomed to interrogation and Bertillon to analysis, and, unlike everyone else present, L'Inspecteur Bertillon did not appear to object to Dubuque's authoritative manner.

Ashanti glanced at Sherlock who nodded his approval.

"Joëlle told me that if I did not do as she told me, she would make sure I never worked with the tigers again."

"What did she want from you, Mademoiselle?" asked Bertillon, breaking his silence.

Ashanti was silent.

"Ashanti, if you don't tell them," Mirabella interjected, her eyes pleading as she wrung her hands, "Dr. Watson will be hanged. And he didn't commit the murder; I know he didn't. We must tell the truth."

Sherlock glanced momentarily at Dubuque before murmuring to Ashanti, "*Even the French Police* will piece it together eventually, Miss Van Horn. Best to tell them."

Ashanti stared at them a long while before answering. "She wanted diamonds."

"Les diamonds in the pouch velvet they were yours?" Dubuque exclaimed.

Ashanti nodded.

Sherlock raised his eyebrows in exasperation. "Obviously Miss Janvier was blackmailing Miss Van Horn."

"Where did you get the jewels, Mademoiselle Van Horn?" Dubuque demanded.

"It is elementary, lieutenant," muttered Sherlock. "It isn't necessary to distress the girl to this degree. The answer is obvious."

"*Bon Dieu*! It is not evident!" sputtered Dubuque.

"My good man. The diamonds," Sherlock rolled his eyes, "were Miss Van Horn's dowry."

Chapter Thirty-one
The Royal George

"I told you, damnit! She was alive when I left the room! The puppy following Miss Janvier around told you that as well!" The Duke of Cambridge twirled his long white moustache which met his white sideburns covering all but his chin, which was bare. He wore his military dress, red jacket, blue sash, black slacks, and knee-high black Hessian boots.

The Royal George, as he was called, looked every inch the monarch. He towered over men. The 2nd Duke of Cambridge, the Earl of Tipperary, Baron Culloden, and the grandson of King George III, was, in fact, the successor to the throne until Victoria was born, and he remained on close terms with his cousin the Queen.

And yet, George William Frederick Charles, born into royalty, was a working man. He entered the military as a colonel in the Hanoverian Army. He served in the 12th Royal Lancers, followed by the 8th Light Dragoons and the 17th Lancers. He was promoted to Major-General in eighteen hundred and forty-five, and to general commander-in-chief of the British Army in eighteen hundred and fifty-six.

"Doctor Watson, do you mean?" Lieutenant Dubuque asked irreverently as he looked up into the eyes of the Duke who was well over six feet. In addition to his own intimidating stature, the Royal George's enormous body guard stood behind his master exhibiting rippling muscles, impressive to even a skilled boxer such as the Great Detective.

But the French lieutenant was neither intimidated nor impressed, not withstanding Prince George's rank.

"I don't mean nothing. I'm telling you what was, you frog, and if I had my way we'd annex your flowery soil into Germany!" he said, showing his Hanover roots. "I've got to get back to London, you ninny hammer!"

"*Arrêtez s'il vous plaît!* We have had a murder here. *Bon.* The French police does not care how important you are in your country, your grand dukeship, that is of little moment to us! We have a dead girl on our hands. And you a married man. Tsk! Tsk!"

"Don't you tsk! Tsk! me" Prince George huffed. "Talking about me when that Romeo doctor—"

"I beg your pardon, your highness." Sherlock interrupted this heated exchange. "But I must inform you in all fairness that the good doctor, like you, has served his country."

"You don't say?" asked Prince George, his opinion of Dr. Watson clearly improved despite the fact that the doctor's innocence was a threat to his own. The Royal George tapped his cane on the bare ground of the courtyard framed by red brick which bordered Joëlle Janvier's second-story room.

"Very true," added Sherlock. "Served in the Second Afghan war as a surgeon. Injured at Maiwand."

"Afghanistan, you say? Must be brave." Prince George nodded, and it was obvious that his assessment of the man whose guilt could save his own neck from the noose was now altered.

"Better to answer the lieutenant's questions, your Highness," Mycroft interjected. "It will be that much sooner that the matter is put behind us."

"I've told you all I know, damnit! If I knew who killed the lovely Miss Janvier, don't you think I would say?" Prince George glared at the Frenchman, his opinion in that court apparently much the same. "So far as I know, it was the lieutenant himself!"

"M-m-moi?" sputtered the lieutenant. "*Sacre Bleu!* What idiocy do you speak?"

"I left, the doctor left, you were the only one remaining guarding the door, you said so yourself!" yelled Prince George. "You went in and killed her! The window was locked. This is as logical an explanation as any."

"It is ridiculous, it is!" replied Lieutenant Dubuque with a sweep of the arm.

"And your companion here?" asked Sherlock, his eyes turning towards the bodyguard. "Surely he saw something?"

Put a sword in his mouth, and Prince George's foreign bodyguard looked to be Blackbeard's larger, meaner brother. The fierce-looking attendant wore a long, twirling moustache and a pointy short beard; his hair was dark. He had a light blue fleece hat resembling a fez, from which emerged an oseledet, a simple long lock of hair whereby the majority of the head was shaved. He had tall, knee-high leather boots. He wore a grey-brown tunic and a light blue shirt-dress of sorts—a beshmet—held together with a long red silk sash at the waist. The *shashka*, as the sword was called, was at his side, along with a whip tied to the beshmet.

"Wh—huh? You mean Kazimir?" The Royal George asked.

"He is presumably your body guard?" Sherlock asked. "A military man? It is his undertaking to watch and protect, is it not?"

"Kazimir is a Cossack. Bravest men on earth." Kazimir's expression did not flinch. But unlike a British guard, who would look straight ahead knowing the conversation was none of his business, the Cossack kept his eyes all over the room. He watched everything unashamedly, true to his heritage of keeping Russia's borders safe in exchange for freedom and independence.

"*Explain*. I thought the Cossacks they protect the Czar?" asked Dubuque, stepping back involuntarily as he studied the threatening stance of the man standing before them.

"Damn straight!" replied the Duke of Cambridge.

"Cossacks are frightfully loyal to the Czar," explained Sherlock, "risking their lives to keep the Czar safe, in order that they might not be under the Czar's jurisdiction. In exchange for their protection, Cossacks do not pay any taxes to the Czar."

"*Comment!* That does not make the sense," murmured Lieutenant Dubuque.

"It don't to you! To a Cossack it makes all the sense in the world," sighed Prince George, clearly exasperated.

"In effect, they give their loyalty that they might have none," stated Sherlock.

"So the Cossack—he is loyal to you?" Dubuque asked. "Or to Russia?"

"To *both*, didn't we just say?" Prince George growled.

"In the Cossack's mind, it is one and the same," Mycroft murmured.

"Can he not speak for himself?" Lieutenant Dubuque asked.

Kazimir glared at the Frenchman, clearly understanding, but he said nothing.

"Do you trust him, le Duc?" Lieutenant Dubuque asked.

"Kazimir has been with me almost as long as my mother has," muttered Prince George. Even with blue eyes, his gaze was fiercely intense. "I won't have you question his loyalty. Kazimir would die for me!"

"*Mais bien sûr!* And where was the Cossack at the time of the murder?" pressed Dubuque.

"Kazimir wasn't anywhere close to the murder scene!" replied Prince George. "He was outside guarding the building! And doing a damn fine better job than you did, lieutenant! The people he guards don't *die*!"

"And your body guard—why did he not stand outside the door while you were visiting?" asked Inspector Bertillon, until now only watching and observing.

"Excellent question," murmured Sherlock.

"Kazimir goes wherever he needs to be. He's not one of your bloody lapdogs!" replied Prince George curtly. "If he thinks he needs to

be outside the door, that's where he'll be. If he needs to be watching the
building, that's where he'll be. And because he does what is needed is why
I'm still alive talking to you bloody fools!"

Sherlock turned to Kazimir. "And where were you, sir, while Prince
George was visiting Miss Janvier and until the murder was committed?"

The Cossack glared at the Great Detective as a wolverine might
study its prey. Sherlock held his ground, envisioning all possible manner of
defense were such a response to prove necessary.

Studying the formidable man before him, Sherlock concluded that
the Cossacks' reputation as a pirate-gypsy race, renowned for their raids
against the Ottoman Empire, was no doubt deserved. When Napoleon
invaded Russia, the French troops feared the Cossacks above all others,
who were famous for guerrilla warfare, their specialty being scouting,
reconnaissance, and ambush attacks, in part the basis for today's special
operations.

Kazimir turned his piercing stare to Prince George who nodded.
"As commander said, outside building watching entrances and exits."

"Where, precisely?" asked Sherlock, undeterred.

"In hallway, then in street, then in courtyard, then in hallway."

"The courtyard outside Miss Janvier's window?" Bertillon pressed.

"Yes," said Kazimir.

"*Pourquoi?* And why were you there, Monsieur?" asked Dubuque.

"Because his highness was inside room," Kazimir stated succinctly
in his deep, baritone voice. He placed his massive hands on his waist. "It
is best place to observe. And if there is someone suspicious, I wish to see
before they approach, not after."

Prince George chuckled at the absurdity of the questions.

"And who did you see, my good man, while you stood outside the
window?" asked Sherlock of the Cossack. The bodyguard was a wealth of
information, having observed all, with the added advantage of being able
to confirm or deny everyone else's account. Sherlock was not sure that the
police understood his importance.

"I saw dark girl in the courtyard, leaving as I arrived."

"And what was she doing?" Dubuque asked.

Kazimir raised his eyebrows. "Leaving the courtyard."

"He just said that, you idiot," Prince George muttered, giving
everyone a taste of that which constituted polite conversation in the military.

"Describe her, s'il vous plaît," the lieutenant insisted. Sherlock
gave the lieutenant credit that, regardless of the abuse hurled upon him, he

went forward.

"She had whip in her hand," Kazimir stated.

"Was she practicing?" Bertillon asked.

Kazimir shrugged.

"You bloody fools!" snarled Prince George. "Kazimir doesn't know what she was doing, he only saw what she was carrying. Ask him what he was doing! How could he know what she was doing before he arrived?"

"We will ask ze questions, *s'il vous plaît!*" the lieutenant reprimanded angrily before turning to Kazimir. "Is this correct? Mademoiselle Van Horn's activities they were not evident?"

"She was carrying whip," Kazimir repeated.

"Did you see her use it?" Dubuque insisted.

"No."

"Was Miss Janvier still alive when Miss Van Horn left the courtyard?" Sherlock asked.

"Yes." Kazimir nodded. "As long as his highness was there, French girl was alive. When the commander left, I left the courtyard to meet him in hallway."

"Did you see anyone else while you moved to meet Prince George, Mr. Kazimir?" Sherlock asked, moving between the two men.

"I saw tiger girl leave building," He replied.

"Miss Mirabella?" Sherlock asked.

"Yes." Kazimir shrugged, indifferent.

"Anyone else?" Sherlock asked.

"Russian was in courtyard with me."

"Monsieur Stanislav Afanasy?" Dubuque asked.

Kazimir nodded.

"And when did you see Mr. Stanislav leave the courtyard?" Inspector Bertillon asked.

"At time his highness left Russian girl's room." He spit on the ground. "Afanasy saw commander in window which caused him anger. Went in building as if headed for girl's room."

"However—you only saw Mr. Afanasy leave, you did not see him reach Miss Janvier's room, did you Mr. Kazimir?" Sherlock asked.

Kazimir nodded agreement.

"And was Miss Janvier alive when Mr. Afanasy left?"

"Yes, I saw her through window. Then I left courtyard."

"*Merci beaucoup, Monsieur*, you've been very helpful," Inspector Bertillon stated.

"Can we damn well get on with it now?" demanded Prince George.

Sherlock thought of the handkerchief found on the floor with the letters "SF" embroidered on them. "Your highness, your wife, is she visiting Paris?"

"Sarah?"

"How many wives do you have?" Lieutenant Dubuque raised his eyebrows.

The Royal George's expression revealed that he considered himself to have none. Sherlock reflected that, though Prince George's devotion to his troops was well known, being called 'The Soldier's friend', he was seemingly undeserving of Sarah Fairbrother's continued devotion.

"When a man through some ill-fated accident makes a great mistake, he must abide by it," Prince George muttered.

"I take it that the great mistake was your marriage, your highness?" Mycroft asked.

The commander-in-chief of the British army suddenly became indignant. "I'll tell you something, you young whippersnapper, when I came into my post, pay was about three pence a day for a common soldier, and the army's idea of discipline was branding and flogging."

"You don't hold to that, sir?

"Damn straight, I don't. The death rate in the *non-active duty* army was five times higher than in civilian life! That tells you something about the food and the conditions. The bloody Parliament treats convicts better than they do the soldiers who serve Her."

Sherlock appreciated the sentiment. The man before him might have been born a prince, but he knew a working soldier's life, and he had a great deal of empathy and a sense of justice. From the depth of feeling in Prince George's eyes, Sherlock had not been surprised to learn that Prince George cried for days after a battle. His stormy temperament hid a deep emotion.

"And Sarah Fairbrother. Is she a jealous woman?"

Prince George suddenly burst into laughter. "Jealous? I should say so."

"And your sons? Is it possible they would avenge their mother's honor?"

"George, Adolphus, and Augustus?" Prince George stopped laughing abruptly. "Too busy gambling and skirting it themselves to be concerned."

In contrast to the words spoken, Sherlock concluded that the sons were quite devoted to their father. The pride he observed in Prince George's eyes did not lie: a father's devotion was almost always returned by sons. All three had promising military careers—which must be due to the Duke of

Cambridge's connections.

"I'll tell you now, as I'm not one to beat around the bush," Prince George continued. "When I married Sarah, I was young and foolish. The love of my life was one Mrs. Louisa Beauclerk, and when she died on December twenty-eighth, it was the sad day which ended the happiness in this world for me. We were together some thirty years."

"And how did Mrs. Beauclerk die?" asked Sherlock without wasting any time on the niceties.

Prince George frowned. "Some claimed it was poisoning, but that's all twaddle! It was a natural death. She hadn't felt well for some time."

"How did some believe she was poisoned?"

"Chocolates they found in the house. But I know for a fact Louisa never touched chocolates."

"It has been my observance that the food women eat in view of men is sometimes different from that which their stomachs reveal to have been consumed," Mycroft murmured.

Sherlock thought of the candy beside Miss Janvier's bed which was even now being tested for poison.

"Was your wife visiting you during your sojourn in Paris?" Mycroft asked.

"And what business is it of yours? I don't like your tone. And you nothin' but a bloomin' civilian!"

"I am a civilian conducting a murder investigation at the crown's insistence, if you please. I'll ask you again, your highness. Was your wife visiting you during your sojourn in Paris?"

"Sarah? Humph! She ain't here. Never travels."

Sherlock considered that a visit to Piccadilly was in order.

Chapter Thirty-two
Office of the Okhrana
Russian Imperial Consulate, 97 Rue de Grenelle, Paris

"It is a fact that Miss Janvier was one of our agents," Arkadiy Mikhailovich Harting, head of the Russian Imperialist Police in Paris, better known as the *Okhrana*, murmured. Mr. Harting, having much the serious appearance of a professor, leaned back in his chair. He was of medium build, muscular, sporting a goatee and slicked back hair, handsome in a meticulous sort of way. He added, "She spied on revolutionary activity, reported it to us and we, in turn, reported it to the Czar."

"We had only just uncovered this information when we called Watson off the case," Mycroft explained. The elder of the Holmes brothers languidly sipped on the tea which had been offered to him, heavily dolloped with cream. Mycroft sighed, his cup momentarily suspended in mid-air, "The next thing we knew she was dead."

"Was she a good agent?" Sherlock asked bluntly. Certainly he had his own assessment of Miss Janvier, but he wanted to hear Arkadiy Harting's.

"One of the best," Mr. Harting replied simply, leaning back in his chair. Through the window behind Harting's desk one could see the Seine River.

"The best . . . in what way?" pressed Sherlock.

"Nothing would stop her," Mr. Harting replied without hesitation. "She knew no limits or boundaries. She was fearless."

"No doubt she will be greatly missed," murmured Mycroft, studying Harting over the rim of his cup.

"The organization will be significantly impacted by her absence, beyond a doubt," Mr. Harting nodded somberly.

"What were some of Miss Janvier's successes?" asked Sherlock.

"She had immense success in pinpointing and communicating arms sales and supply dumps." Mr. Harting inadvertently rearranged the papers on his massive oak desk, sparkling clean, not often seen in government offices. Lestrade's office came to mind.

"Ah, yes," murmured Mycroft, seeming deep in thought. "I recall a store owner by the name of Loewenthal?"

"Precisely," nodded Mr. Harting, his expression suddenly suspicious as his eyes alighted on Mycroft, as if he were displeased that someone outside of his organization should have access to this clearly confidential information. "One of Miss Janvier's greatest successes was discovering and infiltrating a counterfeit operation to fund the revolutionaries. Robert Loewenthal, a Russian émigré, had a small sort of shop which served as a front for the operation. The entire ring was caught red-handed and brought to justice."

"Her convictions must have run deep," said Sherlock, scrutinizing Harting.

Harting raised his eyebrows. He was so polished and practiced that only the slightest disagreement was visible.

"I can see that you do not agree, Mr. Harting?" pressed Mycroft.

Harting patted his lips with his handkerchief, clearly annoyed that he had revealed his opinion. "Among our agents, there are those whose motivation is an abhorrence for revolutionary activity of any kind. There are those for whom loyalty to the Czar is a religion. Then there are those . . . with purely mercenary motives."

"And Miss Janvier fell within the last group," Sherlock murmured.

"Quite so." Mr. Harting nodded.

"And no doubt there are those who are attracted by the excitement and glamour of the life of espionage," Sherlock added with a slight smile.

"You have an excellent command of both the details and the greater concepts of our organization, Mr. Holmes," stated Mr. Harting with both appreciation and apparent discomfort.

"But though the work is perceived as glamorous by some, it is more accurate to call it *dangerous*, as evidenced by Miss Janvier's untimely death," Mycroft surmised.

"Entirely true," Mr. Harting agreed.

"And where did Miss Joëlle Janvier's motivations fit in on the continuum?" Sherlock leaned forward, nonchalantly stirring his tea. "In other words, how greedy was she?"

"Mercenary, with a lust for power and riches," Mr. Harting replied simply. He leaned back in his chair, evincing a slight smile. "And one of the best because of it."

Chapter Thirty-three
A Former Lover

"You were terribly jealous of Miss Janvier, weren't you, Mr. Afanasy? She taunted and demeaned you." Sherlock noted the accused's lack of concern. His hair was long and dark, which he separated into a small braid on each side of his head, allowing the remainder of his hair to flow freely. He wore a white leotard and a gold belt, the stretchy top dipping low on his torso, revealing a muscular chest. His face was clean-shaven.

"This she did to everyone," Stanislav shrugged with indifference.

"You were once her lover, were you not?" pressed Sherlock.

"Once." Stanislav looked away, appearing suddenly emotional.

Sherlock pressed his advantage. "Miss Janvier found out about your activities—she was working for the *Okhrana*—and she threatened to turn you in, which would necessarily result in your being pursued by the Russian secret police. And you killed her."

"Kill her why?" he asked sadly. "I loved her. No reason to kill her."

"You had every reason, I should say," Mycroft said. "It would silence her."

"If had silenced her, why you know so much?"

"There is more to learn, I assure you, Mr. Afanasy." Mycroft narrowed his eyes.

"Will not tell what you don't know. Ha! ha!" Merriment crossed his expression of overall sadness, entirely out of place.

"Ah, your political activities, of course we know about that, Mr. Afanasy," replied Mycroft. "We know that you are involved with revolutionary groups here in Paris. The *Okhrana* has been following you for months."

"Pssst!" Stanislav spit on the ground. "Let follow. I am no traitor to Mother Russia!" There was no fear in his eyes, only courage, as one would expect from a trainer of the big cats. But there was, however, a sadness and determination, revealing an acceptance of misery.

The man is terribly unhappy and expects always to be so, Sherlock considered. "The point is that you are involved with groups plotting to overthrow the Czar. We know this for a fact so there is no point in pretending and wasting everyone's time."

"So to Siberia send me." Stanislav threw back his head, laughing. "Am in France now, cannot touch me."

"I imagine the Czar has his methods if the threat is great enough." Sherlock added softly, "An assassination plot would certainly qualify."

"You care why? Nothing to do with Joëlle."

"Untrue. And maybe you didn't know if she had yet told anyone about your connection to the group—maybe she just held it over you to torture you," Mycroft said. "That combined with your passionate involvement makes you a perfect candidate for murder, Mr. Stanislav."

"I knew. And . . . I not kill woman."

"But you might kill a viper," Mycroft suggested.

"Joëlle not viper! You not know her!"

I knew her as well as I wished to.

Stanislav spat on the ground again, then grew closer, his stance threatening. He placed the whip inside his gold belt which freed his hands. Sherlock held his fists close to his chest in the event he might need them.

Touching, though. And remarkable. In spite of all Miss Janvier had done to him and the threat she posed—the Russian police was well known for its cruel tactics— Stanislav loved her.

Stanislav twirled the whip which was in his hand. "Not afraid of tigers. Not afraid of Siberia. Not afraid of woman."

"Fear and hate are closely linked emotions." Mycroft raised his eyebrows.

"How I did it?" Stanislav pursed his lips. "I not able to enter room." Stanislav pursed his lips and a genuine hatred crossed his countenance. "Wish I had been in room. Might have saved her."

"Were you talking to Miss Janvier through the window before you proceeded to her room, Mr. Afanasy?"

"Yes."

"I thought so. We found your footprints outside the window."

"So what?" Stanislav shrugged. "Many footprints there."

"Was the window open when you spoke with Miss Janvier?" asked Sherlock.

"Yes. How Joëlle she hear me otherwise?"

"And what time was that?"

"Four thirty."

"Precisely?"

"Da."

"How do you know, Mr. Afanasy?"

"I hear ringing of clock tower." He smoothed his hair back on his head and then wrapped his fingers around the thin straps of his leotard which covered very little of his muscled chest.

"And what did you say to Miss Janvier?" Sherlock asked.

"I ask her not turn me in. Not afraid. Just want to see what she say." Stanislav's countenance turned somber.

"What did she say?"

"She laugh. Joëlle she always laugh. She say she already did."

Sherlock watched Stanislav fingering the whip. If, indeed, this were true, it gave Mr. Afanasy no motive unless it were that of revenge.

A strong motive indeed.

Or perhaps Stanislav didn't believe Joëlle Janvier and presumed her to be playing with him as a cat played with a mouse—as she had always done.

If it was a crime of passion, there was often no logic to it. And Stanislav Afanasy didn't appear to care what happened to him.

A perfect candidate for murder.

Chapter Thirty-four
Poison

"There were an enormous amount of foreign substances in Miss Janvier's system. Do you know anything about that, Miss Van Horn?" asked Mycroft, leaning his tall body forward. He was clean-shaven, revealing his fine, chiseled features, and his hair was cut short. He was dressed in light-colored pants, a dark, fine frock coat, and a low-cut vest paired with a slim cravat. Though the mismatched pants and jacket were all the rage in the fashion world, it was uncharacteristically informal for the elder Holmes brother from what Mirabella had observed.

He is obviously going slumming on this particular evening, Mirabella reflected—a fashionable pastime of the privileged for diversion and amusement, instigated with the newly popular East End novels describing the slum conditions in St. George's, Mile End, and, of course, the notorious White Chapel. She herself found nothing amusing in viewing the suffering of others.

"Of course, poison is the method of choice for women," Sherlock said. "In addition, poison could be administered and the murderer not actually be present when the murder took place."

"I gave Miss Janvier medicines, not poisons!" Ashanti shook her head in surprise, seated just inside the circus tent at a makeshift table where interrogations had been initiated.

"So . . . was Miss Janvier poisoned or wasn't she?" asked Mirabella.

"There was morphine in her system. But many people use that drug recreationally." Mycroft glanced at his brother. "Did she take the drug herself, or did someone else administer the drug? And, if it was someone else, did it contribute to her death?"

"Oh, my head is swimming," murmured Mirabella.

"It has only just begun," Sherlock pronounced. "Our bare-backed rider makes an elephant look like a light diner with no appetite. She was hedonistic and indulgent in every way. In addition to the chocolate, strawberries, and champagne in her stomach, there were vast amounts of strange herbs in Miss Janvier's system. Were they in the chocolate or the strawberries? And were they harmful to her? The herbs could be harmless to one person and fatal to another. And were they taken voluntarily or forced upon her?"

"But the sheer variety of substances in her stomach make it highly probable that an attempt at poison was made," Mycroft added.

"Probable but not irrefutable. The first course is, of course, to identify everything that was in her stomach and then to find the corresponding item in her boudoir," Sherlock said. "We then test the item in her boudoir in an attempt to determine if the poisons and questionable substances were in the strawberries, the chocolate, or the champagne. We then attempt to determine who provided each of the items. We know that the champagne was from Dr. John Watson. The chocolates may have come from the mysterious woman who had dropped the handkerchief, either "SF" herself, her carrier, or one who wished to implicate her. The strawberries add yet another suspect. And then there is you, Miss Van Horn and your voodoo ritual with the herbs."

"Since there were so many substances in the stomach of the deceased," Mycroft said, "either everyone was attempting to kill Miss Janvier at once—or a number of people were providing her with unharmful herbs. It seems unlikely doesn't it?"

"Again, unlikely, but possible," Sherlock mused, as if he had already come to some conclusions.

"True. And finally," Mycroft added, "We must conclude if any of these substances were actually the cause of Miss Janvier's death, regardless of who might have made the attempt." He turned to Ashanti. "We start with you, Miss Van Horn. The herbs believed to have come from you—the voodoo elements of herbs, bark, and dried snake—are not known to be poison unless she was fatally allergic to them. Perhaps you had inside knowledge?"

"And, if Miss Janvier wasn't allergic, why were they given to her?" Sherlock asked.

Ashanti shook her head, refusing to answer.

"Just tell us this, Miss Van Horn," demanded Mycroft, brushing the sleeves of his jacket with his hand. "Did you give Miss Janvier the strawberries?"

"Why would I give Joëlle strawberries?" Ashanti was strangely not reluctant to speak on this topic.

"Perhaps the herbs were a ruse to draw our attention elsewhere . . ." Sherlock considered. "Perhaps there was something in the strawberries."

"We found strawberries in your room, Miss Van Horn," stated Mycroft.

"It is no crime to eat strawberries," replied Ashanti, covering her hand with her mouth.

"That's true! I ate some of those strawberries in my tent," Mirabella came to her friend's aid. "They can't have been poisoned."

"Indeed they were," Mycroft said. "The strawberries in Miss Janvier's room were, in fact, poisoned, and the poisons match the contents of Miss Janvier's stomach."

Both Ashanti and Mirabella gasped in unison.

"Ah, so Ashanti gave you strawberries on the day in question, Miss Hudson?" Sherlock asked, his piercing gaze directed at her.

Mirabella bit her lip, nodding, feeling her eyes watering.

"Are you holding anything back, Miss Belle? I forbid you to do so in a murder investigation," Sherlock said.

"Many people ate strawberries on that day, they came from a vendor outside," Mirabella added.

"I am inclined to believe her," Sherlock stated to his brother. "Miss Janvier could have been in no doubt that Miss Van Horn hated her—and Miss Janvier was not stupid however cruel she might have been. She would not have eaten food given to her by Miss Van Horn."

"And yet . . ." Mycroft considered, "Miss Janvier ingested the herbs on her nightstand—and the strawberries."

"B-b-but I did not give her the strawberries!" exclaimed Ashanti. "What was in them?"

Mycroft took a piece of paper out of his pocket and read it out loud. "I've only just received the report. Henbane, jimson weed, angel's trumpets, and corkwood."

Sherlock turned abruptly to stare at Mycroft.

"What is it, Shirley?"

"I don't even know what any of those things you are saying mean," Ashanti wailed.

"It sounds like voodoo herbs to me," Mycroft said. "Very strange names."

"Miss Van Horn is telling the truth," Sherlock said, leaning into his seat.

"I bow to your superior knowledge of chemistry, Shirley. What is it?"

"Carbon 17 Hydrogen 21 Nitrogen Oxygen 4," Sherlock replied matter-of-factly. "Tasteless, odorless, colorless."

"As I said, what is it, Shirley?"

"It has the same function as the substance derived from the borrachero tree--or, in smaller doses, from the belladonna plant."

"Ah, to induce the stopping of the heart," Mycroft considered, obviously perplexed. "But we already know that Miss Janvier did not die from a disease of the heart." Mycroft returned his eyes to the piece of paper, raising his eyebrows.

"Precisely," Sherlock said. "I therefore conclude that the purpose of the substance was entirely different and had nothing to do with Miss Janvier's death. In fact, that the purpose of the one administering the drug was entirely opposed to murder."

"Aha. I see what you mean, Shirley. This is political in nature."

"Quite so. This substance, in lower doses, is a truth serum." Sherlock turned to Mirabella. "What did the street vendor look like?"

"He had auburn hair—and a beard," considered Mirabella, tapping her forefinger to her chin. "I remember thinking that his hair was very neatly trimmed and he looked quite out of place. He had an academic and intellectual way of speaking. Very odd, considering that he was selling fruit from a cart."

"As I thought." Sherlock turned to Ashanti abruptly. "Had you seen the street vendor before, Miss Van Horn?"

"No, never," she exclaimed, her alarm beginning to come to the surface.

"Who was it, Mr. Holmes?" Mirabella asked, turning to Sherlock, as she realized the answer to this question must be important.

"*Professor Moriarty,*" whispered Sherlock.

"If the professor poisoned Miss Janvier, then Ashanti had nothing to do with it," Mirabella said.

"Unless it was her job to transport the strawberries to Miss Janvier," Sherlock considered.

"Miss Van Horn, what do you have to say about the herbs in Miss Janvier's room?" asked Mycroft. "Roots, bark, snake skins, and . . . hrumph . . .dried animal parts."

Ashanti paused for a moment, as if considering denying any knowledge of the items. She lowered her eyes. "Joëlle, she asked me to help her."

"To help her with what?" Mycroft asked.

"My auntie is medicine woman, a *Sangoma*. She taught me the old ways."

"Your aunt is a Witch Doctor?" asked Mycroft.

"No." Ashanti shook her head. "A Sangoma has no black magic. Is shaman or healer. She can also into the future see."

"A clairvoyant," Sherlock said, knitting his eyebrows.

"A Sangoma is good in everything she does. The future of the tribe depends upon it. Is not like the missionaries said. Sangoma is healer."

"Was Miss Janvier sick?" Mycroft expressed his disbelief. "She appeared most healthy to me."

"Was not sick." Ashanti shook her head.

"What were you helping her with then?" Mycroft asked.

"I can say not. I am sworn to silence," pronounced Ashanti.

"Then you may hang by the neck," Mycroft murmured.

"Oh No!" Mirabella covered her mouth with her hand as she felt her eyes water.

"Miss Van Horn, you must tell us to save yourself," Mycroft stated.

"Nein." Ashanti shook her head. "A promise is a promise."

"Can you nod 'yes' or 'no', Miss Van Horn?" Sherlock asked gently, his eyes looking out the window as if he were deep in thought.

Ashanti nodded in agreement.

"Miss Janvier, she was with child, was she not?" Sherlock asked abruptly, turning ninety degrees from where he stood to face her.

Shock crossed Ashanti's expression, then she nodded.

"It is true," Mycroft nodded. "The autopsy revealed it. Good work, Shirley."

"It was obvious," he muttered. "And why would you help her, Miss Van Horn? I gathered you were not the best of friends."

"The girl who danced on horses—she had no friends," murmured Ashanti. "She said . . . she would not hurt the tigers if I helped her."

Sherlock raised his chin in disbelief. "But you didn't have any reason to believe her, did you, Miss Van Horn?"

"No," murmured Ashanti, shaking her head.

"You had already given Miss Janvier the diamonds, and she threatened you again. So you knew her word was not good."

Ashanti nodded.

"Unlike your own," Mycroft added.

"So why did you help Miss Janvier then?" Sherlock asked softly, his expression revealing that he already knew the answer and only wanted to hear it from Ashanti's lips.

"Did not." Ashanti released a slow, sly smile. "Only pretend to."

"So, that leaves us where we started, doesn't it?" Sherlock asked, a slow smile forming on his lips. "If you wouldn't kill the baby, you didn't kill Miss Janvier for dread of harming the baby, either. And neither would you have transported the strawberries—for the same reason."

Ashanti's eyes opened wide, startled that someone would understand her—and believe her. "When Joëlle she die, her baby it was healthy. If the baby was sick, it was not because of me."

Mycroft nodded gravely. "When Miss Janvier died, her baby was presumed to be healthy. But her baby was not old enough to survive Miss

Janvier's death. This was your alibi, Miss Van Horn, why did you not simply tell us?"

"I made promise," she replied solemnly. "And you wouldn't believe me anyway."

"But you did give Miss Janvier a strange herb, didn't you Miss Van Horn?" asked Sherlock.

She nodded. "It was an herb to rid her of the devil in her soul—and to protect her baby from the darkness."

"That was very kind, considering your relationship with Miss Janvier," Mirabella considered thoughtfully.

"What is the name of the herb?" asked Mycroft, appearing deep in thought. "That would be a useful herb—to rid one's soul of . . . unwanted desires."

"It did not work," Ashanti replied, shaking her head sadly.

"I wouldn't expect so," murmured Mycroft, leaning back into his chair and closing his eyes momentarily. "But it was worth a try."

"Sometimes it works," Ashanti explained. "A *Sangoma* can cure those who are sick in head. I have seen Sangoma distinguish between those who are sick und those who cannot be healed. Once in my village, there was a man who was mad—he was verrückt—and the *Sangoma* healed him."

"But it did not work for Miss Janvier?" asked Sherlock.

"She did not wish to be healed of her heart black." Ashanti shook her head.

"And you gave Miss Janvier another herb, did you not, Miss Van Horn?" asked Sherlock.

Ashanti looked pointedly at Sherlock, surprise written all over her face. "It was an herb, so that, when Joëlle died, she would not come back in animal form."

"When she died?" repeated Mycroft, startled. "You knew that Miss Janvier would die?"

"Yes." Ashanti nodded. "The tigers they told me."

"Miss Van Horn," Mycroft straightened his black silk tie. "You don't honestly expect us to believe . . ."

"It is true. I can speak with wild animals. I have always had this ability."

"I believe her," murmured Mirabella. "The tigers *listen* to her. If they didn't, I might be the dead body you are investigating instead of Miss Janvier's."

"I did not kill her!" exclaimed Ashanti, clearly exasperated. "It sounds crazy if I in English say it, but if you speak Zulu, you understand. I was not afraid to kill her, and *I would have* if tigers she hurt. But I saw her death. I knew I did not have to."

Sherlock studied her. "So your alibi, Miss Van Horn, is that, even though you were fully prepared to murder Miss Janvier, the tigers came to you in a voodoo vision and told you the murder was unnecessary—that someone else would do the job for you?"

Ashanti nodded.

Oh, this is terrible, Mirabella reflected.

"And did you see in your vision—*who* killed her, Miss Van Horn?" asked Mycroft with something approaching amusement as he yawned.

Ashanti shook her head. "No."

"And what about the chocolates?" Mirabella asked. "Were they poisoned?"

"The box itself was not," Mycroft answered. "We can't be certain if the one piece Miss Janvier ate was or not."

"And the champagne?" Mirabella asked.

"The bottle itself was not poisoned," Sherlock said.

"Miss Van Horn, I beg you will help yourself." Mycroft stated gently, returning his attention to Ashanti. "Do you know who the father of the baby was?"

Ashanti shook her head. "Joëlle she has hurt enough people in life, I will not let her hurt another in death."

"You must lay all the facts before us or you are obstructing justice and we can put you in jail," Mycroft said.

Ashanti laughed. "Do you think I am afraid of jail? Or even hanging?"

"Are you afraid of anything, Miss Van Horn?" asked Sherlock deliberately, studying her with interest.

"Causing pain to those I love," Ashanti managed to say as she rung her hands.

"And the tigers?" Sherlock asked softly. "Who will protect them if you are not here, Miss Van Horn?"

"Who are you protecting, Miss Van Horn?" added Mycroft. "If he is innocent, no harm will come to him."

"The innocent they are always ones to be hurt," she replied tersely. "The powerful, they go free."

"Ashanti didn't kill Miss Janvier!" exclaimed Mirabella, watching the direction of their pompous gazes. In an instant she felt she would burst with anger. "And I know that you know that! Why do you torture her?"

"Why do you say so, Miss Belle?" Sherlock asked, his sudden

interest obvious.

"Ashanti would have taken the diamonds with her instead of leaving them behind, of course!" replied Mirabella.

"I am inclined to believe you, Miss Belle." Sherlock smiled with appreciation. "An excellent deduction."

"Unless that was what Miss Van Horn wished us to think, and it was—as we have already determined—a crime of passion," Mycroft considered.

"That is entirely illogical, Mr. Holmes." Mirabella shook her head. "Ashanti wanted those diamonds for her tigers. They belonged to her. She would have taken the jewels with her—a crime of passion or not! Ashanti couldn't take the diamonds while Joëlle was alive. And if Ashanti had killed Joëlle, she would have taken the diamonds before leaving. And no one would have known of the existence of the jewels to suspect her. This alone is proof that Ashanti is not the murderer."

"I must admit, this is a convincing argument, Miss Belle," Sherlock considered, his expression approaching admiration. "I begin to wonder if you might yet become a detective."

"And besides—" she paused. "Ashanti doesn't have the kind of passion required for the murder."

"What are you saying, Miss Hudson?" Mycroft pressed.

"Ashanti has been to hell: she has suffered more than any person I know. She would have only killed with *purpose*. She is like the tiger: it would have been efficient and quick, without hesitation. It would not be a moment of irrational rage, it would have *meant something*."

"And if it had been done with purpose," Sherlock nodded in agreement, "she would have taken the diamonds."

Chapter Thirty-five
La Santé Prison

"Not everything works out as it should," murmured Mirabella.

"That's a damn truth if ever there was one!" exclaimed Watson from his dismal jail cell. La Santé Prison's dark grey stone did not improve the mood. The air was damp and it would appear that they were a mile beneath the earth's surface if it weren't for the very high window providing a minimum of light. There was a single bench and a bucket inside the cell, along with a blanket which, though worn, appeared to be clean. It was difficult to discern, however, particularly in the dim light. In many prisons, the blankets themselves were laden with insects and disease.

So Mirabella had brought some blankets and a wash basin, along with wine and food. She started to respond but held her tongue, thinking it better to let John dine in peace and to not disturb him with too many questions, though she was most anxious to know how he fared.

Obviously not well from the look of him. He had not bathed. He was unshaven and his hair ill-groomed. It was such a strange sight—she had never before seen John Watson thus. His three-piece wool suit had been confiscated, he was in a prison uniform, and he looked entirely out of place.

"What do you speak of, Miss Belle?" asked Sherlock.

"I was thinking of Ashanti," she replied sadly, tearing her eyes from John to look at Sherlock. "What happened? I don't understand it. It makes no sense that our country should have invaded her country."

"Why not?" muttered Watson, rubbing his wounded leg with his free left hand, an injury which must have been exacerbated by the dampness. "It is a violent world and the innocent are often persecuted."

The three were situated outside Watson's jail cell, with only Mycroft being seated in a chair which had been procured for him. Ever the gentleman, he had offered it to Mirabella, who had declined.

"Indeed. There have been seventy-two invasions in this century alone," answered Sherlock. "The sun doesn't set on the British empire without some effort on our part."

"Queen Victoria never sanctioned the invasion of Zululand, I assure you," stated Mycroft indignantly.

"Are you quite serious, Mr. Holmes?" demanded Mirabella, her eyes were glued to Mycroft. "Then how . . . ?"

"Shhh! Curb your excitement and lower your voice, Miss Belle. The guards might hear you. We don't want them to confiscate the things we have brought for Watson," cautioned Sherlock.

"We definitely don't want that!" admonished John, gulping down a few swallows from the wine bottle.

Mirabella leaned forward, staring at Mycroft aghast, as she whispered, "What do you mean the Queen didn't sanction the invasion, Mr. Holmes?"

"Sir Henry Bartle Frere undertook the invasion at Isandlwana without the approval of the crown," stated Mycroft. "Neither did Cetshwayo wish to fight, the Zulu were British allies."

"But they did fight," replied Mirabella.

"Naturally, when the British invaded. It was that or surrender their homeland." Mycroft raised his pants legs so they did not touch the ground.

"But the Zulu lost anyway," murmured Mirabella.

"Not at Isandlwana," Mycroft shook his head. "The Zulu won that battle. It was, in fact, the worst defeat in British colonial history."

"It was this defeat which rallied British approval for the final annihilation of the Zulu," Sherlock murmured.

"But how did the Zulu win Isandlwana?" asked Mirabella. "The Zulu only had spears and clubs. And the British had modern rifles and artillery."

"Indeed," nodded Mycroft. "And the Zulu defeated six fully manned companies of the famous first Battalion of the 24th almost to the last man with spears and clubs."

"But *how*?" asked Mirabella, covering her mouth.

"With sheer numbers. The Zulu died ten to one," answered Mycroft.

"They were like dominoes falling left and right," Sherlock uttered, a stark expression crossing his countenance.

"But why did Frere invade without the approval of the Queen?" persisted Mirabella.

"He wished to crush the savage foe," replied Sherlock, shrugging matter-of-factly. "Frere's Secretary of Native Affairs, Sir Theophilus Shepstone, feared a black uprising. And polygamy was repulsive to those stationed in Africa with the charge of uniting the natives and Boers under the British emblem."

"The sexual behavior of those wholly removed from oneself has long been a reason for murder and persecution," Mycroft said.

"Polygamy *is* repulsive," agreed Mirabella. "Ashanti fled from becoming one of a harem."

"You must allow for cultural differences, Miss Hudson," advised Mycroft.

"No I mustn't!" Mirabella replied. "Slavery in any form is wrong. And I understand that polygamy was not so distasteful to John Dunn and his forty-eight wives!" *Give or take a wife.*

"Indeed, Miss Belle? I am most gratified to see that you are expanding your knowledge of the world." She thought she saw a twinkle of laughter in Sherlock's eyes, but it must be that the dim light was obstructing her vision. "To be sure, I expect that there has been no decrease in polygamy as a result of the Anglo-Zulu war."

She paused to reflect. "It is also wrong that Frere acted without the Queen's approval. But in the end, rather than the Queen's government apologizing for their act, they rallied the troops and crushed the Zulu, validating Frere's initial invasion."

"Hello! I'm sure I'm enjoying this history lesson here in this jail cell," exclaimed John Watson. "If you don't do anything about it, I will hang by the neck for the murder of Miss Janvier while you debate the causes of freedom across the globe."

"I'm so sorry, Dr. Watson," Mirabella replied, reaching in her basket for a baguette of French bread and a pear, passing them through the jail bars. "I was merely allowing you to eat your lunch without being interrogated."

"Hmph!" John muttered, tearing into his loaf of bread as he downed the piece with wine.

"Do you have another bottle of wine?" John asked, swallowing. He re-corked the bottle and hid it under his blanket, apparently wishing to save the small amount remaining for later.

"No, but I shall bring you another bottle tomorrow," Mirabella replied.

"Bring two," John muttered. "Or a dozen."

"That is an excellent idea," mused Sherlock. "Watson may be able to bribe the guards for special treatment with a fine bottle of wine."

"I'll drink it myself, thank you for your concern, Holmes," replied Watson with a stinging insincerity.

Mycroft straightened his collar from the seated chair, running his hand along his neckline. Mirabella considered that it was the only time she had ever been in Mycroft's company and not seen him eating. It appeared the atmosphere had removed his appetite, and that was saying something for Mycroft Holmes.

"My good doctor, the Zulu wars do have some bearing on the case," said Sherlock. "It speaks to motive and the character and stability of one of the suspects. Believe me, we are putting our heads together in an attempt to get you out of here."

"Don't speak to me, Holmes," Watson retorted to Sherlock.

"Shirley has the right of it," added Mycroft reflectively. "We must do a thorough analysis of each of the suspects in order to save our friend here."

"Here! Here! Let's not kill the innocent!" exclaimed Watson.

"I would expect Miss Van Horn to be extremely bitter as a result of the Zulu-Anglo war." Mycroft considered the facts before them.

"Most certainly," Sherlock considered. He was the only one of the four who appeared comfortable in this venue. It never ceased to astonish Mirabella that Sherlock looked at home wherever he was, be it before the Queen of England, in the dungeons of a prison, or scouring the sewers. "Essentially a rogue band of our countrymen invaded Zululand, the British got their asses served to them on a silver platter, the sympathies of the English people rose up, we went back in and finished off the Zulu, and then we left."

"Do you believe . . ." considered Watson, suddenly reflective, "That Miss Van Horn is disturbed enough that her violent impulses might be mischanneled? It is her father, her family, and her country we are speaking of."

She considered John's words momentarily, determined to answer truthfully. "And yet . . . Ashanti is *different*. If anything Ashanti is somewhat removed from this world. She only inhabits it a small percentage of the time. It has been a place of great suffering for her."

"But is she capable of murder?" asked Mycroft.

"Most definitely," nodded Sherlock.

"The other possibility, of course," contemplated Mycroft, "is that Miss Van Horn killed Miss Janvier accidentally."

"Accidentally?" asked Watson. "What the devil . . ."

"She might have had the best of intentions in giving Miss Janvier the herbs—to kill the demon in her and to protect the baby—and it might have backfired," Mycroft said.

Her attention turned to John Watson. As she considered the very real possibility of the doctor hanging by the neck, she felt her heart would break.

But neither did she wish Ashanti to hang.

Mirabella had never been so thankful for the genius of Sherlock Holmes in her life. *Everything depends upon it.*

"But we already know that the strawberries had the poison in them, so the case is solved," Mirabella said.

"Ah, yes. The truth serum." Sherlock turned to Mirabella.

"So it is not a poison?"

"In a manner of speaking," Sherlock said. "But it did not kill Miss

Janvier. However, it does speak to motive."

"And, anyway, why do we care?" Mirabella insisted. "Miss Janvier killed Beckham, we solved the murder, why don't we just go home?"

"Ah, well, unfortunately Watson will hang if we do so," Mycroft said, tapping his lips with his handkerchief.

"Just a slight glitch in an otherwise damn fine plan," John muttered.

"In addition," Mycroft added, "It is possible that whoever killed Miss Janvier is an even worse threat to Britain than she was. Miss Janvier was mainly a threat to her own country—Russia—but there are greater considerations from our perspective."

"That's a relief," John growled.

"Hide this in your jacket, Dr. Watson," Mirabella commanded, slipping a candy confection through the bars.

"I'd rather have another bottle of wine," John Watson muttered.

"Are you having the . . . nightmares . . . Dr. Watson?" she asked.

He glared at Sherlock. "As if anyone cares."

"Have you thought of keeping a journal?" she asked, reaching in her basket for a keyed notebook, fountain pen, and ink well. She placed them through the bars. "Sometimes simply writing one's thoughts can bring peace."

"No thank you, Miss Mirabella." John did not accept the items. "Anything I would write now might be used against me in a court of law."

"Or—I know!—have you thought of writing down your cases with Sherlock Holmes?"

John looked up, a certain light returning to his eyes. He stated derisively, "At this very moment I would love nothing better than to tell the world the truth about Sherlock Holmes!"

He moved to the bars and grabbed the items from her hands a bit too forcefully. He added, "Another bottle of wine might help the words to flow, as it were." John ran his hands through his hair. "And a comb and shaving knife."

Mirabella sighed a sigh of relief. A knife wouldn't be allowed, Dr. Watson knew that, but the fact that he was suddenly concerned about his appearance was a sign that he was feeling better.

This was just the response she had hoped for. "And when you have finished, Dr. Watson, I shall call on the English papers and ask if they are interested in your recounting. It may yet further your case."

"But do *not* mention Miss Hudson, Watson," Sherlock interjected. "I do not wish her name in the papers under any circumstances."

"Never fear, Holmes, I have a great deal to say—and none of it about Miss Mirabella."

"Good."

"You might not think so when I am finished," Dr. Watson stated in a low tone.

"And what of the other suspects?" Mycroft asked, clearly ready to leave the environ. "Let us discuss them while the good doctor is still sober."

"I fear that moment has past," murmured Sherlock.

"What about Prince George?" Mirabella asked. "What of his wife?"

"You speak of Sarah Fairbrother, I suppose?" asked Mycroft, crossing his arms in front of his waist as he glanced about the jail. "Technically she's not his wife, although there was a marriage ceremony performed."

"How can she not be his wife, then?" asked Mirabella.

"Prince George, a prince of England, the Duke of Cambridge, and King George III's namesake, cannot marry without the Queen's consent. If Sarah Fairbrother is not apprised of that fact, you can be certain that the king's grandson is," Mycroft pronounced.

"Do you mean that Prince George willingly went through a wedding ceremony knowing that it was not legal or binding?" asked Mirabella, astonished, covering her mouth with her gloved hand.

"How could he not know it?" murmured Mycroft with a raise of his eyebrows, bemused. "Prince George was educated at Cambridge and his grandfather was the king of England. He himself was in line for the throne until Victoria was born. There could be no doubt that he knew whom he could and could not marry and under what circumstances from a very early age."

"Very likely in the womb." Sherlock began to load his pipe with tobacco. "It is quite inconceivable that he would be ignorant of such matters."

"If the dictates of his own family and his superior education are not enough, try the Royal Marriages Act of 1772." Mycroft covered his nose with a white handkerchief as if he found the smell deplorable. "Not to mention that Prince George did not even sign his name on the marriage certificate."

"You can't be serious," muttered Watson, appearing to take an interest in the conversation for the first time. "He had to sign the marriage certificate. Impossible to conclude the ceremony otherwise."

"I didn't say he didn't sign the marriage certificate," replied Mycroft. "I said he didn't sign *his name*. He signed instead 'George Cambridge, Gentleman'."

"In all probability he momentarily forgot his name," stated Sherlock matter-of-factly.

"If so, it was admittedly at a very opportune time," Mycroft mused, now patting his forehead with the handkerchief.

Watson chuckled, and Mirabella was relieved to witness a smile..

"Why would Prince George go through such a charade?" asked Mirabella, tapping her finger against her cheek.

"Perhaps to get the woman off his back," considered Mycroft. "She is reputably quite strong-willed—and jealous."

"And so that he might continue to partake of the marriage bed," said Sherlock.

"Really Holmes, most unsuitable conversation," Watson said, nodding his head towards Mirabella. "There is a lady present."

"Glad to see you're reviving, Watson," said Sherlock, taking a puff on his pipe.

"And what is the Queen's objection to Miss Fairbrother? Why wouldn't she let Prince George marry her?" Mirabella asked, ignoring John's censure, her curiosity getting the better of her as often happened.

"Miss Fairbrother is a stage actress. Reputedly the greatest beauty of her day," Mycroft explained.

"The Queen objected to the match simply because Miss Fairbrother was a working woman?" huffed Mirabella, placing her hands on her hips.

"At the time of the wedding Miss Fairbrother had four illegitimate children by three different fathers," added Mycroft. "If the second coming had commenced and Jesus Himself had asked her royal highness to approve the match as a personal favor to the Father, Son, and Holy Ghost, the Queen would not have consented to such a marriage."

"I see," murmured Mirabella, biting her lip.

"Never mind that two of those four children were by Prince George," interjected Sherlock. "And she pregnant with a third at the time."

"And yet he is taking up with a bare-backed rider in sequined tights!" fumed Mirabella.

"Excellent observation, Miss Belle. And if the morals of everyone present as well as all of the world's countries meet with your approval, may we continue with the case?"

"Yes, sir," she replied, adding softly, "I'm sure I think of nothing else."

"Good. Prince George is a weak man where women are concerned. But he is not alone among royalty in that." Sherlock glanced at Watson. "Or among men in general."

"And yet—"considered Mycroft, "It is not that Prince George is incapable of love or loyalty. Or even that he requires a younger woman. The Duke of Cambridge had a second mistress, a Mrs. Louisa Beauclerk, whom Prince George has described as the idol of his life and his existence. She died only months ago after a love affair spanning over thirty years."

"It is no wonder he is seeking consolation. Though possibly in places where he shall not find it," murmured Dr. Watson. "And Sarah Fairbrother still lives?"

"Oh, yes. But the Duke and Miss Fairbrother live in separate residences in Piccadilly," Mycroft said.

"And how old is Prince George?"

"Sixty-five years of age," Mycroft replied. "And still going strong. With no legal heirs."

"Indeed. All of his illegitimate children unrecognized by the crown. And yet all are direct descendents of Queen Elizabeth 1 and every other British monarch as well as being related to all the royal families of Europe. Something very few respectable people are able to say," said Sherlock.

"I wonder if any of the prince's children are bitter?" mused Mirabella.

"Aha! Finally! Now we are getting somewhere," Sherlock exclaimed approvingly. "Let us solve the case with haste!"

"How could they not be?" asked John, his interest in the conversation growing. "Their mother ill-treated, her devotion completely undeserved and unreturned, and their own status one of shame."

"And yet Prince George is a devoted father, I understand, and has paid off his sons' gaming debts more than once," Mycroft mused. It was amazing the information that man stored in his head, Mirabella reflected, not for the first time wondering how he came by it.

"And what are their names?" asked Mirabella, her interest intensifying. "The children of Prince George and Sarah Fairbrother?"

"George, Adolphus, and Augustus," Mycroft replied. "All with the surname of 'FitzGeorge', and all in military service like their father."

"And all great-grandsons of King George III," murmured Sherlock.

"I wonder," mused Mycroft, touching his index finger to his chin.

"I as well," nodded Sherlock, their eyes locking. "I wonder if any of the three might have had strong objections to their father cavorting with a young woman in sequined tights while their mother lives."

Chapter Thirty-six
The Royal Mistress

Sherlock stood outside 6 Queen Street in Mayfair, London, neat but not extravagant by any means. Certainly the address was in a desirable part of town.

All the homes were terraced, sharing walls, and 6 Queen Street was a four-story white washed building with three doors and wrought iron balconies on each of the levels.

Inspector Tobias Gregson, a tall, formidable man, took his peaked cap off his head and nervously twirled it in his hands. His full beard was neatly trimmed and he was dressed in a frogged jacket.

Gregson knocked on the door and was soon after greeted by a maid. "Is Miss Fairbrother home?"

The maid scrutinized the two gentlemen. "And who do you be?"

"Sherlock Holmes. And Inspector Gregson of Scotland Yard." The great detective stepped forward, removing his hat and bowing, but the gesture was lost on the plump woman who had already turned away and was yelling, "Madame, Scotland Yard is here to sees ya. Will you sees them?"

"No," a response was heard from the other room in a robust voice. Clearly the room's inhabitant had the gift of projection which had been put to good use on the stage.

"The mistress ain't at home," the maid said.

"Excuse me, madam." Sherlock brushed past her into a small parlor where he bowed again before an older woman, seated, who stared unapprovingly at him even as Gregson joined them. "I am Sherlock Holmes, here on behalf of the Duke of Cambridge."

"Shall's I call the police Madame? I couldn't stop 'im!"

"I am the police, Madame," murmured the inspector. "Inspector Gregson at your service."

The older woman shook her head in the negative. "Bring some tea, please, Dorothy."

Sherlock remained standing, watching her. She had classic features and large blue eyes. Her hair was now white and braided in a style which must have been popular when she was young: in loops around her ears and across her head in a Grecian fashion. Though she had had a shapely figure in her youth, it was apparent that she was not now very active. There was pain in her eyes, emotional or physical, he surmised it was both. He glanced about the room in search of a cane and saw none—most unexpected—but he did see an unusual amount of clutter for a home which was four stories high, as if everything of importance was crammed into this one level. His eyes ran to the hem of her skirt to see excessively flimsy shoes which would not support a woman of her weight.

"Would you like a seat, sirs?" Her expression was calm and accepting, but her eyes were those of someone who had experienced much disappointment. Somewhat ironic since all about the room were paintings of Miss Fairbrother in her theatrical successes.

"Thank you, Miss Fairbrother," Gregson replied politely while seating himself. Sherlock moved to stand beside the fireplace.

"My husband sent you?" she asked, looking at Gregson.

"Well, no, Ma'am," the inspector replied. "But his Royal Highness is in a bit of trouble, and I'm wondering if you could help me with that. We'd like to clear his name if at all possible."

"A woman?" she asked.

"Yes, Your Grace," nodded Sherlock, studying the photographs on the mantle piece. If, in fact, she had been married to the Duke of Cambridge, she would be the Duchess of Cambridge and he extended the proper address in the hope of winning her confidence, a ploy Gregson had clearly overlooked. Sherlock felt the woman who had borne the Duke three children deserved such an address, though the law didn't agree.

And I who have always been a stickler for the law. What is becoming of my ordered world? He knew who was stirring the pot: a Miss Mirabella Hudson.

Fighting his distracting thoughts, Sherlock answered the lady. "A circus performer. Found dead."

Sarah shook her head. "George is a lot of things, but he would never kill a woman."

"And why is that, Miss Fairbrother?" asked Gregson.

"Loves them too much," she replied simply.

"And you, Duchess, when was the last time you saw the Duke?" murmured Sherlock, moving about the room.

"About a month ago, sir." Her gaze rested favorably on him.

"Does Prince George visit often?" asked Sherlock seating himself beside Gregson even as the tea arrived.

The woman who had borne three children fathered by the grandson of the King of England and whose children were cousins to the Queen of England shook her head, adding a lump of sugar to her tea while unable to hide the longing in her eyes. "He pays his respects. And he takes care of the boys."

"There was a handkerchief found in the dead woman's room with the initials 'SF'" said Sherlock, taking a sip of tea. "How do you suppose it got there?" Sherlock watched her, noting that there was no surprise in her expression, which ordinarily would have been indicative of her guilt. Unfortunately, nothing about this case was ordinary.

"I would expect that George dropped it accidentally," she replied, her blue eyes steady and her lack of concern remarkable. She must know that the question inferred that she was a murder suspect. "He always picks up the lace for me when he travels to Paris."

"I need to ask, when Mrs. Beauclerk died—" Gregson began.

"George married me. He didn't marry her, you know." She glanced at a photograph on the mantle, her expression suddenly youthful if belligerent. "You've come from Scotland Yard, 'ave you? That case is closed." Sarah Fairbrother grew very stiff and her lips pursed together, as if she were finished with the conversation. She smoothed her blue taffeta dress around her which was of a fine material, and plenty of it. The furnishings were of fine quality, if outdated, and Miss Fairbrother had a maid. It was obvious that Prince George was taking care of her even if he was no longer in love with her.

"There were chocolates in Mrs. Beauclerk's room," Gregson continued. "There was an identical box in the room of the deceased circus girl."

"You sent those chocolates, didn't you Duchess?" Sherlock asked gently, already knowing the answer.

"And poisoned them?" Gregson muttered.

Sarah Fairbrother came quickly back to the present, but her eyes rested favorably on Sherlock. She then glared at Inspector Gregson, demanding, "You didn't find any poison in the chocolate, did you?"

"Not in the remaining chocolates," Gregson replied. "We can't be certain there wasn't any poison in the chocolate she consumed."

"Do tell us, Your Grace, I have a friend rotting in jail for the crime who will surely hang if I don't get to the bottom of this." Sherlock added, "Forgive the inspector. He is not accustomed to be in the presence of royalty."

"You know I was the most celebrated actress of my day, Mr. Holmes."

"And the most beautiful. It is easy to see now that I have met you."

She smiled at him, her blue eyes twinkling, and he began to see the sparkle that had attracted so many men. "And yet—Mrs. Beauclerk lived for thirty years with my husband—the best thirty years of my life. If I didn't kill her when she was young, why would I kill her when she was an old woman?" She sighed heavily, dotting her eyes with her handkerchief.

"George is the only man I have ever loved, you know."

"That I gathered, Madame. But he never deserved you," stated Sherlock consolingly. "Although you must admit, it's an odd coincidence that there would be chocolates in the room of two of your husband's dead mistresses."

"It don't mean it was me." She added under her breath, "And possibly they should stay away from other women's husbands."

"And you, Miss Fairbrother, where were you on the night of Thursday last?" asked Inspector Gregson.

Both she and Dorothy chuckled, who was now adding hot water to the teapot.

"Gregson," Sherlock glanced at the blanket thrown over the back of the boxy chair Sarah Fairbrother was sitting in. "She was here, of course."

"Why of course?" demanded Gregson.

"I'm an invalid, sir," replied Sarah Fairbrother, pulling at the blanket to reveal wheels on her chair. "I haven't been able to walk for fifteen years."

Chapter Thirty-seven
A Prisoner of his Own Mind

"I cannot believe you, Mr. Holmes! You have truly stooped to new depths this time!" Mirabella exclaimed, enraged, as she paced Sherlock's sitting room in the Le Grand Hôtel de la Paix, the whimsical embossed velvet curlicues in the wallpaper in direct contrast to her mood. "Your friend is in prison and you sit here smoking your . . . your . . . *substances*."

"I am smoking the *substance*, as you put it, in order to assist Watson." Sherlock stared into the fire smoking his pipe without looking at her, dressed in his maroon velvet robe though it was only three o'clock in the afternoon. "And . . . do you really think you should be alone in a man's room, Miss Hudson?"

She threw her arms in the air, the sleeves of her man's suit tightening around her wrist. "I'm dressed as a man! No one could know. And anyway, I am alone all the time with you and Dr. Watson in your apartment in Baker Street."

"In the first place, Miss Hudson, you are working when you are in my flat in London. Here, you are only annoying me. In the second place, you really should give up trying to dress as a man, Miss Belle. It's entirely unconvincing. Even a pillow at your waist cannot hide your curves."

"Now see here, Mr. Sherlock Holmes!" She moved closer to him and pointed her finger in his face. "We were not discussing my curves!"

"I certainly was." He took another puff on his pipe, a smile forming on his lips.

"Do you see what I mean? This is not like you. You sound utterly foolish. You're smoking your illicit substances and speaking gibberish—and you pretend to be on the case?"

His grey eyes were reminiscent of a troubled storm as he ran his free hand through his coal black hair. Quietly he added, "I'm up against a wall."

"Are you quite serious, Sherlock? You're using drugs because you can't solve the case!" She was not accustomed to questioning her employer in this disrespectful manner, but she was utterly infuriated. John Watson's life was at stake and Sherlock was using his pleasure drugs! If he had to do such a distasteful thing, at least it should be between cases.

"Indeed. The illicit substance, as you put it, helps me to see clearly. What other reason could there be?" He glanced up at her from his chair.

"Really, Miss Hudson, have you learned nothing in all your time in my presence?"

"I have learned a great deal," she sighed, moving to sit in the adjoining chair facing the fireplace but with a view of the Eiffel Tower. "The reason you indulge has nothing to do with the case. It is boredom and the need to be constantly stimulated, Mr. Holmes."

"I am bored, in fact," Sherlock said, but his expression was one of interest.

"You're bored? Well then have a cup of tea and look out the window at the birds—or at the fashionable people strolling by." She sighed. "Heaven knows I would love to have the time to do such things."

"Would you, Miss Belle?" he asked, but his expression was unmoved. "For me it is an abomination."

"Clearly I don't know the pain of being alone with myself as you do."

"I am longing to know the pain of being alone right now, in fact."

"God gave you this great mind and talent. Why do you wish to destroy that which you have been given, Sherlock Holmes?" She took the offensive pipe from his hand and placed it on the Louis IV stand between them but he made no move to reach for it. "You're one of the greatest minds alive today."

"Of the century, I should say," he shrugged indifferently.

"Then why do you abuse your body—this gift you have been given?"

"Only think, Miss Belle. Do try." He stretched his long legs along the cream-colored carpet. In this setting of cream and taupe, his maroon satin robe stood out favorably, showing his physique to advantage.

"There is no understanding you, Sherlock. It is hopeless."

"Only consider. I'm brilliant, my mind never stops. I don't know how to function outside my mind." He appeared suddenly somber and pensive.

"Very true." She poured a cup of tea for him, adding one lump of sugar and a generous dollop of cream, which she held out to him. "You are absolutely held captive by your mind."

"Precisely!" He took a sip of the tea. "Which is generally to be desired."

"But not in this case?"

Sherlock closed his eyes momentarily. "Logic and deductive reasoning will generally solve the case, but at times, in my line of work, sometimes the answer only becomes clear when the mind stops and all the confines of thought are dissolved." He closed his eyes momentarily, an expression of bliss present for only an instant. "One must be free of all limitations and be free to soar."

"Mr. Holmes, are you saying you can't come to the answer without drugging yourself into sedation?" she pressed, sighing heavily.

"Without question."

"Because your mind is too brilliant."

"Yes."

"How utterly ridiculous!"

"Ridiculous or not," he shrugged, opening his eyes and taking another sip of tea. "It is true. I don't know how to stop my mind and, as you pointed out, my friend's life is at stake." He placed the teacup on the stand distractedly, appearing suddenly morose.

"I'll tell you why you use drugs, Sherlock Holmes. *Because you like them.* Any excuse will suffice."

He turned to raise his right eyebrow at her.

"You prefer the drugged state because you cannot tolerate your own company," she continued. *And I can certainly sympathize with the feeling!* "When you can't come to a solution, when your mind is stale, you are forced to be with yourself. You are so uncomfortable with the solitary state that rather than persevering through it and learning to utilize it, your lack of discipline allows you to give up."

"Lack of discipline?" he chuckled. "You can't be serious, Miss Belle."

"You are a most undisciplined person, Mr. Sherlock Holmes! Right after your brother."

Sherlock huffed indignantly, his eyes taking on a sudden intensity. "Mycroft is most undisciplined, I'll give you that, Miss Hudson, only doing that which pleases him. But I live for discipline, logic, and order."

"You, Mr. Holmes, give the appearance of one who is tireless and relentlessly determined," she argued, "but yours is a drive born of an insatiable curiosity rather than the need to force yourself to do anything you do not wish to do. You only do precisely that what you wish to do: a luxury your exceptional intelligence and abilities have afforded you."

"How can you say that, Miss Belle, when I am scaling the sewers, on my hands and knees along the railroad tracks, tracking criminals in the middle of the night, and going without sleep until the case is solved?"

"If one wishes to do something it cannot be considered discipline, can it?" she asked pointedly. "Perhaps you and your brother are alike in that: you only do that which you wish to do. You have merely been blessed with a great deal more energy and drive than your older sibling."

"Mycroft is assuredly the most hedonistic person of my acquaintance, and will accept nothing but the most luxurious of accommodations."

"The fact remains, Mr. Holmes, that you do not know how to do anything which does not please you. Every attribute has its corresponding detriment, and this is yours."

"I thank you for your unsolicited assessment of my character, Miss Hudson, though one might ask why you, who are financially dependent upon the talent, enterprise, achievements, and intelligence of that same character, consider yourself qualified to do so."

"I am sorry, sir, I merely wish for you to enjoy the life which is available to you—and which is inaccessible to most of us. And I cannot help but wonder if you, Sherlock Holmes," she added deliberately, "the most gifted, amazing, and blessed person of my acquaintance, are happy."

"Happy?" he laughed, throwing his head back, his unruly dark curls flying everywhere. "Irrelevant."

"Hmph!" she exclaimed, now truly annoyed. "It is utterly repulsive to me that one of the most gifted men of all time destroys the vessel the rest of us would kill to have!"

A seductive smile formed on his lips which she found somewhat disconcerting. "I do hate to see you in this repulsed state, my dear. Though it is quite becoming in its own way."

"And what is so horrid about your own company, Mr. Holmes?" she asked. "The more you give into the drug, the more difficult for you it will be. Now it is a simple distraction, but it will change your chemistry, and one day it will become something you crave. *Your body will forever crave the drug.*"

"Miss Belle." He took another puff on his pipe, closing his eyes momentarily. "Solve the case or leave me to my tried and true devices to solve it. If you have nothing to contribute, you are excused."

Mirabella pursed her lips, fuming. Sherlock was right. Until she was far more capable and had skills which could impress him into taking note of her opinion, she was wasting her breath as well as endangering her position. *I cannot help him.*

She made a sudden resolve. *I must study and learn everything I can from Sherlock Holmes so that I might be a worthy assistant.* Until she was truly useful to the Great Detective—until she had earned his respect—she had no right to reproach him on any subject.

She stood to leave. He took her by the hand and, for a moment, those stormy grey eyes held her frozen where she stood, as if there was something he wished to say to her but could not.

"Miss Belle?"

"Yes?" she asked, almost breathless from the grip he had on her hand.

"Before you go, would you kindly draw my bath and call for a fresh pot of tea?"

Chapter Thirty-eight
Alone in a Man's Boudoir

Mirabella did not leave the *Paris Le Grand* that night. She stayed, sleeping in Dr. Watson's room. She was too worried about Sherlock to leave him alone. Thankfully, Ashanti had her return performance with the tigers, leaving Mirabella free for the evening.

Naturally Mirabella availed herself of a hot bath while she was at the *Le Grand*. One must be clean, after all. Oh, my goodness, the hotel even provided a new bar of soap! The remains of which she put in her purse wrapped in a handkerchief.

What is happening to me? I am not the respectable girl my mother and father raised! Thievery, but that was the least of her sins. They would be absolutely mortified to know that she had stayed in a man's boudoir alone overnight!

And if anyone else found out, she would be ruined. She should have paid more attention when Sherlock taught her disguises.

"Good morning, Miss Belle." Sherlock looked like a man who had indulged in a drunken orgy the night before. He was unshaven and his skin was ashen, his eyes red, and the curls of his dark, uncut hair rebellious. He had a decidedly masculine scent, though she knew he had bathed as she had drawn the bath herself. The only undisturbing thing about the Great Detective was his maroon velvet dressing gown, pressed and clean.

She rang the bell for tea and toast, retiring to the bedroom while it was delivered. Once the bellboy had left, she attended to the preparations.

Sherlock took the hot tea she offered, and she was relieved to see that his hold on the teacup was firm and steady.

"You ought to be ashamed, Mr. Holmes! Here you sit in your luxury hotel—no doubt recovering from an orgy of hedonism—while your friend sits in jail, *alone*. And you not any closer to solving the case."

"Not any closer? *Au contraire*, Mademoiselle Belle." He stared out the window sipping his hot tea, appearing to savor it. Quite different from his disturbed countenance of late.

"Excuse me?" She spun around, her hands now on both cheeks. "What do you mean Mr. Holmes?"

He raised his eyebrows at her. "You really must improve your French, Miss Belle."

"Are you . . . did you . . . solve the case, Mr. Holmes?"

"I did."

"Who is the murderer?" she demanded.

"Ha! Ha! I am not a puppy dog at your beck and call, Miss Hudson. Nor will I condone the lazy of intellect."

Thank goodness. He is himself again.

"If you are unable to piece it together for yourself, you shall know in due time," Sherlock added.

"How did you solve it, Mr. Holmes?" she asked excitedly. She wanted to scream with joy from the top of the Eifel Tower. She might do just that.

"The way I always solve it. I told you mine was a tried and true method."

She shook her head in disapproval. "Mr. Holmes, I'm quite sure you could solve the case without the use of hallucinogens."

"Possibly. But, as you say, Watson was in jail, and the clock was ticking. Moreover, I rarely use hallucinogens. Now *that* is purely a drug for play." He held his teacup as if toasting her, a devilish smile on his lips. "Stimulants are more in my line."

"Sherlock Holmes!" she exclaimed, exasperated.

"Yes, Miss Belle?" he asked as he studied her, for once completely attentive, a smile on his unshaven face. She had to admit that Sherlock had a lovely smile on those rare occasions when he chose to utilize it, enlivened by his silver eyes which were always intensely focused.

"Are you certain that you know who the killer is, Mr. Holmes?"

"I do."

"When will Dr. Watson be out of jail?" She felt a heavy sigh emerge from her lips, as if she had only begun breathing again.

"Soon. Very soon."

She moved closer to him, attempting to divert her eyes from his masculine form. "Who is the murderer, Mr. Holmes? Please tell me."

Sherlock laughed, throwing his head back. "Do you think I am simply going to tell you, Miss Belle? Show me that you have exercised your brain cells and made the slightest progress. You who have accused me of being undisciplined can provide me with nothing."

She gulped. Oh, so Sherlock remembered that conversation, did he? *I might have known.*

"Show me some effort on your part," he insisted. *"Tell me who killed Joëlle Janvier."*

"Well," she gulped. "It had to be someone who hated Miss Janvier. So that would be . . . me, Stanislav, Sarah Fairbrother, or Ashanti. And possibly Joëlle's estranged husband."

"The list of people who hated Miss Janvier is much longer than that, Miss Hudson," Sherlock chuckled, taking another sip of his tea. "And who had the opportunity to kill her?"

"John . . . er, I mean, Dr. Watson or Prince George."

"Wrong on both counts, Miss Belle." He shook his head, his disappointment evident.

"But the only people who had access to Miss Janvier were Dr. Watson and Prince George."

"Incorrect. They are the only two people I didn't suspect from the beginning."

"But—"

"Who is the murderer, Miss Belle? If you don't answer the question correctly an innocent man will hang." He placed his teacup on the mantle and moved closer to her, his robe open at the neck revealing his bare chest. His proximity made her a bit on the agitated side. Softly he added in an ominous tone, "I'll give you a hint, although you have not earned it. It was a whipster."

"But I don't see . . . ? The murder weapon cannot possibly be a whip!" she exclaimed, utterly perplexed.

"The murderer must of necessity be someone who is able to use a whip. Since neither Prince George nor Doctor Watson are whipsters, neither of them could be the murderer. All the evidence points to someone else, it could not have been either of them anyway, but this is added confirmation."

"You are saying that the murder weapon was . . . *a whip*?" she asked, disbelieving.

"Miss Belle, you astonish me," murmured Holmes, leaning against the fireplace mantle. He left the teacup on the mantle and returned to his seat abruptly, moving to light his pipe. "I did not say a whip was the murder weapon. To the contrary, I said the murderer is someone who knows how to use a whip."

I am completely confused. But regardless of whether or not she understood the words of Sherlock Holmes, she did not doubt their accuracy for a minute.

Oh, dear. It had to be Stanislav or Ashanti. Stanislav had an alibi—he was seen—at the time of the murder. *It has to be Ashanti.* Oh, heavenly Father, *no.* Please not Ashanti.

"Answer me, Miss Belle," Sherlock implored her. "*Who was the murderer?*"

This was one of the most surreal moments of her life. "I think the murderer was . . . it was . . . *Stanislav.*" She studied Sherlock's expression, hoping against hope that his countenance confirmed it.

"And what is the reasoning which led you to that conclusion, Miss Belle?" She could see his pulse beating rapidly at his neckline, a match to her own, she was sure.

"Because . . . he . . . because . . ."

"Because you like Mr. Afanasy the least of all the suspects?"

She nodded. It was so infuriating when Sherlock knew precisely what she was thinking. Of all Sherlock Holmes' annoying qualities, this was the one she liked the least. It was much too intimate. Especially now.

"Tsk. Tsk. We are British, Miss Belle." He set his pipe down. "If you wish to decide cases in that manner, you will have to move overseas, I fear."

"Move overseas? Whatever do you mean, Mr. Holmes?"

"There may very well be a place for you in the American judicial system, Miss Hudson."

Chapter Thirty-nine
A Meeting of the Minds

It was a veritable party of Europe's most powerful and influential law enforcers. Chief Arkadiy Harting, head of the Russian Imperialist Police in Paris was present. Lieutenant-Colonel Sir Edmund Henderson, head of Scotland Yard, had crossed the English channel to be one of the esteemed party. Prince George, supreme commander of the British army, as well as cousin to and confidante of Queen Victoria, was reluctantly in attendance, along with his Cossack bodyguard Kazimir who stood near the door in his gypsy attire, as colorful as it was billowy, a saber strapped to his side. Also present was Alphonse Bertillon, Head of the French Forensic Identification Department.

Never to be absent from any gathering of importance, Mycroft Holmes was present, who some said had far too much influence in the British government, along with his younger brother, Sherlock, fast climbing the ladder of fame and beginning to catch the notice of both Scotland Yard and the Queen of England.

Here some of the leading minds in criminology spanning three countries converged.

"All for the death of a circus bare-backed rider," Mycroft Holmes murmured under his breath as his eyes scanned the room, seated beside his brother at a round table.

"Ah, but Mademoiselle Janvier was so much more than a circus performer to have warranted such a gathering," replied Sherlock quietly, only heard by Mycroft as everyone else was chatting amongst themselves. Sherlock was not only a master of disguise but had learned to control his voice so that it was only audible to the intended party.

"True," replied Mycroft. "She represented revolutionary unrest across Europe, in France, England, and Russia, and, in fact the entire continent. Monarchies have ruled for centuries, a remnant from feudal times. Whether that which is to come will be better or worse is yet to be seen, but everyone knows that change is in the air." He took a sip of the tea already served. "Miss Joëlle Janvier was an affront to the *old school* represented here, desperately clinging to the status quo."

"Do you think so, brother dear?" Sherlock murmured. "I should say Miss Janvier was an affront to almost everyone."

Mycroft shrugged with indifference. "True. But was her death politically motivated—or was it personal, an act of passion?"

"And have you worked out the answer to that question, Mycroft?"

"Of course. But do carry on, Shirley." Mycroft yawned, having no need of the glory—or the effort required to obtain it. "Should you like to go for an early drink when this is concluded? I fear it has taken a toll on my nerves."

"Naturally. I worry for your continued health, Mycroft. You must learn not to exert yourself to such an extreme." Sherlock glanced at Watson, in chains, accompanied by Dubuque, who had escorted the good doctor here from La Santé Prison.

"Quite so." Mycroft put a large dollop of cream in his tea. "I can't seem to contain myself."

"You're not the only one, my dear brother." Studying Watson more closely, Sherlock concluded that Watson didn't look any worse for wear, the color having returned to his complexion. The good doctor was looking well if unshaven and unkempt. No doubt the news that he was soon to be released from his chains had elevated his mood.

No, the ordeal had not hurt the handsome philanderer and had no doubt given Watson time for reflection. Of which he was seriously in need. Sherlock had always known Watson to be a lady's man but had been dismayed to learn just how much of a rake his friend could be given enough blunt and encouragement.

There are some places a man of honor should never go. Sherlock pursed his lips as he thought of Miss Belle. Even a rake should keep his actions confined to those ladies who understood what the game was about.

Sherlock forced himself to observe all those present as his thoughts were momentarily more uncontrolled than was comfortable for him. In addition to the criminologists, also present were the murder suspects: the maid Francine, Stanislav Afanasy, Ashanti Van Horn, Veronika Vishnevsky, and, of course, Dr. John Watson and Prince George.

Sarah Fairbrother, Prince George's mistress and the mother of his children, sent her regrets due to her infirmity, and was excused.

The party sat in a large room overlooking the River Seine in a building near to the Ministere de la Culture. The air was dark with the smoke of coal-burning tug boats putting along on the river, mixed as they were with pleasure boats and fishing boats. Despite the black smog, a more beautiful city was difficult to imagine with its cathedrals and palaces, exquisite architecture, elaborate formal gardens and statues, quaint bridges and fashionable people.

"Gentlemen." Sherlock rose at the head of the table, seated beside his brother Mycroft. "And ladies." He nodded his head towards Miss Ashanti Van Horn and Miss Francine.

And among these powerful players there was yet another woman here by invitation, at Sherlock Holmes' insistence: a Miss Mirabella Hudson, chief bottle washer and of no use to anyone—except, apparently, to the Great Detective.

Those seated about the table turned and stared at her disinterestedly as she entered the room carrying a notepad and pen as Sherlock had instructed her to do. The Cossack glanced at her from the door for only an instant. No one would question the need for a transcriptionist.

"My secretary," Sherlock said.

***

Mirabella took a seat at a small table in the corner, showing her deference to those at the grand table.

In an instant all the hardship I have endured is worth it. The tiger's fangs, the bloody corpses, the fencing and pistol lessons, even the lace doilies. Mirabella was thrilled beyond belief and thought her eyes might never close again as she scanned the room wide-eyed.

There was no reason for Sherlock to include her, she knew that.

Why did he? She knew very well that Sherlock Holmes didn't need a note taker: every word spoken, every gesture was committed to his memory. Why had he taken this action which he must know would mean the world to her and which afforded her the utmost respect?

Sherlock Holmes might push her to the extremes, but, underneath it all, she was finally beginning to realize that his forcefulness which bordered on persecution revealed that he had faith in her. As he had in so few people.

And here is my reward.

"As you know, we are here to shed further light upon the murder of Mademoiselle Joëlle Janvier, a Russian spy of some resolve," Sherlock began. "Technically she died a married woman and was a Mrs. Bezborodov, but for purposes of this inquiry we will refer to the deceased as Miss Janvier, as we all knew her."

Some knew her better than others. Mirabella glanced at John Watson.

"We know the following," continued Sherlock. "Joëlle Janvier was married in Russia to a Dr. Bezborodov, who in recent months strongly desired to remarry."

"Divorce is only possible through a church court in Russia," Bertillon said. "Since divorce was exceedingly difficult, there could be only one infallible solution to his problem."

"If you ask me, Bezborodov did it! The swine!" interjected Prince George.

Chapter Forty
A Terrorist Plot

"I wouldn't think so," replied Mycroft, taking a sip of hot tea lavishly adorned with cream. "There was a large monetary payment made to Mrs. Bezborodov, presumably to entice her not to put anything in the way of the proceedings. There is generally a way if enough money is involved— even for the church." Mycroft shrugged.

"The existence of the bribe indicated, at least, that someone believed there was a way," Sherlock added. "In some cases divorce is possible if infidelity can be proven—particularly by the woman—and there was certainly evidence of this."

"For reasons better left undisclosed, the divorce had to be kept secret: the doctor could not afford the publicity. Much associated with Miss Janvier was better kept secret." Mycroft stared pointedly at Prince George, appearing every bit the royal dressed in his regal attire: a red uniform, a pale blue sash across a not inconsequential torso, and a vivid display of gold braid and medals.

"However that might be, let us address Miss Janvier's allegiance," Sherlock continued. "Through the expert detective work of Dr. John Watson, we discovered that during the early days of her marriage, Miss Janvier took a vow to serve each the revolutionaries and the Okhrana. It has been a mystery to many which of those vows inspired her true loyalty."

Chief Arkadiy Harting spoke up at this point. "Miss Janvier chose allegiance to the Okhrana. Thus, she became a double-agent as regarded the revolutionaries."

"So, in effect," Lieutenant-Colonel Sir Edmund Henderson, studied Chief Harting, "You were her boss."

Mycroft frowned. "In so far as anyone was Miss Janvier's boss, yes."

"That's precisely the point, isn't it, Chief Harting?" Sherlock asked. "Miss Janvier was betraying the Okhrana as well, wasn't she? She took the money, but she had no allegiance to anyone. She was a *triple agent* in point of fact. And you were one of the few who had her number early on."

"Certainly not," Chief Harting retorted, his expression suddenly stone-faced.

"Please do give us some credit, Chief Harting," Sherlock continued. "Otherwise, how can you explain the fact that Czar Alexander II was not aware of the attack on that fateful Sunday, and that the terrorists were so strategically placed? There can hardly be a bigger clue to Miss Janvier's allegiance than the murder of the Czar, can there? And it gets worse, doesn't it?"

"How can it possibly get worse than the murder of the Czar?" Chief Harting replied somberly.

"*The duma*," Mycroft stated.

"The council assemblies to be elected by the people? But those were reversed by Alexander III," Chief Harting argued.

"Precisely," Sherlock continued. "Miss Janvier was in a position to know—she had to have known about the duma—and with that information she might have calmed her group and used her position for the future good of her country and its ninety-seven million inhabitants."

"She had the power to save everyone—her people *and* the Czar," Mycroft murmured.

Sherlock leaned closer to Harting. "But, instead, she fueled the fan—potentially destroying her country's future hopes. For that, you despised her, didn't you?"

"Yes," Harting nodded, anger suddenly evident in his reddened complexion. "The sorceress betrayed the Mother Russia. She betrayed *everyone*. When she left Russia, it wasn't because of her husband, it was because there were those in the *Okhrana* who suspected her. So she came to Paris and joined the circus. Not until later did she regain favor with the Okhrana—against my protests."

"But because the terrorist group was successful in its assassination of the Czar, understandably the revolutionaries were more positive towards her." Sherlock paused, frowning. "But the Okhrana had its doubts. The Czar had died after all. So she had to do something to regain favor with the Russian government: she had to sacrifice a few men to the cause. She gave names of the revolutionaries who had killed the Czar to the Okhrana."

"Yes, the men who were executed: those who had thrown the bombs." Chief Harting nodded.

"On the alter of Joëlle Janvier," Mycroft murmured.

"Some might say that Mademoiselle Janvier was the one who threw the bomb, though she never touched it?" Sherlock pressed.

"Yes." Chief Harting nodded, regaining a modicum of his control. He had, after all, been trained not to reveal his true emotion.

"But you were ordered to work with her, weren't you, Chief Harting? Those above you are not as perceptive as you." Sherlock asked. He tapped his fingers on the table. "And you held her personally responsible."

Chief Harting nodded.

"But despite the reality, Miss Janvier appeared to be very successful, did she not, Chief Harting?" Mycroft asked. "Those in high places believed that you were the two best agents in the entire Russian Imperialist Police. A great team. The Circus was an effective front for her political activity, and Paris is the center of Russian revolutionary activity."

"She was a master of deception," replied Chief Harting, nodding. "Miss Janvier once even stopped a bomb plot in St. Petersburg, saving Alexander III's life."

"Possibly a plot of her own planning?" Sherlock asked.

"Possibly." Chief Harting closed his eyes momentarily. "But she was in good standing with the Russian government, who would hear none of my protests."

"As it is, the oppression of the people is much stronger than it was under Alexander II, and the revolutionary groups much more active as well," Mycroft noted. "Miss Janvier created more work for herself on both sides."

Chief Harting sighed, grief crossing his expression. "Now the country is reduced to people executing each other, and it doesn't make a great deal of difference. But on that fateful day when Alexander II was executed, it made all the difference in the world. If that had not happened, the tide would have turned." Chief Harting took out his handkerchief and dotted his eyes, as if he wept for every one of his countrymen.

"Ah, but it can always get worse, can't it, Chief Harting?" Sherlock interjected. "If Miss Janvier had lived, no doubt she would have made an attempt on the life of Czar Alexander III as well."

Mycroft added, "Miss Janvier was planning a trip. The letter found near her nightstand from the Czar inviting her to the palace was proof of that. If she had access to the Czar—Miss Janvier was a favored person at this point after all—she could get into the palace and kill him herself."

"Wouldn't a personal letter from the Czar indicate that Miss Janvier was on the Czar's side?" asked Lieutenant-Colonel Sir Edmund Henderson.

"I believe the letter indicated that Miss Janvier had wielded an invitation and planned to kill the Czar personally," Sherlock stated. "Recall that we have more than this letter to support our conclusion: if Joëlle Janvier was on the Czar's side, she was sadly ineffective in protecting Alexander II from the assassination. Did she assist with the murder of Alexander II as retaliation for the death of her father? And was she still plotting to kill Alexander III?"

"But she would be caught and hanged," Lieutenant-Colonel Sir

Edmund Henderson objected, clearly incensed at this travesty to justice.

"Perhaps. But the relevant point is that she didn't believe she would be—and therefore might have made the attempt." Mycroft said. "All the success had gone to her head."

"Precisely," continued Sherlock. "Miss Janvier had been successful for so long at having other people take the blame for her crimes that she began to think herself invincible and the rest of the world idiots. She was extremely narcissistic and believed that everyone else was inferior."

"What an odd thing for you to say, Holmes," Watson murmured, his hands still in chains.

"Arrêtez vous !" Dubuque commanded Dr. Watson. "Be silent !"

"Some of us use our gifts to benefit mankind," Sherlock continued, his eyes resting on Dr. Watson. "But back to Miss Janvier. As much as Miss Janvier loved money, I believe that she loved power more."

"Indeed," Mycroft agreed. "She used her sexuality . . ." he glanced at Watson "she used whatever she had. She reveled in the knowledge that she had the power to put revolutionaries in jail, that she could kill people without getting her own hands bloody, that she could control all sides and every side. She knew how to manipulate and deceive. The idea that she might kill the Czar of Russia and get away with it—a person who had felt so powerless as a child—was intoxicating to her."

"She cherished delusions of grandeur," Sherlock pronounced. "She imagined that she could control not only those around her but the fate of entire countries—millions of people—and therefore the course of the world. It made her feel . . . safe."

"And, in the end, it killed her." Mycroft added.

"You have no proof of this. It is only a theory," stated Lieutenant Dubuque.

"Ah, but there is a great deal of proof of Miss Janvier's mental state," replied Sherlock. "She was a triple agent, Chief Harting will confirm this. We know that she sent many men to the hangman's noose, her purported comrades. Did she appear to have any remorse over this? Not at all. She tormented Mr. Stanislav Afanasy and Miss Van Horn continuously. She kept her husband in a state of purgatory, and enjoyed making new conquests." He glanced at Watson and Prince George. "A woman interested solely in money or in protecting her country would have behaved differently, with a different focus. It was primarily about the power."

"It is difficult to believe that she deceived so many," Inspector Bertillon mused.

"Sometimes the mentally demented are far more successful than the normal person because the deranged believes his inner lie so unequivocally that he is able to convince everyone else of it," Mycroft replied.

"There is someone she did not deceive, however," murmured Sherlock, looking at the group of suspects before him. "*The murderer.*"

"*You* killed her!" Prince George exclaimed to Chief Harting. "You should have turned her in!"

Chief Harting grew somber. "I did not kill her."

"True, you were not at the scene of the murder," Sherlock stated. "Logically, there could have been only one person to have killed Miss Janvier."

Everyone leaned forward at the table.

"The last person to enter the room," Sir Edmund Henderson stated. "And the person no one suspected. Miss Francine."

"Moi? I did not kill her!" Francine, the maid, exclaimed.

"If Prince George did not kill her and Dr. Watson did not kill her, it had to be you, Miss Francine," Sir Edmund continued. "Lieutenant Dubuque swears that no one else entered or left the room."

"Non! Non! I did not!" Francine exclaimed, throwing her head into her hands.

"Ordinarily you would not have been strong enough to kill such an athlete as Miss Janvier was," Mycroft murmured. "Unless she had been drugged."

"She was drugged," Dubuque offered. "There were odd herbs in her system. Even morphine."

"Yes, in trace amounts," Dr. Watson offered. "In quantities which might have drugged an ordinary woman, but recall that everyone has a different tolerance to drugs. I don't believe the amount present would have impacted Miss Janvier significantly."

"Oh, and why is that?" Lieutenant-Colonel Sir Edmund Henderson asked.

Dr. Watson added under his breath, "You would be astonished at how much champagne she could drink."

"I must say that I agree. I believe the herbs in her system were for a different purpose altogether." Sherlock turned to alight his eyes upon Ashanti, seated next to Francine.

"*Arretez!* Enough of this!" exclaimed Lieutenant Dubuque. "Whatever the political intrigue you seek to confuse us with, Mr. Holmes, it matters not! We all know, Mr. Holmes, that vous amie, *your friend*, Dr. Watson, was the murderer!"

"Impossible, Lieutenant Dubuque," replied Sherlock with a heavy sigh. "Please listen this time, so I do not have to repeat myself unnecessarily."

"And why is it impossible that Dr. Watson should be the murderer?" asked Bertillon.

Watson's eyes were glued to Sherlock in intense interest.

"Dr. John Watson could not have strangled Miss Janvier with his bare hands as the marks on her neck were not those made by hands," explained Sherlock. "And there was no weapon found on his person. It is very simple, really. The murderer could not have been Dr. Watson."

"Hmmm," replied Bertillon, tapping his cheek in thought. "Prince George, on the other hand—"

"*Oui*, the handkerchief with the initials 'SF'," muttered Dubuque.

"An interesting point," considered Bertillon. "*Voila*! Sarah Fairbrother is a very interesting suspect from the beginning."

"Did Miss Fairbrother kill Miss Janvier?" asked Sir Edmund Henderson, his bushy eyebrows knitted together, not one to beat around the bush. "Were the chocolates from Miss Fairbrother?"

"They were," replied Sherlock. "It is inconceivable that both Miss Janvier and Mrs. Beauclerk would have had an anonymous gift of the exact same chocolates from two separate people, particularly since Miss Fairbrother was so resentful of both."

"Are you saying Sarah was the murderer?" Prince George asked, as if he believed her fully capable of performing the deed despite her infirmity.

"No." Mycroft repeated. "The remaining chocolates in the box were not poisoned, and we do not believe that the one she ate was poisoned either—or that the cause of death was poison, despite the odd contents of her stomach."

"I will unveil the murderer to everyone's satisfaction," said Sherlcok.

"Do continue, Shirley, I don't wish to miss afternoon tea," murmured Mycroft, dipping a cookie into his hot tea in an elaborate blue china cup.

"That would be a travesty," muttered Watson, jingling his iron chains.

"Very well. Miss Fairbrother sent the chocolates, but they were not poisoned. No doubt they arrived with a note of warning in the vein of 'Stay away from other women's husbands,' words Miss Fairbrother uttered to me herself. It would not surprise me in the least if Miss Fairbrother believes the words to have some power in ensuring that justice will prevail."

"Particularly since two of her rivals have perished shortly after reading them," murmured Mycroft patting his mouth with a handkerchief.

"You can't mean the chocolates and the note were a threat and nothing more?" sputtered Lieutenant-Colonel Sir Edmund Henderson.

"Indeed I do," Sherlock stated definitively.

"Do you have any intention of revealing the real murderer during this lifetime, Holmes?" Prince George demanded. "I don't think it necessary to bring the mother of my children into it if she has nothing to do with it!"

"Everyone has something to do with it," retorted Sherlock. "From the beginning, this was a difficult case to solve as there were so many people who had reason to hate Miss Janvier."

"Difficult but not impossible," murmured Mycroft.

"Agreed. As we established, Miss Janvier investigated revolutionary activity and reported it to her boss, Chief Harting." Sherlock turned to stare at Stanislav, no amusement in his expression. "*Your* revolutionary activity, Mr. Afanasy."

"I am not murderer! Only attended meetings," exclaimed Stanislav. His eyes grew suddenly soft. "And I loved her."

"Did you?" asked Mycroft.

Sherlock then turned to Ashanti, who looked particularly beautiful in a white linen day suit with bustle which was cut to her athletic form, her dark eyes and skin radiant. "And Miss Janvier was blackmailing you, was she not, Miss Van Horn?"

"Yes," nodded Ashanti. "She said she would hurt tigers if I did not give her diamonds."

"But you were saving the diamonds to build better facilities for the tigers, were you not? So, no matter what Miss Janvier did, it hurt the tigers, the creatures you love most in all the world."

Ashanti nodded.

"And you drugged her with the intent to kill her?" Mycroft asked.

"No. I did so she would not come back in animal form—and to help the baby."

"The baby who was Stanislav's?" Sherlock asked quietly.

Ashanti did not answer.

"O Bozhe moi!" *Oh my God!* Stanislav's eyes grew wide open in obvious surprise. He clearly hadn't known. He took his head in his hands in sudden grief.

"I do not believe that you killed her, Miss Van Horn," Sherlock nodded. "Someone beat you to it."

"Yes," agreed Ashanti, a hint of disappointment in her expression, as if she might have wished it to be her. "But I could not have killed her.

I could not harm the innocent baby." She added quietly, "I have seen too much killing and pain."

"You are not on trial for the desires of your heart, Miss Van Horn— or we would be able to convict many in this room," added Sherlock.

Ashanti stared at the Great Detective aghast as if she had fully expected to be the scapegoat for the murder.

"As we have learned, Miss Janvier was ever in search of greater reward, both in terms of riches and excitement." Sherlock returned his gaze to Chief Harting. "And she was not a double agent but a triple agent. Subsequently, she betrayed even you, did she not, Chief Harting?"

"Of course, I already said . . ." He stood up, but his demeanor was perfectly calm.

"No, I am speaking of her betrayal of you, personally, not of her betrayal of Russia. It wasn't that you had attempted to inform the Czar of her duplicity—but that you dared not. She was blackmailing you as well. That is the source of your guilt, is it not? That because you kept quiet, the Czar died. She threatened to reveal your secret to the newspapers, did she not, in spite of the fact that your alliance had given her everything she had."

"All the information was there! It was as clear as the red blood on the white snow!" Harting exclaimed. "It would have made no difference!"

"We'll never know, will we, Mr. Harting?"

Mycroft's cookie paused in mid-air as he stared at Chief Harting, suddenly very interested in the proceedings.

"She knew," Sherlock leaned forward, "as you must, that you are the convicted terrorist Abraham Hackelman, and an escapee from prison."

"You idiot! You can't be serious!" exclaimed Prince George, jumping up out of his seat, "The head of the Russian Imperialist Police a *terrorist*!"

"Doesn't surprise me at all," remarked Bertillon, smiling.

But a splash had been heard and Harting was out the window, landing in the Seine below. In a short time he was out of view amidst the steamboats, although the commotion was further aggravated with people shouting and bells whistling.

Chapter Forty-one
Loyalty

"Attrapez-le ! Attrapez le meurtrier!" *Catch him! Catch the murderer!* Lieutenant Dubuque yelled out the window.

"Oh, but it wasn't Harting who killed Miss Janvier," remarked Sherlock, staring distractedly out the window as he moved to stand by the lieutenant.

"*Mon Dieu!* But you said—" demanded Bertillon. "He's jumped out the window!"

"I didn't direct Harting to jump out the window!" replied Sherlock, shaking his head in disapproval. "I hardly think I can be blamed for that."

"Possibly he has always had a longing to do such a thing," Mycroft added.

"Why did Harting run then, if he wasn't the killer?" demanded Bertillon

"I should think it would be obvious by now," murmured Sherlock, wrinkling his brow in disappointment. "He ran because he was found out. Harting was a double-agent for years, acting as one of the revolutionaries, even being convicted and going to jail to maintain his cover, and eventually rising to the rank of Chief of Police in the Okhrana."

"Harting is not, in truth, a terrorist," considered Sir Edmund Henderson, who understood the workings of espionage as the head of Scotland Yard. "He was merely convicted as one. He was an underground agent."

"Precisely," added Sherlock. "Harting was playing his role so well that no one knew he was working for the other side. He was sent to jail as one of the revolutionaries. It is extremely dangerous work to be a double-agent."

"He might have learned something in jail," considered Dr. Watson reluctantly. "He had to keep his faith with the revolutionaries."

"Even so, you can't have the Director of the Russian Imperialist Police exposed as a convicted terrorist. Very bad for the image," argued Mycroft. "What if the Prime Minister of England, or the President of the United States were exposed as a convicted terrorist? Do you think they would long stay in power?"

"But only *think*—" insisted Dr. Watson, joining the conversation.

"We may certainly think, Watson, but we can never force anyone else to do so, nor will we," murmured Sherlock.

"*Alors!* I assure you that the publicity alone will damage the reputation of both the Okhrana and the Russian Czarist government," considered Lieutenant Dubuque. "Not to mention the French police that it was under their nose."

"I am sorry to ask question, but . . . do you think they will catch Harting?" asked Ashanti. Clearly she knew what it was to be hunted and to be in hiding.

"No possibility of that whatsoever," stated Mycroft.

"Why?" demanded Prince George, inadvertently touching one of the medals on his sash. "He should be tried. It is the law. If he is not guilty he will be released."

"Remember that when Harting was convicted, many others were too," considered Sir Edmund. "Why was he never executed? Because he was on the side all along of the Czars and he was merely doing his job."

"Then why did he run?" persisted Prince George.

"Because the police would be forced to arrest him, it's on the books. But they won't go after him, and they won't report it to the papers – unless there is a leak," muttered Henderson, the head of Scotland Yard, adding with a command as he turned to glance at Mirabella. "Don't put that in your notes, girl."

"The reading populace is . . . easily swayed," considered Mycroft. "All the opposing political side has to do is to slant the story and the populace is eager to believe it."

"But shouldn't Harting stay and face the music?" demanded Prince George.

"He certainly had motive to remove Miss Janvier," considered Mycroft. "Hers was a crime against Harting, against their friendship, against the French and Russian governments, and even against the Czar. It is a betrayal against not only the French police but the czarist police."

"And the Russian people," agreed Sherlock. "But Harting didn't kill Miss Janvier and he had nothing to do with it."

"Why then did you expose him, Mr. Holmes?" asked Bertillon, appearing to be curious.

"I have not exposed Harting to the press. I merely stated the truth for our inner circle. I do not see how I can be blamed for his dramatic exit. I certainly did not ask Harting to leave." Sherlock appeared amused with the proceedings.

"ENOUGH!" exclaimed Chief Henderson. "We have expostulated long enough. Who killed Mademoiselle Joëlle Janvier?"

Sherlock turned to Prince George. "Why don't you tell us who killed her, your highness?"

"But it couldn't have been Prince George," interjected Watson. "He left before I did. And she was alive when I left."

"True."

"And you said it had to be someone who knew how to wield a whip," Sir Edmund said.

"Yes, that limits the playing field, does it not?" agreed Sherlock.

"A whip? *Are you mad*?" exclaimed Lieutenant Dubuque. "There were no rope marks on her neck!"

"But we know that she was killed by asphyxiation. Meaning that she was strangled," Sherlock reiterated.

Lieutenant Dubuque was almost red in the face. "If there were no rope marks on her neck, how could she have been strangled?"

"Correction. There were marks. Small, round, uniform marks," said Sherlock. He turned to Mirabella, who was writing in the corner. "What do you say, Miss Hudson? Who killed Miss Janvier?"

"If it was a whipster, it had to be Miss Van Horn, Mr. Stanislav, myself, or you, Sherlock," Mirabella said quietly.

"*Bon.*" Bertillon turned to Ashanti. "For my money, I think it was Mademoiselle Van Horn, if those they are the parameters. Of all the candidates, she had the most reason to hate Miss Janvier to my way of the thinking."

Sherlock shook his head in disagreement. "Look at Miss Van Horn, only now recovering from a terrible accident. She still has slashes and bruises, though she has done her best to cover them." He added softly, "A tiger attack has saved her from suspicion."

"With her injury, it is very unlikely that Miss Van Horn would have been able to kill another human being, particularly an athlete such as Miss Janvier," Mycroft agreed, taking time away from pouring cream into his tea. It was a wonder there was any left in the creamer to pour. "The Russian spy would have put up a formidable fight."

"And yet Mr. Afanasy had an alibi for the time of the murder," considered Bertillon. "And we do not seriously consider Mr. Holmes or his assistant."

"There is one other it might have been, is there not Prince George?" Sherlock asked. "Besides the four mentioned."

"You're a damn fool," he muttered, and I'll have you court-martialed when we go back to England."

"Very unlikely," said Mycroft, taking a sip of tea and appearing quite blissful.

Mirabella covered her mouth with her hand as the realization hit her. "*Mr. Kazimir.*"

Sherlock smiled, turning to admire the huge Cossack. "Yes, Prince George's bodyguard – and a defender of the Czar. Kazimir had two reasons to want Miss Janvier dead and it was his duty to kill her on both counts: she was a threat to the Czar and she was a threat to Prince George."

All eyes turned to look at the Cossack bodyguard, whose fierce expression did not waver.

"No!" Prince George exclaimed, jumping from his chair. "Kazimir wouldn't! He is the most loyal guard I've ever had."

"Precisely," murmured Mycroft.

The Cossack appeared indifferent to the proceedings, not making the slightest move to jump out the window, Mirabella observed.

"It was the Russian—the man who loved her," Prince George exclaimed. "Jealousy. A crime of passion."

"And kill his own baby?"

"But he didn't know. That was evident," objected Bertillon.

"Yes, but Miss Janvier knew. And she would have told him to protect her own life," surmised Mycroft, dipping another cookie in his tea.

"Kazimir told us himself that Miss Janvier was alive when Mr. Afanasy left the courtyard and that he himself lingered in the courtyard after Mr. Afanasy—after everyone had left, in fact."

"You're a damn liar!" sputtered Prince George. "What does the courtyard have to do with it? He wasn't in her room. How did he do it?"

"I was fortunate to have been in contact with the Chinese Embassy not so very long ago when working on a case," began Holmes, standing to move towards Kazimir. "While I was there I took advantage of the situation to learn some of the eastern martial arts, generally not shared with Westerners. I found much to be remarkable, but, being a bit of a whipster myself, one of the arts I found of particular interest."

"And that would be?" asked Sir Edmund Henderson.

"The Chinese have a silk sash," Sherlock began, turning again towards those seated, "which has weights sewn into it but appears to be a decorative piece of apparel when worn. It can be slung precisely like a whip."

"I fail to see how that explains the closed window," stated Lieutenant Dubuque.

"It is elementary, my dear fellow," Sherlock said. "Miss Janvier leaned out the window. The silk sash was thrown and wrapped around her throat, strangling her. Silk does not leave a mark. *But the coins do.* When she fell backwards, the rope was retracted. Her flailing body grabbed the window, closing it shut from the inside. The door was already locked from the inside."

"But why does that implicate my man?" demanded Prince George, "even if there were a grain of sense in that?"

"Your highness, there are only a handful of men in the world who could have executed that maneuver," murmured Sherlock with obvious admiration.

"Don't mean it was my man," proclaimed Prince George, admirably coming to the defense of his companion despite the possibility that the Cossack may have killed his lady bird.

"I don't know that even I could have done it. Miss Belle might have been able to do it if she could but apply herself, so unlikely. Miss Van Horn, though skilled, does not favor using the whip on animals and therefore does not practice much with it, she will tell you so herself. Her strengths are more in acrobatics and animal training. She is not motivated enough in using the whip to have learnt to that degree."

"Still don't prove it was my man!" exclaimed Prince George.

"In protecting the Russian borders, one of the borders of particular interest to the Czar is the Mongolian border. And who lives in Mongolia? The Chinese. Cossacks protecting the border have some contact with the Chinese."

Sherlock moved to Kazimir and held out his hand. The warrior looked at Prince George, who nodded.

The Russian removed the red silk scarf from his waist, wrapped several times around his waist until it became evident it was some twenty-four feet long. *Clank!* As the bodyguard handed the silk scarf to Holmes the sound of metal rubbing together was heard.

Sherlock examined the silk scarf with gold coins attached until he found a spot where the gold coin was missing, holding the scarf up for all to see.

The Great Detective then pulled a gold coin out of his pocket, the coin which had been found at the scene of the murder.

It was a perfect match to the coins on the scarf.

Chapter Forty-two
A Criminal Offence

"Brilliant work, Monsieur Holmes," Dubuque smiled warmly, kissing both of Sherlock's cheeks, despite Sherlock's hesitancy. "How can I ever thank you for solving ze case, *mon amie?*"

"Well there is one thing I would very much like," replied Sherlock with some degree of formality.

"*Bon!* Perhaps it can be arranged, *non?*"

Sherlock whispered into the lieutenant's ear, who appeared startled at first and then smiled. He bowed to Sherlock before exiting, stating, "It is against the law, this. But I will do my best."

"Well, the case is closed." John Watson expressed intense relief as the chains were removed from his hands. He walked over to Sherlock and there was a bit of a stench from his proximity.

"KPOW!" Watson punched Sherlock in the jaw, adding softly. "All's well that ends well."

"Dr. Watson, how could you?" exclaimed Mirabella.

"I do apologize, Miss Mirabella," Watson replied. "I shouldn't have done that with ladies present."

Sherlock rubbed his jaw. "I can see that your prison stay has not affected your strength, old boy."

"I should say it has increased it, Holmes."

"Very good. Glad to hear it." Sherlock began moving his jaw back and forth, relieved to learn that it was not broken. "And would you like to join Mycroft and myself for drinks before dinner, Watson?"

"Indeed I would. If I might freshen up in the hotel room first?" Watson asked politely. "I'm in dire need of a bath and shave."

"Of course, my fine fellow," Sherlock replied, thinking that he might need a sherry sooner rather than later as the throbbing pain began to set in.

"Mr. Holmes, do you need a doctor?" Mirabella insisted.

"Nothing of the sort," Watson replied. "I am a doctor."

"You don't seem to be in the business of healing today, Dr. Watson," Mirabella said.

"To the contrary," replied Watson. "I'm feeling better already."

"Mr. Kazimir won't be prosecuted?" Mirabella asked.

Mycroft laughed. "Not a chance. Diplomatic immunity, don't you know."

"He'll probably receive the highest honor from the Czar," muttered Sherlock.

"So Miss Janvier's death will go unpunished," Mirabella whispered, biting her lip.

"Miss Janvier's greed and her inability to know right from wrong caught up with her," stated Sherlock. "It was only a matter of time."

"The Cossack, on the other hand, saw everything in black and white terms. He knew where his duty lay, and he responded courageously without regard for the consequences to his person." Mycroft shrugged, adding under his breath, "Perhaps it was done for the best. *She was a loose cannon.*"

Mirabella stared at the two Holmes brothers. "How can you both be so laissez faire? You are defenders of the law."

"I solved the case," muttered Sherlock, taking his pipe out of his pocket and beginning to fill it with tobacco. "It is up to the law to take over now. The government. That is Sir Edmund Henderson's position and I leave it to him. I assure you that my hands are tied."

"Hmph! I see how it is!" exclaimed Mirabella, crossing her arms in front of her chest. "If there is a woman who has power over men, you will not come to her defense."

"Not at all, Miss Belle!" chuckled Sherlock, lighting his pipe, a smile forming on his lips. "Such a thing is delightful."

"We care very much that justice was done." Mycroft frowned. "But making the Cossack accountable has nothing to do with justice. In this situation, justice will never be done."

"Whatever do you mean, Mr. Holmes?" Mirabella asked.

"The Russian monarchy is focused on suppressing the anti-czarist movement," Mycroft replied. "They should, instead, be focused on providing a more democratic society—then there would be no need for an anti-czarist movement and no opening for such an unscrupulous person as Miss Joëlle Janvier. In attempting to squelch the people's movement, they may create a more extreme government than would otherwise occur."

"The pendulum is swinging, that is a fact. It cannot be stopped," agreed Sherlock. "The establishment for which we work is fighting the anti-Czarist groups, but the Russian Czar would be better served to address his people. In the end, if the Russian government does not, there will eventually be an uprising by the people. This is inevitable. This is out of our hands."

"What we do here is to apprehend individual criminals who are hurting others," Dr. Watson added. "Can we fight the bigger tides of human history?"

Mirabella turned to look at Mycroft, her eyebrows knitted together. "Then why is Mr. Mycroft Holmes here, if this case has nothing to do with the British government?"

"This case is much bigger than a single criminal," Mycroft nodded. "There has been a French Revolution, trouble is brewing in Russia, will there be an English revolution? As a result of the Industrial revolution, the move to the cities, and the child labor?"

She gasped, covering her mouth with her hand. "You wish to stop an English revolution, Mr. Holmes?"

"Don't you, Miss Hudson?" Mycroft smiled at her.

"Indeed, some of the things we do may yet have far-reaching implications." Sherlock sighed heavily.

"Why did I get in the cage with the tigers if not to make the world a better place?" Mirabella demanded, placing her hands on her hips.

Sherlock's expression was suddenly thoughtful, even warm. "You did it for yourself, Miss Belle."

"I most certainly did not!"

"Are you not a changed woman?" he asked, a sudden tenderness in his eyes, his pipe paused in mid-air.

"Yes, but—"

"And will you not take that change with you when you leave Paris?" Sherlock persisted.

"Well, of course. Naturally—"

"Well then," the Great Detective shrugged, blowing another ring of smoke. "Most things work out for the best, don't they, when you follow the path of right?"

"The world is progressing, Miss Hudson," Mycroft added. "Anyone who believes in doom has the wrong of it."

"Still, I think you miss the point," she objected. "You are very happy that an innocent girl should go—"

"Innocent?" Dr. Watson raised his eyebrows, suddenly part of the conversation. "I think not."

Chapter Forty-three

Isandlwana

Closed the kind eyes
nevermore the clasp of the faithful hand.
But the clamour and wrath of men are still
where they sweetly rest
And the loved dust is one with the dust of the well-loved land
Earth has taken the wronged and the wronger both to her breast
Cetshwayo sleeps in Inkandhla
Rhodes on Matopo height
Escombe and Osborn alike in the dear Natalian soil
Do they dream?
And what dreams are theirs in the hush of the kindly night?
Never, since time began, has any come back to tell....
O brave, true, loving hearts, at rest from long strife and toil
Mandiza, Sineke, Mamonga, Kebeni, Magema
Hail and farewell!
--Alice Werner
"Myths and Legends of The Bantu"

Ashanti caressed the cheek of her beloved, Ekundayo, the warrior whose bride she was soon to be. She was a coveted princess of the king, but she knew in her heart that Ekundayo loved *her* rather than her place of prestige in the tribe.

She looked past the paint on Ekundayo's face and into his eyes. She saw the ferocity which was mirrored in her own spirit and the pride and concern for his people which was so like her father, King Cetshwayo.

"Long live the Queen!" The red coats were lined up on the hillside in the intense African heat, shoulders touching, fighting for what they believed to be God and country. But how many countries did they need? And was not their God the God of all?

They were brave men, many of whom would die today, and they obeyed their orders. Whatever they were asked to do they did.

Twenty-five thousand Zulu warriors descended upon the central column, the main body of the three-pronged invasion force. The British rifles were aimed at them, but as the Zulu dropped, more came from behind.

The British could not re-load faster than the African warriors could descend. The black men in war paint did reach the redcoats and in *every* case it was one-on-one in the end: one man with a rifle and one man with a spear. There was no other scenario.

And in every case there was no more than one survivor and no prisoners taken.

Ashanti saw the bullet hit Ekundayo's chest and she saw him fall back, replaced by another young body, as if he were only a painted black body to be replaced, of no meaning to anyone.

To no one except to her, his brothers and sisters, his parents, the children who would have been and the nation which was no more.

"Stop! Stop!" Her sisters grabbed her, holding her back as she sought to die alongside her love.

Each man who dropped, on either side, represented not one life, but all the lives intertwined with that one.

The odds were against the young Zulu warriors though they outnumbered the British ten to one: one in three of the Zulu would die. And most of them would simply be a place holder, having no contact with the enemy.

There would be no prisoners, only death. Within six months an entire generation of the feared Zulu would be almost obliterated.

And what did the winner take away from this battle? The knowledge that they had won, had obtained their revenge and nothing more. Very little territory would exchange hands.

King Cetshwayo, a friend and ally of the British, would go to his grave not understanding why.

As tears rolled down her cheeks, Ashanti looked to the sky and saw diamonds falling from the sky in her mind's eye, like raindrops.

In the end, Ashanti reflected as she watched the blood flow over her beloved land, it was absurd to feel superior as a result of the technology and the weaponry belonging to the culture one is born into. To have been born into an advanced culture makes one fortunate and privileged, nothing more.

Her auntie, the *Sangoma*, had taught her that we are all human and the only characteristic which warrants any claim to superiority is one's heart.

How do we deal with the poorest and most destitute among us? Her Auntie had asked. *The answer to this question defines us.*

A single hyena watched the blood flowing on the ground from the hillside. He laughed, and then he turned around and returned to the forest.

Chapter Forty-four
A Good Beginning

"Did you get your diamonds back, Ashanti?" Mirabella hugged her friend.

"I have not proof they were mine." Ashanti shook her head while touching her ears, now devoid of jewelry.

"Where are the diamonds that were in your ears?" Mirabella asked, alarmed.

"Just these two they were enough to build habitat—like the tigers' homes in their native India."

"Not quite enough," Sherlock stated, entering the tent. "The French Police may have confiscated the diamonds, but Mycroft *persuaded* them to use the proceeds to buy the land surrounding the circus."

"How did he persuade them to do that?" asked Mirabella, suspicious.

"In exchange for keeping Harting's terrorist tendencies out of the paper, naturally."

"But you can't guarantee that no one will find out," argued Mirabella.

"True, we can only guarantee that *we* won't be the originator of the information." Sherlock's expression was emotionless. "And Mycroft has certain *persuasive* methods."

"That sounds like blackmail to me," murmured Mirabella.

"In governmental circles it isn't called that," replied Sherlock matter-of-factly. "It's called *diplomacy*."

Mirabella thought of asking her friend to come with her again, but she had never seen such a glow in Ashanti's expression. Ashanti had had a dream, and, for once it had come true.

Oh no! "But did you get anything in writing, Ashanti, when you handed over the diamonds?"

"Yes, I did." nodded Ashanti, a smile forming on her lips.

"Miss Van Horn received a small lesson in how to deal with the European," added Sherlock, now standing at the opening to the door of their tent.

"It is difficult system to understand," Ashanti admitted, "But I am learning. The more I learn, the more I wish to spend rest of my life with tigers."

"And Mr. Afanasy . . . are you quite safe with him?" asked Mirabella.

Sherlock tipped his hat and exited from the doorway.

"Stanislav?" Ashanti laughed. "He is quite harmless. I will teach him how to handle the tigers in time."

"Stanislav? Harmless?" repeated Mirabella in disbelief, thinking of the huge man who had shown so much passion and anger.

"At least he tells truth," stated Ashanti. "Stanislav never lies. I always know what he is thinking."

"Well, yes," agreed Mirabella reluctantly.

"And he is fearless, brave. Nothing frighten him. Not even tigers," she smiled shyly. "It is a good beginning."

Chapter Forty-five
Au Rocher de Cancale, Paris
The World is My Oyster

"I'm so thankful to be able to eat in public again. It appears that you are no longer mortified at being seen with me!" sighed Mirabella, taking a hard-won bite of oysters on the half-shell while sitting outside at the sidewalk café of Au Rocher de Cancale. She glared at the oysters: she had thought it would be quite an elegant thing to order, but it was a very odd taste, almost as odd as caviar, and much more difficult to transfer to her mouth. She wasn't certain that she liked either.

It's not always true that the more expensive it is, the better it is.

But she very much did like having had a hot bath and being able to dress as a woman in public, wearing her best day suit, a form-fitting pink linen day suit, the long fitted jacket hitting her at the hips with a skirt which was looped and draped over a lace ecru underskirt to create a bustle along the hip line. Her satin slippers were much the worse for wear, but no one was likely to see them.

"We were never mortified to be seen with you, Miss Belle." Sherlock glanced approvingly at her chestnut brown hair arranged atop her head in curls. A wicked smiled formed on his lips. "Only to be obligated to listen to your tongue lashings."

"You shall hear a great deal over the next few weeks, I assure you, Mr. Holmes," she retorted.

"No doubt we shall." But his grey eyes were laughing instead of turning to daggers. Certainly he would not have tolerated these remarks from her even a month prior.

She studied Sherlock's appearance, which was always interesting, but today was particularly notable in a navy corduroy jacket, a lavender and white striped silk sash around his neck, and a handsome conductor's hat ornamented with silver embellishments atop his head.

"What is the hat you are wearing, Mr. Holmes?" she asked. "It is most elegant—and decidedly unusual. It has an almost military look to it."

"I am most disappointed you do not recall it, Miss Belle."

"It is the good Lieutenant Dubuque's headgear if I am not mistaken," said Mycroft. "And a bit of a tight fit, I should say."

"Indeed it is," nodded Sherlock. "On both accounts."

"I hate to be the bearer of bad tidings among all this admiration, but it is illegal to bestow one's uniform as a gift," mentioned Dr. Watson, familiar with rules of the military. "Dubuque could be dismissed from the police force for giving you his hat."

"*Au contraire*, my good doctor," stated Sherlock, patting his lips with his handkerchief. "The good Lieutenant—now Capitaine—would merely say I had stolen it, if questioned, which I highly doubt he will be. His reputation is greatly advanced with our recent success. He even has a new office."

"I for one am very glad to have the case closed," muttered Dr. Watson.

"Ah, but it was the best of times, my good man," countered Sherlock.

"It was," murmured Watson. "And the worst."

"Speaking of which, Mr. Holmes, you never told me who it was who tried to kill me—in the tigers' cage that is."

"Ah, I suppose I didn't." He wiped his mouth with his handkerchief.

"Do you know who it was?" Mirabella pressed.

"Of course I do."

"Was it Miss Janvier?"

"Yes."

"But why? I was no threat to her!"

"Ha! ha!" Sherlock laughed. "You underestimate yourself, Miss Belle. Of course you were a threat. Miss Janvier guessed that you were working undercover—I suspect she learned of your questioning Miss Veronika—or else she didn't like the attentions bestowed upon you by Watson. I expect the former because the latter would have put Watson in danger as well."

"There is something else that still confuses me about the case," considered Mirabella while struggling with the oyster and her fork. "It doesn't make sense."

"Yes, Miss Belle?" stated Sherlock. "What is there to perplex you?"

"The strawberries," Mirabella said. "Why would someone give Miss Janvier a truth serum?"

"Are you quite serious, Miss Belle?" Sherlock laughed. "The truth serum was administered by someone who wanted to know what Miss Van Horn knew—which was considerable. She knew a great deal about the Czar and about the revolutionaries. And who would want to know what she knew? Many people, I expect."

"In particular, someone who was involved in arms sales,"

Mycroft added.

Mirabella sighed heavily. "So the administrator of this drug wasn't at all interested in killing Miss Janvier!" Mirabella exclaimed. "He was interested in keeping her alive."

"Indeed," Sherlock said. "And at that . . . he failed miserably."

"Well then . . . the other perplexing thing was . . . of course Harting was a double agent—he would have to be. So why would he run? He had nothing to hide. It makes complete sense that as an agent working for the Czar he would be spying on the revolutionaries as one of them from within the ranks. And a person successful in that capacity would naturally rise to a higher position in an espionage organization."

"Yes, it is entirely logical that he would be a double agent in the course of his loyalty to the Czar. And in pretending the part, he might be sent to jail," laughed Sherlock. "And that is precisely why it would be so damning. Have you learned nothing about the human race, Miss Hudson?"

"But it isn't *true* that he was working for the terrorist side," she objected.

"Yes, but he was a *convicted terrorist*. The truth has very little to do with it," stated Mycroft. "You have a great deal to learn about politics, Miss Hudson. The opposing side will take the facts and twist them until they don't resemble the truth at all—and this is precisely what is believed."

"Speaking of gossip," Mirabella considered, "I have often wondered about this. I thought there was no talking at the Diogenes Club which you founded, Mr. Holmes?"

"Most assuredly," nodded Mycroft somberly.

"How could that be conducive to gossip?" she wondered. "How can a social club have no talking?"

"And who would wish to join such a club?" asked Watson, polishing off the last of his pommes frites and taking a swig of beer. "I'm surprised that you ever have any new members."

"People frequent the library to read because the information is readily available as it is not in their own homes," Mycroft replied, unmoved. "There are more academics in London than one might think."

Ahem. Sherlock wiped his mouth with his handkerchief before muttering, "In point of fact, there's a surprisingly large roster at the Diogenes Club."

"You are certainly full of questions today, Miss Hudson," Mycroft remarked.

"Today and every day," Sherlock said.

"I can certainly understand wishing to go to a place to read in complete silence," considered Mirabella, taking a sip of warm coffee. "But

I've heard people have been kicked out for *coughing* at the Diogenes Club!"

Sherlock coughed. He muttered, "Perhaps that is just an excuse to get rid of the undesirables."

"I would truly like to meet the couple who parented you two," considered Watson, adding in low tones. "Persons or aliens as they may be."

"Nothing of it, quite an ordinary parentage I assure you, my dear Watson," replied Sherlock. "Country Squires in Sussex. Our mother is a sparkling society matron. She loves nothing more than a grand party. Her greatest sadness is that she is not a blueblood."

"She wishes to be of aristocratic birth?" Mirabella asked.

"It is too late for that, I'm afraid," Sherlock muttered. "She might have wished to marry someone who was."

"That is to say, a member of the peerage. Our dear mother is . . ." Mycroft bowed his head as if in prayer, ". . . *a mere gentleman's daughter*."

"And, heaven forbid, a working farmer's wife," Sherlock added, amusement making his grey eyes appear silver.

"No, although I do believe our great-great-great grandfather on our father's side was a baron." Mycroft laughed, waving his hand in dismissal. "Sadly, one must be at least an earl to be considered a member of the peerage."

"Oh, yes," Mirabella said, "Baronets and Knights are not peers, and thus do not sit in the House of Lords."

"At any rate, I do not think that esteemed branch of the family would recognize us at this point," Sherlock added.

"Mother would have settled for marrying an earl," Mycroft conceded. "But a Duke? That would have thrilled her beyond measure. And she might have accomplished it. She was beautiful and very well connected, related to the Vernets of Paris, a family of enormously prestigious painters. Her grandmother Violet was a sister of Horace Vernet, who was born in the Louvre in hiding during the French Revolution."

"And your father?" Mirabella asked. "He is a country squire. Very impressive!" Being a curate's daughter, she was sufficiently impressed. The country squire was the most important man in any country parish. The country squire owned a good portion of the land, had at least one tenant, and lived in the largest house, the manor house.

"But being the country squire, no doubt your father is the lord of the manor and the local magistrate?"

"He is," Sherlock nodded. "The local Justice of the Peace. And the manor will pass to Mycroft, the eldest son. But it isn't the largest house in

Sussex, which belongs to the 7th Duke of Devonshire."

"Why isn't the Duke of Devonshire the local magistrate of Sussex then?" Mirabella asked.

"Because the JP will be the most important local man—outside of anyone who is in the House of Lords, which is a conflict of interest," Dr. Watson said. "Lords are generally not permitted to be magistrates."

"It explains a great deal," Mirabella said, deep in thought. "Sherlock and Mycroft must have grown up seeing their father presiding over every manner of civil and legal case. They must have learned the criminal justice system and the law from an early age."

"Oh, we did," Mycroft laughed. "Even when court was held in the local pub we were often permitted to be present. It was the stuff of a great childhood: drunkenness, profane swearing, highway robbery, and rioting."

Sherlock sighed happily, closing his eyes momentarily. He added, "Smuggling, assault, and burglary. *Pure bliss.*"

"Why did your mother not marry a man of title if it was so important to her?" Mirabella asked, studying the two brothers with more than a little confusion.

"Because our father was positively smitten," Mycroft replied. "She had the good sense to know that life with a man who truly loved her gave her the greatest chance at happiness." He added somberly. "Though she still laments to this day that I shall never inherit a title."

"I see." Watson nodded as if understanding had dawned. "So Mycroft takes after the mother and Sherlock the father."

"In a manner of speaking," Sherlock agreed, glancing at his brother.

"Although I am the smarter of the two," Mycroft forwarded with a smile.

"And the laziest," Sherlock added.

"Mycroft smarter than you, Holmes? Truly?" Watson laughed, turning suddenly to Mycroft. "No offence, your imminence."

"Oh, yes indeed," Sherlock replied, suddenly solemn. "But that still puts me in the top ten most intelligent people in the world, so I don't fret much over it."

"So . . . you don't have siblings? Sherlock must not have had much exposure to girls, hence his low opinion of the female sex," Mirabella murmured slyly.

"I would say it was all the dresses Mycroft paraded me in when I was yet too young to fight back against my much older brother," retorted Sherlock. "It gave me a complete distaste for the feminine. Although I did learn how to use make-up for the purposes of disguise." He frowned, his gaze suddenly fixed on Mirabella. "An art about which you have much to learn."

"There is only Honora between me and Sherlock," Mycroft explained. "She is almost exclusively concerned with appearances, and frankly, not the brightest bulb on the tree. The younger twins, Annabel and Rutherford, were much younger, about your age, Miss Hudson. We didn't have much to do with them, with Shirley a full ten years older and myself seventeen."

"As for the social mother that I supposedly take after, I must be off, business awaits," Mycroft stated as he rose from his chair, motioning to his entourage standing outside the *Au Rocher de Cancale*.

As Mycroft sauntered away, Dr. Watson chuckled to himself while attacking his repast of mushroom omelet, sausages, pommes frites, champagne, and orange scones with the ardor of one who had been without decent food for some time. "Probably has another luncheon to attend."

"Where he will no doubt gain valuable information," added Sherlock.

Sigh. Mirabella watched the stately and debonair elder Holmes brother turn the corner. He was so pleasant and easy to be with. She glanced at John Watson. She was so happy that he was out of jail—and safe.

And happy to be out from under his spell as well.

That was a match that never could have been. As lovely a person as John was—and the best of friends—she made a resolution then and there that no man would be the recipient of her love unless he were able to be true to her alone. A man who needed more than one woman was not for her. And no doubt she was not the woman for him either—or she would have been enough.

"I saw your article about the case in *The Gazette*, Dr. Watson," Mirabella said.

"As promised, I wrote nothing about you in the article, Miss Mirabella, and never will."

"You more than made up for your restraint in your exaggerations of me, Watson," Sherlock stated, but there was amusement in his expression.

"It had to be done, old chap," John replied. "Surprisingly, it was a cathartic experience. I may even end up writing about the Afghan war."

"First hand accounts are fascinating to the reading public, Dr. Watson," Mirabella agreed.

"The interesting point about this case to me, upon reflection, was that Miss Van Horn understood Joëlle's weaknesses. Perhaps better than anyone," murmured Dr. Watson, his sea green eyes glistening even more than usual as they all lounged about on the Parisian sidewalk café with their champagne brunch.

"Very good, Watson," Sherlock nodded. "I believe that Miss Van Horn would have found a way to kill Miss Janvier had she persisted in her actions against the tigers. And it would have been a more vicious attack— perhaps by the tigers themselves."

"But only after Ashanti had given Miss Janvier every opportunity to right the wrong." Mirabella shuddered. "And Mrs. Beauclerk? Do you really believe that her death was innocent?"

"Ah, the mistress who jilted the former mistress," Sherlock said. "I have seen the autopsy, and I believe Mrs. Beauclerk to have died of natural causes. In addition, none of the chocolates in her room were missing."

"Mrs. Beauclerk never ate any of the chocolates?" Mirabella asked.

"A most fortunate happenchance, as this was what convinced me of Miss Fairbrother's innocence despite all the similar scenarios," Sherlock replied. "And the fact that I don't believe any of the numerous substances in Miss Janvier's stomach were intended to kill her."

Sherlock took a small wrapped package out of his suit pocket. "But enough of this, I have a gift for you, Miss Belle."

"Why? . . . What is this for?" she asked suspiciously, looking up from her endeavor.

"You did an excellent job, Miss Belle, and showed great courage. I was very impressed with your devotion to the case. I think . . ."

"Oh, go ahead, Holmes, ask her!" commanded Dr. Watson, popping a mushroom into his mouth.

"I believe you are now, officially, to be an operative on our cases. If you would wish to be?" Sherlock asked, showing far more shyness than he was inclined to show.

"Are you quite serious, Mr. Holmes?" she exclaimed, letting her fork drop. "Oh, I would love that above all else! You'd let me work on the cases?"

"As needed," Sherlock said. "Of course, you would still need to keep my laboratory in order and cook our meals."

"Of course!" she agreed, so thrilled that her status had risen and that there would be more cases.

"It is a very dangerous work, Miss Belle, you must be fully aware of this."

"Oh, please, Mr. Holmes, I believe I have deduced that by now! If I were so stupid that I did not know this, you would not wish to hire me, I am sure."

"Are you certain you are prepared to risk your life every day, Miss

Mirabella?" Watson admonished. "I advise you not to agree to it."

"Oh, I am! I love this work. Except when I hate it. I would like nothing better than to walk away from this job—but I find I cannot bear to. I always surprise myself with what I am able to do." She wanted to hug herself. "And will I be receiving an increase in my salary?"

"Absolutely not," Sherlock replied.

"I thought not." She giggled.

"You are a bright girl, Miss Belle, and, I believe you to be capable of anything I shall give you. My only concern is that you are too reckless and lack focus. Also, you are much too prone to intruding into my private life, acting as if I am the employee and you the employer. If you can correct those shortcomings, we shall discuss compensation."

"So there will never be an increase in salary," she replied softly.

"Yes, of that I am well aware, Miss Belle," he replied, pushing the package towards her.

She steadied herself in her chair, unaccustomed to any type of praise from the Great Detective. She opened the package, and there before her was a beautifully wrapped bottle of Lorenzy-Palanca's *Nuit d'Arlequin* perfume. "This is terribly expensive."

"Terribly."

She wondered if Sherlock and Mycroft had some family money of their own. Though they didn't lack for anything, they were clearly working men. She knew that Sherlock made a considerable income from boxing alone—and betting on himself. He was also an investor. In addition to his other skills, he was a shrewd financier.

And yet, Sherlock made a considerable amount of money, but her guess was that he parted with a great deal of it as well; his expenses were considerable. The informants on his payroll alone must require a bit of blunt. And so far as she could see, Scotland Yard paid him a mere pittance for his consulting work—if at all.

No, it wasn't about the money for Sherlock: *it was about the work.*

She turned the crystal bottle in her hands, glistening in the sunlight, longing to keep it. "Would it be proper for me to accept it?"

"When have you ever been concerned about being proper, Miss Belle?" Sherlock laughed, his grey eyes alight.

"I am a respectable girl," replied Mirabella, indignant. Though she knew very well that it was completely unsuitable that a single woman should receive should a gift from any man other than her intended.

"Respectable, yes. Proper, *never.*" Sherlock smiled with more warmth than she was accustomed to see on his face. "As it should be."

Her hands tightened on the crystal jar.

"It is a gift from Mycroft who made the selection at my request, and I fear I could not catch up with him now," continued Sherlock.

Mirabella knew very well that a slow-moving snail could catch up with Mycroft—and certainly Sherlock Holmes could!

She knew also that the gift was from Sherlock.

"Open it," he commanded. "Name the scent if you will."

She obeyed, as she was accustomed to do with Sherlock, however she might argue at times. "Gardenia and black current?" she asked after a moment's reflection.

"Yes, with secondary scents of pink orchid and vanilla," replied Sherlock. "Do you like it?"

"Oh, it is heavenly. I *do*." She looked longingly at the bottle, the nicest gift she had ever received, before looking disbelieving into Sherlock's intense eyes, so focused on her. She found that she liked it though her heart was a-flutter. She hoped she might not fall over in her seat.

"It is a complex scent which may or may not deserve you. But whatever your feelings, you should wear a scent which reflects you, Miss Belle," he added softly.

"Very nice," agreed Dr. Watson. "It does seem like Miss Mirabella."

"Cheers, then!" Sherlock raised his champagne glass. "To our new lady detective!"

"To Miss Mirabella—" Watson chimed in.

Mirabella raised her glass, smiling. She wondered if she had ever been happier than this moment. She was finally a member of the team. She had been fully accepted by Sherlock Holmes and Dr. John Watson. She might not be an equal partner, but neither was she a third wheel who could be discarded at a moment's notice.

They believed in her. *They trusted her.* She was valued for what she could do; she had a function and a purpose. Her job, though extremely difficult, demanded something of all aspects of her being. She loved having a position which utilized all that she was instead of a small fraction of her abilities.

I wish this moment might never end.

"What ho?" said Sherlock, his eyes suddenly alighting on a fashionable lady with dark hair only just seated next to the street. A magnificent purple feather protruded from her maroon velvet cap which matched a fitted walking maroon satin suit.

Who is she? Curious, Mirabella turned to look in the direction of Sherlock's gaze while tipping the rim of her large modish hat so as not to be seen—she was learning *always* to be on the case as Sherlock had taught her. And more importantly, she was enjoying tipping the chic hat, only just purchased from a Parisian milliner with Mycroft's assistance, so she knew it must be quite the thing.

A slow smile began to form on Sherlock's lips. The dark-haired beauty turned to smile at Sherlock while chatting amiably with her companions: a man of average appearance in a brown tweed suit, and another woman with strawberry blonde hair wearing lavish sapphires and diamonds, also splendid in a lavender gown. How did such a plain man as that, who looked like a bank examiner and intensely boring, warrant two such ravishing beauties?

Even more disturbing was Sherlock's reaction. His expression was wistful, and the air was, well . . . *charged.*

The air was always charged when Sherlock was present, but this was different. The electrical field currently was between him and the woman in red.

"Who is the lady in red?" asked Mirabella with only a moment's hesitation.

"The woman," Sherlock replied with obvious admiration.

"Yes, I can see it is a woman, but whom?" she asked as cordially as she could muster.

"*The* woman," he repeated himself, not meeting her eyes, as if it were a matter of complete indifference to him whether or not she were there. When only a moment ago he was focused on her, giving her an expensive bottle of perfume as if they were an item.

Which, of course, they were not, but she was not averse to the attention from the great Sherlock Holmes—or the kindness.

That moment was past. Little had she known how short-lived it would be.

John Watson was now truly indignant, slamming his hand on the table as Mirabella would have liked to do. "Holmes, you have been fooled by Miss Adler since the moment you met her! You have never seen her for what she is!"

Mirabella had never before seen Sherlock distracted by anything outside of a case. In astonishment, she studied Miss Adler whom she now recognized from the photograph, a brunette, small and petite, so unlike herself. She was elegantly dressed, with dimples which made her face light up when she smiled. *Irresistible.* Mirabella swallowed hard.

"Believe me, I know precisely what Miss Adler is." Sherlock pursed his lips, as if the knowledge were ambrosia to him.

Detestable!

"I wonder, my dear Holmes, would you consider Miss Janvier and Miss Adler to be of the same cut?" asked Watson in an apparent attempt to bring Sherlock back to this planet.

"Oh not at all," Holmes replied vaguely, his eyes still glued to the table without attempting to hide that fact. "And—Miss Adler is much more intelligent than Miss Janvier—who was not lacking in intelligence. We never would have caught Miss Adler, she would not have died, and we would very likely all have gone to jail to pay for her crime."

"Most deserving of our respect and awe, indeed—one who would betray her friends and sacrifice innocents to serve her ends," muttered Watson.

"I respect nothing more than intelligence," Sherlock stated simply.

"It is the heart that matters," said Mirabella. "The brain is only wiring, and combined with the wrong heart will go terribly wrong."

"The heart more important than the brain?" Sherlock turned to look at her, shaking his head. "I think not."

"And who is the woman with Miss Adler? And the gentleman?" Mirabella asked, pointing to an auburn-haired bearded man, who was strangely familiar to Mirabella. Where had she seen him?

"Oh, my heavens! It is the man with the strawberries," she whispered, aghast. She had been so focused on the woman commanding Sherlock's attentions that she had not fully seen him.

"As I suspected, a gentleman of some renown. The woman, if I'm not mistaken, is a concert violinist," Sherlock said."

"Do you recognize the gentleman?" whispered Mirabella.

"Indeed I do." Sherlock shook his head in contemplation. "Professor Moriarty."

"The fiend!" exclaimed Watson, standing up in his chair, apparently ready for battle, but Sherlock motioned to the good doctor to return to his seat, which he did begrudgingly. "And if Miss Adler is such a saint, why is she with Moriarty?"

"Oh, I believe it is the other woman who interests Miss Adler, my good doctor, not the professor." Sherlock took his pipe out of his pocket and began to fill it with tobacco. "It appears, my revered associates, that we have yet another case."

Sigh. "And I thought we might rest for a bit, Mr. Holmes," Mirabella said.

"Rest? Ha! ha!" Sherlock laughed. "We shall rest when we die." He glanced at the table of three. "Which, from the look of things, might be sooner than we think." He turned to her. "Are you quite certain you wish to be a detective, Miss Belle? It is a dangerous life, but I have finally reconciled myself to the fact that it is your choice. You are a woman fully grown who will make your own decision, and I clearly have nothing to say to it."

"I don't object to being in danger," she considered, swallowing hard as his words sunk in. "Naturally I would not wish to be, but it comes with the position. Still, isn't there some puzzle we might unlock which is *safe*? Must we always rush in where fools fear to tread?"

Sherlock returned his gaze to her, a smile forming on his lips, which she found strangely alarming. "Charming girl, you have only just been promoted. You are now a detective, with all the advantages and disadvantages which are associated with the profession."

She motioned to the table of three with her chin. "Might we at least finish our lunch before we hurl ourselves into life-threatening danger, Mr. Holmes?"

"Indeed," Dr. Watson muttered, rubbing his wrists as if the memory of the chains was still fresh in his mind. "Why did they have to show up *now*?"

"That is precisely my question," muttered Mirabella, taking the last piece of bread from the center of the table and buttering it with gusto, as if she were engaged in a sword fight with her worst enemy.

Sherlock raised his eyebrows at her, but she observed pride and amusement in his stormy silver eyes. "My dear, it is providence. *Show us what you can do*, my esteemed Miss Belle."

Another Case brought to a Successful Close

Or was it . . . ?

If you enjoyed this book and wish to see more of the series, the surest way to insure that an author can continue writing for a living is to write a review. Reviews are the bread and butter of authors today: without reviews, our books have no visibility on Amazon – and the readers who would like our books do not find them. Feed an author, write a review. It is sincerely appreciated! :)

Other books by Suzette Hollingsworth

SHERLOCK HOLMES & THE CASE OF THE SWORD PRINCESS

THE PARADOX: *The Soldier and the Mystic*
THE SERENADE: *The Prince and the Siren*
THE CONSPIRACY: *The Cartoonist and the Contessa*

To be released in 2016:
Sherlock Holmes & The Chocolate Menace

To sign up for future releases and my newsletter:
www.suzettehollingsworth.com

Acknowledgements

Naturally, first and foremost, I must acknowledge Arthur Conan Doyle, who created the captivating characters of Sherlock Holmes and Dr. John Watson, who are so real in our minds that many consider them as historical figures rather than as fictional characters.

This book is inspired by one of the radio shows which starred Basil Rathbone and Nigel Bruce. The New Adventures of Sherlock Holmes was an old-time radio show which aired in the USA from October 2, 1939 to July 7, 1947. Most episodes were written by the team of Dennis Green and Anthony Boucher, to whom I owe particular thanks.

I wish to thank my extraordinary editors: K.J. Charles (an award-winning author), Caroline Tolley, and Callie Burdette.

This book would not be possible without my husband, Clint Hollingsworth, who is artist/writer/editor and the light of my life.

If I could, I would kiss the feet of the voice actor who produces the audiobooks, Joel Froomkin, but I haven't met him. Joel is a phenomenal talent who brings my books alive and truly turns my books into theatre. He is an amazing actor and director (Joel has directed Molly Ringwold and Charles Shaughnessy, of "The Nanny" fame.)

Thanks to Clint Sterry, who is fluent in Russian and Russian culture. I am certain I did not do his brilliance justice, and he will no doubt take issue with my depictions, but I am better for having spoken to him.

I sincerely thank the community of brilliant authors who offer assistance, inspiration, and guidance. I particularly wish to thank the Beaumonde chapter of RWA for their incredible insight and research assistance. No one becomes an author overnight, and the assistance and inspiration these talented authors/marvelous people provide is invaluable and critical. In particular, Susanna Ives, Nancy Mayer, Delilah Marvelle, Delle Jacobs, Charlotte Carter, Jo Beverly, Leslie Carroll, Allison Lane, and many others who have helped me over the years (knowingly or unknowingly!), giving generously of their time and encouragement.

And to those persons who have believed in me throughout: my husband Clint Hollingsworth, my BFF Charlsie Sterry, Harvey Gover, Sue Bartroff, Donna Weiss, Keli Lock, Gloria Stookey, and THE BEACH GIRLS (Girls of SHS '75), my forever friends. I also wish to thank Amy Brazil, Virginia Hashii, my mom Mary Denison; and readers and friends Rena Kohr, AnaMaree Ordway, Rex Gordon, Denae Lancaster, Wendy Edwards, and Patsy Cantrell. Also check out Wenatchee Book Co. on facebook, my favorite bookstore.

I am forever grateful to Pam Bruner for my book signing party, for being the truest of friends (to everyone she meets), and for being the most unique, charismatic, and effective person I know. If you want something to happen, give it to Pam. Therefore, I am giving Pam a challenge: world peace. If Pam accepts the challenge in between her other gigs, I guarantee it will be here by 2020.

And, of course, to all true friends everywhere who keep our dreams alive when they falter in our hearts.

Dreams are more real than reality itself, they're closer to the self.
--GAO XINGJIAN, Dialogue and Rebuttal

Author's Notes

This is a work of historical fiction, meaning that some of the settings and characters are based on actual historical fact and that some of the characters and settings, as well as the plot, are fictional but possible given the right set of circumstances. In the best of worlds one wishes to time travel through books.

In line with Arthur Conan Doyle's depiction of Sherlock Holmes and John Watson:

>   January 6, 1854: Sherlock Holmes' birthday. Mycroft 7 years older
>   John H. Watson's birthday on July 7, 1852   1.5 years older than Holmes

>   Mirabella's birthday: Nov. 7, 1863

Many of the characteristics depicted in this book were introduced by Arthur Conan Doyle, e.g., the description of John Watson's campaign in Afghanistan and resultant insomnia, the description of Mycroft as a lazy but brilliant mid-level bureaucrat, the description of 221B Baker street, and the statement of Sherlock's parents as being country squires. Although not explained by Arthur Conan Doyle, it is a fact that a country squire might live on the largest manor, and would very likely be the local Justice of the Peace. All the explanation surrounding the local J.P. is consistent with the history of the day. The location of Sussex as the family home is my own invention, but is in line with Doyle saying that Sherlock retired to Sussex.

Arthur Conan Doyle made very little mention of Sherlock's family, parents, home, and no mention of siblings outside of Mycroft. My additions were in line with the framework established by Arthur Conan Doyle and were written with the idea of "making sense" within that framework. Mirabella Hudson is my own creation.

It does seem very likely that Sherlock Holmes would need a female operative, doesn't it? Some readers have made it clear that they do not want a feminine presence in any books containing Sherlock Holmes as a character. Because, naturally, there were no women in Victorian times.

Perhaps it is the greatest irony in the history of the world that the future of Russia and her ninety-seven million inhabitants (at the time) was determined by the terrorist Ignacy Hryniewiecki who threw the bomb which killed Alexander II, Czar of Russia, on March 13, 1881. On that very morning, Alexander II had signed a duma initiating a constitutional monarchy (a monarchy which shares power with a democratically elected branch). The duma was thrown out by the new Czar Alexander III with the death of his father. In that moment Hryniewiecki destroyed any hope of democracy for his people and sentenced twenty million to death in the century to come under the regime of Joseph Stalin, not to mention all the lives affected by living in a communist regime in the forfeit of a government by the people. There can be no doubt that the Czarest regime was replaced by another, and more brutal, autocratic regime. This is not a political statement but a recording of history: this author has nothing to say against socialism or even communism in theory, which, on paper is a government which puts the people first (unlike Fascism, which makes no secret of the fact that it dislikes certain groups of people and which has racism built into its by-laws). Unfortunately, it is a fact that Joseph Stalin ruled with an iron hand, had no regard for human life, and killed twenty million of his own people. http://www.ibtimes.com/how-many-people-did-joseph-stalin-kill-1111789

Essentially Alexander II was trying to help the peasants, it backfired, he put together a new plan which would have helped, a terrorist shot him before it could go into place, which sealed his son's (Alexander III) conservatism, who retaliated against the peasants, which led to the eventual downfall of the Czars (Nicholas II, 1917, Bolshevik revolution). The terrorist killed the only person in power who was on his side.

It is true that Alexander III (along with Nicholas II) witnessed the brutal murder of his father. The Czar was transported to the palace and lived another 15 minutes in that mutated state and, in fact, died, in the room where he had signed the "Emancipation of the Serfs" almost twenty years prior to the date. The inner thoughts of Alexander III and the conversation inside the carriage I cannot know of course. It is true that Alexander II rescinded the duma the next day and that his regime was totalitarian.

The Russian way to spell Czar is Tsar. Tsar and Tsarevich is the next in line, the equivalent being the crown prince.

There was an actual person Arkadiy Harting, who was both a convicted terrorist and the chief of the Okhrana. This stuff is so good I could not make it up.
OKHRANA: THE PARIS OPERATONS OF THE RUSSIAN IMPERIAL POLICE By Ben B. Fischer
"Harting may be the most interesting character in the essays, see "The Illustrious Career of Arkadiy Harting". He rose from informer to master spy to spymaster, eventually becoming chief of the Paris office. As noted above, his top agent, Zhitomirsky, penetrated Lenin's inner circle during the Bolshevik party's underground days. Before he quit the espionage business in 1909 following his exposure by the French press as a Russian spy, Harting had served tsarist Russia, imperial Germany, and republican France, receiving decorations from all three.
Harting met his match in Vladimir Burtsev (see the third reprinted article, entitled "The Sherlock Holmes of the Revolution"). Burtsev was a revolutionary by profession but a counterespionage expert by talent. He organized what in effect was a highly professional counterespionage bureau for Russian radicals. In 1909 Burtsev personally unmasked a major Okhrana agent, Evno Azef. Also in 1909, after years of relentless effort, Burtsev succeeded in proving that a ter-

rorist known as "Landesen", who had escaped from the French police in 1890, actually was Harting. This was leaked to the press, prompting Harting to flee to Brussels, where he went into hiding and was never heard from again."
So far as I know, Harting did not jump out a window. In addition, I have no reason to think that Harting withheld any information from the Czar or was in any way disloyal to the Czar. He was no doubt a hero and extremely brave: being a double agent is a notoriously dangerous profession. As in the book, the fact that Harting was a convicted "terrorist"—and the head of the Okhrana. I can't make this stuff up, people: it's too far-fetched. Yes, truth is stranger than fiction, that is why historical fiction is my genre of choice.

Prince George, the Duke of Cambridge, cousin to the Queen and head of the British army, was an actual historical figure as was Sarah Fairbrother, his mistress and the mother of this three illegitimate sons. The Royal George, as he was called, did NOT have an affair with a circus barebacked rider to my knowledge. I canNOT know Prince George's true character or conversation. It is clear that Prince George was a devoted father and that he was apparently in love with one woman in his lifetime (Louisa Beauclerk), which is more than many men can say. He did provide for Sarah Fairbrother and the address of 6 Queen Street in Mayfair, London was her abode.

Prince George was considered to have an eye for the ladies, but I question his reputation as it may have only referred to his relationship with the great stage actress of the day, Sarah Fairbrother, his three sons with her, and the false marriage ceremony he had with Miss Fairbrother. All those facts are accurate. His relationship with Sarah Fairbrother did not appear to be a happy one despite their having three children together.

However, it is apparent that the Duke of Cambridge was in love with another of his mistresses, Mrs. Louisa Beauclerk, and that their relationship spanned over thirty years (1849 – 1882 when she died). Prince George himself claimed to love Mrs. Beauclerk above all others, stating that she was the sole source of his happiness. He called Mrs. Beauclerk the "idol of my life and my existence", and, when referring to her death on 28 December 1882 stated that "Friday next, 28th, was the sad day which ended my happiness in this world". Therefore, despite Prince George's numerous affairs, I think it must be concluded that Prince George was able to love a woman, he did not require a younger woman, and Sarah Fairbrother's advancing age was not the cause of his lack of devotion and the lack of harmony in their relationship.

Any representation of Sarah Fairbrother which might be interpreted as maligning her character in this novel is completely unfounded and a fictionalized version of her character. The only account I read of her was that she was "jealous", I have no knowledge of Sarah Fairbrother sending chocolate, poison or otherwise, to Louisa Beauclerk.

A "wedding" did occur between Prince George and Sarah Fairbrother 12-17-1846, but Miss Fairbrother was not legally recognized as his wife, which Prince George would have known even during the ceremony. They were not

legally married according to the Royal Marriages Act of 1772 and he did sign a false name to the marriage certificate.
http://anthonyjcamp.com/page12.htm

It is estimated that there are only 350-450 Siberian tigers left in the wild. Almost all wild Siberian tigers live in the Southeast corner of Russia in the Sikhote-Alin mountain range east of the Amur River. Their former range included northeastern China and the Korean Peninsula, and as far west as Mongolia. They are the largest of the tiger species and can grow up to 13 feet in length and weigh up to 700 lbs.
The Siberian is considered a critically endangered species with the primary threats to its' survival in the wild being poaching and habitat loss from intensive logging and development.
To help Tigers In Crisis http://www.tigersincrisis.com/siberian_tiger.htm.

A gift from Bahadur, the white-bearded yogi, if you wish your meditation period to be more exotic:
http://hansonrecords.bandcamp.com/album/sounds-of-the-indian-snake-charmer-vol-two

The events surrounding Cetshwayo, the last king of an independent Zulu nation, are accurate according to my research, as was the granting of 38 wives to John Dunn. The character of Ashanti is fictitious.

Ashanti is modeled after both Irina Bugrimova (b. 1910, d. 2001), first female lion tamer in the Soviet Union, and Mabel Stark (b. 1889, d. 1968), the world's first female tiger/tamer. Both ladies were mauled by the big cats—and both loved them nonetheless. After working so many years with tigers, Mabel committed suicide because she was fired from the ring.
In 1923, Mabel starred in the Ringling center ring, but two years later in 1925, the circus banned all wild animal acts. After a sojourn to Europe where she performed in a circus, she came back to the U.S. in 1928 and began work with the John Robinson Show. In Bangor, Maine, she lost her footing in a muddy arena and was seriously mauled by her tigers. She would suffer a wound that almost severed her leg, face lacerations, a hole in her shoulder, a torn deltoid muscle and a host of other injuries. She was rescued by fellow trainer, Terrell Jacobs, and returned to the ring in a matter of weeks, swathed in bandages and walking with a cane. She suffered numerous maulings and serious injury over her nearly 60 years of working with tigers. At one point in her career, she faced 18 big cats in the ring.
In 1968 Jungleland was sold to a new owner who disliked Stark and fired her. Soon after she left, one of her tigers escaped and was shot. Stark was angry and hurt about the animal's destruction and felt that she could have safely secured the tiger if the owners had asked for her assistance. Three months later, she killed herself by an overdose of barbiturates. In the last pages of her auto-

biography, Hold That Tiger, Stark writes: "The chute door opens as I crack my whip and shout, 'Let them come,' Out slink the striped cats, snarling and roaring, leaping at each other or at me. It's a matchless thrill, and life without it is not worth while to me." She died on April 20, 1968.

The University of London in 1878 was the first university to admit women and University College London laid claim to be the first institution to run co-educational lessons.
http://www.london.ac.uk/history.html
University of London Senate House Malet Street London WC1E 7HU
In 1878 London became the first university in the UK to admit women to its degrees. In 1880, four women passed the BA examination and in 1881 two women obtained a BSc.
In 1900-1, there were 296 women students at Cambridge and 239 at Oxford. Women did not become full members of the university in Oxford until 1919 and in Cambridge until 1948.

Author Bio

Suzette Hollingsworth grew up in Wyoming and Texas, went to school in Tennessee (Sewanee), lived in Europe two summers, and now resides in beautiful Washington State with her cartoonist/author husband Clint, Barney D. Barncat, and Tinkerbelle the dachsie.

She collaborates on an autobiographical web-comic with her husband, Clint Hollingsworth, www.startingfromscratchcomic.com. Visit her website at www.suzettehollingsworth.com. You can contact her via facebook "Suzette Hollingsworth". If you enjoyed this book, please write an honest review and post it on Amazon, which is a great help to the author in finding her fan base.

Suzette's writing style combines wit with elegance and can be described as "A Jane Austen and Robert Downey Jr. meet on the African Queen type of Historical Romance".

Her goal in writing historical fiction is that you, the reader, will engage in a magical journey and time travel through her books. She is very excited about her current Sherlock Holmes series in which Mrs. Hudson's niece is a potential love interest amidst this Victorian mystery. Sherlock Holmes is a great, fun hero to write because he is liked from the get-go despite being pompous and insufferable (or perhaps because of it!), something which might result in an unsympathetic hero in another narrative. The series draws on the imagery surrounding the beloved Sherlock Holmes and Dr. Watson (in particular, Robert Downey Jr. and Jude Law), incorporates the witty banter into the relationship between Sherlock and Mirabella, and lends itself well to Steam punk, blending the "Age of Invention" with something old-fashioned, elegant, and slower-paced.

Enjoy. *The game is afoot.*

www.ingramcontent.com/pod-product-compliance
Lightning Source LLC
Chambersburg PA
CBHW051426170626
46809CB00006B/2336